A GOOD WAY TO GO

A GOOD
WAY TO GO

A Detective Inspector McLusky novel

Peter Helton

Severn House Large Print
London & New York

This first large print edition published 2015
in Great Britain and the USA by
SEVERN HOUSE PUBLISHERS LTD of
19 Cedar Road, Sutton, Surrey, England, SM2 5DA.
First world regular print edition published 2014 by
Severn House Publishers Ltd., London and New York.

British Library Cataloguing in Publication Data

Helton, Peter author.
    A good way to go. – (Liam McLusky series)
    1. McLusky, Liam (Fictitious character)–Fiction.
    2. Police–England–Bristol–Fiction. 3. Murder–
    Investigation–Fiction. 4. Detective and mystery stories.
    5. Large type books.
    I. Title II. Series
    823.9'2-dc23

ISBN-13: 9780727872654

Severn House Publishers support the Forest Stewardship Council™
[FSC™], the leading international forest certification organisation. All
our titles that are printed on FSC certified paper carry the FSC logo.

Typeset by Palimpsest Book Production Ltd.,
Falkirk, Stirlingshire, Scotland.
Printed and bound in Great Britain by
T J International, Padstow, Cornwall.

The story, all names, characters and incidents portrayed in this novel are fictitious. No identification with actual persons is intended or should be inferred.

One

It was late, much later than she had planned to get home, but it had been a good evening and for once she had really enjoyed herself. Jasmine Rogers took her mobile from her handbag before dumping the bag on the hall table. Shouldn't have had the coffee of course, it was back to work first thing tomorrow, or today, to be precise, but she was always faintly nervous around other people's dinner tables and it was good to have something to hold on to, a glass of wine, a cup of coffee, a cigarette. No one smoked anymore of course, she was the last of her friends to have given up and it was at gatherings like tonight's when she longed to be able to reach for a cigarette. She was glad there were none in the house right now, the urge was so strong. In the sitting room by the sofa she kicked off her shoes – you were seventy per cent more comfortable with your shoes off, she had read somewhere – and went into the kitchen without bothering to turn on the light. Jasmine had lived in this tiny two-bedroom house for twelve years now and was sure she could navigate every inch of it blind-folded. Having filled a tall glass with water from the tap she greedily drank from it, then refilled it. She'd had too much wine too and hoped the alcohol would win over the caffeine

1

once she got to bed. There was nothing worse than . . . than . . .

A sudden feeling of unease appeared as if from nowhere. She lost the thread of her thought and stopped halfway to the door. Standing very still in the dark she sniffed the air. What was that smell? A strange smell. No, not strange, *unfamiliar*. A smell that didn't belong here. A faint whiff of something like cheap aftershave or air freshener. Perhaps she had brought it with her from the party though she didn't remember smelling it there. Did she carry it with her from the minicab? That certainly had smelled of all sorts of things, some best not too closely analyzed.

Jasmine tried to shrug off the feeling of unease and left the dark kitchen. She carried her glass of water, a nightly ritual, to the bottom of the stairs where she flicked off the downstairs lights. Just as she did so an after-image of the little dark wood mantelpiece tugged at her eyes and once more made her stop in the dark. Was something missing there? She flicked the light back on and went to examine it.

The house was sparsely decorated and there were few ornaments – you had to show restraint in a house this small – and the same five items, dutifully dusted once a week, had stood on top of the mantle for years: a tiny fake bronze of a satyr brought back from Crete; a heavy lump of pink quartz inherited from an aunt; a black ceramic candle stick holding a red candle she never lit; a framed picture of her younger self cuddling a dog now long dead; and a

2

hand-carved wooden bowl with a rose motif around the rim, always empty. It was all there, all five items.

Then why did it make her feel queasy to look at them? Perhaps she was more drunk than she realized. A sip of water. She didn't really feel sick, it was more a mental queasiness, like having been asked an urgent question in a language she barely understood. She tore herself away, turned off the lights again and this time climbed the short stair, automatically avoiding the spot that creaked on the third step from the top.

On the narrow landing she halted and sniffed again: those refreshment towels soaked in eau de Cologne that you got with finger food? As always she had left the narrow window on the landing ajar since all the kitchen odours seemed to waft upstairs, so perhaps that was how the smell had drifted in. In her bedroom – she used the smaller, quieter one in the back – she undressed. What a relief. The place felt stuffy. It was unnaturally mild for the middle of March but she just knew that the moment she turned the heating off the weather would turn icy again. She flicked off the light and opened the window a crack to let in some air. Below, quietly, almost imperceptibly, her little low-maintenance garden was awakening in the mild air. Yet even here at the window she thought she could smell the faint, alien perfume. She had it in her nose now, she supposed, no point in obsessing about it. Living alone could turn people peculiar; she always worried about that, worried she was becoming eccentric. Peculiar habits. Obsessions. Talking to yourself.

'Talking to yourself,' she said aloud to her reflection in the bathroom mirror. The buzz of her electric toothbrush was loud in her ears, drowning out the little night noises. She was glad this was a quiet neighbourhood – quiet for Bristol, anyway – and her neighbours on both sides elderly. Never a noise. Probably asleep since ten. As she replaced the toothbrush on its holder the smell came strongly into her nostrils. She had it now: deodorant. All-over body spray. One of those things that made men irresistible in television adverts. Someone out there must have seriously overdone it.

She padded back into the bedroom in the dark and slid into bed. The sheets were cool on her skin but that wouldn't last. She really liked her days warm and her nights cool. Lying on her back she plucked the blanket loosely around herself and closed her eyes.

With the window and the door to the landing open a tiny breath of air stirred from time to time, caressing the skin on her exposed arms. *Forty-six years old and all that touches me is the wind. Don't go there, or you'll never sleep.* She reached for her glass of water, always in the same place so she could find it in the dark.

The mantelpiece. Jasmine shot upright, pulled the bed sheet up to her neck and swung her legs out of bed. She *knew* now. The phone, the phone, where was her mobile? Now she knew there was someone in the house. It didn't come from outside, the smell was here, on the inside.

4

Because someone was here. Her feet tangled with the bed sheet on her flight to the door where she ripped her dressing gown off the hook and frantically struggled into it. She couldn't smell it now but she knew someone was hiding. The proof was downstairs. Why did she leave her phone there? Never let your phone out of reach, it's not safe, not even in your own house. Irresolute she stood on the landing. *The spare bedroom.* Its door was closed. *He had to be in there.* It was the only place she hadn't been in tonight. Her nostrils flared as she tried to sniff out the intruder. He was waiting in there. Get to the phone. Downstairs. Get to the phone. Holding her breath she backed away from the closed door to the top of the stairs. With infinite care she let herself down along the handrail, backwards, avoiding the stair that creaked, step by step, down to the bottom. Her hand fluttered as she groped for the light switch, never taking her eyes off the top of the stairs.

She forced herself to look at the mantelpiece again, eyes wide, unblinking. Her stomach contracted into a twisted ball of fear. Yes, there were the same five ornaments that had always been there. But the order had been reversed as though she was looking at it in the mirror. Her eyes sought other surfaces. The top of the television: ceramic dog and glass paperweight, *reversed*. The bookshelf: pine cone, sea shell and Moroccan lantern, *wrong way around*. Even the cushions on the sofa: *swapped over*. The telephone on the writing desk by the window looked miles away. She felt she might never make it

5

across the room. Her mobile lay on the coffee table. She tiptoed across to it, scrabbled it off the shiny surface of the table and dialled the emergency number.

Two

The ashtray was full. And the tray appeared to be stuck. Perhaps it really was time to buy a new car then. *If and when.* McLusky dropped the cigarette end out of the window where it expired with a hiss on the wet tarmac. The country lane was quiet. Magically the rain had stopped at the precise moment he had left the pub and now he could see the clouds were breaking up, revealing the first stars. It was still too warm for the time of year but the air felt clear now, and wonderfully breathable.

He worried with his thumbnail at a small crack in the windscreen. Of course the old Mazda had more serious faults than a cracked windscreen and an ashtray that couldn't be emptied. He had bought the sports version, which meant the engine was thirsty. Neither heater nor air con worked. Driving below thirty made *something* under the bonnet – all things mechanical were mysterious to McLusky – screech in protest. He also thought the front right corner sagged a bit, which might explain why the steering always pulled a little to one side. *If and when*, he would buy a new car. Not a *new* new car obviously, but perhaps not another impulse buy.

He was thirsty again now. Beer created its own thirst. Normally there'd be a bottle of water rolling around somewhere but he knew it was empty. The problem with drinking in country pubs was the whole thing about driving back afterwards; if you stuck to the drink-and-drive limit it was hardly worth going there and if you didn't then you risked your licence. And if you were a detective inspector, your job.

If and when they gave him his job back. He'd find out soon. But if he added a drink-and-drive charge to his tally his career would definitely be finished, Superintendent Denkhaus would see to it. Which is why he had pulled over just a couple of miles from the pub when he realized he really had overdone it this time. He'd been sitting in this passing place, just beyond a crossroads of single-track lanes for half an hour now. He should have eaten something at the pub but the only things they'd had left were a few sandwiches and some samosas. McLusky hadn't been tempted. If at all possible he avoided triangular food. Food shouldn't be triangular, it simply wasn't natural.

Let the effect of the beer wear off a bit. Normally the chances of being stopped weren't that high, unless you drove like an idiot right in front of a patrol car. His problem was that he had managed to make himself conspicuous by getting a suspension for unauthorized firearms use, the firearm in question being a confiscated sawn-off shotgun. Which was another argument for buying a new car: since he had been suspended, everyone on the force seemed to recognize an olive green Mazda 323 with a long scrape along the passenger side and an unearthly engine noise.

He lit another cigarette. *Nine weeks of enforced idleness.* What could have taken them so long? Nine weeks was more holidays than he had taken in years. He had spent all of it in the city, reading in steamed-up cafés, brooding in pubs, rattling about in the flat he rented above Rossi's, the Italian grocer's in Northmoor Street. He had adopted *The George*, a countrified pub just north-west of the city, for some of his drinking after twice running into CID colleagues from Albany Road station in his more usual haunts. It was the solicitous questions as much as the gossip he found hard to cope with. Many officers drank at the *Green Man* of course, a pub virtually monopolized by CID. McLusky was glad for the *Green Man*; he thought of it as 'bunching the idiots' and studiously avoided the place.

He took a deep drag from his cigarette and gave the ashtray another try. Perhaps if he pulled hard enough and twisted upward at the same time . . .? The tray flew out of its socket, showering him with cigarette butts and enveloping him in a thick cloud of bitter ash.

'Marvellous.' He could taste cigarette ash on his lips and spat out of the window. Then he got out and started brushing ash and fag ends off the seat, the steering wheel and himself. 'Filthy habit, Liam,' he admonished himself. McLusky had given up smoking several times but never for longer than a few ill-tempered weeks.

The sound of an engine made him stop and listen. He got back behind the wheel. The lane was very narrow, despite the passing place, and

9

the approaching car, definitely a car, sounded as though it was travelling at speed. A sudden attack of paranoia made him take the keys out of the ignition, so as not to appear drunk in charge of a vehicle. He slid down low in the driver's seat, stirring up more ash that tingled in his nose. In no time at all the car appeared in the rear-view mirror. Being a police officer he recognized the make of the car even in the dark from its silhouette: a clapped-out, ancient Golf. He looked around. Only one headlamp was working and the interior lights were on. Two young men in the front, wearing identical blue baseball caps. Going too fast. Looking panicked. Now McLusky could hear the wail of a following police siren, getting closer. There came the tyre-screech of hard braking. He watched with disgust as the Golf snaked to a stop just past the narrow turn-off, reversed, then disappeared up the lane. The car's lights disappeared, the cabin lights winked out at last. Seconds later a small, rural patrol car blew past his window, the driver never giving him or the turn-off a glance, carrying straight on.

'You won't catch them like that, laddie,' McLusky called after him and started his engine. It screeched like a banshee. He accelerated away hard, turned into the lane the Golf had taken, and accelerated some more. Because of his suspension from duty he no longer carried his airwave radio or it would have been simple to let control know which way the suspects had taken. He also had no siren on the car but he did manage to lay a groping hand on the magnetic blue beacon, reached through the window and stuck it on to the Mazda's roof. Of course he had no idea why the patrol car was chasing them but it hardly mattered; if they refused to stop for a siren then they were always worth checking out. He could no longer see them and the patrol car's siren had disappeared too. He was pushing hard along the narrow lane. It rose and fell, curved left and right as it followed the contours of the fields, hidden on both sides behind dense hedges. It might of course simply be a drunk driver trying to avoid losing his licence. It occurred to him that so was he, and for a moment his foot went light on the accelerator. But after all he, McLusky, was on the side of the angels. Generally speaking. And anyway, he felt fine now, was probably barely over the limit.

He caught a faint glow of brake lights far ahead and pushed on. He was unfamiliar with these lanes. Another narrow crossroads, fingerposts unreadable as he flew past them, following the beacon of brake lights ahead. More than once he had to brake heavily to avoid ending up in one hedge or another. The steering really was a bit vague but the engine was fine, it really did move, this thing.

Then all at once he was right behind them. He could see the panicked white face of the passenger as he squinted over his shoulder. McLusky flashed his headlights. 'Yes, it's the feds, you morons!'

The fleeing driver responded by speeding up. McLusky thought he saw wisps of steam or

11

smoke escaping from the bonnet of the Golf as the distance between the two cars increased once more. He hung back. Somewhere in a stone-cold sober corner of his mind he knew that the responsible thing was to lct the two idiots go before they crashed their car. But the greater part of him, the one in charge of this evening's entertainment, really wanted to see the little buggers stuff their car into a hedge. His foot pressed hard on the accelerator. Steering through the corners required an equal mix of skill and luck now, then all of a sudden he had caught up with them again. He drove as close to their rear bumper as he dared, his lights on full beam now, dazzling in the fugitives' mirrors.

Then he saw it coming, long before the fleeing driver did: a sharp, almost right-angled corner, marked by three cat's-eyed poles. McLusky braked hard, dipped his lights and wrestled his car to a stop just in time to watch it happen.

By the time the other driver reacted it was already too late. He stood on the brakes, locking the wheels. From that moment on he was just another passenger: locked wheels don't slow down. Unstoppable, the old Golf skidded, turning to the right until it arrived at the corner sideways. Its nearside wheels briefly dipped into the ditch before the car flipped over and flew through the hedge. It disappeared in a cloud of leaves, dust and smoke on the other side.

McLusky pulled forward around the corner beyond the scene of the accident and got out. A few yards further on he vaulted a five-bar gate into the field that the hedge was protecting.

The car was lying on its roof. The single head-light still miraculously burnt in the crumpled front. Both doors were open, the occupants had disappeared into the dark. McLusky stood for a moment by the ticking, hissing wreck and listened. Nothing. He stuck his head in at the door of the upside-down car. Even through the reek of burnt rubber and spilled petrol the aroma of cannabis was strong. He inhaled deeply. McLusky hated drugs. But he simply loved the smell. Just as he flipped open his mobile to report the crash the lonely police siren re-appeared, getting stronger. He folded his mobile and climbed back into the road. The patrol car soon approached and stopped at the black tyre marks.

PC Oscar Weisz didn't let the mere absence of any car put him off, he knew an RTA site when he saw one, having attended enough Road Traffic Accidents in his six years of rural policing. He got out of his car to investigate. As he rounded the corner he encountered McLusky who by now had managed to hide his blue beacon under the driver seat and held his warrant card out to the searching beam of the PC's torch.

'DI McLusky. I was on my way home when I heard the crash. Car's on the other side. No sign of the occupants. Did you want them?'

'They were driving like idiots and with one headlight missing. Wouldn't stop for me.'

'Stopped now. I could smell weed and I thought I could smell booze as well.'

'That figures,' said PC Weisz who thought he could also smell drink.

'Well, it's all yours. I doubt you'll find them without air support. Have a good shift.' McLusky got into his car and with a screech of the engine disappeared down the lane.

The PC watched him drive away. He could have sworn he'd seen blue emergency lights earlier but he had called it in and been told there was no one doing a blue-light run in his area.

DI McLusky. So that's what he looked like. Well, if you asked him, that man needed a shave and a haircut. And perhaps a change of clothes. He smelled like an ashtray.

7.31 a.m. One minute after his alarm went off McLusky lit the ancient gas boiler in the bathroom, waited for the water to warm up then squeezed himself under the shower. This consisted of a drooping plastic shower head connected via a plastic tube and rubber cups to the hot and cold taps on the roll-top bath. He had become quite adept in getting the mixture right but one or the other connector not infrequently slipped off its tap, resulting in scalded feet and icy shocks to the body, or vice versa. Either was apt to wake a hungover DI in the morning but McLusky found that even the anticipation of water torture was enough to keep him alert.

Not that McLusky needed alerting this morning. Today the decision of the disciplinary board would be made known to him at a nine o'clock meeting with Superintendent Denkhaus at Albany Road station. Not since he had first walked through the doors at police college had a day felt so momentous. Back then he had felt positive,

14

elated even, now he felt gloomily at the mercy of forces beyond his control.

He managed his ablutions without mishap, shaved without cutting himself. For the inquiry itself he had dressed conservatively and had felt like a delinquent wearing a borrowed suit at a trial. To McLusky nothing shouted 'liar' louder than an ill-fitting suit worn purely for show but he had been 'strongly advised' to wear one when up in front of the board.

Today he dressed less formally: chinos, black shoes and socks, slate grey shirt and black leather jacket. No tie. His only concession was the shirt. The board had made its recommendation, all decisions had been taken; how he dressed today made little difference. The important thing was not to feel like an idiot when he got out of the superintendent's office, whichever way it went. The mirror above the bathroom sink was the only one in the house. It was still steamed up. McLusky couldn't be bothered to wipe off the condensation just to catch a partial view of himself. Pretty enough for the super, he presumed.

Outside it was unnaturally mild again. He didn't wear the leather jacket for warmth. It was more a place to stow some of the gubbins that a uniformed officer would hang from his stab vest or service belt: radio, mobile, pepper spray, notebook, as well as things like warrant card, cigarettes and lighter. It might also make him feel less naked under Superintendent Denkhaus' lizard stare.

When he opened the Mazda's door even to him

15

the smell seemed unhealthy. Last night he had kidded himself that he had brushed most of the ash and cigarette ends out of the front but in the bright light of this morning it looked appalling. He checked the time: nothing he could do about it now. He found an old edition of the *Bristol Herald* among the mess on the back seats and sat on that. He hoped the print would not come off on to the back of his trousers. Traffic was curiously light as though conspiring to hasten him towards his doom. This morning he would have welcomed gridlock.

Oh, grow up. That's what Laura would say. Would have said. Frequently had said. Before she dumped him. Since his short and disastrous fling with Louise Rennie he found he thought even more about Laura than before, certainly more than he did about Dr Rennie. Hardly surprising, when he had spent three years living and quarrelling with Laura in Southampton, while he had seen Rennie no more than a dozen times. And now Laura was here, in Bristol some-where, as a *mature student*, of all things. He was in his thirties now and ought to feel grown up, take what life threw at him calmly and competently, but somehow that plateau of serenity still seemed a far-off prospect. If he were a truly grown-up person, he thought morosely, he would have stayed home and sober last night, not got drunk and hared around the countryside in a clapped-out motor that smelled like a cremation.

A quarter to nine, perfect timing. Not so late that he had to rush, not so early that he had to

16

hang around chewing his nails. His parking space was still there. Good omen or an oversight on the part of management? He insinuated his car into the narrow space and left it there with the windows wide open to air it. If your car wasn't safe in the police car park, then where was it?

Albany Road police station was a crumbling cube of 1970s concrete not far from the harbour. Its architect had not imagined it to age gracefully. He had seen it as disposable, expecting it to turn overnight into instant junk around the year 2000, which it duly had. Instead of pulling it down and replacing it, however, the powers-that-be had 'refurbished' it. It had happened before McLusky's arrival and he suspected rightly that refurbishment had meant a lick of paint and change of furniture, not rewiring or updating the plumbing. And naturally there was still no air conditioning.

Sergeant Hayes greeted him casually as he passed the lobby, as though the detective had been away for no more than a weekend. Upstairs he walked swiftly and with a brief nod past the windows of the CID room, not waiting for a response.

DS Sorbie looked up as McLusky passed. So today was the day. Fingers crossed and with any luck he'd be rid of McLusky before the day was out. The man was a menace, to Sorbie's career as well as in general. He'd blasted a suspect's car with a sawn-off shotgun and when it crashed simply walked off to have a quiet ciggie. That ought to be enough to get anyone thrown off the force; people had lost their jobs for much less.

And in the current climate . . . Sorbie briefly crossed his fingers, then returned to the report he was reading.

At the end of the corridor McLusky opened the door to his tiny office with a certain amount of trepidation. He hadn't really expected to find someone else working behind his desk but in his worst-scenario imaginings the door had been locked or his office emptied. He found all as he had left it: two chairs, one in front, one behind the desk, a couple of gunmetal grey filing cabinets and a grey metal waste bin. It had the dimensions of a broom cupboard and just enough floor space for him to get behind the desk. He looked at it all with something approaching fondness. What he liked most about his office was the fact that the window faced towards the back, the drab service area of the station, affording him a view of the delivery ramp and the wheelie-bins. It allowed him to sit in the window, precariously balanced on the sill, unobserved by his colleagues. McLusky was convinced that it was easier to think that way. His DS, James 'Jane' Austin, was convinced that one day McLusky was going to nod off and fall into the wheelie bins below.

Five minutes to go. Denkhaus had a habit of keeping his underlings waiting outside his office in the presence of his steel-eyed secretary so McLusky had honed his skill in arriving upstairs exactly at the appointed hour, thereby cutting down on waiting time. He opened the window and lit a cigarette – strictly against regulations – and smoked greedily. He really was nervous. The suspension had allowed him plenty of time

18

to realize just how important his work had become to him. He had also asked himself often enough why, if it was that important, he was seemingly incapable of playing it straight, of sticking to the rules? Ninety seconds to go. He flicked the cigarette through the open window and set off towards the superintendent's office. He hoped that when he got there nobody asked him that very question since he had found no real answer. He admitted to himself that he was too disorganized. Secretly he suspected that he didn't fully fit into a grown-up world.

He entered the outer office precisely on time. Lynn Tiery, the secretary, acknowledged this fact with a brief glance at the electric clock on the wall and announced his arrival to the superintendent on the old-fashioned intercom. McLusky had no time to sit. 'Send him in,' the super's voice squawked back from the plastic loudspeaker.

McLusky had expected there to be several people but he found Superintendent Denkhaus alone in his large and minimalist office. He noticed that the usually bare windowsill had now acquired an unhappy-looking cheese plant with a minimal amount of leaves. Denkhaus was seated at his desk, framed by the window behind him. Sun glittered on slivers of the harbour waters, visible here and there between the crowded buildings. McLusky was not asked to sit down so stood, fighting the urge to hide his hands in his pockets; instead he linked them as though in prayer. When he felt the irresistible urge to twiddle his thumbs he clasped his hands behind his back instead.

Denkhaus took a theatrical minute to peruse a pile of papers in front of him, then looked up.

'DI McLusky, I'll try and make this as short and as painless as I can. Naturally there ought to be a representative of the board present but he was taken ill. I don't see any point in postponing this meeting so we will proceed without him. The board has mysteriously accepted your explanation that you were only carrying the shotgun because you felt it was unsafe to leave it in your car and that you aimed the shots at the tyres of the approaching vehicle to stop it from running you down in the narrow lane. The board is not normally given to flights of fancy but there we are.' He sighed. 'Of course it was not simply the matter of unauthorized gun use but several other breaches of the Police and Criminal Evidence act regarding unauthorized surveillance and false imprisonment that earned you a lengthy suspension. The false imprisonment matter resolved itself when the suspect in question was persuaded to withdraw his complaint.' Denkhaus breathed in deeply. 'By me.' He allowed himself another dramatic pause during which he focused unblinkingly on the troublesome inspector. He gave a grunt as though articulating the next sentence gave him physical pain. 'You have been reinstated with immediate effect and will resume your duties. *However—*' he let the gold fountain pen he had been holding drop on top of the file and leant back in his chair – 'I have several things to add. One: you can expect to be invited to attend refresher courses on PACE and other aspects of policing soon, together with similarly forgetful officers from around the county. Two: and I want you to listen very carefully to this—' he dropped his voice as though fearing a listener at the door – 'the slightest misdemeanour or anything *at all* unorthodox and you'll be out on your ear. I'll make certain of that. Any questions?'

'No, sir.'

Denkhaus' voice returned to normal amplification. 'Then carry on, get yourself up to speed. Oh, and for the time being you'll report directly to me.' Denkhaus observed just the tiniest movement of McLusky's eyebrows and sighed impatiently. 'Not because of any chicanery on my part but because DCI Gaunt is off sick. He . . . suffered an accident while on compassionate leave.'

'What kind of accident?' McLusky came alive. Not many people at Albany Road would shed a tear if the chief inspector took his time recovering.

The superintendent shifted his bulk in his seat and pretended to busy himself with McLusky's file again. 'Ah, er . . . an *automotive* accident, I believe. That is all, DI McLusky.'

Back in his own office McLusky logged on to the network, opened and shut drawers on his desk. His office had been unlocked all these weeks and pilfering was not unheard of at Albany Road. Yet it all seemed to be here, including his tiny travelling kettle, half a bottle of Glenmorangie and a couple of glasses pinched from the canteen, as well as a backlog of unreturned and unwashed

21

coffee cups and saucers. He'd smuggle those downstairs later. Right now he needed to get himself up to speed, find DS Austin and get himself a mug of coffee, in reverse order. He found Austin clacking away at his keyboard in the CID room. The DS looked up apprehensively, trying to read the inspector's face. He read it correctly and smiled with relief.

McLusky checked the kettle for water and flicked it on. 'I'll need you to bring me up to speed quickly, Jane. I'm making coffee, want one?'

DS Sorbie had stopped reading and sat staring unseeing at his computer screen. *Unbelievable.* It didn't stick. That man had to be Teflon-coated. How had he got away with it again? If he, Sorbie, or DI Fairfield, say, had kept a stolen shotgun in their car and blazed away at a suspect with it he'd fully expect them to end up in court. He looked around the room. Even DC Dearlove stopped eating crisps long enough to congratulate McLusky on his reinstatement and DS French was *smiling* at him. French hadn't smiled for years.

McLusky carried the mugs, Austin the files. In the inspector's office they sat either side of the twelve-inch tower of CPS papers and case files and blew on their instant coffees. The radiator under the window had been designed for a much larger office, which meant it was very warm in the room, despite the open window.

'How bad was it?' Austin wanted to know.

'Surprisingly painless. Compared with the grilling I got during the inquiry it was nothing at all. He'll be sending me to a refresher on

PACE, together with other miscreants. And he did warn me he'll be keeping an eye on me.'

'He always has for some reason.'

'I know. Probably because he distrusts university graduates. But this time I think it might actually mean spyholes in ceilings.' He couldn't help looking up towards the yellowing ceiling tiles. 'So what's been happening?'

'Not a lot while you were away, strangely enough. And you know what that means.'

'Yes. You haven't noticed yet whatever it is the bastards are up to.'

'Aye, that'll be it. I've been working on these from where you left off—' Austin patted the files on the desk – 'initially with DCI Gaunt but he's off sick.'

'Car accident was it? Denkhaus said something like that.'

'Is that what he told you? I heard different. Gaunt went up north on compassionate leave because his father had died. And while he was there broke several bones in a go-carting accident.'

'Go-carting? That's one way to distract yourself from your grief.'

'Rumour has it he'll be out of action for weeks. I call that a result.'

'OK, I'll dive into some of these then.' McLusky pulled a few inches of the pile towards himself. 'Any of these you don't want to part with speak now.'

'Lord, no, you go ahead and dive.'

'Anything else around here I ought to know about?'

23

Austin scratched the tip of his nose while he gave it some thought. 'Nothing earth shattering. The drinks machine now dispenses only mushroom soup. Or mushroom *flavour* soup, to be precise. DC Dearlove is devastated. I think he only comes in for the soup, he's on at least six a day. Chicken was his favourite.'

'He'll want counselling, next.'

Austin cranked up his usually mild Edinburgh accent. 'Och aye, if you ask me he could do with some of that anyway. Then you'll have noticed the heating is still on full despite the unnaturally warm spring. Apparently it'll take an act of parliament to turn it off before the usual date, whatever the weather and never mind the cuts. Naturally it'll snow the day they do turn it off. Apart from that, a few muggings, suspicious car fires and two stabbings outside the Dakota Club, nothing fatal. Oh yeah, and the odd riot in Stokes Croft.'

'I did notice. I live round the corner, remember?' McLusky got up and yanked open drawers on the filing cabinets. 'Half of my files are still missing, purloined by the enquiry. I wonder how long they'll sit on those with their big overpaid arses.' The phone on his desk rang. He ignored it for half a minute while he flicked through the files, trying to get an idea of what was there and what wasn't. 'Answer that, will you?'

Austin picked up the phone. 'DI McLusky's office. Yes . . . okay . . . I know where it is. You can tell the super DI McLusky is on his way.'

McLusky glowered at Austin. 'DI McLusky is on his way where exactly?'

'Netham Lock. Body in the water.'

'Suspicious?'
'Highly.'

McLusky slammed the cabinet door shut. 'Marvellous,' he said, and meant it.

Three

Traffic on the Feeder Road was light. The road was as straight as the Feeder Canal which it followed and McLusky was driving fast, the narrow canal to the left, industrial estates to the right. *To Let* signs flew by, too many of them, a sure indication that the recession had bitten deep.

'And they said the body was still in the water?' McLusky asked.

Austin was glad it was a warm day because it meant they could drive with both windows open. He let his left arm dangle over the sill to catch the breeze. 'Yup. *Suspended in the water*, I think is what they said.'

'How do you suspend a body *in* the water? Dangling from the bridge?'

'I've no idea. We'll find out in a minute, that's the lock over there. Erm, Liam . . .?'

'Yes?'

'This car.'

'I know.'

'It smells bad. It sounds bad.'

'I *know*.'

'It looks awful.'

'DS Austin, would you like to walk the last quarter of a mile?'

'I'm only saying.'

The lights turned red just as they reached the lock that sat below the bridge. The lock gates

26

were closed. Heavy traffic flowed in all directions on the road around the lock-keeper's cottage below. 'Welcome to Netham Lock,' said a large sign beside it. Trees lined the towpath on the opposite side right up to the ninctcenth century stone cottage. Several small motorboats were moored along the path. A narrowboat was manoeuvring to tie up behind them, another was puttering slowly towards the lock. Below them they could see uniformed officers and civilians standing by the water's edge near the cottage. The lights changed and McLusky turned on to the bridge. Several police vehicles were already creating a bottleneck on the Netham Road. They left the car behind a police van and walked down the slipway to the canal. As they did, McLusky's eyes darted everywhere, registering the entire scene.

He recognized PC Hanham who was talking to a civilian by the water's edge. PC and civilian looked remarkably similar, both tall, broad-shouldered, serious, with greying hair.

'Here they are now,' Hanham said to the man. He greeted the arrivals. 'Morning Inspector . . . Sergeant. This is Mr Marland, the lock-keeper. He found the body and made the call.'

McLusky held his ID up for the lock-keeper to inspect. 'I'm DI McLusky, this is Detective Sergeant Austin. The body is still in the canal?'

'It is. Out there,' said Hanham, nodding his head downstream.

'Male or female?'

'A woman. Mr Marland is pretty sure it's a woman.'

'Can we not get her out? Isn't there a boat we can use?'

'That's my boat there,' said Marland. He indicated a small wooden dinghy tied up at the bottom of stone steps leading into the water. 'But it won't do you any good. I tried to get her out, she must be snagged on something.'

'Where exactly did you see the body?'

Marland pointed to a buoy some twenty yards away, more or less mid-stream. 'The red buoy.'

'Ah, you tied a buoy to it,' said McLusky, relieved. 'Good thinking.'

'I didn't. It was the buoy tied to the body that alerted me. There's not supposed to be a buoy right in the approach to the lock.'

'Could it be the result of some kind of boating accident, perhaps?' Austin suggested.

'Not unless she was in the habit of sailing with a buoy tied round her neck. Anything's possible, I suppose.'

'Right, you'd better show us,' decided McLusky. 'Does your boat take three people, Mr Marland?'

McLusky and Austin sat on the thwart facing the lock-keeper who operated the tiny, puttering outboard. It took all of thirty seconds to reach mid-stream. Marland expertly cut the engine and they glided slowly alongside the buoy.

Austin noted with resignation that naturally the buoy ended up scraping along the boat on his side. He pulled on a pair of latex gloves and reached down. 'Got it.'

'Let's have a look then, pull it up.'

Austin found the chain on the bottom of the

buoy and pulled. After only a few inches he felt strong resistance.

'Well, go on,' McLusky urged.

Austin pulled harder. Even though he knew there was a dead body on the end of it he recoiled when the slick top of a head broke the surface of the dark water. The boat swayed precariously as he pulled and the inspector leaned over for a better look.

'Steady!' warned the lock-keeper, 'You'll have the boat over.'

It was the head of a woman, middle-aged, Austin guessed. The skin looked grey and a little pink as light reflected off the plastic buoy. The eyes were shut, the features distorted.

'The chain's round her neck,' Austin said. 'And I think there's stuff in her mouth. It's definitely stuck on something, though, it won't come up higher, I'm pulling quite hard. I don't want to pull any harder, I might mess things up for forensics.' He gently let the chain run through his hands and the head slid eerily back under the surface.

'Right, let her be, at least she won't go far.' McLusky turned to the lock-keeper. 'No voracious fish in here that'll strip her to the bones, I take it?'

'In the Feeder? Not many fish of any kind.' He started the engine and reversed gently away.

McLusky took in the tree-lined towpath and the stone cottage on the north side. 'Must have been quite idyllic here once, a hundred years or so ago.'

'Don't you believe it,' said Marland, making

29

the turn. 'It was a lot filthier back then. Heavy industry all round, you couldn't breathe for smoke and fumes round here in those days. As for the canal water, forget it. I doubt fish could have survived in it then.'

McLusky pointed downstream. 'Those two narrowboats, are they normally moored here?'

'No, there's no mooring for those here. They're waiting to go through the lock and upriver but they can see the lock's closed, that's why they're tying up there.' They had reached the bottom of the steps again and Marland steadied the boat so they could get safely ashore. 'And if they're not completely blind they'll have spotted the red buoy in the middle of the canal and police just about everywhere.'

Both narrowboats were now stationary alongside the towpath. 'Those three boats in front of them, are they always here?'

'Yes, that's permanent mooring,' Marland said. 'The one closest is mine.'

'No one lives on them, do they?' Austin wanted to know.

'On those little tubs? They only have one tiny cabin below. No, and they're hardly ever used.'

'We'll need the names of the owners all the same.'

'I can give you those.'

'And there isn't a boat missing, or anything?' McLusky asked. 'Nothing amiss?'

'Not a thing, as far as I can see.'

'How about this dinghy? Is that secured at night?'

'At night it's chained and padlocked to that metal ring there.'

'OK,' said McLusky. They were all back in front of the cottage. 'When did you first notice the buoy?'

'A few hours ago. About nine thirtyish.'

'And you went to investigate.'

'Not immediately. I had a couple of enquiries on the phone so I had to deal with those first, but I kept the lock closed and then came out again to have a look at it. It was quite a shock when I pulled up a dead woman, I can tell you that for nothing.'

'I can imagine. Not pleasant.'

The lock-keeper wrinkled his nose in distaste. 'I had to fish a dead dog from the lock last summer. *That* was not pleasant. But a dead woman is something else, Inspector.'

'I agree. Thanks for your help. Someone will take a statement later. In the meantime, if you could find the names of those boat owners. Oh, and you might as well tell those people on the narrowboats that there won't be any traffic through the lock for quite some time. Tomorrow at the earliest, depending on what we find.'

Marland set off down the towpath. 'They'll be ecstatic. It's not like you can set up a diversion.'

Next McLusky went to find Hanham who was busy stretching police tape across the footpaths approaching the lock. 'Go and stop those people from getting off their boats. Tell them to stay where they are. Get their names and addresses and the boat registration and see if they know anything at all. I want to know why they're here and where they thought they were going and where they'll be for the rest of their natural before you let them go again.'

Back at the cottage McLusky turned to Austin who had just finished a phone call on his mobile. 'When can we expect the Underwater Search Team?'

Austin pulled a face. 'They're busy with a lorry that slid into the river.'

'So what? The lorry can wait, it won't go anywhere, will it?'

'It was full of pigeons.'

'Pigeons?'

'Homing pigeons. And the driver is missing.'

'Marvellous. How long?'

'Your guess is as good as mine.'

In the event that proved to be true. Austin had guessed 'probably by lunchtime' while McLusky had muttered that in his experience they could wait 'all bloody day'. The Underwater Search Team arrived after just over an hour. The large Mercedes van of the unit caused even more of a bottleneck on the road above.

McLusky recognized the team leader but couldn't remember his name. He was an athletic man in his thirties with a tanned face. McLusky vaguely wondered how people who spent their working lives underwater got a suntan. 'Did you find your pigeon man?' he asked him.

'Please don't mention pigeons to me. Ever again. But yeah, we found the driver. In a pub near the site of the crash. Pissed as a fart. He was adamant he was sober at the time of the crash.'

'Naturally. Hard to prove otherwise.'

'Quite. We charged him with leaving the scene of an accident. Is that it out there?'

'The red buoy, yes. There's the body of a

32

woman underneath, we couldn't get her out, she's snagged on something. The lock-keeper will let you use his boat, I'm sure.'

'No, ta, we always use our own gear. Who thought of tying a buoy to her?'

'The killer did.'

'Considerate.' The officer walked off, calling instructions to his team of three. Thirty minutes later a diver let himself drop from a Rigid Inflatable Boat near the buoy and disappeared bubbling under the dark surface of the water.

'Rather him than me,' McLusky said. He was sitting next to Austin in the little boat, kept expertly at station by the lock-keeper at a respectful distance from the search unit's RIB. The buoy bobbed a few times, then lay still on the water again.

Austin dunked his hand into the cool murk, pulled it out, sniffed at it. 'How can he see anything down there? It's like brown ink. Smells OK though. Riverish. I quite like it.'

'Riverish, eh? Shouldn't that be canalish?'

'Same water, surely.'

The diver broke surface next to the RIB and spoke to the team leader in the boat. He reached inside for a tool – McLusky couldn't see what kind – and slid under again. The walkie-talkie McLusky was holding crackled into life as the team leader called him. 'We have a dead female chained to the buoy by the neck. Also tightly bound with some kind of rope or other material. There's another chain round her feet and at the other end of that chain some kind of weight. That's down in the mud at the bottom.'

'You can't tell what it is?'

'Not yet. We'll free the body first. Then we'll bring up anything else we can find. I'm sending down a second man.' As he spoke a further diver let himself glide into the water. By now the railings at road level above them were lined with spectators and so was the bridge above the lock. Every one of them appeared to be holding a mobile phone, some to talk into but mainly to take pictures with. On the north side of the Feeder, crime scene officers in white overalls had arrived. They too took copious photographs. Closest to the water stood the cameraman, taking continuous video footage with a large shoulder-held camera.

To McLusky and Austin in the puttering boat of the lock-keeper it seemed like an age before anything else happened. Then the heads and shoulders of both divers appeared. Straps were secured around the body, then all four men, two in the water and two in the boat, strained to manoeuvre the dead weight out of the water and into the RIB. McLusky noted the near shoulder-length blonde hair, a dress made from dark, patterned material. The body was trussed up tightly, arms stiffly by the sides. He thought he caught a glimpse of gold as the body disappeared into the waiting body bag. He nodded to the lock-keeper who gratefully returned the detectives to dry land.

By the time they had suited up to take a first look at the body the pathologist had also arrived. Dr Coulthart was in his fifties, had a suspiciously full and dark head of hair and wore delicate gold-rimmed spectacles. He was standing on the towpath over the unzipped body bag, which was roomy enough to accommodate even the largest corpse, or one of medium height with chains and red plastic buoy attached. 'Ah, McLusky.' He nodded at the detectives. 'Sergeant . . .' He searched for the name, then remembered. 'Austin.'

'Well?' McLusky asked.

'I've been here less than two minutes, Inspector. Please spare us both the traditional pathologist and police officer chit-chat, we're not on television.' He looked up, saw the scene-of-crime officer with the camera looming close, and added: '*Yet.*'

'I don't know what you mean, I'm sure,' said McLusky, who knew all too well. It was a well-worked cliché that CID wanted instant results while pathologists liked to hedge their bets for as long as possible, lest the post mortem contradict any pronouncements made at the locus.

'She's in her forties, late forties, I'd say, well groomed. The dress looks expensive enough too. She is still wearing her watch.'

'What make is it?'

Coulthart bent down to it. 'Gucci.'

'Not cheap, then.' He glanced at his own watch, which had stopped again, despite a new battery.

'We can rule out robbery, I think,' Austin said, 'watch or no watch. Who goes to all this weirdness for a robbery?'

'Quite, quite,' Coulthart agreed.

McLusky became aware of another white-suited figure in his peripheral vision. It was DSI Denkhaus. 'Time of death?' McLusky asked.

'Couldn't say.'

'How long in the water?'

'No more than twenty-four hours, I'd say.'

'Was she strangled? With that chain?'

Coulthart gently moved the dead woman's head from side to side. 'Not sure. There are bruises on her neck so I can't rule it out.' He stood up. 'And that's all you're going to get until I've had her open.' He turned to Denkhaus. 'Hello, Rob, what brings you out into the fresh air . . .?' Denkhaus smiled and walked wordlessly off down the towpath. Coulthart joined him for a stroll along the canal.

The detectives watched them go while three SOCOs zipped up the bag and removed the body. 'He's definitely checking up,' Austin said. 'Either that or he was pining to see the pathologist.'

McLusky shrugged. 'I think those two play golf together.' He sniffed the air. 'Can you smell something?'

The RIB of the search team was out in midstream again. Austin sniffed. 'Canal? Rubber boat? Petrol fumes? Unwashed SOCOs?'

McLusky was already walking towards the lock. 'No. Worse than that.' He reached the cottage, still sniffing.

'I can smell it now,' Austin said behind him.

McLusky was about to knock on the closed door when his nose led him past it and around the next corner: two uniformed constables, beakers of coffee in one hand, half-eaten baps in the other, mouths full, frozen in mid-chew. One of them was PC Hanham. 'What's going on?' McLusky demanded to know.

Hanham swallowed down a large unchewed

chunk of food that an hour later would give him heartburn. 'Sorry sir, we were starving.'

'You're not the only ones. What's that you've got there?'

'Bacon buttie. And coffee,' said Hanham. He looked as though he was afraid he would be asked to hand it over.

'Where from?'

'*Wheelies Diner*, just up the road.'

'Genius. Don't get caught, DSI Denkhaus is on the prowl.'

'I know, we nearly ran straight into him, that's why we're hiding here.'

The afternoon ebbed away while dark clouds rolled in over the city. As soon as the superintendent had left in the Range Rover that he used for police business, McLusky and Austin had stocked up on coffees, bacon butties and chocolate bars at *Wheelies*. Now they were standing by the edge of the canal with the team leader, watching the last dive of the search unit.

'We'd initially cut the chain in order to free the body,' the team leader explained. 'We had one hell of a time finding it again in the sediment at the bottom. At the other end of it was that radiator.' He indicated the rectangular, ribbed object on a tarpaulin nearby. 'Same style as I have in my house, as a matter of fact. I hope that doesn't make me a suspect.'

'You never know,' said McLusky encouragingly. 'The chain. How long was it? I mean was it exactly the right length for the depth of the canal?'

'Not quite, no. Far too long in fact, by several

37

feet, I'd say. The body was actually like *that* under water.' He indicated the slant with one hand. 'The current dragged the body a bit sideways and the radiator anchored it about so far away.' He stretched out one arm.

'There goes that theory,' McLusky said, draining the last of his coffee. 'I had hoped it was the right length. That would at least have pointed to someone who knew the depth of the canal.'

The diver came up empty handed on his last dive, made a hand signal to his boss and heaved himself into the boat.

Apart from the radiator the team had also brought to the surface a dozen drinks cans, bottles, a folded pram and a bent bicycle wheel.

'That's it, said the diver. There's nothing else down there in the vicinity except mud and darkness.'

It was getting dark. Impatiently, DI Kat Fairfield followed the trundling tractor and trailer along the B road, too narrow and winding to overtake safely. This was not what she had come here for. She had driven out of the city for a blast around the back lanes to let off steam. It hadn't really been a row but it could easily have turned into one had she not left Louise's place when she did. Louise had sprung dinner with her two friends on her and she had felt unprepared and on the back foot all evening. She was no match for Louise Rennie's intellect and education, she had known that when they became lovers. Then it had not looked like a problem. Louise, being a lecturer, was patient and never patronized her when they were alone together, but when her friends were around and the wine was flowing she seemed to take a delight in talking about subjects she knew full well Kat could barely follow. Tonight it had felt as though those three were secretly laughing at her and she had made her excuses – early start, busy day – and no thanks, she'd see herself out. And had driven out of Bristol for a blast in the countryside. In her beloved, zippy little Renault.

Zippy? Presently she was doing twelve miles per hour! She hung back a few yards, took a deep breath and floored the accelerator. It was a stupid place to overtake, a slight rise too, it seemed to take forever to get up to any sort of speed. Headlights appeared in front of her out of nowhere, the tractor slowed, a horn blared, she threw the car onto the correct side of the road just as a dark 4 × 4 slammed past her in the opposite direction, the driver still leaning on the horn. Her Renault dipped one wheel into the sandy verge and fishtailed before she finally managed to straighten up the car. Only then did she let out her breath again, giving voice to her shock in short, Anglo-Saxon syllables. She drove on sedately while her heart rate slowed to normal. *Stupid, stupid, stupid.*

And now McLusky was back, too. He had been suspended from duty at just the time when she had usurped his place in Louise's bed. She hadn't seen him since, which meant she had never had to deal with the consequences of it. But now, against all the odds, McLusky was back. So far she had managed to keep her relationship secret from her other colleagues. Her only two remaining girl friends – both in straight relationships and busy bringing up small children – had reacted with guarded bemusement. But she had been *married* once? What had *happened*? Where had *that* come from? Well, nowhere, it had always been there, only Louise hadn't, end of story. But at work this story had the potential to run and run, especially if it became known that she had pinched a colleague's girlfriend. She'd never hear the end of it and it probably wouldn't help her career either.

She speeded up now, no longer in the mood for a blast but wanting to get home quickly. She had drunk a large glass of wine at Louise's but its effects had worn off, leaving her feeling scratchy and wanting more. She shifted easily through the gears, swung smoothly through the bends with one hand on the wheel. Then she saw it.

A moving flashlight by the side of the road. Seconds later her headlights caught a camper van, half pulled off the road at an awkward angle, just where the fields were giving way to trees. The engine cover at the back was raised. Next to it stood a blonde woman. Fairfield slowed right down. No, it was a young man, with shoulder-length hair, mid-to-late twenties, she guessed. 'If you can't tell them apart anymore, Kat, perhaps you should take early retirement,' she chided herself.

She stopped her car, lowered her window. 'Trouble?'

The man skipped lightly over to her side of the

car. He was wearing walking boots, jeans, a white tee-shirt with a fresh streak of car grease across it and a short denim jacket. Fairfield stored away the descriptive details automatically, without thinking about it. 'Thanks for stopping, ma'am. I've been here for half an hour and lots of folks drove by but nobody stopped.' He spoke with a soft transcontinental accent she was unable to place yet it somehow made her think of surfing and beach parties, even as the fumes from her car engine wafted around them. He was quite good looking, she supposed. She hoped he wouldn't say something embarrassing, like 'dude'.

'You've broken down?'

'Yup, sure have.'

'Called the RAC? Breakdown recovery?'

'I'm not a member of anything, I'm just a visitor to your fair country. I had sort of hoped not to break down.'

Fairfield nodded towards the broken-down van. 'I see. That's why you bought a thirty-year-old VW camper.'

'Bit retro, I know. But it's been good to me so far and I only need it to get me back to London now.' He patted his jacket pocket. 'I've got my plane ticket home.'

Fairfield smiled. Americans. Forever *goin' home*. 'I'm afraid I'm not a mechanic. But I'd be happy to call a breakdown service for you.'

'I was hoping that wouldn't be necessary. I know what's wrong with it, it's just a broken fan belt.' He indicated the frayed fan belt on the ground at the rear of the van with his torch. 'I

41

don't suppose you're carrying replacement fan belts, ma'am?'

'I'll have to disappoint you there.'

'Well . . .' He shifted awkwardly on his feet. 'There is one thing I know that works.'

'Yes?'

'It's kind of embarrassing. Erm, I know that pantyhose work as a fan belt. Or, or stockings. You, you don't have a spare pair of those, either?'

Fairfield had heard of using tights or stockings as fan belts. 'Not a spare one, no.'

'I couldn't persuade you . . . I mean, I'd buy them off you, obviously . . . I know it's quite an imposition.'

Oh, what the hell. It was quite a mild evening and she was going straight home anyway. 'Oh, all right, if it gets you on your way.' She released her seat belt and stepped out of the car. The road was still empty and it was quite dark now, except for the lights of her Renault.

The young man looked up and down the road. Just then a car appeared, travelling in the opposite direction. 'You're welcome to use my van to change in, obviously.'

'That won't be necessary. You just stand by your van so you don't get yourself run over. And turn around for a minute.'

'Oh, of course.' The young man trotted off as he'd been told. 'This is very kind of you,' he said, facing the other way.

'I know.' The car passed by without slowing and disappeared into the darkness. Standing on the near-side of her Renault Fairfield pulled up her knee-length skirt, popped off one shoe, and with three quick movements and a changeover of feet took off her tights. 'Right, you can turn around.' She felt slightly awkward herself as she handed over her tights to the stranger who accepted her offering with an air of reverence.

'I . . . I don't know how much . . . what do I owe you for these?'

'Forget it. In my job you get through a lot of those. As long as they get you going again you're welcome to them.'

'Thank you, I'm much obliged. In your job? What is your job?'

'I'm a police officer,' Fairfield said, walking back to her car, 'who is glad she shaved her legs this morning. Goodbye. And good luck.'

'Thank you ma'am. I'll be fine.' He waved as Fairfield drove off fast. 'Police woman,' he said as he watched her tail lights disappear into the distance. For a moment he buried his face in the crumpled tights and inhaled deeply. Then he stuffed them into his jacket pocket and went to fit the fan belt back on the engine with practised ease.

Four

'It's a weird one.' DC French voiced the opinion of most of the detectives in the incident room.

With his first coffee of the day getting cold in his left hand, McLusky pushed the squeaking pen across the whiteboard. He was no good at drawing, and drawing underwater scenes from imagination was an added challenge. He stepped back. 'Yeees, and she wasn't really eight foot tall, either.' He wiped at the drawing with the eraser and re-fashioned the lower half. 'That's the second chain around her feet here and that's supposed to be a radiator at the bottom there. That's how we found her.'

DC Daniel Dearlove, 'Deedee' to his friends and enemies alike, piped up: 'Strange way to dispose of a body. Why hang it from a buoy like that?'

McLusky dropped the pen into the tray of the whiteboard, apologizing with a shrug for his drawing. 'Well, you get the idea. Why hang her from a buoy like that? You tell me, Deedee. There's some chicken soup in it for you.' Scattered laughter in the room. Everyone had worked late last night without result and the mood in the room was flat.

'Perhaps he meant to let the body go and was disturbed before he could do it?' French suggested.

'No. You want to hide a body, you wrap it up,

44

you weigh it down and drop it in the canal, then get the hell out of there before someone clocks you. No, this was how we were supposed to find her. Not simply washed up somewhere. The body was arranged like that and it took some doing. This body wasn't disposed of, it was being displayed.'

French tilted her head as she stared at the drawing. 'Displayed yet out of sight.'

'Yes.'

Austin squinted at the board. 'The way you drew that makes it look a bit like an exclamation mark.'

McLusky sounded irritable. 'Meaning?'

'Nothing, just saying.'

'Never mind what it looks like, let's concentrate on what it is: a dead woman suspended in the water in a canal smack in the middle of Bristol. Who, how, why and when? We have no one reported missing that even vaguely fits the description. About five foot eight, mid forties, well groomed, blonde hair, about shoulder length. We'll have more to go on after the autopsy. Talking of which.' He looked at his watch. It had stopped at ten to seven. McLusky turned around to check the clock on the wall. It showed ten twenty. 'Is that the right time?' Nods and affirmative grunts. 'The autopsy is scheduled for eleven.'

Austin nodded. The inspector hated attending autopsies so it usually fell to the sergeant to be there. 'Am I going?'

'No, not this time. See if you get any joy on the victim's Gucci watch, instead. French, chase up the owners of the moored boats, Deedee, all

45

the witness statements . . .' McLusky rattled off a few more instructions and left for the mortuary, west of the city in Flax Bourton. He left behind a relieved DS. Austin hated attending autopsies even more than the inspector did and often suffered bad claustrophobic dreams after witnessing them, something he had never mentioned to any of his colleagues; in this job you were meant to be tough, unaffected, being able to take it. No one would offer you counselling because you witnessed a corpse being eviscerated.

What McLusky had not mentioned to Austin was the superintendent's insistence that from now on he, McLusky, attend all autopsies personally and, while DCI Gaunt was away, reported directly back to him. Which was why the inspector stood outside the mortuary one minute before the appointed time, fortifying himself with a hasty smoke. Judging by the amount of cigarette butts littering the ground outside the entrance this was a well-observed practice among visitors to the place. A curiously mild, blustery wind carried away his cigarette end when he flicked it towards the car park.

'Inspector McLusky, what a pleasant surprise.' Dr Coulthart squinted theatrically over the top of his gold-rimmed glasses at him. McLusky answered with a childish grimace. He had been reliably informed that Coulthart couldn't see a thing without his glasses and peered over them purely for schoolmasterly effect. 'I had expected your Scottish deputy,' Coulthart continued. 'Mr Austin is not unwell, I hope?'

'In fine fettle.'

'Glad to hear it. You are just in time.'

The now naked body of the victim lay on the table, still often casually referred to as 'the slab', though the high tech, adjustable stainless steel support had little in common with the marble slabs of old, apart from the facility to drain away the fluids leaking from the body. In the viewing suite, separated from the procedure by a wall of glass, McLusky nevertheless thought he could smell death. He knew what it smelled like, and his nose, like an elephant, never forgot.

Coulthart indicated bagged-up clothing on the counter behind him. 'Knee-length dress, a leaf pattern, green on darker green, natural cotton fibre. Silk underwear. It all goes with the Gucci watch, I'd say, though the dress is mass produced, but not cheap, it's silk lined.' A quick look over his spectacles. 'Try Debenhams, Inspector. Apart from the chains, which were of medium gauge, rusted and old, she was also trussed up like a pig on a spit with two lengths of nylon clothesline. Both have already departed to forensics. She couldn't have moved a muscle.' Coulthart's quiet assistant, the video camera and microphone were all in place. 'Let us begin, then.'

McLusky settled down on the bench. On the wall to his right a monitor showed everything the movable camera saw. If there was one place where smoking ought to be allowed it was this one, McLusky thought. He had now given up giving up smoking but was once more trying to cut down. The very thought of smoking less

47

seemed to stoke his cravings. 'Was she strangled with the chains round her neck?'

Coulthart moved the camera for a close-up of the area. 'There is some bruising around the neck but she wasn't strangled. She drowned, Inspector.'

'You mean she was alive when she was thrown in?'

'She could have been drowned elsewhere but I think once we open her up,' Coulthart made the first, Y-shaped incision, 'we'll find she drowned in canal water.'

McLusky looked elsewhere, at the white, antiseptic walls and stainless steel fittings. He tried to imagine the scene of the murder. 'Was she conscious?'

'There are no contusions, so she wasn't knocked unconscious. Toxicology will tell us if she was drugged or not.'

'She'd have screamed. Someone would have heard. The lock-keeper's cottage was only yards away.'

'She was gagged. With adhesive tape, quite broad. It eventually fell off under water but there are still traces of the adhesive on her face. Quite broad tape, electrical. Gaffer tape, I believe it's called.'

'Bastard.'

'Yes. Her head must have been only just below the water and she drowned, taking in water through her nose. Not a good way to go, I agree.'

'Did she put up a fight at all? Would the killer have scratches or bruises?'

'There are no signs that she fought him off, no

48

defensive wounds, nothing under her fingernails that would be consistent with her having fought her attacker. Obviously, immersion in water always messes up trace evidence like that. I'm not hopeful.'

'That could mean her killer was convincingly armed or she knew him.'

'Yes, Inspector. Or both.'

At lunchtime, in the neon-lit cavern that was the Albany Road staff canteen, McLusky surprised himself with an undiminished, post-autopsy appetite. There was not much left at the counter that looked edible. A few misshapen meatballs, some ladlefuls of potato-topped mystery mince and slices of pizza curling under the heat lamps. McLusky appreciated good food, only he rarely got to eat it. While his eyes travelled wearily over the offerings perishing under the heat lamps he filled his pockets with several types of chocolate bar, which he planned to use as replacements in his new reduced-smoking regime. Eventually he opted for what he considered the safest option, the all-day fried breakfast, a cholesterol bonanza known at the station as the '999 breakfast'. He found Austin drinking coffee at one of the tables, a puddle of mystery mince on a plate in front of him.

'How did it go?' Austin prompted.

'I'll call another briefing for three o'clock, after I've seen the super, tell them when you get upstairs, Jane. She died of drowning, almost certainly where we found her. The bastard stuffed a rag in her mouth, gagged her with tape, took her down there, got her on to a boat or something

49

and chucked her in the canal. When the bubbles stopped he knew his work was done.'

'He must be quite a charmer.'

McLusky speared a wrinkled sausage. 'Absolutely.' He nodded grimly at his sergeant. 'I have a bad feeling about this one.'

'Don't eat it, then,' said Austin. 'It looks like yesterday's.'

The picture board in the incident room had acquired a few more photographs, of the victim's dress, underwear and watch, close-ups of the chains and of the woman's face. McLusky had the room's attention. 'We still have no ID. Someone must miss her. She had had recent intercourse but there are no indications of rape. She was dressed, though her legs were bare and she was minus her shoes. She had no piercings or tattoos, which makes a change. Someone must have noticed she's missing.'

French tapped her chin with her biro. 'Could she be a high class pro?'

'It's possible but we have nothing to suggest it. The watch . . .?' McLusky turned to Austin.

'No joy. Gucci watches are a bit expensive but they're hardly rare. That one,' Austin pointed to the photograph on the board, 'is about six hundred quid on Amazon.'

'Definitely not robbery then,' said Dearlove.' You'd hardly leave that on the body.'

'That depends,' said McLusky. 'If she carried a briefcase with a hundred grand in it you might not want to bother with the watch. However, would you bother to tie her up with string, gag her with gaffer tape, put a buoy round her neck and chuck her in the canal? It's hard work, takes time and forethought. Organization.'

'And it's risky,' French added.

McLusky nodded. 'And it's risky. But as it turns out, no one appears to have seen it happen. *As usual.*' The general public's immense capacity for being unobservant was one of McLusky's many pet hates. 'According to the autopsy results she went into the water between one and four in the morning. There's of course very little light and no lighting at all on the north side of the canal.'

'It's an awful lot to carry, too,' Austin said. 'Are we perhaps looking at more than one perp here?'

'Please don't say "perp", Jane, when you mean "deranged killer", it makes him sound like a bit of indigestion. You'll be calling suspects "crims", next. But yes, by all means let's keep an open mind about that, though the MO has a touch of the insane about it, and that would suggest a single perpetrator. OK, we're looking for the transport that was used, a car and a boat of some description. I want to know where he got the buoy and we need to find out where the radiator came from.' There was a perfunctory knock at the door before a constable entered the room, holding a sheet of notepaper. 'Yes, what is it?' McLusky asked him.

'We think we may have found the dead woman's car, sir,' the constable said.

McLusky took the note from his hand. 'And what makes you think that?'

51

'The car was abandoned in a lay-by on the A369. We found a sort of jacket inside that appears to match the dress she was wearing.'

'A "sort of jacket", Constable?'

'Yes, you know what I mean', the constable said, undaunted. 'It's part of a woman's outfit but quite useless as a garment, really.'

There were giggles among the officers. 'Yes, thanks, I can picture it.' McLusky gulped down the cold coffee then picked up his radio and his jacket. 'OK, you all know what to do, so do it. Jane? You and I are going to take a look at the motor.'

Five

'The car is registered to a Barbara Steadman,' said PC Weisz who had found the silver BMW abandoned in the lay-by and had guarded it ever since. He recognized one of the CID officers. It was that McLusky character he had come across the other night, only he looked less dishevelled now and didn't smell of booze. But he could still do with a haircut. 'Her date of birth fits with the age of the victim from the canal.' A thin mizzle of rain was falling. McLusky turned up the collar on his jacket. The luxury car gleamed wetly beside the greening hedge. 'That jacket on the passenger seat,' Weisz was saying, 'matches the dress of the victim.'

With gloved hands McLusky moved the driver's backrest forward and back, had a thorough look at the inside without passing more than his hand and arm through the door. Crime scene technicians didn't like anyone to so much as breathe inside a car that was a possible locus of a crime. The keys were in the ignition. He closed the door to keep the increasingly intense rain out. Crime scene investigators were just arriving, filling the area with more cars and vans. 'She didn't leave here of her own free will. No one moves too far from a car with the keys in the ignition, and she left her jacket.' He turned back towards the car, took another look at the jacket through the wet car windows. 'Not exactly equipped for all weathers, was she? I mean it's strangely mild but not that mild. Unless she's got gear in the boot.' He looked about. It was a rural stretch of the Pill Road, already busy with afternoon traffic. 'It's a bit of a miracle the thing's still here. Unless . . .' McLusky bit his lip, and squinted sideways at the car.

'Unless what?' Austin asked.

'Unless of course it *isn't* still here.'

Austin scratched the tip of his nose. 'I don't follow.'

'Might not have happened here at all,' McLusky said cheerfully. 'The car could have been dumped here recently. If she was snatched from her car it *may* have happened here or it may have happened somewhere else entirely.'

'Registered driver has a Bristol address, just outside Ham Green,' said Austin. 'That's not far up the road.'

McLusky walked off and took out his packet of Extra Lights. 'Let's give the crime-scene techies some room.' After a moment's hesitation he put the cigarettes back in his pocket and took out a chocolate bar. He unwrapped it and offered Austin half. 'Want some? It's one of those twin things.'

Austin accepted the stick of chocolate-covered biscuit. 'Chocolate? Since when?'

'Helps me cut down on the fags. Her car is pointing in the direction of her home, which suggests she was on her way back from wherever she was. We'll wait for the details to come through then pay her home a visit.' He crunched the last bit of the chocolate bar and crumpled the wrapper into his pocket. 'Not bad.' He took out his cigarettes and lit one, despite the rain. He called across to the crime-scene technicians. 'Anything good in the boot? Money, guns, illegal immigrants?'

'Pair of green wellies,' called the woman examining the boot. 'Tartan rug, tiny torch.' She twisted the little red thing. 'Batteries flat.'

'That's it?'

'That's your lot.'

He turned back to Austin. 'So, unless her coat was stolen then she drove that thing wearing a dress and matching jacket. Now that says to me she wasn't on her way to do the shopping. Wherever she was going she didn't expect to be walking anywhere. Garage to garage, perhaps.' McLusky, shielding his cigarette from the rain under his cupped hand, gestured at the BMW, which was now surrounded by white-suited figures. 'Assuming she was the one driving it, why would she stick it there?'

'What do you mean?'

'Well, look at it: it's right at the entrance to the lay-by, there's space for lots of cars. But the car's right at the entrance.'

'The lay-by was full? No. She was meeting someone? Someone who was already parked there, perhaps.'

'Yes. Most likely.' A raindrop squarely hit the end of his cigarette and extinguished it. McLusky let it drop unceremoniously and without comment.

'Or she saw something else in the lay-by and went to have a look.'

'Like what?'

'Dunno.'

'Or she stopped for the killer who was flagging her down.' He accepted a sheet of notes from a constable. 'Right, few more details. She was 49, married.' He widened his eyes at Austin before continuing. 'And her husband just this minute reported her missing. Lovely. He only just noticed he'd mislaid his wife. I think we should have an urgent word, don't you?'

The large detached house west of Ham Green matched the price tag of the BMW yet managed to do so without ostentation. Solid, Victorian, partially clad with ivy.

'Four bedrooms?' McLusky let the Mazda crawl slowly up to the open gate of the tarmac drive.

'More than that, I'm sure,' Austin said. 'Looks like someone's at home, you can ask.'

McLusky stopped the car where it would block the drive, though the Range Rover standing in the slate-roofed car port would have no trouble escaping through the large gardens. At the porticoed front door McLusky pressed the brass doorbell. He thought he could hear a faint chime inside but no one came to answer. After rapping a few times on the door he stepped back out into the drive. The rain provided no more than a fine misting now but he felt damp and uncomfortable nevertheless. 'Let's have a look round the back.' They peered in by the ground floor windows as they rounded the solid building.

'Not short of a few bob,' Austin commented. 'Looks nice and comfy.'

The inspector stopped at a tall sash window, cupped his hands on the glass to look inside and gave it his appraisal. 'Bit overstuffed perhaps but yes, looks comfy enough.' McLusky, who owned six pieces of furniture if he counted the mattress on the floor he called his bed, rarely felt comfortable while awake. He briefly thought of Louise Rennie's flat in Clifton. That had been comfortable yet at the same time full of light and air. He had concluded quite early that Louise needed a lot of space around her.

At the back of the house they found a large Victorian conservatory in need of repainting, a terrace and a garden that gently rose towards a stone wall behind a line of trees that separated it from the fields beyond. At the end of a stone-flagged path, halfway between house and trees, stood a wooden summerhouse. Smoke twirled thinly from a metal stovepipe. Behind a window shaded by the rustic porch McLusky thought he detected a slight movement. 'In the Wendy house.'

As they walked towards it a bearded face appeared at the window, then the door opened and a man stepped on to the tiny porch. In his late fifties or early sixties, he was tall, with short, thin grey hair and a grey, angular beard. 'Can I help you? Oh, police,' he added when McLusky and Austin held their IDs aloft.

'I'm DI McLusky, this is Sergeant Austin. Are you John Steadman, sir?' The man nodded. 'And you reported your wife missing?'

'I did. About an hour ago. You got here quickly. I was led to believe the police would take ages to respond to a missing-persons call.'

'Led to believe by whom?' McLusky asked.

'Well, you know. Just . . . general opinion. Yes, I am getting worried.' He gestured behind him. 'Do come in out of the rain, please.'

The summerhouse was simply furnished. The Persian rugs on the floor were worn but genuine. There was a desk that held an old-fashioned doorstep of a laptop and a profusion of papers. In front of it a beaten-up leather chair. A rickety chaise longue at the other end. A small, pot-bellied stove sat in the centre of a tiled circle. The walls were lined with books, the chaise longue was stacked with them. There was a faint note of damp leaves but the strongest note was that of red wine, a half-empty glass by the side of the computer. 'Sorry, it's a bit cramped with all three of us in here,' Steadman said.

'It's fine,' said McLusky whose own office was less than half the size. 'Mr Steadman, could you describe your wife, please?'

'I did all that over the phone just an hour ago. I gave the officer a detailed description.'

'I'm sure you did. Would you describe her again for me? I'd like to hear it for myself.' Steadman repeated the description, quickly, and with a slight air of irritation. McLusky nodded sympathetically throughout. 'What was your wife wearing when you last saw her?'

'A red-and-gold dressing gown, as far as I recall.'

'So you didn't see her leave the house?'

58

'No. I have no idea what she was wearing when she left the house.'

'When did you first notice your wife was missing?'

'Yesterday morning, really. I mean, she hadn't come home by the time I went to bed the night before but when she wasn't there in the morning either that's when I realized.'

'Realized what?'

'That she was missing, Inspector.'

'But you waited until today to report it.'

'I know you don't take it seriously for the first twenty-four hours anyway.'

'I think you'll find that we make decisions on an individual basis and we would have at least looked out for her car. A silver BMW, registration . . .' McLusky read the index number from his notebook.

'That's right.'

'Mr Steadman, yesterday the body of a woman was recovered from the Feeder canal. It was widely reported.'

'I, er, I don't follow the local news. I'm busy here with . . . wait, wait. Are you saying . . . you mean . . .' He faltered, looking from one officer to the other.

'We can't be certain,' McLusky said gently. 'Did your wife wear a watch?'

'Yes, a gold one.'

'A Gucci watch?'

Steadman breathed in deeply and shrugged. 'It could be. I really should know, I gave it to her. But I'm not sure of the make.'

'We found your wife's car in a lay-by a few

miles south from here. There is a possibility that the body found in the canal is that of your missing wife. It would help us if you could come to see if you can identify the body. Or if you would like someone else to go, preferably a relative . . .'

Steadman turned away from them, reached for the glass of wine, drained it. He spoke without turning around, standing very straight. 'I'll do it. I'll come. In the canal? But . . . if her car is nowhere near . . . I don't understand.'

'Neither do we yet. DS Austin will arrange for an area car to take you to the mortuary.'

Austin nodded and stepped outside to make the call.

'When we came and rang the door bell earlier there was no answer.'

Steadman turned to face him. 'Yes, there's no one in the house. I can't hear it back here. The bell. So I can work undisturbed. Cleaner, gardener and so on all have keys.'

'But you had just reported your wife missing. Wouldn't you be anxious for news?'

'I did give them my mobile number.' He indicated his phone on the desk.

McLusky fished the sheet of notes he'd been given earlier from his jacket and squinted at it. 'So you did.'

'You must understand, we have been living quite separate lives. I'm retired now and working on a book, so I spend whole days in here. My wife left sometime late afternoon on Saturday. I presumed she had gone for a drive.'

Control sent a car for Steadman; McLusky

followed it a few car-lengths behind with Austin beside him. 'What do you make of him, Jane?'

'Shocked, but not overwhelmed. He wasn't exactly screaming "Oh God, please not *that*", but he's quite . . . I don't know. More surprised than anything. It takes people in different ways, of course.'

'His wife worked for Western Energy, apparently.'

'Not as a meter reader, I expect. And how come *they* didn't miss her?' Austin wondered.

'She'd taken today off to make it a long weekend. Not due back at work till tomorrow, according to him.'

'Let's hope it is his wife, then,' Austin said.

'Yes, please. And if possible a radiator missing from their house. But in the absence of that I'll settle for the body being that of Barbara Steadman.'

When the sheet that covered the body's face was drawn back by the mortuary assistant on the other side of the viewing window the detectives' eyes were on John Steadman. His nostrils flared, his eyes widened, his mouth fell open. He stepped closer to the glass. 'How did she die?'

'For the record: can you identify the body as that of your wife?'

'Yes. That's . . . Babs.' He enunciated the name as if saying it for the first time. Or for the last. He swallowed hard. 'How?'

Austin nodded at the assistant to cover the face. 'There's an office we can use,' he said. 'We'll talk in there.'

Steadman accepted a cup of sweet tea. The details of the case had been withheld and McLusky was determined to keep as much of it from Steadman for as long as he could. Husbands were always the most likely perpetrators in a woman's violent death. Looking at him now, McLusky tried to visualise the tall, almost gangly man bundle up his wife, drive her to the canal, row her out towards the lock. McLusky noticed that apart from his hair and trimmed beard his eyes, too, were grey, making him think of a timber wolf. Did wolves have grey eyes?

'And she was murdered? Someone *drowned* her? My wife was a strong swimmer. How do you drown someone?'

'Do you know of anyone who might have wanted your wife dead? Any enemies? Disputes? Rows?'

'No one is liked by everybody, Inspector, but we don't all get . . . drowned.'

'How was your relationship with your wife? Would you say it was a happy marriage?'

'It was a normal marriage.'

'You mentioned you were leading quite separate lives. Could you elaborate on that?'

'I thought that was self-explanatory.'

'Indulge us. It will help us get a clearer picture.'

'We took separate ways, quite a while ago. We no longer shared many interests. Or friends, even. Expectations.'

'Expectations of what?' McLusky asked.

'I'm retired, as you know. I simply wanted to concentrate on my writing now.'

'In your Wendy house.'

'In my writing shed, yes.'

'Your wife disapproved, somehow?'

'No, not disapproved. Let us say that she found the prospect less than exciting. Writing is not a spectator sport.'

McLusky watched Steadman's dry, manicured hands, resting quietly in the man's lap. 'And what would your wife have found more exciting, Mr Steadman?'

'Scraping dog shit off her shoes.' He gave McLusky a sour smile. 'Almost anything, Inspector.' He made as if to drain his tea, then changed his mind and set down the cup. 'I want to go home now. If that's all right.'

'Of course. Just one more question. Where were you on Saturday, between, let's say midnight and six in the morning on the Sunday?'

'Is that when it happened? I was at home. Asleep. And no, there's no one to confirm that.'

The area car was still waiting. Outside the mortuary entrance they watched him being driven off. 'Did he do it?' Austin asked.

'There's a lot of resentment there. We'll obviously have to go back and interview him properly when we know more about both of them. Would you put money on him?'

'A fiver each way. He wants a quiet life. There are no children. Much quieter without her around. Plus it would explain why the car was found so close to the house.'

'Would it?'

'Would if they were in the car together.'

'Let's see,' said McLusky. He half-closed his eyes. 'He uses her car so he can leave it somewhere away from the house to make it look like she was attacked by a stranger. He ties her up,

63

sticks her in a boat, rows her into the middle of the canal. Tells her he's had it up to here, gives her the heave-ho, dunks her like a teabag, waits for the bubbles to stop, then drives back. He abandons the car away from the house but close enough to walk home.'

'Something like that.'

'Stranger things happen at sea.' McLusky sniffed at a wrapped Mars bar as though it were a fine cigar, then peeled off the waxy paper.

'Careful,' warned Austin. 'Before you know it you'll be on twenty a day.'

The head office of Western Energy occupied a five storey building by the river; forbidding plate glass from the outside, efficient luxury on the inside. Security was tight. The man at the front desk had asked him to wear his visitor's pass visibly at all times. 'During last week's protests we had a couple of environmental activists sneak into the building and they got nearly all the way to the top floor. So if security see anyone without a pass they're likely to pounce on you.'

'I'm not easily pounce-able,' he assured the man yet did as he had been told. A few minutes later, walking along the corridor of the personnel department behind a blue-suited woman – a Ms L. Williams according to her own pass – McLusky quietly wondered what five floors full of employees could be doing in the computer age if you supplied two products and sent out bills only every three months. Once seated in the glass cube of her office he asked the question in

64

another way. 'I suppose selling energy is not a simple business?'

'Far from it, inspector. It's immensely complex, fiercely competitive and lies absolutely at the heart of our economy. Without us everything stops. To make sure it doesn't is what we are here for.' Ms L. Williams smiled, but not too much, having already been told what the inspector's visit was about.

'Thank you, perhaps I'll read the brochure for myself later. And what part did Barbara Steadman play in all this?'

'It's hard to take in. I didn't know her well but I had come across her at some meetings and several functions.' Her eyes left McLusky's for a split second as they flicked to the computer screen at the corner of her desk. 'Mrs Steadman was management, head of domestic telesales.' She added, helpfully, 'Acquisition and retention.'

Acquisition and retention of customers, he assumed. 'Any problems at work?'

'No, quite the opposite, she was doing extremely well and will be difficult to replace. Her salary reflected that.'

'That would have been my next question. How much did Mrs Steadman earn?'

'That really is confidential, Inspector. You might send a written request for that kind of information but it's company policy not to reveal to outsiders . . .'

With difficulty McLusky managed to stop himself from rolling his eyes to the ceiling. It never ceased to amaze him what some people

65

considered too sensitive to reveal to the police, even in a murder investigation. He spoke with the patience of a ticking time bomb. 'Barbara Steadman was murdered and I am hunting for her killer. I know what type of underwear she preferred, I have watched her naked body being cut open and I can tell you that her liver weighed two pounds and four ounces. By the end of this investigation I will know more about her than she ever did herself. How much did she earn?'

Ms Williams didn't blink. 'Ninety-six K a year.'

'And after bonuses?'

'Last year just under a hundred and sixty.'

McLusky thought of John Steadman and wondered what the man's own pension plan looked like. 'Did Mrs Steadman have direct contact with customers?'

'Not personally, no. Her department did of course.'

'Have there been any disputes she was involved in? With customers, I mean.'

'She didn't deal with things like that. Her work was more strategic planning, Inspector, not running after customers waving red bills.'

'Did she have enemies in the company? Did she tread on any toes to get where she was?'

'Not that I am aware of.'

'Or was Mrs Steadman particularly friendly with anyone?'

'Again, I am not aware of any personal attachments within the company.'

'Lonely at the top, was it? Did she have lovers?'

'You mean *did she have affairs*? I really wouldn't know, Inspector. This isn't a corner shop, you know. If Mrs Steadman was conducting an extra-marital affair I'm sure she had the . . . the *means* to conduct it discreetly. Not that it's a shooting offence but we don't encourage employees to bring their private lives to work.'

Private lives, lonely deaths. McLusky wasn't sure he believed that a complete separation of private life and work was such a good idea. You worked for a company for years and all they knew about you was what you were worth to them, of the rest they were 'not aware'. Standing in the rainy street near the Western Energy building, trying to remember where he had left his car, he thought that leaving your private life at the door for the duration of your working day felt too much like suspended animation.

When he remembered where he had left his car his vague hope that it had been stolen was dashed. The old Mazda sat untouched by the kerb, scratched, lopsided and with the keys in the ignition.

Afternoon had turned to evening and the skies had cleared by the time McLusky left Albany Road Station that day. He started the engine, then just sat in the driver's seat, for a moment undecided. He knew there was no food at home and lunch was a long time ago but shopping and cooking seemed altogether too much effort. Fish & chips from Pellegrino's was often his answer to this recurring problem or, lazier still, cheesy chips at Rita's near his flat, but he felt too restless even for that tonight. He drove to a sandwich bar near the harbour where he could be sure of a doorstep egg-and-bacon sandwich with brown sauce that would not be subject to geometric mutilation. He'd wave away the offer of tea or coffee; he was saving his thirst for a few pints at the Barge Inn opposite his flat in Northmoor Street. Yet when he found himself back behind the wheel of his car it seemed to develop a will of its own. Instead of heading for Montpelier and the pub he found himself again driving down the now lamp-lit Feeder Road alongside the shadowy canal to Netham Lock. Traffic on the road was sporadic. He left his car unlocked just beyond the bridge.

A narrow slipway led him down to the edge of the canal opposite the lock-keeper's cottage. A lantern illuminated the area directly in front of the closed lock. No light showed behind the cottage's windows. With less traffic noise around he could hear the small watery sounds in the dark. The buoy no longer marked the spot where Barbara Steadman had been murdered but McLusky thought he could tell exactly where it had floated, marking the evil that was hidden below the surface, marked so it would be found. Was the killer trying to say something? Was the manner of the killing meant to signify something? Surely the manner of her death and the way the body was left meant something to the killer, but what and how?

Not a good way to go, the pathologist had said. He made a mental note to ask him just what constituted a good way to die. Most of us hoped to die peacefully in our beds, possibly surrounded by our loved ones after a long fulfilled life, yet he doubted many lives were blessed with that kind of ending. Most ended in hospital beds, many on hospital trolleys, unobserved by loved ones. Most people died at three in the morning, because it was always darkest before the dawn. McLusky had attended many murder scenes in his time at CID which had given him a mental catalogue of bad ways to go, with vivid pictures that refused to fade. He remembered the smells that went with them, too. Barbara Steadman's death smelled of wet rubber, damp canvas and of canal water. It was an earthy, not unpleasant smell. Perhaps that was what one ought to aim for, he thought, a death that smelled pleasantly, earthy, that didn't reek of disinfectant or scream with blood.

McLusky's eyes had been fixed on the empty spot on the water. Now he looked up. He had no idea how long the figure had been standing there, on the opposite bank. It looked to him like a man in a hooded top or coat. It was hard to make out since the figure remained a few feet outside the pool of light created by the lantern in front of the cottage. The figure stood tall, motionless, looking directly at him across the width of the dark water. McLusky could see the light skin tone of the face but could not make out sex or age. Then the man, surely a man, lifted one hand and briefly held up one finger.

McLusky called across. 'I'm a police officer. Stay there, I want a word.' But even as he started up the path towards the level of the bridge he could see the figure turning away, retreating into the darker shadows of the towpath opposite. 'Wait, I want to talk to you!' McLusky called but

69

his voice was swallowed up by a passing lorry. He began to jog across the bridge and down behind the lock-keeper's cottage. By the time he stood breathless on the towpath it was empty.

Six

'I walked along for a bit, checked the moored boats and the vegetation, but he'd gone.'

They were sitting in Austin's blue Nissan Micra, parked opposite the Steadman house. Austin had insisted on travelling in his own car and McLusky had reluctantly joined him. He hated being driven, especially in tiny cars. Austin waved away the inspector's wordless offer of a share in his chocolate bar. 'He probably made off across the playing fields.'

'It was pretty dark down there and I didn't have my torch. I could easily have walked past him if he hid in the bushes. The thing was, when he was still opposite me, just before he ran off, he made some kind of gesture. Like giving me the finger but I think it was his index finger. As though he was admonishing me. Or pointing towards heaven. Then disappeared in a puff of smoke. I should have been quicker off the mark there.'

In his frustration McLusky stuffed the entire chocolate bar into his mouth with three angry bites.

'What made you go back there at that time of the day in the first place? Did you think we had missed something?'

McLusky worked hard to free his teeth from the caramel goo of the chocolate bar before

71

answering. 'I often do that. Go back on my own when it's quiet. After the circus has packed up and the gawpers have gone home. You can't really see a place properly while it's infested with personnel. So I go back when it's quiet. Get a feel for the place. It helps me think. Somctimes. Not this time. I ended up running up and down the towpath, effing and blinding.' After which he had driven home and drunk several angry pints at the Barge Inn.

'Talk about disappearing acts. You should have seen Fairfield this morning.'

McLusky leant back against the passenger door to get a better look at Austin. 'Should I? I haven't seen her at all since I got back.'

'I think that's because she's avoiding you. She was walking down the corridor, I was some way behind her, I'd just dropped some files off in your office. You were coming into the corridor, talking to Dearlove. The moment she heard your voice she did an about-turn and darted back into her office.'

McLusky had lost Louise Rennie in the drug-white snows of the last winter. Austin had been the only soul whom McLusky had told about finding Kat Fairfield in bed with Louise who at the time he had – wrongly as it turned out – thought of as his girlfriend. He had felt he just had to tell someone. Immediately afterwards he had threatened Austin with justifiable homicide should he spread it around the station. 'Fairfield on the run. That's gratifying to know.' He winkled a cigarette from a battered packet.

'Do you mind not smoking in the car?' Austin asked. 'Eve is giving me hell about the smell.'

72

'Another bloody no-smoking zone. You might have told me before you made me come along in your car.'

'I thought you were cutting down. You just had a chocolate bar.'

'Yeah, but after eating you need a fag, don't you? It aids digestion.' With a groan he levered himself out of the car. 'OK, I'll pollute Steadman's air instead. Let's see if we can rattle the man. I think I detect less than perfect grief there.'

McLusky lit a cigarette and waited for a delivery van to pass before crossing the street. The van slowed in front of him and turned into the drive of Steadman's house.

Austin blipped the central locking. '*Dauphin* deli and caterers. No supermarket own-brand for John Steadman, I'm sure.'

'Posh, are they?'

'A round of their sandwiches and you'll be remortgaging the house.'

'Count me out, then, I'm renting.'

'Given the Steadmans had been living quite separate lives,' Austin mused, 'what if Barbara was planning to go her own way altogether and leave dear John to it? Take half the house and his writing hut?'

'Now that would be upsetting the prof's regime. She's not going anywhere now. Peace and quiet for Mr Steadman. Let's see how the professor is consoling himself.'

The delivery man, carrying a green plastic tray full of goods, was just being admitted by Steadman when they reached the porch. 'Morning, Mr Steadman, mind if we come in too?' McLusky

73

didn't wait for an answer and followed the delivery man into the hall.

Steadman was visibly annoyed. 'Close the door behind you, Sergeant, before any more people stray in.'

The caterer stood with his heavy load in the hall. 'Straight into the kitchen, sir?'

Steadman nodded at him. 'If you would. No, *this* way, Inspector,' he said to McLusky who was following the delivery man's broad back along the passage to the kitchen.

'Oh, the kitchen will do for me,' McLusky said over his shoulder and carried on. 'I know my place.'

Steadman took a deep breath during which he fixed Austin with an exasperated stare.

'After you, sir,' Austin said with exaggerated politeness.

The kitchen was classic country house style, yet, despite stone-flagged floor, scrubbed oak table and Aga, managed to look curiously sterile, like the kitchen of a show home. The caterer knew his way around and sorted the delivery away, including champagne and a side of smoked salmon that went into the fridge. McLusky pretended to take a close interest in the delivery, following the man around and ignoring the fuming Steadman until all had disappeared into fridge, freezer and pantry.

'Thank you, Mr Steadman.' The caterer had his pad signed and was left to find his own way out.

'Have you made any progress at all?' Steadman challenged McLusky.

'Early days, sir,' McLusky said while pretending

to take an interest in the furnishings. 'Murder investigations take time.'

'Then what can I do for you?'

'Oh, just routine questions. Murder inquiries are full of routine. All of it boring but necessary. And very effective. We have a very good clear-up rate for murder. Not so good on burglary, I'm told, but murder, we're very good at that. Actually,' he turned to Austin. 'you might make a start on questioning the neighbours. I'll join you in a moment.'

'Questioning the neighbours?' Steadman asked as Austin left. 'What about? What would they know?'

'Oh, again, you see, it's just routine, sir, nothing to worry about. Are you friendly with your neighbours? Was your wife?'

'We never really had much to do with them. Our properties are far enough apart, it's not like we'd chat over the garden fence, Inspector. That's what large gardens are for, getting away from the neighbours.'

'Is that what they are for? I often wondered,' McLusky said. He had lived at his own address for over a year and had barely noticed his own neighbours even without the help of a few acres.

'Do you have any idea where your wife went when she left the house?'

'None. As I think I told you, she liked driving. She loved that car and she liked being on the move.'

'Was your wife having an affair?'

'I don't know. It's possible.'

'Do you know with whom?'

75

'No. I said she was *possibly* having an affair, Inspector. Not that it would have made much difference.' There was a pause. 'I didn't kill my wife in a fit of jealousy.'

'It appears not. Who benefits from your wife's death?'

'I do. We have no children. I didn't kill her for the money, either. My pension is quite adequate, I assure you.'

'That must be gratifying. Yesterday you mentioned people who have access to the house.' McLusky flicked open his notebook, found the relevant page. 'You said several people had keys, you said *cleaner, gardener and so on all have keys*. Who is "and so on"?'

Steadman caressed the slight stubble beyond his neatly trimmed beard. 'Just . . . services. My wife was not a very domestic sort of person. She left that kind of thing to professionals. The laundry, for instance, there's a laundry and ironing service she employed. They come into the house and hang up your cleaned and ironed clothes in your wardrobe and leave again. *Pressing Business*, that's what the company is called. That's it for people with keys. Gardeners, cleaner, laundry service.'

McLusky snapped his notebook shut. 'OK, that clears that one up at least,' he said, hoping it would sound as though he had a long list of suspicious inconsistencies in his notebook.

'If you don't mind, Inspector, I would like to get back to my work now.' Steadman indicated the direction of the summerhouse with a nod of his head. McLusky could just glimpse a corner

76

of Steadman's writing shack through the kitchen window.

'Of course. It must be a great solace. Thank you for seeing me. I'm sorry to have bothered you at what must be a difficult time for you.' Especially with nothing but smoked salmon, venison pâté and champagne to sustain you, McLusky thought uncharitably. Steadman led him to the front door. 'If you have any questions yourself, don't hesitate,' McLusky said.

'There is one. My wife's car. When can I pick that up?'

'You'll be informed when forensics have finished with it. I can't say how long it might take, it all depends.'

'On what, Inspector?'

'On what they'll find. Oh, I do have one more question,' McLusky said, already outside. 'Did you sleep with your wife the day she disappeared?'

Steadman gave him an expressionless stare that lasted several seconds before he answered. 'What could you possibly . . .' He faltered.

'Only there were "signs of recent intercourse", as the pathologist would put it. Are you sure you don't know whether your wife was having an affair?'

'I have no idea. And I don't want to know. Perhaps my wife's driver would know. Why don't you ask her?'

'Knickers, sir?' DI Kat Fairfield tried to keep the incredulity out of her voice but since Superintendent Denkhaus was standing with his

77

back to her, pretending to enjoy the view from his office window, she briefly let her eyes go cross-eyed.

'Yes, Fairfield, underwear. And I want you to look into it. So to speak.' Denkhaus tore himself away from the view and gave the sickly cheese plant a disgusted look before sitting down behind his desk, still not meeting the inspector's gaze.

'But surely that's not a CID matter, uniform deals with that sort of thing quite admirably.'

'It's not just underwear disappearing from clotheslines anymore. He's now breaking into people's houses, going through . . . *women's things*. Photographing them.' Denkhaus made an impatient gesture with his hand, as though he could wave the subject away like an unpleasant smell. 'Usually while the women are in the house. It's got to stop.'

'I still don't see why us, sir.'

Denkhaus sighed and lent back in his chair. 'Because a couple of nights ago it happened to the ACC's wife, that's why! And Anderson asked for you. He remembered meeting you and was impressed. You should be flattered.'

Fairfield also remembered Assistant Chief Constable Anderson, a barrel-chested man with a booming voice, and was reasonably certain that it was not her achievements as a police officer that had impressed him when she had been introduced. He had only spoken a few words to her and those he had addressed mainly to her breasts. 'I see,' said Fairfield neutrally.

'Good. Get stuck into it. Catch the little pervert

78

before he does something worse. These things have a nasty habit of escalating.'

'Yes, sir. Before I go, sir . . . Every time I come in here that cheese plant looks more miserable.'

Denkhaus made a sour face. 'It was a present from the ACC's wife.'

'And you've been trying to kill it ever since, haven't you? Well, I'm taking it into protective custody,' she said and walked past his desk, snatching up the suspiciously light pot.

'Thank you, DI Fairfield,' Denkhaus said, turning to his computer screen, 'I hope you two will be very happy together.'

'Her driver? She had a driver?' Austin looked back at the Steadman house in consternation. 'And he tells us now?'

They had met up again by Austin's Micra. McLusky insisted on having a smoke before getting back in, so they talked across the roof of the car. 'Until about two weeks ago. She'd lost her licence for drink driving and got a lengthy ban. She needed a driver to carry on with her work. She only got her licence back ten days ago.'

'So Steadman could be telling the truth when he said she liked to just drive around. Must still have been quite a novelty, being back behind the wheel.'

'It's possible. She had a nice enough car. Her driver's name is Lisa Burns.'

'Do we have an address?'

McLusky flicked his cigarette butt into the

centre of the road. 'No. But I know what she's doing, now that she no longer drives Barbara Steadman's beemer.'

Nowhere in the tiny taxi cab office in Whiteladies Road was private enough, so all three of them sat in the back of the blue taxi. Lisa Burns took the fold-down seat, facing Austin and McLusky. Burns looked older than her forty years, with very short hair dyed silver, a sharp nose and straight, thin lips. Her quick, pale blue eyes darted across the officers' features as though she was trying to store away every detail.

'Yeah, I stopped chauffeuring Barbara two weeks ago. That was sad enough. I quite liked her. And now she's dead, it's hard to believe. I knew it was coming of course. I mean her getting her licence back. So I managed to have a job lined up. Lucky, I suppose, considering the times.'

McLusky started gently. 'What was Mrs Steadman like to work for?'

'Oh, all right. She was . . . yeah, she was OK. And she paid well.'

'How did you come to work for her? Were you with an agency?'

'No, nothing like that. I did do a chauffeur course, once. Well, didn't stick the whole course, too poncey, but I'd learnt the basics. Nah, I was driving a cab when I met her. I picked her up from court the day she got banned from driving. She just couldn't stop crying, that's how we got talking. By the time we got to her house she'd hired me. She offered me more money than I'd been making driving the cab and without any of the hassle you get with punters. I jumped at it. Seven series Beemer, no pukers, no drunks, no aggro. It was a no brainer.'

'And where did you drive Mrs Steadman? To work and home again, presumably. Where else?'

'Oh everywhere. To work, of course, and between cities, London quite often, she hated trains, Swansea, Cardiff, mostly for work. She was quite a high flyer.'

'What about outside of work?'

'Where did I drive her? She didn't seem to have that many friends but she went to restaurants, she liked Browns for lunch for some reason.'

'Drinks?'

'Yes. Not with me, you understand. But yeah, she liked a drink, quite a lot of it, to be honest. It's what lost her her licence in the first place. And now she had me to drive her everywhere she could of course drink as much as she liked.'

'Any special friends?'

'Well, yes, she did have affairs. She did go out with men, though she never discussed them with me. Not *a lot* of men, I don't mean that. Mustn't start false rumours. I think she tried internet dating for a while.'

'Could you describe any of them?' Austin asked, notebook at the ready.

'Not really, she was very discreet. I never had any of them in the car. Not once. I only ever caught a glimpse of two of them and they both had dark hair and they were a bit younger than her. Well dressed but you'd expect that. She wasn't out there for a bit of rough.'

'When did Mrs Steadman last meet one of these men?'

'It's hard to say. I often dropped her at restaurants or near the harbour and she'd later call me and say I wasn't needed, you know what I mean? The last time was the day before she got her licence back.'

'Where did you drop her?'

'Near the harbour. She often went to places in the centre. Once or twice it was the Isis.'

'Nice.' McLusky had eaten at the luxurious restaurant once, a command performance in public relations organized by the superintendent. 'She didn't say where she was going that last time?'

'As I said, she was very discreet. She never chatted much about her private life, not to me. And she didn't use the car or me as a way to impress people. I wouldn't roll up in front of the restaurant and hold doors open for her and stuff. I was always around the corner. I was spiriting her away.'

'Did you ever drive her husband?'

'No, never.'

'But you have met him?'

'No, just saw him once from afar at the house.'

'Did you notice any change in her patterns, her mood or her behaviour over the past days or weeks?'

'She did go up and down a lot recently. But she was always a bit like that. You can't smoke in here,' Burns warned McLusky who was getting ready to light up.

McLusky opened the door. 'Okay, thanks for

talking to us. Leave your address with my sergeant.' He stepped outside and lit his cigarette and waited curbside for Austin to join him. When he did, Austin stood upwind from him. He had given up smoking himself and being around the inspector still tested his resolve.

'What do you think?' McLusky asked.

'Sounds genuine. She always knew the job would end, there's no grudge there.'

'And what about the Steadmans?'

'Classic marital stalemate, I'd say. Both drink and can afford to do it in style, wife has affairs and hubby says he doesn't care.'

'If she was internet dating we'll have to find the agency and see who she met up with. She might have run into her killer there.'

'I'll get Deedee on to it.'

'Anyways, let's grab some lunch.'

Anyone eating at the Albany Road Station canteen quickly learnt to avoid any dish with the word 'bake' in its name, with the result that the caterers continuously renamed the same dishes to sneak them in under the radar. That was how McLusky ended up jabbing his fork aimlessly into a yellow crust of strangely insubstantial potato mash to hunt for evidence of food below. 'How's your hotpot?' he asked Austin.

'Well, it's hot and they probably made it in a pot, that's about it. What's yours?'

McLusky pushed out his bottom lip and lifted up a loaded fork to stare at it. 'Mystery White Fish in Gloopy Sauce. With mash on top.'

'Which used to be called *Ocean Bake*. How could you fall for that? Call yourself a detective.'

'I know. I'm a total failure,' he said and shovelled some of it into his mouth.

Austin's mobile chimed and he answered it. He listened, dropped his cutlery on to his plate in disgust. 'You're kidding, right?'

Seven

'It's hard to believe,' Austin said. 'Honestly, it was so quiet while you were suspended.'

'Oh, yeah, apart from a couple of riots,' McLusky said. He was driving at speed in his Mazda on Brunel Way across the river. 'I'm surprised you're not blaming me for those as well.'

'You have to admit, two murders in your first week back is quite surprising.'

'No, Jane, what's surprising is that they want us to attend a second one when we're nowhere yet with the first body. If it had also been found in the canal I could understand it. But on an allotment?'

'Not actually on the allotments, right next to them where it goes down to the railway line.'

'Whatever,' said McLusky, fighting the steering of the car. 'I just want to know why we're suddenly the only two detectives in Bristol.' As McLusky took the roundabout at forty miles per hour the limitations of the suspension became all too apparent and he had to work hand over fist at the steering wheel and slow right down to keep the car from mounting the pavement. 'Sorry about that. I'll get it fixed, I promise,' he said as he slewed into Clanage Road.

'It wants fixing with a new one,' Austin said primly. 'Turn right at that little lane at the end of the allotments.'

85

When he did, McLusky could see that they were probably the last to arrive at the scene. A few hundred yards further on stretched a long line of vehicles. Brightly marked police cars, red, yellow and white against the green of the playing fields to their left, forensics vans, the Range Rover of DSI Denkhaus, the dark blue Jaguar of the pathologist, the sombre coroner's van and even a big command vehicle had been crammed into the narrow lane. McLusky stopped well before he reached the line of vehicles, performed a six-point turn on the ungenerous width of tarmac and parked.

'Planning a quick get-away?' Austin asked.

'I live in hope.'

'Hope, Liam? That's called delusion round here.'

It may have been unseasonably mild but on the allotments beyond the fence not much seemed to grow yet among the browns and greys of their winter livery. DS Austin entertained vague notions of one day creating a vegetable patch for his fiancée, Eve, in their tiny back garden but the inspector, he knew, was always happiest with solid tarmac under his feet. McLusky walked along without giving the allotments a single glance, eyes fixed on the figures busying themselves around the white tent on the slope of the railway cutting. From a distance most of the figures in their white crime-scene suits looked the same but McLusky spotted the unmistakable shape of the superintendent. He made straight for him.

'Afternoon, sir. What have we got?'

'Male, mid-thirties. Various wounds.'

'Killed here?'

'Probably deposition site.'

'ID?'

'Nothing so far.' Denkhaus gave him a joyless smile. 'So why did I call you?'

'That would have been my next question, sir, yes.'

'Well, have a good look at him and have a word with Coulthart.' Denkhaus checked his watch. 'Report to me back at the station, I'm late for a meeting.'

McLusky who had automatically checked his own watch – still stopped at ten to seven – made for the command vehicle where he donned a protective suit while quietly grumbling at no one in particular. Austin knew not to inquire. Suited up, both of them trod carefully along the marked path, took deep breaths and entered the tent. It had been erected with difficulty on the slope of the railway cutting. All around the tent a fingertip search was on the way, but here inside only the video man and the pathologist attended the dead body.

The corpse lay with head pointing down the incline, one arm twisted under the body, head to the side. The face appeared to McLusky hideously contorted, as though frozen mid-scream. The hair was a matted, bloody mess and both face and neck were covered in smears of blood. The corpse was dressed in a dark suit and white shirt. Its feet were bare.

'Ah, you finally made it,' was how the pathologist greeted them. He had been squatting by the side of the body and straightened up now.

'And a good afternoon to you too,' McLusky said with bitter cheerfulness. 'Deposition site, I was told.'

'Indeed. Though I don't think *deposited* is quite the word I would use were I asked to describe it.'

'I'm asking.'

'This one was dumped. Flung into the weeds. A bit like fly tipping.'

'There's certainly enough of that going on round here.'

'*Flung*?' Austin repeated. 'Does that mean we're looking for more than one person? Hard to fling a man that size.'

'Just the one,' Coulthart said. He gestured up the slope. 'SOCOs think they've identified one group of heavy footprints, deep imprints coming in and lighter ones going back up. One man, acting alone. He carried the dead man, hence the deeper footprints, tipped him down the slope and walked back, hence the lighter footprints. You are looking for one strong man.'

'I'm not sure I'm looking for him at all,' complained McLusky. 'I'm in the middle of another investigation and so far I can see no connection. Unless you're telling me this one was drowned, fished out of the canal and had his suit pressed before he was dumped here.'

Coulthart looked at McLusky over the top of his glasses and allowed a pause to develop that, better than words, said 'are you quite finished?'. Then he peered through the bottom of his glasses at the body by his feet. 'Two things. It's hard to see with all this blood, but this man was gagged.

He had a rag shoved inside his mouth and had it taped up. The tape is missing but the tell-tale signs are there. Discoloration and I'm sure we'll find trace evidence of adhesive on his skin. Here's the other thing I thought might make it of interest to you.' Coulthart delicately pulled at the suit sleeve of the dead man's arm, revealing a darkly discoloured wrist. Circling it was a single thin bracelet of dark blue cord.

Both McLusky and Austin squatted down to take a closer look. 'It's a bit of clothesline,' Austin said.

'Yes. Nylon clothesline. Different colour from the stuff on the woman but definitely clothesline. He has ligature marks on his wrists and ankles. Other marks too.'

'Yes, what are those?' Austin asked. 'Looks blistered. Burn marks?'

'Possible. Can't say for sure until I get him on the table.'

'When will that be?' McLusky wanted to know.

'Not today, perhaps not even tomorrow. We're busy.'

'When did he die?'

'Some time last night, that's as close as I can get.' He consulted his watch. 'Probably between six or seven o'clock and midnight. It all depends.'

'What on?' Austin asked.

'The temperature wherever he was killed. The temperature of the vehicle that brought him here and so on and so on. Too many unknowns. You've been at this game long enough to know that whatever I say out here is no more than educated

89

guesswork. But he was dumped here during the early hours.'

Outside the tent McLusky approached the uniformed sergeant in charge of the area search. 'So who found the body?'

The sergeant made himself comfortable on his feet, glad to be asked. 'Couple of kids from the allotment, running after their dog. They're still with their mother somewhere over there.' He gestured over the fence towards the mosaic of plots and sheds. 'Will you be questioning them?'

McLusky pulled down the corners of his mouth. 'Did they remove anything from the site? Find anything?'

'They didn't approach the body. Just retrieved their dog and ran back to tell mum.'

'She call us?'

'Yup.'

'Anyone else approach the site between the kids finding it and you lot turning up? Did the mother go near it? Anyone?'

'It appears not.'

'Small mercies. As long as you have their contact details I'll be happy. Halle*lujah*!' McLusky had just found an unexpected Mars bar in his jacket and pulled it out like a conjurer who has surprised himself with his own trick. As he ripped the wrapper off the bar and sank his teeth into its soft sweetness he wondered whether he needed distracting from his cigarette cravings or was now developing an additional chocolate addiction. Either way, he would have to stock up again soon. He left the sergeant to direct his officers in the fingertip search and joined Austin on the tarmac where they struggled out of their scene suits.

'Any thoughts, Jane?'

'You'll ruin your teeth.'

'Your concern for my dental health is gratifying.' McLusky crammed the last of the Mars bar into his mouth, making his next utterance barely comprehensible. 'Anything else you want to contribute?'

Austin tried to make sense of it. 'We have no ID for the bod and no one of his description has been reported missing. Both were gagged at some stage. We've got one bit of clothesline to link the two, but it's the wrong colour and what house doesn't have clothesline in the garden? You don't look convinced.'

They started to walk down the line of cars. 'I told you I had a bad feeling.'

Austin just nodded; McLusky always had a bad feeling. He probably woke up with a bad feeling every single morning. Perhaps that's why he became a police officer.

'But until we identify him,' McLusky went on, 'we'll only have forensics to go on. Let *them* come up with something to link the two.'

'Apart from that bit of clothesline everything says it's a different killer.'

'Go try that line on the super,' McLusky said and gestured ahead to the superintendent's Range Rover. Denkhaus was sitting at the wheel, waiting. As they drew level the driver window slid down.

The superintendent had watched the two detectives come up the lane. For some reason he was feeling his age today and those two looked too bloody young. Austin of course really was young, still just inside his twenties, with a fashionable haircut and suit. And McLusky. Half gifted, tenacious police officer, half Peter Pan. And now he had chocolate round his mouth like a five year old.

McLusky had just been told about it by Austin and was licking his lips while hunting for a tissue in his jacket.

'What do you make of it?' Denkhaus asked him.

'What happened to your meeting, sir?'

'Postponed. Well?'

'It's a possible,' McLusky admitted. 'It's thin so far but two similarities is a lot: the gag, the clothesline. Three major differences, though. Barbara Steadman was drowned. She was alive when she went into the canal and the whole thing has a ritualistic feel about it. Killing her there in that fashion had lots of unnecessary complications. Unnecessary unless it somehow made sense to the killer.' McLusky nodded the back of his head towards the tent which was barely visible from here above the lip of the railway cutting. 'This one wasn't killed here, he was dumped, and I mean *dumped*. Driven to the end of the track and tipped down the slope. No attempt at concealment, no ritualization about it. Just got rid of. If it really is the same killer then it's almost as though the first victim meant something to him, while the second didn't.'

'Yes, I buy that. You said three major differences.'

'Yeah. First one's a woman. This one's a chap.'

Denkhaus sighed. 'It hadn't escaped me. Right, keep looking for similarities. And why was he dumped here? Why choose this place?'

'You can get to it without passing CCTV. Fly-tipping down the railway embankment is quite a sport round here.'

'But you'd have to know about this lane, first. Perhaps there is a connection with the allotments.' McLusky just pointed over the super's shoulder. 'Ah, of course,' Denkhaus nodded. 'The playing fields. Yes, you're right. I very much hope these two bodies aren't connected.'

'I'll do my best, sir.'

Denkhaus nodded, then nodded some more, thinking. 'Would you excuse us a moment, DS Austin?'

'Sir.' Austin nodded and walked off down the road.

Denkhaus waited until the sergeant was out of earshot. 'It's your show, McLusky, unless something suggests the two are definitely unconnected. I don't have to remind you that both your conduct and progress will be minutely scrutinized.'

'I never doubted it, sir.'

'What will also be scrutinized is your continued work relationship with DS Austin. Fortunately he was uninvolved in your misdemeanours or you'd have found yourself paired with someone new. But make no mistake, everything is up for review, depending on your future conduct.'

'I'll bear it in mind.'

'I hope so. But if you do decide at any point to throw away your career, don't drag DS Austin down with you.'

'I won't, sir.'

'Good, good. Well, you'll be busy, McLusky.' He started the engine. '*Very* busy.'

Standing a few yards apart on the tarmac the two detectives watched their superior drive off. 'Anything I need to know about?' Austin asked.

'Nope, not a thing. He just wanted to tell me again how happy he was to have me back.'

The sun was sinking behind a bank of dust-grey cloud by the time the site was wound-up. The fingertip search had yielded a large selection of detritus that generations of Bristolians had flung towards the railway lines: broken glass, broken trowels, bicycle tyres, condoms, a hamster wheel and a car door were among the items recovered. Nothing that immediately suggested a connection with the dead body; the corpse was merely one more thing a citizen could not be bothered to put where it belonged. They had now rectified this: the body had been sent to the mortuary, the rubbish removed. McLusky had spent another hour in the incident room, talking, talking, talking and asking rhetorical questions of the team: why, how, where. Some of these questions would not be answered until the autopsy had been done, others would take much longer. Forensic laboratories worked slowly and were getting slower. Now samples were sent off to whatever laboratory lay within a reasonable radius from the locus of the crime and had the smallest backlog to work through.

When McLusky left his car unlocked near his flat he was thinking of what constituted a reasonable radius to solve his nutritional problems. He needed a drink but also something to eat. Rossi's was closed. He had no appetite, yet too many chocolate bars and instant coffees had left his stomach fizzing acidly and something had to be done about it before he added a few pints of stout to the mixture. He considered the Barge Inn directly opposite, only he could see through the windows that it was quiz night. Apart from the daftness of the occasion it meant there was no food to be had apart from rounds of tiny triangular sandwiches for the quizzers. McLusky turned away and walked the quarter mile up to Rita's on Stokes Croft. It was while he was making his way back towards the pub, eating cheesy chips with a plastic fork, that he heard her laugh. Laura's laugh. He would know the sound anywhere. For three years that sound had been his reward, though quite a rare currency in their last year together in Southampton. Now that she had moved to Bristol for her studies, rarer still. He only saw her occasionally now, mainly through chance encounters, and to this day she had not told him her Bristol address.

There was nowhere to hide. He walked on and seconds later Laura rounded the corner. She was flanked on one side by a much younger woman, a teenager still, he guessed, and on the other by yet another of those attractive, long-haired young men which archaeology courses appeared to attract. Laura slowed as she recognized McLusky and stopped in front of him. Her hair had grown longer and her clothes become younger since she had started her studies.

'Liam!' She seemed genuinely pleased to see

him. 'This is Liam, guys. Erm, this is Val, and that's Ethan.'

Val smiled at him, Ethan said: 'How're you doin? You must be Laura's policeman friend.'

'I must. You're American?'

'Canadian!' Ethan and Laura said in happy unison. Ethan waved McLusky's apology away. 'I get that all the time. I don't blame you. I'm only just beginning to tell all your Scotch and Welsh accents apart.' All three of them were flushed with drink and all were carrying hold-alls, rucksacks and sleeping bags.

'Off to a festival?' McLusky suggested.

'Not this time of year,' Laura said. 'We're going on a dig tomorrow. Three days, close to Stonehenge. Chance of a lifetime.'

McLusky was beginning to feel self-conscious about the parcel of chips he was holding. 'Three days in a tent? In the first week of April? In England?' he asked.

'I know,' said Ethan, 'they're mad in this country.'

'It's Val and me in the tent,' Laura said, impressing the point on McLusky with a well-rehearsed look. 'Ethan's in the year above us and says he's learnt his lesson. He's invested in a van to kip in. I'm thinking of getting one myself, maybe in autumn . . .' Laura stopped herself, realizing that the bottle of wine she had shared with Val earlier was making her gush. 'You're . . . back at work?' she asked.

'Yeah. Just knocked off.'

'The murder? Are you working on that? The woman in the canal?'

He nodded. 'And a second body has been found. A man this time.'

'Another one!'

'Perhaps it's not a bad time to get out of town,' Ethan said.

'You may be right,' McLusky said without taking his eyes off Laura. 'Well, have a good dig. I hope it stays dry for you.' He walked on with a nod at Laura's companions while a small irritable part of him began to pray for three days of heavy rain. His chips had cooled down to an unpleasant temperature and he ate them quickly out of a sense of duty to his stomach. He dropped the remains of the parcel into a wheelie bin and made for the Barge Inn. *Laura*. All excited about digging holes and staying in a tent. She had previously always said she hated camping, like all sensible people.

Laden with supermarket shopping, DI Fairfield fumbled open the door to her maisonette, squeezed through it, then shouldered it shut. For a moment she leant her back against the door, letting out a deep breath through puffed cheeks. What a bloody awful day. She thought she could fall asleep right here, leaning in the hall, shopping bags and all. After a few seconds, however, she launched herself forward towards the kitchen. She set down her shopping on the kitchen table and, still wearing her coat, she attended to priorities, like opening the bottle of wine she had bought to allow it to breathe. She let it breathe for as long as it took to get a clean glass from the draining board, then poured it brimful of the ruby liquid. It would breathe more freely in a glass, surely. She took a large, thirsty gulp out of it before setting it down on the worktop next to the cooker, turned on the oven, then shrugged out of her coat. *I wish someone would uncork me and let me breathe*, she thought, then berated herself for being melodramatic again. She sometimes thought it was being Greek that made her prone to exaggeration and melancholy. Not depression. She preferred the word *melancholy* to describe the long grey moods she fell into, and it was a good Greek word after all. Kat Fairfield, née Katarina Vasiliou, had after her divorce thought hard about going back to her maiden name but had decided that Fairfield was an easier name to make a career with in CID. Detective Superintendent Vasiliou . . . DSI Fairfield. Would either of them make it that far? Neither of them would impress Louise, she felt sure. Fairfield took another gulp of wine and started clearing away the shopping, all except the lasagne ready-meal she would shove in the oven later. Hey, it was a step up from the microwave, so moving in the right direction. No, rank would not impress Louise. Neither would a supermarket's own-brand lasagne from the *Pay the Difference* range. It was the culture thing. She just didn't have the schooling. Louise and her friends could talk so easily about stuff like history and the classics. They knew all the characters of classic novels and could quote from poems. They could tell all the Jane Austen stuff apart and it wasn't from the telly, either. She had tried to catch up. She had started reading one of Louise's books, *The Mill on the Floss*, picked almost at random off one of her crammed shelves. She had fallen asleep over it several times. How tedious could books get? Surely there was more action in her average work day than in that entire tome. She really did want to improve her mind, and she would go back to her art classes next term. She enjoyed life drawing and it wasn't something she had done to impress anyone either. Unlike the thing with the telly. Louise had convinced her that television was vulgar and that it ate up what little free time Kat had. Get rid of it, she'd advised, and suddenly you'll find you have time for all sorts of things you'll otherwise never get around to.

Like cooking. Fairfield drained the glass, ripped the packaging off the lasagne and shoved it into the noisy fan oven. Yup, it was true. She hadn't gone as far as selling the thing but had unplugged it and stuffed it into the cupboard under the stairs and so she would be awarded a gold star by Louise for it. At first this had made her feel mature and sophisticated but recently, on those many evenings when she was too tired to read, the siren call of the banished set had become louder.

In the sitting room, in place of the TV set, now stood a radio. She turned it on but reception in her area was notoriously bad and she soon gave up trying to find anything appealing and turned it off. A ticking silence ensued, only enhanced by the background hum of the fan-assisted oven next door. Fairfield let herself sink on to her sofa. She wanted to get into some comfortable clothes but found it hard to summon up the will power to go upstairs. She was looking at the mantel-piece. The little black mantel clock said it was eight thirty. Only, the clock wasn't in its usual place. Fairfield stood up to look at it. It was usually on the left, where she could easily see it from her favourite corner of the sofa. Now it had changed places with the Moroccan sugar bowl, usually on the opposite end. She must have somehow put them down the wrong way around last time she dusted. Weird. She swapped them over. And went upstairs to change out of her work clothes.

Eight

Two in the afternoon in the incident room. McLusky had talked himself full circle around everything they knew about the two killings. He was no longer standing by the whiteboard addressing the rest of the detectives in the room, he was sitting at a desk like all the others, arguing. They had talked for a long time and no one had come up with a new avenue to explore. Frenchie – DC Claire French had given up trying to resist her nickname – had only one Jaffa cake left to get her through the rest of the shift and struggled to resist it. DC Dearlove sat tapping a plastic spoon against his front teeth: his thinking pose. Austin sat staring unhappily at the brown sludge at he bottom of his coffee mug and decided to give up dunking biscuits. McLusky was holding a full cigarette packet between the nails of his index fingers, twirling it with his thumbs. 'The first killing has something weirdly ritualistic about it.' He stopped twirling and sat up straighter. 'OK, I'm killing someone. I'll either do it in a fit of temper; I'll hit them, stab them, strangle them or if I have a gun handy, shoot them. Then I think: shit, I killed her, what am I going to do with the body. Right? *Or* I plan it. I'm cool and calculated. I work out beforehand where to kill them, how to kill them, how to flee the scene or how to get rid of the body, possible alibis, the works.'

'Unless you have a degree in forensics and/or a lot of luck you'll get caught,' Austin said. 'Eventually.'

'*Hopefully*. But this one is different from either of those. Yes, it was planned. But that woman was alive when she went into the canal. She was snatched from in or near her car. Trussed up and gagged. Transported across town, brought by boat to the place where she was drowned. That's not cool and calculated, that's sustained rage, surely. Or insanity, of course. He had plenty of time to think about what he was doing. Plenty of time to change his mind, relent, find some compassion with the struggling woman. But no. There doesn't appear to be a sexual motive, either, though her tights were missing. We checked with her husband who says she would not normally walk around with bare legs. But otherwise she's fully clothed and has not been raped.'

'She had had recent intercourse,' said French. 'Perhaps she laddered her tights in a passionate clinch.'

There were a few titters. 'Possible,' McLusky said. 'Good thinking.' Then he returned to his previous thought. 'Killing her the way he did meant taking an awful risk. Even in the middle of the night he could easily have been spotted lowering her into the water from a passing car. The second bod had his head bashed in and was unceremoniously dumped by the railway line. The *way* Barbara Steadman was killed must mean something to the bastard.'

'Unless that's what he wants us to think,' French said. 'Make it look like the killing is down

102

to some weirdo with a psychotic agenda. To make us look in the wrong direction?'

'Still too complicated, too much effort. If you were faking the weirdness surely you'd leave a weird note or stuff her mouth with butterflies or something corny out of the movies, but this was hard work. And too risky. No, Frenchie, he meant it.' McLusky was tapping his desk to the rhythm of his speech for emphasis: 'This is your *ac*tual, *ge*nuine, *bo*na *fi*de weird shit.'

And everyone knew McLusky hated weird shit. French gave a Gallic shrug and realized she had popped her last Jaffa cake into her mouth without thinking; now the rest of the day stretched like a desert in front of her. Unless she went to buy more, of course, but that would probably mean she'd end up eating two whole packets in one day. Again.

'Ordinarily a killer is most concerned with concealment,' McLusky went on. The phone nearest him rang and he snatched it up. 'Incident room . . .' He listened, nodded, nodded. The superintendent had managed to bully the mortuary into bringing the autopsy of the second body forward. Even so there had been a day's delay. McLusky hung up and kept talking while gathering his things to leave. 'We have a PM at last. I may return with words of wisdom but don't hold your breaths, and get on with all the routine stuff. We still haven't identified the boat he used.'

McLusky was trying to resign himself to a life punctuated with post mortems: having to look at corpses being cut open, have their innards taken out, inspected, weighed and bagged up; prodded, scraped and poked in every orifice, filmed and photographed in this state of ultimate undress until eventually most of it was returned into the corpse in more or less the right order and the cavity neatly sewn up. McLusky had always maintained that he didn't much care what happened to him after his death, by which he meant whether he'd be buried or cremated, yet he definitely hoped to die in a bed and of known causes and so be spared the procedure he was about to witness.

'Your superintendent can be quite persuasive.' This was how Coulthart explained the fact that the autopsy had been given priority.

'Don't I know it.'

'Ah. Would that also be the reason why you are yet again gracing these procedures with your presence?' He flashed McLusky a look over his glasses but didn't wait for an answer. 'Let us begin, then, I have a busy schedule here and a lecture to deliver in town later. Dead male, in his early-to-mid thirties . . .'

'Are you sure?' McLusky interrupted. 'Hard to tell from what I saw of his face of course but his hair is completely grey.'

'Yes. Dyed grey. Perhaps a disguise but I think more an affectation. His real hair colour is closer to that of his eyebrows and pubic hair, a rather boring, mousey brown.'

'He'd have coloured his eyebrows too if he wanted to really change his appearance enough to deceive anyone, surely. Did he die from his head wounds?'

'He did. However . . .' Coulthart moved the

camera first to one of the wrists, then one of the ankles so McLusky could get a close-up view on the monitor. 'Both wrists and ankles were scored and blistered.'

'What the hell am I looking at? Burns, are they? Was he tortured?'

'I'm sure it was torture for the deceased but I have a notion that the object wasn't torture. I think someone made an amateurish attempt at electrocuting this chap. He was tied to a chair or something similar and connected to the national grid. Only it didn't kill him. Now if you'd want to torture someone you'd connect electricity to bits of the body, his genitals for instance would be quite effective. You wouldn't pass electricity through the entire body; that always risks stopping the heart. This bloke was fit enough to withstand having quite a lot of current run through him. So the killer bashed his head in instead.'

'Oh, marvellous. Why can't I get a nice and simple murder for once? What wouldn't I give for a stabbing outside a pub with a couple of witnesses and some CCTV right now.'

'I'm sure you'll get lucky one day. And yes, the perpetrator definitely used clothesline to tie him with. It was cut off the body before he had his jacket put back on him and was dumped, but one ring of the material remained in place, probably moulded into place by the heat of the electric current.'

'Same stuff as we found on the first body?'

'Can't say. It went off to forensics yesterday. Don't hold your breath, Inspector.'

'I won't. It'll come back in a week's time with

a note saying "Yup, it's definitely clothesline" and an invoice for half my monthly salary.'

'Such cynicism in one so young. You never know, it might be more elucidating than that. We'll compare trace evidence of course to see if we can connect the two bodies but the immersion in the canal makes that a rather hopeless endeavour. In the meantime, and even before we have opened our friend up, I can offer you quite a bit more right here. When I said he wasn't tortured I meant his killer didn't. There are quite a few older, healed and partially healed marks on the body that are consistent with sexual violence. His nipples were damaged at some stage, probably with needles. Several puncture marks. Let's roll him on his side for a minute,' Coulthart said to his assistant, who obliged. 'And as you can see he was also beaten, regularly, and quite hard, on his back and buttocks.'

'Caned? Whipped?'

'Whipped. Cane marks aren't as long as these and don't curve round so far.'

'OK, you're the expert. If some of the marks are fresher than others that says to me he submitted to it. He wasn't attacked.'

'Quite. For our grey-haired friend here it was a way of life, I'd say, and he did have regular anal intercourse, too, though not immediately before his death.'

'Damn.'

'Yes. No DNA for us there. Right, let's put him on his back and let's get stuck in. So to speak.'

By law McLusky was obliged to witness the autopsy, yet nowhere was it written that he had

to focus too closely on the process of eviscera-
tion that followed the Y-shaped incision which
opened up the body cavity. From then on the
inspector let his eyes unfocus or studied the stainless steel starkness of the operating room's facili-
ties. It was enough to listen to the running
commentary on the internal organs of the corpse.
According to Coulthart, the victim had been in
fairly good shape, had done a lot of cycling too,
judging by his leg muscles, either on an exercise
bike or a real one. The pathologist was just
remarking on the apparent absence of any obvious
pathology when DS Austin entered the viewing
suite.

'Jane, what are you doing here?' McLusky
asked, forgetting that Coulthart could overhear.

'Jane, is it?' Coulthart said, looking up. 'Oh,
of course, it's *Austin*. Inescapable, really.'

Austin ignored it. 'Someone has just reported
a man missing, fitting his description. His
employer, in fact. Went missing three nights ago.
Everything fits.' Austin handed McLusky a sheet
of printed notes.

After speed reading what it said, McLusky
stepped closer to the pane of glass. 'Dr Coulthart,
meet Stephen Bothwick, 34 years of age.'

Austin shook his head, muttering: 'Bit late for
introductions when you've already got both hands
inside a chap.'

They had driven back into town in separate cars
and were now standing outside a tall Georgian
building in Clifton where they had arranged to
meet with the police locksmith to open up the

dead man's flat. McLusky knew the area well. It was only a few houses away from Louise Rennie's place and just around the corner from the Primrose Café in Boyces Avenue. 'You're late,' McLusky told the locksmith when he arrived two minutes after he had finished his cigarette. Austin was willing to bet that, had the locksmith arrived before McLusky had finished smoking, he'd have accused him of being early.

The man gained access to the second floor flat with worrying ease, making McLusky wonder, not for the first time, how safe anyone's place of abode really was, and tangentially why locksmiths didn't more often embark on a career of housebreaking. Not wanting to be accused of putting ideas in people's heads he refrained from asking. He pulled on latex gloves, thanked him and went inside.

'For a man in his early thirties he has quite mature tastes,' Austin said as they walked past a Regency hall table with gold-framed mirror above. The large sitting room also looked peculiarly conservative, with a dominating fireplace, dark carpets, gold-trimmed black curtains at the windows and solid period furniture.

'His hair was dyed grey. Perhaps it was all an attempt to give himself more gravitas. Or perhaps he inherited the lot.' McLusky left Austin to check out the sitting room while he looked around in the kitchen. It was large and tried less hard to look like the nineteenth century. He went straight for the fridge. 'Not quite so sober in here!' he called over his shoulder. 'Stuffed olives, squeezy processed cheese, instant whipped cream in a can! Suitable for vegetarians! Who knew?' He walked back through the sitting room. 'Talking of whipped, let's check out the bedroom. Found any kinky videos?'

Austin was holding up a clutch of DVDs. '*Better Golf from Tee to Green, Story of a Golfing Genius, Augusta Open Championships 2013.*'

'Definitely a weirdo, then.' He entered the master bedroom. Here, too, wall-to-wall old-fashioned solidity was unrelieved by any sign that Stephen Bothwick had ever been young. The brass bedstead looked a genuine antique, so did the enormous wardrobe and the heavy dressing table. There was a large snake-charmer's clothes basket in one corner. It was big enough to accommodate a man so he looked inside. It was empty. 'This guy was my age. Where did I go wrong?' he softly enquired of the room. McLusky still made do with a mattress on the floor and a bin liner full of dirty washing in one corner, not because he couldn't afford anything better but mainly because he never felt settled enough to do much about it. It had been another point of friction between him and Laura, her knowledge that deep down he didn't care much about the lifestyle she had carefully constructed for them. As for Louise Rennie's place around the corner from here, that was all expensive air and contemporary light and beauty. Here, however, something heavy hung in the air, quite apart from the whiff of deodorant or perhaps perfume in this room. The curtains looked too thick, the duvet too heavy, the wardrobe too looming. McLusky opened and closed drawers gingerly, leaving it for the crime scene technicians.

'Anything?' Austin asked as he joined him.

'Bugger all. Not even one lousy pair of handcuffs. It's like a show home in here. Look at this bed. You said this guy lived alone?'

'According to Mr Lamb, his employer.'

'Is that the same guy who told you Bothwick had a "small flat in town"? This place is huge. What's in the second bedroom?'

'A second bed and one of those old-fashioned little writing tables.'

'Have you found a computer yet?'

'No. But there's a printer and the, er, gubbins for a laptop. *Charger* is what I mean.'

'Is it,' McLusky said absentmindedly. He left the master bedroom and stuck his head in next door to see for himself. 'All right, mobile phone records, internet history, if possible, the usual, Jane.' He moved on to the generously proportioned bathroom. It was spotless and polished. 'We'll let forensics crawl over this place. Tell me, in your experience, do all thirty-four year olds leave their bed neatly made and the bathroom like this?'

'Ask me again in six years' time. Only if they're hoping to get laid, I should think. Or because mum's on her way over.'

'Or someone comes and cleans up after them. But perhaps he has a cleaner. Right, let's go and talk to Mr Understatement, his employer.' He picked up the few unopened letters on the hall table. None were private correspondence. Two were charity appeals, a third with a printed

110

address label had a Bristol postmark. '*Wait*. How did they get here?'

'Someone put them there?'

McLusky held up the letter. 'Yes, Sherlock, look at this postmark.'

Austin did. 'Posted yesterday. So it arrived today when he was already in the mortuary.'

'Find out if he has a cleaner or a housekeeper or whatever. Someone's got here before us. I think this someone cleaned up Bothwick's flat. Somebody definitely collected his mail from his box downstairs and left it here.' McLusky carefully slid open the letter.

'What's it say?' Austin asked.

'His check-up's due at the dentist's.'

McLusky let himself be persuaded to be a passenger in Austin's tiny no-smoking car. His resistance was weakened since he had to admit that the now-completely-broken front suspension made it difficult to get his Mazda around corners. He left it parked, unlocked and with the keys in the ignition in the hope that someone would drive it away and torch it after skidding into a ditch. Austin drove them south out of the city on the Bridgwater Road and eventually through the affluent village of Barrow Gurney. He stopped in a lane flanked by birch trees, opposite a large converted farm complex a short way outside the village. Only one leaf of the wrought-iron gate was open so Austin left the car in the lane. It was a blustery day and snatches of music were riding on the wind. Someone was practising the cello; short phrases of something McLusky did not quite recognize were being repeated. He ground a cigarette end into the tarmac with his shoe while exhaling the last puff of smoke.

'Did Mr My-PA-has-a-small-flat-in-town by any chance say he himself had a little cottage in the country?'

'Mr Lamb, Bothwick's employer, is Deputy Chief Executive of Somerset County Council; that must make him master of euphemism and understatement.'

'Oh, I remember him now. He's the guy who was making a statement outside the council offices about the cuts and how we all have to make some sacrifices and someone flung a wing nut at him. He got his cut right there. It nearly put his eye out.' McLusky marched through the open gate up the drive and towards the horseshoe of buildings, converted barns and stables. There was a yellow Lotus parked in an open double garage with wooden hinged doors; in the cobbled yard stood a grey five-door Mini Countryman. He took in the cars, the immaculately restored nineteenth-century buildings, the new cobbling of the yard. The place looked large enough to house five families in comfort.

'This place looks full of sacrifices,' McLusky growled. 'Other people's. Just how much are we paying this guy out of our rates and taxes?'

'I'm sure it amounts to several pounds. Though if you get to do his job you've probably made your millions already.'

'Probably,' McLusky mused. 'If you were that rich, though, wouldn't you rather retire young in a small cottage than keep on working to pay for all this lot?'

Austin staggered in mock horror. 'And muddle through without the indoor swimming pool? Are you mad?'

'Sorry, I wasn't thinking.'

They had crossed half the yard when a door in the main building opened and a woman appeared. She had short, blonde hair, wore large pearl earrings, a cream raw-silk dress and matching shoes. An enthusiastic Labrador shot past her and came barking across the yard to inspect the arrivals.

'Are you the police? My husband . . .' She broke off to shout at the dog. 'Zora! Come here! No, here!' The dog took no notice and continued to dance around the two officers. 'It's all right she's just friendly. And very stupid.'

McLusky held his ID aloft. 'Are you Mrs Lamb?'

'Yes, my husband has gone for his swim. Let me lock up the idiot dog and I'll take you to him.'

McLusky gave Austin a wide-eyed look. Austin shrugged. 'I didn't know he had a pool. I was joking when I said it.'

Mrs Lamb reappeared and led the way. A double cross of brick paving had been set into the cobbles, connecting the various outer doors of the buildings, which allowed Mrs Lamb to negotiate her home in four-inch heels. The swimming pool was housed in a long, low building. They entered through a door into a well-heated vestibule, then through another door into the pool area. The pool was long and narrow. The only additional luxury was provided by several large

113

potted palms surrounding a couple of wicker chairs and a table. McLusky breathed in deeply. The smell brought back childhood memories of swimming lessons at a municipal pool which had been high on chlorine and short on potted palms.

Mrs Lamb called to the large, white-skinned grey-haired man swimming lengths. 'Darling? Your police officers have arrived.' Then she turned and click-clacked away on the tiled floor, leaving by a different door.

David Lamb turned on to his back and eyed them without acknowledgement while he continued swimming for a while, then turned back on his front and made for the nearest steps in a leisurely, efficient crawl. 'Damn it, don't you people make appointments? You could have called before turning up here.' He kept on talking as he turned his back on them to fetch his bath-robe from a chair. 'And I *had* expected you a lot earlier than this. I called about Stephen disappearing several hours ago.'

McLusky walked up to him, showed his ID. 'I'm DI McLusky, this is Detective Sergeant Austin.'

'I don't really appreciate people walking with street shoes through the pool area, but since you're here you might as well stay where you are.' He sat down in the chair and made a gesture that McLusky took for an invitation to sit down in the second chair. Austin stood, feeling hot in his suit and wondering what it must cost to heat an indoor swimming pool and keep the air temperature of the entire building this tropical.

Lamb, wrapped in a short, wine-red

monogrammed bathrobe, gave him an impatient look. '*Well*? Have you any news yet?'

Now that Lamb was out of the water and covered up McLusky recognized him. He remembered him being interviewed on the local news, talking about the cuts. McLusky gave him the nod and Austin spoke. 'I'm sorry to have to inform you that we have reason to believe Mr Bothwick may be dead.'

'Dead.' Lamb stared straight ahead across the still turquoise of the pool.

'Yes, a body fitting the description you gave was found the day before yesterday. Did you not hear it on the news?' asked Austin.

Lamb looked up but not at Austin, and said to McLusky: 'There were no details, I didn't connect the two.'

'I see. Stephen Bothwick worked for you. In what capacity?'

'Stephen was my PA. How? How did he die? Did he have some sort of accident?'

'No accident,' Austin said. 'He was murdered.'

'Murdered,' Lamb said, still addressing McLusky as though the inspector was using Austin as a medium to speak through. 'A mugging, do you think? But where?'

'We don't know the motive for his murder yet,' McLusky said. 'But it wasn't a mugging. His body was found near Ashton Gate on a piece of waste ground. Would Mr Bothwick have any business in that area?'

'How did he get . . .? No, no business at all, Inspector. As far as I know. And how was he . . .?'

'He died from a head wound,' McLusky said.

Austin allowed a respectful pause before asking: 'Did Mr Bothwick drive?'

'Yes.'

'What make of car did he drive?'

Lamb sat up straighter. 'A VW, a Golf. Silver.'

'Tell me, when did you last see Mr Bothwick?'

'Three days ago. In the evening.'

'Where was that?' McLusky asked.

'Here, it was here.'

'And you didn't miss your personal assistant until this morning?'

'It wasn't like that, Inspector. Of course I missed him. Only one doesn't run to the police the moment someone hasn't shown up for work.'

'He would have been due to, what, come here? That would have been two days ago in the morning. And when he didn't appear what did you do?'

'I called him. But his mobile was switched off.'

'When he left here, what time was that?' Austin asked, notebook at the ready.

'It was six o'clock.'

'He left here to go home?'

Lamb stood up. 'Look, I think I told all that to the policewoman I spoke to on the phone. He left here at six, I never saw him again, now you're telling me he's been murdered. Perhaps *I* can ask a question now! Are you two in charge of this investigation?' McLusky simply raised his eyebrows and Lamb didn't wait for confirmation. 'Then tell me, Inspector, who's looking for Stephen's killer while you're here asking useless questions?'

'Routine questions need to be asked,' said

116

McLusky, 'and procedures followed, I'm sure you'll appreciate that, Mr Lamb. I'm afraid I'll have to ask you some more obvious questions. How long had Mr Bothwick been working for you?'

'Not quite three years.'

'So you'd have got to know him pretty well, wouldn't you say?'

'I suppose so. What are you leading up to?'

'He was not married, we understand. Was he in a relationship, do you know?'

'He never told me of any.'

'Did he seem different at all, lately? Scared, preoccupied?'

'He seemed to have things on his mind. Yes, now that you mention it.'

'But he didn't voice any concerns . . .?'

'Nothing like that.'

Austin's mobile chimed a text alert. He checked it. 'His car's just been found.'

'OK, good,' McLusky said. He turned back to Lamb. 'Can you think of anything else that may throw light on his disappearance?'

Lamb shook his head. 'No, I can't. If I could throw light on it I'd have thrown it. And now if you don't mind, I have work to do.' He took off his bathrobe and dropped it on the chair, pushing past Austin to the edge of the pool. 'Call me when you actually know something.' He dived heavily into the water and swam to the other end where he heaved himself out and without looking back disappeared through the door his wife had used earlier.

There was a moment's silence during which

Austin flapped the air with the sides of his open suit jacket to cool himself. 'What are you thinking?'

'Good exit,' McLusky said. 'Nice bit of theatre. We'll talk to him again later. Let's get out of here, unless you fancy a swim.'

'In an empty, heated private pool?' he said as they walked out. 'Wouldn't mind.'

'If we have to question him again you can take your cozzie.'

'I haven't had a swim since my last holiday.'

'Where did you go?'

'The Lakes. The water was bloody freezing. But I had to try it once.'

McLusky could not remember when he had last taken a holiday. Oh, yes, he could: three years ago with Laura. *Italy*. Too hot, too many art galleries. 'OK . . .' They were back outside in the yard. A blonde girl wearing boots, black jeans and a black jacket was stuffing a cello case into the back of the grey Mini Countryman. McLusky skipped over, showing his ID. The girl, who looked about nineteen or twenty to him, acted unimpressed and got into the driver's seat but she left the door open. 'You're here because of Stephen. Dad's chap? I've just heard.'

'You're Mr Lamb's daughter?'

She gave a brief nod. 'Chloë.'

'Did you know Stephen well?'

Raised eyebrows and a smile. 'Not my type, Inspector. Best ask Dad. I have a rehearsal,' she said, reaching across to close the door.

McLusky laid a hand on the sill. 'Where does your father usually park his car?'

118

'His Lexus? In there, next to Mum's.'

'It's not here now yet your father is. Why is that?'

'Oh, didn't he tell you? Stephen pinched it.'

Nine

'Knickers? Are you serious?' DS Jack Sorbie was so disturbed by DI Fairfield's news that he found it hard to concentrate on his driving.

'Careful, Jack, you nearly knocked that cyclist over.'

'Well, he should try looking in his mirrors and using his indicators. I have a court appearance to prepare for, not to mention our usual insane workload, and the super sends us to catch a bloke who nicks women's underwear off people's washing lines. Tell me I'm dreaming this because it has all the hallmarks of a nightmare.'

They were driving across town to see ACC Anderson's wife at home, top of Fairfield's list of the underwear thief's victims, though of course not the first victim, only the most high-profile one. Fairfield was hoping that the sooner the ACC was satisfied that something was 'being done about the pervy little scrote' the sooner she could return to duties more fitting to an inspector of CID.

'You haven't read the reports, then. He's no longer content with taking underwear from washing lines; he's breaking into people's houses. While the women are there.'

'Yeah, all right, all right. I did skim the reports. Does he stick to certain neighbourhoods? Posh underwear round here, I expect.'

Fairfield flicked the tablet computer she was holding with a fingernail. 'No, he's all over the place. We've no idea how he chooses his victims yet. Turn right here, I think.'

'I know the way, ta,' Sorbie said and turned into the leafy street of solid detached houses. 'So how are we going to catch him? Does the perv leave samples of his DNA behind for forensics? If you know what I mean by his DNA?'

'He doesn't. But forensics isolated fingerprints at the houses where he broke in. He's not on file, though.'

'Still, handy if we do get him.'

'*When*, Jack,' Fairfield admonished despite feeling no more confident about it than he did. It's this one,' she said, pointing at a house. 'Blencathra.'

Sorbie found a parking space opposite. 'And what's a Blencathra when it's at home?'

'It's a mountain in the Lake District. Did you never watch *Wainwright Walks*?'

'You've lost me again.'

'Easily done, Jack.'

Assistant Chief Constable Anderson and his wife lived in a solid suburban house with a large garden and a double garage. It was surrounded by a neatly clipped hedge and protected by a wrought-iron gate. So this was what one could look forward to if one's CID career plans came to fruition. Automatically she assessed the security aspects of the property and even before she had crossed the road knew that neither hedge nor gate would keep burglars or prowlers out. The hedge was a burglar-friendly privet and the gate carried so much ornamental scroll-work it was practically a ladder. There was a state-of-the-art CCTV camera prominently visible on the front of the house but when Fairfield rang the bell beside the gate it remained stubbornly pointing away from her at something in the deep front garden.

'Hello?' The disembodied voice coming from behind the speaker grill above the bell sounded confident.

'Detective Inspector Fairfield and DS Sorbie, we have an app . . .' Noisily they were buzzed in. '. . . ointment,' Fairfield said belatedly, raising her eyebrows at Sorbie and walking in.

'I really don't know why both of us should have to do this,' Sorbie said.

Fairfield stopped. 'If you want to do it by yourself that's OK with me.' She walked on up the drive.

'It's not that. It's just . . . if you're going to be discussing underwear and stuff, the women are just going to be embarrassed with me there as well.'

'How considerate of you,' Fairfield said. 'It's not because *you* are embarrassed of course. *Good afternoon*,' she said briskly to the woman who had opened the door. She had briefly met the ACC's wife before, at a police function.

Sarah Anderson was fifty, with uniformly nut-brown hair, wore too much make-up but dressed in immaculate and understated fashion. She raised a polite smile. 'I remember you, DI Fairfield,' she said, waving away the proffered ID. 'Sergeant Sorbie.' She acknowledged Sorbie with a slight nod and from then on pretended that he wasn't there.

'You've had a nasty scare,' Fairfield began.

'It was nothing, really.' Once they were all seated in her generously proportioned drawing room Sarah Anderson retold the story briskly; how she had forgotten to take in the washing, much of it delicate things, including underwear and stockings, and then went to fetch them late in the evening since rain had been forecast. It was dark and she hadn't bothered to put on the patio lights. 'I hadn't turned on the kitchen light yet, there was enough light coming from the corridor which is probably why he didn't know I was coming. It was when I opened the door to the garden that I switched on the lights and nearly ran straight into him. He was right by the house.'

'Can you describe him?'

'He was slightly built but he wore a balaclava and black clothes.'

'How tall would you say?'

'I really couldn't say. He was sort of loping along when I startled him and he was busy stuffing my stockings into his jacket. He started to run off, stumbled over the stone border out there but didn't actually fall. He ran off into the back of the garden and disappeared. The officers that came before said he probably came through the hedge. You can squeeze through in some places where it isn't as dense as it should be. I think the trees shade it out here and there.'

'Would it be all right if my sergeant had a look round your garden?'

'Of course. Through the French windows.'

Through the French windows Fairfield could see a large expanse of lawn and a broad border, showing a few drifts of early flowers. 'What about eye colour?'

'Oh, I remember those, they were blue. And startled, obviously.'

Fairfield made a note. Behind them Sorbie let himself into the garden. 'Did he say anything to you at all?' she asked.

'No, he made a sort of "wah" sound of surprise – quite a childish sound, I thought later – then he ran off.'

'Did you say anything to him?'

'No, I was too shocked really. Until he was gone, then I could have said quite a lot to him, I promise you.'

'So he took your stockings? All of them?'

'A couple of pairs. I'd hung up three.'

'Two out of three. Mm. Anything else?'

'Nothing else, no. I really don't see what the fuss is all about. We already had a constable and a sergeant out here. He's unlikely to come back and it wasn't as though he'd attacked me.'

'No, but these things have a habit of escalating and you're not the only victim. He has sneaked into people's houses, too. Is there anything on your CCTV?'

She comically pursed her lips, shook her head and smiled. 'My husband only had it installed yesterday and I have no idea how to work it. I'm not looking forward to the tutorial either. It makes me feel as though we are under siege.'

Sorbie came back into the room, shrugging his shoulders behind Sarah Anderson's back. On a

124

small side table a phone rang. 'If you would excuse me while I answer that,' she said.

'Oh, Mrs Anderson, I think we're finished here anyway, we'll let ourselves out if that's OK. You've been most helpful, thank you for your time. And we'll keep you informed, naturally.'

Outside a wind had sprung up, driving grey clouds across the sky. 'Anything of interest in the garden?'

'Yeah, a plastic gnome that was the spitting image of the super. Sitting on a toadstool. You?'

'Nothing, really. He'll never be caught like this, I'd bet my pay cheque on it. He'll be caught *in flagrante delicto* or by accident, mark my words.'

Austin and McLusky watched as Chloë drove away, the rear window of her car obscured by the cello case. The second leaf of the gate opened automatically for her and closed rapidly as the Mini disappeared down the lane towards the village.

'His personal assistant nicks his Lexus and he forgets to mention it.' McLusky turned around and stood facing the main building. He lit a cigarette and inhaled deeply.

'Oh aye, minor detail, easily forgotten. Are we going back inside?' Austin asked.

McLusky made a non-committal sound while thinking about it. He found a half-eaten chocolate bar in his jacket pocket and took a bite from it, then took a drag from his cigarette.

'Smoking and chocolate bars at the same time now. It'll end in tears, Liam.'

'It won't as long as I don't get the two mixed

up. No, we'll leave it for the moment. Deedee was doing a background check on Bothwick and Lamb, let's first see what he digs up.'

Back in Austin's Micra McLusky called DC Dearlove for the background check.

Austin started the engine. 'Back to Albany Road?'

'Oh no,' said McLusky, 'I'm very happy here. Relax.' Austin quickly checked that the answer hadn't been sarcastic – not always a given – then turned off the engine, folded his arms and sank down in his seat. He was quite used to McLusky sharing only half of his thoughts, or sharing them in his own sweet time.

'Yes, Deedee, shoot,' McLusky said down the phone. 'And could you stop eating crisps for a moment?'

'Mini pretzels,' Dearlove corrected him. 'OK, we have nothing on file for either of them. Bothwick is Bristol born and bred, studied economics at Bristol Uni. Flat in Clifton, but we knew that.'

'Find out the status of his mortgage et cetera. David Lamb, anything interesting?'

'Varied career. Got rich in property developing, in Clevedon and Portishead mainly, went into politics and has ambitions, by all accounts. Somerset Council Deputy Chief Executive. That's a big deal, apparently. Married with a son and a daughter. Son's up at Oxford, reading history, daughter is heading for the other place, to study music.'

'All right, Deedee. Lamb drives a Lexus. Get the reg and try and find it because it appears

Bothwick drove off with it. Pinched it, according to Lamb's daughter. Jane says we have Bothwick's own car – where was it?'

'Outside his own flat, sir,' said Dearlove. 'It's with forensics now.'

'Waste of time, it'll be as clean as Barbara Steadman's BMW. Only, Bothwick's car was where you might expect to find it, unlike hers. Another difference. OK, cheers, Deedee.'

Afternoon had turned to early evening with a sudden change of the light. Austin's stomach gurgled in protest. McLusky had managed to subdue his appetite with chocolate and nicotine and sat humming contentedly while they watched the house. After twenty-five minutes of McLusky's humming, just as Austin took a deep breath to ask if he could a) stop doing it and b) tell him why they were still there, a taxi came up the lane. The taxi slowed and stopped in front of the gate. The driver spoke into his mobile and the gate opened.

Once the cab had gone in McLusky said: 'Pull back fifty yards. We don't know which way he's going so get ready for a u-ee in case the cab goes the other way.'

Austin reversed swiftly up the lane and stopped by the side of the road. Engine off, eyes on the gate to Lamb's property. They didn't have long to wait. Soon the blue cab emerged into the lane and drove sedately away from them. 'Was it him?' asked Austin as he started the engine.

'Couldn't be sure but I expect so. Get going.'

Austin accelerated away and soon regained sight of the cab. 'If I hang back too far we'll easily lose him but if I always keep him in sight on these narrow lanes he'll soon spot us.'

'The cab driver sees a baby blue Micra, how threatening is that? And Lamb himself is hopefully too preoccupied. I don't think he even knows what car we came in. You're doing fine.' After a while he added: 'Are you sure I can't smoke in here? Tell you what, I'll smoke out of the window.'

The lane soon emerged on to a wider B road. The cab moved north and Austin hung back, giving the target a lot of room, even allowing a white van to overtake and insert itself between them. They lost the white van when they crossed the A370 and soon found themselves back on narrow country lanes with fields to either side of them. 'Can't be far now, these lanes don't lead anywhere much,' McLusky said. While under suspension he had taken the opportunity to explore the city and the country surrounding it on his own terms, not driven by any investigations. He had crisscrossed it, absorbed it and held in his mind not only the network of its streets, its landmarks, pubs, restaurants, but also the patterns its denizens wove across it, the ever-changing, ever-evolving web of drug dealing, prostitution, late-night violence and muggings, its music scenes, student populations, artistic enclaves and ethnic groupings. Barely a year after arriving on the force his mental picture of the city and the surrounding towns and villages was every bit as accurate as any of his colleagues could boast. McLusky was always happiest while moving about the city streets, trying to walk in other people's shoes, alive or dead, the victims', the perpetrators', the fearful bystanders' shoes.

They passed a working farm, the smell of fresh manure mingling with that of McLusky's cigarette. A short while later the cab turned up an even narrower lane. 'Easy now,' McLusky cautioned. Austin slowed the car. As they rounded the bend an isolated cottage came into view, with the cab stopped in front. Off-road beside the cottage stood a silver Lexus. 'Squeeze past and keep going until we're out of sight and earshot,' McLusky said, getting out of sight himself by sliding down in his seat until his seatbelt tried to strangle him.

'Think he clocked us?' Austin asked.

'Doesn't really matter,' said McLusky. 'I just want to creep up on him and shout *boo* in his ear to see what happens, that's all.'

The cottage stood near the edge of Cook's Wood and was itself surrounded by trees on three sides. Having left the car in front of the gate of a field entrance they jogged back to the house along the lane. They hurried, in case Lamb only stopped long enough to fetch his car. They had worried unnecessarily; the car was there, and no sign of Lamb.

'So here's his Lexus,' said Austin. 'But what's he up to?'

'Let's have a look-see, but quietly.'

Bramble Cottage was built from dark freestone in an L-shape, and was slate-roofed. A wooden patio with two garden benches and a cast-iron chiminea sat in the nook of the L. The house was surrounded by a small neglected garden consisting mainly of grass and a few anaemic daffodils. Standing forlorn in one corner of the lawn a rotary dryer devoid of clothesline pointed its bare arms at the sky in supplication. A glassless cold-frame housed a desolate collection of empty flower pots.

Ignoring the front door they approached like thieves through the garden, keeping close to the wall, McLusky in front. At the first window he peered in. The sitting room looked comfortable but impersonal; no sign of Lamb. The furniture looked too cheap for Lamb, and not baroque enough for Bothwick, which meant the place was borrowed or rented. He moved on, signalling Austin to follow. He rounded a corner and soon found himself at the back, peering into the kitchen window. The kitchen too had a 1980s holiday cottage look; in his mind's eye McLusky could see the sad assortment of cutlery in the drawers and the floral-pattern enamel cooking pots in the cupboards. McLusky made himself small at the window as Lamb entered the kitchen. He was carrying an open hold-all which he threw with some force on to the table in the centre. Each cupboard he opened he closed again with impatience or frustration. McLusky ducked away and shooed Austin in front of him.

'Good moment to come through the front door,' he murmured.

Austin turned the worn metal knob slowly and opened the door quietly. The place even smelled of a holiday cottage, reminding Austin once more of his two weeks in the lakes. As they sneaked into the narrow hall there were still impatient

130

noises coming from the kitchen, conveniently masking Austin's rumbling stomach. On the floor of the hall by the steep and bare wooden stairs lay a small rolled-up rug. They stepped gingerly over it on their way to the kitchen.

Lamb jumped and let out a shout when McLusky, standing in the door, knocked loudly.

'Hello again,' McLusky said gently.

Lamb recovered swiftly. 'How dare you come barging in here unannounced?'

McLusky strolled into the kitchen and stopped to look down into the open holdall without touching, hands in his pockets. 'There was no one to announce us. And I assure you there was very little barging involved. You didn't barge, did you Sergeant Austin?'

'Hardly at all.'

'You can't come in here without a search warrant,' Lamb insisted.

McLusky looked surprised. 'Do you want us to get one?' Lamb looked uncertain. 'Because it would be a waste if, having been granted a search warrant, we were not going to then search the place.' He nodded at the holdall. 'And everything that's in it.' Even from where he was standing he could see that apart from studded leather items, lengths of red ropes and assorted knick-knacks it also contained a camcorder and some DVDs. 'Of course we don't need a search warrant at all if we have reason to believe that vital evidence may about to be removed or destroyed.' He gave Lamb a friendly smile. 'Or if a suspect belonging to that household has just been arrested. For withholding evidence, for

131

example.' His smile vanished. 'Or tampering with it.'

Lamb passed a hand over his face, suddenly looking very tired. Then he crossed to the table and reached inside the holdall. After extracting a bottle of Scotch he zipped the bag shut and fetched glasses from a cupboard. 'I need a drink,' he said in an apparent lightening of his mood. 'Care to join me, Inspector?'

McLusky opened his mouth to refuse until he caught sight of the label on the bottle the councillor was holding. It was a twenty-one year old Glenfiddich. 'Don't mind if I do. My sergeant, though Scottish by birth, won't, since he's driving.'

Standing in the door, Austin gave his ironic-disappointment impression. He preferred almost any drink to whisky and right now even an instant mug of soup would have suited him far better.

'Oh, then perhaps I shouldn't either,' said Lamb meekly, hesitating with the open bottle near the two glasses.

'Nonsense, you go ahead. You won't be driving anywhere either since you haven't got a car. Because Stephen pinched it, didn't he?'

'It's outside. I brought the spare keys with me.' He poured the first glass.

'Ah yes, I'll take those keys.' McLusky held out his hand and snapped his fingers. 'We'll let you have them back once forensics are finished taking your car apart.'

Lamb corked the bottle without pouring a second glass. 'Shit.' He drained his glass in one and set it heavily back on the table.

McLusky shrugged. 'You said it first.' He turned to Austin. 'Get forensics up here, get the car collected and ask for transport to the station for Mr Lamb. I don't think the councillor and his luggage will fit in the back of your Micra.'

Lamb uncorked the bottle again and this time poured himself a large one.

Twelve minutes on full power. Stir. Let rest for one minute. Another six minutes on full power, let rest for one minute. Stir. Somehow these microwave instructions were more annoying than having to cook it yourself. Fairfield let the packet fall back into her freezer and rummaged some more while her fingers went numb from the cold. Lasagne verdi – boring. Economy cottage pie – what had possessed her? Moussaka – sorry mama. The rest appeared to be just packets of peas, mixed vegetables and fish fingers so old they actually still had real fish in them. She slammed the freezer door shut and warmed her frozen fingers in her mouth. It was just as well Louise hadn't shown any interest in the content of her freezer or she would never have heard the end of it. Louise with her yards of cookery books, flamboyant cuisine and effortless style. Fairfield took another gulp of wine from her glass then tilted the bottle to read the label and made a doubtful noise. A few days out of her lover's orbit and already she had slipped back into old habits and bought cheap supermarket wine. She had been perfectly happy with this stuff before Louise, now she noticed how uninspiring it tasted. It just had no depth to it. She drained the glass

133

and put the screw top back on the bottle while her eyes unfocused. Louise would probably be at home now, cooking or eating a meal, at the dining table of course, not on the sofa with a tray on her lap and the telly burbling rubbish at her. For a few more moments she stood by the kitchen counter, drumming her fingers against the side of the bottle, then she pushed herself off, snatched up her jacket and left the house.

She had only had one glass so she was perfectly OK to drive. Well, a largish glass, but she felt more or less sober. Of course she could have done the sensible thing, she thought while driving up the hill towards Clifton, and rung first to see if Louise was in and if she was welcome but she had not yet made up her mind what she was going to Louise's for. Even as she squeezed the car into a space in Boyces Avenue and walked around the corner to her house Fairfield was undecided: was she here to smoke a peace pipe – or peace cigar in Louise's case – or was she here to finish with her? The lights were on so she'd find out in a minute.

'You're back.' Louise Rennie stood aside to let her into her first-floor flat. She was wearing her grey-and-cream cardigan and her grey slacks and had not taken off her narrow reading glasses. 'I'm glad,' she added.

'Are you?' Fairfield's heart sank the moment she saw Louise. She had very little defence against that woman. It was evening, she was alone, yet she was immaculately dressed, wore her rings, silver necklace and bracelet and her delicate little watch. Her short blonde hair looked just so, her nails were perfect and her toenails manicured. The sight of her bowled her over every time. She marched past her through the hall and then stood irresolute in the large, airy sitting room. The shutters of the tall windows were still open and the darkening sky was a deep indigo that resonated behind the warm glow of the lamps and the open fire.

'Yes, I am,' said Louise, shutting the living room door behind her. 'Or should I leave the door open in case you feel the need to storm out again?' When Fairfield simply shrugged she said: 'Come into the kitchen, I was just going to eat. Hungry?'

'*Ravenous*.' Fairfield shrugged off her jacket and dropped it across the back of a two-seater sofa, something she knew annoyed Rennie's tidy mind. Louise didn't know the meaning of the word 'slobbing'. Not only did she not lie on the sofa eating pizza out of the carton in which it was delivered, she didn't own the kind of clothes to do it in. Even the snow-white chef's apron she now put on was blindingly spotless.

'So you got annoyed and ran away,' Rennie said in the kitchen, tending to a couple of sauce-pans on the gas range.

'You were annoying me on purpose. You know I can't compete with your university chums and all you talked about all night was—' she helplessly waved her arms in the air, trying to remember – 'nineteenth-century poets and what have you. Your mate Morva quoted huge chunks of it, in French, no less, and you all just went "Oh yes, isn't it superb" and I sat there like an idiot.'

135

'What did you want me to do, say *please don't mention poetry, Kat doesn't believe in it*?'

'No. But I think you were enjoying it.'

'Of course I was enjoying it. I love Rimbaud.'

'You were enjoying the fact that I felt completely lost. I was supposed to sit at your feet and adore.'

'Or learn something. You don't have to go to university to learn things.'

'I thought it was supper, not a seminar.'

Louise gave her a sideways look over her shoulder. 'We didn't set out to make you uncomfortable, we were already a bottle of wine ahead when you arrived, remember? And if we had changed the subject *because* you had arrived you'd have felt equally awkward. And so would we.' She moved briskly to the polished oak table and set cutlery and glasses for two.

Fairfield remained standing near the gas range, arms folded across her chest. 'But that's just it,' she said, complaining. 'I'm always made to feel weird around your friends.'

'You might be feeling it, but you're not *being made* to feel it.'

'Same difference.'

'Not quite. But OK, perhaps next time we'll talk murder.'

'Quite possibly.' Fairfield let a pause develop, then said hesitantly: 'Lou . . .? I'm not sure this is working.'

Rennie had been getting ready to plate up the food and froze. 'Oh, rubbish. Pour us both a glass of wine. You can't dump me now, we'll be eating in a second.'

Fairfield sighed. The food smelled delicious.

136

She went to the table and poured out two measures from the open bottle. No screw-top label this one. 'Food smells great. What is it, anyway?'

'Oh, just a réchauffé of boeuf bourguignon.'

'And what's a *re-sho-ffay* when it's at home?'

'It's polite French for re-heated.'

'Then why can't you *bloody say so*? You knew I wouldn't know what it means!'

'Oh, for *Christ's sake* it's not my fault you went to a crap school where they didn't teach you anything! Am I supposed to dumb down for the rest of my life so as not to offend your ignorance?'

Fairfield picked up her glass of wine in her fist, her eyes blazing. Louise licked the wooden spoon she was using and pointed it at Kat. 'Don't you dare throw that at me, that wine costs a bloody fortune!'

'Wouldn't dream of it!' She drank it down in one long draught and set it on the table with an exaggerated, appreciative 'ah'. 'Have a nice life, Lou. I'm sure you will.'

'I'd prefer it if you were in it.'

Fairfield was already through the door, snatching up her jacket as she went. 'We can't always get what we want! I think I'll grab some chips and curry sauce on the way home!' She clattered down the stairs and out into the street. The glass of wine had been a large one and the rush of it was just hitting her pleasantly as she breathed in the mild evening air, walking along on light feet in search of a shop where she could buy some more cheap wine.

And a TV guide.

Ten

'*God*, you people are stupid.' David Lamb had protested all the way to Albany Road, non-stop during processing on arrival at the station, and he sounded no happier now in Interview Room 2, though he had waived his right to have a solicitor present for the time being. To McLusky and Austin, who were sitting opposite him, that meant nothing. Suspects often played the I'm-so-innocent-I-have-no-need-of-a-solicitor card, only to scream for one the moment their threadbare stories unravelled under questioning. McLusky listened unmoved to Lamb's tirade, which showed little sign of abating. 'Not only are you wasting your own time with this nonsense, you are also wasting mine. I have work to do. I don't know how you can complain about cuts to the police numbers and budget if you have leisure to harass innocent citizens while *out there* murderers run free. I, in case you hadn't heard, have a county to run, despite incompetent clowns like yourselves.'

'Then perhaps we should get on with it?' McLusky said. 'My last question was: did Mrs Lamb know about your sexual relationship with Stephen Bothwick and that you had rented a love nest for the two of you?'

'Of course she bloody knew, she's not stupid.'

'You know her better than me. And how did she feel about it?'

'What have my wife's *feelings* got to do with it? Could you have found a more irrelevant question to ask?'

Austin chipped in. 'Mr Lamb, we realize that you must feel great sadness and anger at losing your lover but you are directing your anger at the wrong people.'

'Hark at him! Is he a sodding psychologist now? I'm angry at the waste of time and your useless line of questioning.'

Austin shifted impatiently in his seat. 'Mr Lamb, if you are going to dispute the validity of each question then this could take all night.' He checked his watch. His shift should have finished two hours ago and he had had no chance to call Eve to tell her. But Eve would not be surprised.

Automatically McLusky looked at his own watch, still stopped at ten to seven. It showed the right time twice a day and he had missed it again.

Lamb himself shifted on his chair and threw up his hands in resignation. 'All right, all right. Yes, my wife was *fine* about it, OK?'

'Was she not perhaps upset that you were carrying on a sexual relationship with a male employee?'

'Good grief, Inspector, we've been married twenty-five years.'

'She didn't mind you having a bit on the side? And a gay relationship at that?'

'Please spare me your bourgeois morality. My wife and I have always been sexually curious and . . . *explorative* in our relationships. We have an *arrangement*. It's called being grown-up and *discreet.* Perhaps you chaps are just too immature to fully understand such matters. So if you think that my wife killed Stephen out of jealousy then that's just childish fantasy.'

'Did *you*?' McLusky asked. 'Kill Stephen out of jealousy?'

'No.' Lamb glared at him.

McLusky didn't mind being glared at or shouted at or called names. That was what you came to expect as a police officer, from day one. It did not affect him. His only interests were the emotions and motives behind it, and how to exploit them. In the interview room, in a murder investigation, the end justified the means. But tonight McLusky felt himself become increasingly irritable and he knew why: he had now developed a sugar craving on top of his smoking habit and he was desperate for both a cigarette *and* a chocolate bar. 'Are you quite sure you didn't kill Stephen? You can't provide an alibi for the night in question since both your wife and daughter were away, something you knew about in advance. Also, on the night he disappeared up to your love nest, taking your car without your permission, you had an argument. What was it about?'

Lamb pushed forward his bottom lip, then wrinkled his nose. 'Stephen felt . . . hard done by. It's always problematic having a relationship with people you work with.'

'Is it always?' McLusky asked. 'I wouldn't know. This is not your first such relationship, then?'

Lamb ignored the question. 'There are

140

inevitably power issues. He thought he didn't get enough recognition for the work he was doing. He said I was treating him badly, that I was taking him for granted . . .' Lamb's voice trailed off, sounding tired.

'I expect there to be quite a lot of power issues in relationships that involve sado-masochistic practices, yes. His hair was dyed grey, why was that?'

Lamb crossed his arms in front of his chest and stared sideways at nothing. He looked as though he was ready to cry. 'Because he was an idiot.'

'In that case you choose your lovers carelessly. Would you mind elaborating on that?'

Lamb deflated. He sighed loudly. 'Stephen was going a bit grey here and there. At the temples. I suggested he dye it.'

'And he dyed it *all* grey.'

'Yes.'

'To wind you up. Because you wanted him to hide his age.'

'Yes.'

'And were you wound up?'

'It annoyed me. He was just making a silly point. And he looked stupid with grey hair.'

McLusky leant back in his chair and looked at the ceiling as though searching for inspiration there.

Austin took over. 'Did Stephen have other lovers besides you?'

'No.'

'How can you be sure?'

'I would have known.'

'How? Presumably Stephen had time to himself?

141

And you must have spent *some* time with your family.'

'You know, I'm not sure I like your tone.'

'Then you definitely won't like the prosecutor's tone.'

A pause, then he sat forward in his chair as though he had finally come to a decision. 'Yes, yes. He . . . I, er, I spied on him. We'd had arguments before, I was afraid he might be . . . thinking of leaving me. I really was afraid of losing him.'

'Did you employ a private investigator?'

'No, nothing like that. I confess, I followed him.'

'And what did your own spying reveal? Was he about to leave you?'

Lamb paused, looked at the blank wall to his left. 'Perhaps. I don't know. I'll probably never know.'

'Did he meet other men?'

'I think he was trying to. I followed him to a club a couple of times but each time he left by himself.'

McLusky pretended to look up a piece of information in the papers in front of him. 'So,' he said as though he had arrived at an important landmark. 'The rotary dryer at the cottage.'

Lamb looked baffled. 'What's a rotary dryer?'

'It's a metal structure often found in gardens, Mr Lamb. It consists of a pole with several spokes connected with rows of clothesline.'

'I still don't follow you.'

'The clothesline from the dryer in the garden is missing.'

'Is it?'

'Any idea where it went?'

'I have no idea what you are talking about. Of course I don't know! Stephen and I didn't go there to do laundry together, you know.'

'You didn't, for instance, use the clothesline to tie him up?'

'You're being absurd now.'

'So it was Stephen, then?'

'What was?' Lamb looked worried.

'Not Steve?'

He subsided, seemingly relieved at the turn of the questioning. 'He disliked having his name shortened. I think his mother called him Stevie and he hated that.'

'Do you have a key to Stephen's flat?' Austin asked casually. 'Of course you have, you're paying for it, aren't you?'

'I help. That's not a crime now, is it?'

'Was it you who tidied up his flat?'

'What do you mean?'

'Well, someone cleaned up Stephen's flat after his death, we're pretty sure of it. And that someone collected today's mail from his downstairs mailbox and left the letters on the hall table. So unless you were wearing your marigolds already then we'll find your fingerprints on them. Won't we? Will we?'

Lamb sighed. 'Yes, that was me.'

'And what did you remove from the flat?'

'Exactly what you would expect.'

'S&M paraphernalia, photographs, anything that would connect you to him. Exactly what his killer would have done of course.'

'For the last time—'

McLusky cut across him. 'Did you take his laptop?'

'Yes, I took that.'

'Why?'

Lamb shrugged. 'Pictures. And some videos we made.'

'Nice. Where is it now?'

'At home. In my office.'

McLusky nodded to Austin who left the interview room to arrange for it to be collected. 'What else?' he asked Lamb.

'Some DVDs, some sex toys and such.'

'Why?'

'I can't afford the publicity, I only took away anything that might have hinted at the nature of our relationship. The same at the cottage. I didn't do it to destroy evidence of any crime. It's a private matter and knowing what the police are like the press would soon have been all over it because the police *always* leak information to the press.'

McLusky suddenly leant forward as though his interest was aroused for the first time. 'Now that *is* interesting. Because when we spoke to you earlier today you appeared surprised that your lover was dead yet by then you had already removed all evidence of your involvement from the flat. In other words: *you knew.*'

'Yes. No! I didn't know for sure. But Stephen had gone missing and when I heard the body of a man had been found I thought it might be him. And when I went to the flat it was obvious he hadn't been there. Somehow . . .' Lamb appeared to be struggling with his emotions. 'I know this sounds idiotic, but somehow Stephen was the kind of person that would happen to. I just had this strange premonition.'

'Premonition? *Excellent.* The jury are going to love that.'

Lamb ignored it. 'There was no sign of a struggle or anything but it was obvious he hadn't been home. From there I took a cab to the cottage. My car was there. But I didn't have the keys to the cottage and hadn't been able to find the spare keys to the Lexus so I went home. When I finally found the spare keys I went out again. That's when you followed me. This sort of thing could ruin my career.'

'I understand your concern.'

'Good.'

'Only, both flat and cottage were possible crime scenes. You cleared up the cottage even though you thought Stephen had been murdered and since he had driven your car there and subsequently disappeared it was bloody obvious that it was the most likely place he was attacked by his killer!' McLusky was almost shouting now. 'You were clearly more concerned about keeping the nature of your peccadilloes from becoming public knowledge than you were about seeing his killer caught, so perhaps it would be a good idea not to complain too loudly about the work we do and how we do it unless you want *that too* on the front page of the *Herald*. Right, you will be asked to sign a written statement then you are free to go and resume your very important, grown-up and discreet life. Sergeant Austin can arrange for a police car to drive you home.'

'No thanks, I'll manage.'

'Good, we don't want to waste police time *and* taxpayers' money, do we?' McLusky gathered his papers, already reaching for the tape recorder. What he needed now was a cigarette, a coffee and a Mars bar. 'Just one more question. Do you know or have you ever met a Barbara Steadman or her husband John?'

Lamb pursed his lips. 'Steadman? I have as a matter of fact. Yes, I have met both of them.'

McLusky withdrew his hand from the off button. 'I do wish you hadn't said that.'

Nodding her head to the beat of the music Ellen Fraser rattled off another burst on the keyboard of her laptop. Sitting in a small pool of light from the lamp on the sitting room table near the large sash window she cupped her chin in one hand and read the sentence through, changed *discreet* to *discrete* – she always got those two mixed up – and turned up the volume. Just because she was a mature student didn't mean she couldn't listen to music at immature volume levels – through her headphones so as not to wake the neighbours – and write last-minute essays late at night. And because she was a mature student she could touch type, not just clack away at the keyboard and hope for the best. Ellen had to admit she paid a higher price for burning the midnight oil than the nineteen year olds on her course. Thirty-eight, and old age had somehow crept up on her. She no longer tried to keep up with the pubbing, clubbing and partying; she was too busy trying to keep up with the mortgage and the course work. She had tried to do what was expected of students but after the first few weeks decided that she had definitely reached the age where she preferred to get at least seven hours sleep and wake up in a bed, preferably her own. Not that young men had been throwing themselves at her. Not even one of them had asked her how she liked her eggs in the morning. Which was a shame because she was ready and waiting with the killer retort of 'Unfertilized, thank you'. She had been waiting so long for an opportunity to use it she was no longer sure if it was at all funny. Or even true.

It was her mind that needed fertilizing tonight. Ellen yawned expansively and reached for her coffee mug. Only a cold mouthful lurked at the bottom. She would brew fresh coffee and then make one more effort to get to grips with *The Economics of the Late Medieval Village*.

Ever cautious, she saved the document and slid the headphones from her ears. As she dropped them on to the table the booming music was transformed into an irritating high pitched noise, barely recognizable as music. She paused the player.

Sudden silence. She had been so lucky with this place, a garden flat right at the end of a Montpelier cul-de-sac, it was miraculously quiet yet right in the heart of the city. Of course there was that kind of background noise that all cities had, but you got used to that, you had to consciously listen to hear it, really. She stood and listened, mug in hand. Yes, OK, she could hear it now, very faint, the hum of the city. She was sure that if she had double-glazing fitted she wouldn't hear it at all. Ellen shivered. There seemed to be a slight draught all of a sudden. And now there was a creak, on the other side of the door, in the hall. That was old houses for you. The floorboards creaked, the plumbing groaned and the windows rattled but we still love them because we think they have more soul than new ones. She opened the door to the hall and stepped forward and then stopped, stood immobile. The door to her bedroom was ajar. She was sure she had closed it earlier. In fact she always kept it closed. Perhaps it had opened by itself and that was what she had heard? Did doors open by themselves? Old doors in old houses? There was a squirming anxiety at the bottom of her stomach as she stood and breathed and listened. It was a while before she could bring herself to slowly push at the door with one finger, widening the gap, while trying to tell herself not to be silly and get spooked just because it was late. She slid one hand inside the room and felt for the light switch, found it and flicked it on. She pushed the door open wide. It was quite a small and cosy bedroom. Everything looked normal except for the chest of drawers beside the bed. The top drawer stood open and she knew for certain she had not left it like that. Ellen stepped forward and stood between bed and drawer, looking down into it. It had been messed up. Her tights and her knickers had been messed about and mixed up like a stew. Someone had been in here. She let herself sink down on the bed and immediately shot up again. The patch she had sat on felt warm and damp.

'We still don't have a direct link, then?' DSI Denkhaus took a sip of coffee from his cup, which looked fragile in his large fleshy hands, and returned it to its saucer.

McLusky had not been offered coffee – he could smell it was the real stuff – but at least this time he had been invited to sit on one of the two hard chairs in front of the super's desk. McLusky was tired. Last night's interview with Lamb had dragged on and the morning had been spent collating information and reading witness statements. He knew that if he closed his eyes for longer than a minute he would start snoring.

He sat up straighter. 'The Lambs occasionally met the Steadmans socially, at one function or another, over the last couple of years. The impression Lamb was trying to give was that Barbara Steadman was a social climber, that he disliked her and that he spent no more than five minutes talking to either of the Steadmans.'

'So we have two murders, the drowned woman in the canal, the electrocuted and battered chap in the weeds, and the connection is: the chap's employer and lover had met the first victim, and the second victim had also at one time been tied up with lengths of clothesline.'

'Four inches of clothesline, that's all we have. Without it we would definitely have started separate investigations.'

'What did forensics have to say about the clothesline?'

'They said "it's clothesline", and that was that.'

'Surely more than that?'

'They said "It's definitely clothesline, of a type similar to that used on the first victim". I'm paraphrasing. All bloody clothesline are similar to each other, as far as I'm aware. But they managed to spot that it was a different colour. The woman was tied up in green and blue line, this stuff had once been red but looked greenish, discoloured through age, exposure to sunlight, etcetera and it was affected by the heat of the electricity. The victim had wires attached to his ankles and wrists and someone tried to fry him and it got hot enough to frazzle the clothesline he was tied with.'

'Our man is quite a sadist then.'

'It's possible. But I think he actually tried to electrocute Stephen Bothwick as a method of killing him. Not for sport. Perhaps he hates mess.'

Denkhaus frowned. 'What is that supposed to mean?'

'Perhaps he doesn't like blood. You stab someone or bludgeon someone and you're bound to get blood everywhere. But electrocution could seem to someone a cleaner alternative. Ditto drowning.'

Denkhaus folded his hands in front of him and touched his knuckles lightly to his desk top. 'You are convinced of the connection, then. The MO is very different.'

'Oh, absolutely. It's the same nutter, he just likes variety. Admittedly, without the bit of

150

clothesline we would not immediately have connected the two. Without the clothesline I might not have asked Lamb if he knew the Steadmans.'

'It's thin, though, isn't it?' Denkhaus looked at the ceiling for inspiration. He spotted a ceiling tile that hung lose at one corner and frowned at it for a second, then scribbled on a notepad. 'OK, always assuming they are connected, could the different MOs have been chosen to throw us off the scent? Make us believe in separate perpetrators?' Denkhaus saw McLusky shaking his head. 'Oh, of course not, you're right. You wouldn't leave bodies where they could be found within hours. Left there *in order* to be found.'

'Yes, we were definitely meant to find them.'

'Which is worrying. Someone is trying to make a point. But what about? And for whom? A manager of an energy company and a no doubt underpaid PA of a council exec? Keep digging, McLusky. And run a tight ship, everyone's watching you. And don't get people like Lamb more narked than is necessary. He has influence and he's not a friend of ours.'

'Oh, absolutely, sir. Kid gloves at all times, sir.'

'Oh, yes.' Denkhaus nodded towards the now blind monitor set in the bookshelves to his right and smiled grimly. 'I watched the recording of last night's interview with Lamb. Actually, I thought you handled that rather well. OK, good work. Now get the bastard. And if it turns out to be Lamb, so much the better.'

'Thanks.'

'Have we got mobile phone records for the first victim yet?'

'Yes, we have. I had people wade through them but so far nothing out of the ordinary. The only interesting thing is that Barbara Steadman's husband knows all of the contacts, or knows of them and so far none of them qualify as lovers or look good as suspects. It's a shame we didn't find the phone itself.'

'Quite. Well, keep digging. It's all out there.'

McLusky was already at the door when Denkhaus added: 'Oh, McLusky? That *thing* you drive round in?'

'I'm buying a new one, sir.'

'I'm glad to hear it. When?'

'What time is it now?'

McLusky went back to his office, piled the files he had been carrying on top of a filing cabinet and squeezed himself behind his desk. In the bottom of it lived a tiny travelling kettle amidst coffee-making paraphernalia. McLusky checked it for water, flicked it on and while he waited for the water to boil fell asleep. Just over an hour later he woke up with a start and a crick in his neck. He yawned, flicked the kettle on again, massaged his painful neck and grunted as he stretched his back until it clicked. He stirred whitener into his instant coffee and with irritation poked his spoon at bits of coffee granules that remained floating on top of the grey liquid. McLusky sipped at it and checked his computer. Nothing new. He scratched his head, tried to wake up properly. Two murders, one nutter? Drowning. Electrocution. Clothesline. A high-flying manager, a lowly PA. Who hated you? Who did you two piss off? He finished his coffee and checked the time on his phone: four thirty. Just enough of the day left to go and quickly buy a car, he supposed.

Eleven

A Mercedes 500 SEC. For the past two hours McLusky had been driving around just for the joy of it. Austin would probably say it was another impulse buy, Laura, with her environmental concerns would have screamed, but surely no one could complain that its image let the force down. This thing was more comfortable than his flat. It smelled of leather. It had heated seats. It had a decent sound system. The walnut dashboard made him think of a classic yacht. OK, it might be twenty years old but its shiny black body and the interior were immaculate and it moved like a dream. It had been surprisingly cheap, too, no more than a newer, much smaller car would have cost him. Paying for it had not been a problem since McLusky had little outgoings, living as he did in a rented flat without even the pretence of heating and with a minimalistic wardrobe. And with the compensation payment for being injured in the line of duty still sitting untouched in his bank account he felt he could easily afford this bit of luxury. Even here, parked opposite the Steadman house in Ham Green it didn't look out of place. It was obvious there was some kind of party going on. A wake? There was a *Dauphin* catering van parked in the street outside and both street and drive to the house were crammed with cars, some, but by no means all of them, quite expensive. McLusky had come on the spur of the moment and in order to unnerve John Steadman by asking him about having met David Lamb and so possibly the other victim; a party he had not expected. Perhaps this wasn't the time.

He could hear music, not the kind of music you would expect at a sombre gathering. McLusky walked up the drive to the house and the closer he got the clearer it became that this was no wake. A window was being opened just as he reached the side of the house and music spilled out, the kind of anodyne jazz played by people who did not like jazz. A couple were strolling in the garden at the edge of darkness. He found a bar and buffet in the brightly lit conservatory, helped himself to a bottle of Becks and walked out to Steadman's writing hut, which showed light. McLusky made his way there along the unlit path and peered in through the window. On the chaise longue, which had been cleared of books – hastily, by the looks of it – lay John Steadman. He was delving into the green dress of the blonde woman who sat astride him, unbuttoning his shirt. 'Bereavement counselling,' McLusky said to no one in particular. He dropped the empty bottle into a planter beside the path and checked his watch. Still ten to seven. No matter, there was a clock in the Merc.

'It's huge!' Austin said for the third time. 'Absolutely massive. How much did you pay for it?'

They were standing next to each other at the window, looking down into the Albany Road

155

station car park. 'It was actually quite cheap,' McLusky offered in defence and yawned. He had driven around in it for another two hours the previous night.

'I'm not surprised. Twenty years old.'

'Ycs, but it's immaculate, just look at it.'

'I am. Does it really have a five litre engine?'

'Five litre V8.'

'Economical, is it?'

'Oh, yes,' McLusky said, 'it does several miles to the gallon.'

'I thought so. That's why it was cheap. It'll drink you out of house and home.'

'OK, that's enough boy's talk.' They tore themselves away from the window and walked back towards the incident room.

'Forensics called with a preliminary to let us know there was no blood in the interior or the boot of Lamb's Lexus.'

'How kind of them.' From the other side of the corridor advanced DC French who peered at them through the carrier bags and objects piled high in the cardboard box she was carrying. She stepped aside to let them pass but McLusky stopped to admire.

'Moving house, French? What's all this junk?'

'Collateral damage from DI Fairfield's knicker-thief hunt,' French said and rested the box like an infant on her hip. 'They found prints at a place where he was interrupted while sneaking into a house and got a match. Turns out it's nothing to do with the pants sniffer but the place had been burgled earlier and they found all this junk at the bloke's address, he was a burglar-cum-window cleaner. All this stuff's nicked. And they couldn't be bothered to properly bag it up and label it there and then so guess who got landed with it?'

'I hope his window cleaning was better than his thieving.' McLusky randomly picked up a few of the objects: fake pearl necklace, scratched, gold-plated bracelet, broken clasp. Fake Rolex watch, stopped. 'Ha, look, it stopped at exactly the same time as my own crap watch.' Somewhere in his jacket his phone chimed. 'File it under assorted junk in a couple of bags, Frenchie. Don't spend more than ten minutes on this.' He found his phone and answered it as French moved on. 'McLusky.'

It was DC Dearlove. 'Sir, we have someone reporting their boat stolen.'

'That's something,' Austin ventured when McLusky told him.

'Yeah, but hold back on the champagne.'

Back in the incident room McLusky's computer flagged up an urgent email. 'Hallelujah!'

'What?' asked Austin.

'Someone found a phone lying in the grass by the layby and handed it in. There's a chance it could be Barbara Steadman's.'

'How did SOCO miss that?'

'Don't know,' said McLusky gleefully, 'but I'll not let them forget it in a hurry. It's downstairs apparently.'

Sergeant Hayes handed over the phone in an evidence bag. McLusky scowled at it. 'Are you taking the piss, Sergeant? Barbara Steadman took home a hundred grand plus and this is a pay-as-you go phone. Ten quid in any supermarket.'

'Don't shoot the messenger, sir,' said Hayes when McLusky stomped back upstairs.

First he went off to fortify himself in the canteen. He loaded his pockets with chocolate bars and took his cup of black coffee upstairs with him, covering it with the saucer to keep it hot until he had reached the sanctuary of his office. Outside, typical April temperatures reigned; in his office, with the enormous radiator under the window grilling his back, McLusky luxuriated in fresh air from the open window. He distributed the chocolate bars among drawers and pockets for later. As he did so he felt something unexpected in his jacket; he fished it out and stared at it for a moment before remembering where it came from: it was the fake Rolex from among the recovered tat from the burglar arrest that French had been given to bag up. He must have pocketed it without noticing. Only now it was working. He realized it was one of those perpetual motion watches that wound themselves through the movement of the wearer. He set it to the right time, took off his own stopped watch, dropped it into the bin and put on the Rolex. He logged on to the computer. The list of emails was endless and depressing. This was the part of the investigation he found most difficult to cope with: nothing but conjecture on offer, hoping for a forensic miracle. One miracle would be if they could do their job in less than two weeks. Losing the Forensic Science Service hadn't exactly helped, either. The government had closed it down because *it had been losing money*. Since when did justice have to turn a profit, McLusky

158

wondered. They were now processing some things 'in-house', but anything more than finger-print matching still took forever. He wished TV producers would screen a murder investigation on telly in real time and see how many viewers were left after three weeks when the first forensic results came in.

He took a closer look at the phone and suddenly his mood lightened. He called Austin. 'They said she was discreet. It's Barbara Steadman's shag-ging phone of course. Off to Technical Support with it.'

As the door of the Royal Oak shut behind her, Fairfield looked up at the sky. Any promise of a warm and early spring had disappeared, it was cold April weather and would rain again any minute now. Her hand closed around the tin of small cigars in her jacket pocket; she hesitated only for a fraction before pulling it out and opening it. Only four left. She lit one of the long, slim cigars with a match and slid the tin back into her pocket. She should pack it in, really. It was Louise who had introduced her to smoking cigars but then it had been fine brandy and cigars at her flat. Exiled out here it was nearly impos-sible to have a drink and a smoke together, at least on a freezing cold night in April. What a time to start smoking, just when it became the leper thing to do. Naturally, Louise being Louise, they hadn't been smoking Hamlets from the newsagents; the cigars Fairfield had become used to smoking were Davidoff Exquisitos, at £26 for a tin of ten. 'Here's another fine mess you've gotten me into!' She sighed, blowing smoke in the direction of Louise's flat.

Fairfield was standing in The Mall in Clifton Village, just a few streets away from Louise's. She had deliberately come up here without her car to give herself options: go and see Louise or go and get drunk. Or go and get drunk, then see Louise. Or go and see Louise, have a flaming row and then get outrageously drunk. So far she had been to three pubs, having a pint in each of them, putting things off, mulling things over. Going round in circles, if she was honest. Blaming all of it on *her*.

Fairfield had always been a pub person. She drank wine at home but when she went out on the town she drank beer. Pints. Pints in traditional pubs. When she was out with Louise of course it had usually been brasseries, like the one just opposite, and bistros and restaurants which meant that not only was she now standing and smoking outside pubs, she was smoking outside pubs she no longer felt entirely happy with. But as long as they sold beer she could never go completely off pubs and the Royal Oak wasn't so bad. The other problem with smoking bloody cigars was of course that you were meant to take your time with them – you couldn't really pop out for a 'quick cigar' like you could with a cigarette. Another punter had come out after her, smoked his cigarette and disappeared inside again. 'Freezing!' was all he had said, and he was right. And now a thin, miserable rain began to fall. She took her tin of Davidoffs from her pocket, used it to stub out her half-smoked cigar on it and returned them separately to her jacket pocket. Then she went back inside and ordered another pint of Sharps Doom Bar, simply because the name suited her mood.

McLusky drove, drove through the city. His new car had transformed it for him. Where before he had struggled in a screeching, limping motor he now glided across lanes, cornered with poise and surged up hills. There was no CD player but it played cassette tapes! At home he had nothing to play them with but now at last he had somewhere to play the huge box full of tapes he had lugged from flat to flat for the last decade or more. Several times he had come close to throwing the lot out but now he had a mobile tape deck with a five-litre engine and leather seats. Stone Roses, *I Wanna Be Adored*. He had been driving around most of the evening, stopping for fish and chips at Pellegrino's, quartering the city, feeding cassettes into the machine. Some he flicked straight out again after the first few bars, music that reminded him of Laura; Laura in the bad old days. It was Laura who, while he was in hospital after having been deliberately run over by suspects in Southampton, had packed that very box of tapes along with the rest of his belongings and dropped the lot off at the section house. But not all the music plucked at the wrong strings, he was all right as long as he stuck to the loud stuff, Stripes, Chili Peppers, Led Zeppelin, and music Laura had hated, like Throwing Muses and early Bowie.

He crossed the river in the dark. Raining again.

161

It didn't matter now; the wipers worked and the windscreen didn't leak, which was unusual for a McLusky-owned vehicle. He turned off Clanage Road on to the lane along Bower Ashton allotments and zoomed to the end where it crossed the railway linc. He left the headlights on as he got out of the car, zipped up his leather jacket and turned the collar up. He had forgotten to bring a torch. It didn't matter. He hadn't come back here to examine the place, and the car's headlights were enough illumination for his purpose.

He didn't have a name for it. It wasn't murderers who were irresistibly drawn back to the locus of the crime, it was DI Liam McLusky. The places where the victims were killed or their bodies had been discovered exerted a strong pull on him, bringing him invariably back to the locus once forensics teams were finished, police officers and coroner had departed and SOCOs had packed up. Something lingered there, like an invisible stain on his mental map of the city, or like an elusive smell that teased his nostrils, leaving him restless and tingling with impatience to find the perpetrator. The place was witness. Stubborn in eloquent silence.

And there were other reasons why he came to dark, dismal places like this railway cutting when no one was around. Ever since the attack – or the *incident in Southampton* as his attempted murder was sometimes referred to – he had been prone to sudden spikes of anxiety. They flew at him from nowhere, at odd times, in unexpected places, and for no reason he could discover. There never seemed to be a logical trigger; the dread appeared to fly at him on the wind or rise through his shoes from the ground, unannounced, unstoppable. He usually managed to shake it off by keeping busy, which was never difficult in his job, or by having a few beers; he had never felt anxious in a pub as long as the bar was open. But he came to these kinds of places to challenge himself, throw down the gauntlet to the irrational side of his mind.

Standing beside death, that's what it was. Standing in precisely the place where a victim had been killed or discovered, the place any ordinary citizen would avoid at all cost, was where McLusky looked for inspiration, and sought to purge his anxieties. Tonight he felt good, had enjoyed his driving, yet in the end his worries about the investigation had won: he needed to stand here on top of the railway cutting and breathe. Sometimes he hallucinated smells, very brief snatches that went with the thoughts he was having at the time, flowers or coffee or fresh laundry, and just now, looking down on the overgrown embankment, the aroma of railway carriages as he remembered them from his childhood. The smell vanished after a moment, overwhelmed by the very real one of damp earth close by. The rain intensified. It was stupid to stand here in the freezing rain when he had a warm and comfortable car waiting for him.

It was as he turned away that he thought he saw a movement below him on the slope of the embankment, in the dark where the beams of his car's headlamps did not reach. He thought he had

163

heard a crack, too, like a twig snapping underfoot. Animal, vegetable or mineral? The sound of the rain made it difficult to decide what was moving down there. What would anyone be doing there in the dark at this hour? Even the most hard-bitten drug addicts could surely find a more salubrious place. He took a few steps down the slope but suddenly thought better of it and stopped beside a twisted shrub. 'Who's down there? I'm a police officer!' He became uncomfortably aware that standing up here he was well illuminated by his car's headlights while whoever was moving down there was hugging the darkness. He climbed back up the slimy slope and turned. The beams of the headlights reached as far as the opposite side of the railway cutting but left a black chasm in between. From it, on the other side, emerged the figure of a man, surely a man, tall, in a dark hooded rainproof and dark gloves, moving away swiftly to the right. 'Stop! Wait right there!' Without slowing or turning the figure lifted one arm and gestured back at him, briefly holding up two fingers. McLusky shouted and ran forward. Almost immediately he slipped; he saved himself from landing on his back with his hands and dug his heels in to stop the slide. When he regained his footing and looked across the tracks the figure had disappeared into the dripping darkness. McLusky too stood in the dark now, an unpleasant sensation of sticky mud on his hands. It was about here that Bothwick's bludgeoned corpse had lain. The desire to be clean, dry and back inside his car was stronger than the urge to crash after the hooded figure. He slipped twice more on the slick mud before he gained the top of the embankment.

Had it been the same man that he had seen standing stock still like a sentinel from across the canal? Back then he had held up one finger, now he had flashed two fingers at him: a good old-fashioned insult or the number two? Had he just seen the killer of Barbara Steadman and Stephen Bothwick and let him get away? His stomach went into freefall and fear of failure made his skin tingle. He wiped some of the mud off his hands on a wet tuft of grass and got behind the wheel of his car where he found the wrapping paper from his parcel of chips and completed the job as best he could. Then he turned his huge car in a six-point turn and drove furiously towards Clanage Road and the light.

Light, that was what he wanted, light and clarity and so far this investigation had neither. As he crossed back over the river he thought he understood what he liked so much about his new car, it reminded him of Louise Rennie and the way she surrounded herself with simple, uncluttered luxury, something his own life lacked in spades. And perhaps that was why a little later he found himself cruising up through Clifton into Clifton Village where Louise lived. He felt ready for a drink, the only thing capable of signalling to his brain that his workday was over. Somehow the thought of his usual refuge, the Barge Inn, left him decidedly unexcited tonight but before he could make up his mind which pub to aim for instead, all his attention was taken up by a figure trudging towards him on the pavement through the cold west country rain. It was Kat Fairfield. He only hesitated for a fraction before pulling over. She did not spare the car a single glance. McLusky parped his horn and let the passenger window down. Fairfield slowed, frowned, approached the car and bent down to look inside. Her face was streaming with rain. Her frown deepened when she recognized him. 'Liam?'

'Get in, Kat, before you drown.'

A moment's hesitation in which she made a show of examining the interior before getting in. 'What are you doing with this thing?' she asked once she had slammed the door shut. 'Don't tell me this is yours?'

'Bought it yesterday.'

'It's enormous. It's monstrous. How do you park it?'

'I can't, I have to keep driving it.'

'Ha! Tricky. You'll be moving your office in here then.'

There was a short pause during which McLusky tried to calculate just how much Kat had had to drink. A fair few, he was sure.

'What you doing up here, anyway?' she asked.

'I was thinking of having a drink.'

'I could definitely do with one.' Not once since McLusky's arrival in Bristol had the two taken a drink together or socialized in any other way. First professional rivalry, then their mutual interest in Louise Rennie had kept them apart, but tonight Fairfield didn't care or merely didn't mind or perhaps she was even glad he had turned up, she wasn't sure. When McLusky suggested

166

the Royal Oak she said: 'Just come from there. Let's try the Albion.'

McLusky drove. 'Gastro pub,' he commented. 'I'm not in the mood for spit 'n' sawdust tonight.'

'Me neither, come to think of it.'

The Albion was fairly quiet and they managed to find a table close to the bar. It was only when he lifted his pint of Guinness to his lips that he noticed his black-rimmed fingernails. Fairfield noticed too. 'That doesn't go with the image, Liam. Immaculate Merc and filthy fingernails. Have you taken on an allotment?'

'Slipped in the mud earlier.' He didn't feel like discussing his excursion to the deposition site. Talking shop of course was a simple ice-breaker but tonight there seemed to be a lot less ice, though at the moment Fairfield was definitely avoiding his eyes.

'Can't believe we're sitting in the pub together.' Fairfield sipped her pint. 'I'm as wet as a drowned rat, your hands look like you've been digging potatoes . . .'

McLusky let her talk. She had suggested this drink, more or less, which meant there had to be something behind it, and until he knew what it was he was happy to keep quiet.

There was a pause, into which Fairfield blurted: 'That thing with me and Louise . . . I'm sorry that happened. I'm not in the habit of pinching colleagues' partners.'

'She was hardly that. I'll get over it.'

'Actually I think it's all over between me and Lou.'

'For once I can honestly say that I can imagine how you must feel. What happened?'

Fairfield poured the whole thing out as though McLusky was an old friend and ally, and she found herself saying things like 'you know what she's like' and 'as I'm sure you can imagine'. McLusky bought a second round, even while wondering if it was wise to let Kat have another drink.

'I've always been crap with relationships,' she continued. 'I jus' can't do it, I always manage to louse things up. Right from my very first shag. My first boyfriend. Imagine . . . shy Katarina Vasiliou, as she was then. I was seventeen. He had his own flat. It was my first time at his place. We were about to go out and I went to the toilet to powder my nose. Had a crap. It wouldn't flush away. I flushed twice. He asked if everything was all right in there. No, I'm fine, I said. I was mortified he'd come home and find that huge thing floating in there, I'd have been so embarrassed, so in the end I fished it out, wrapped it in layers and layers of toilet roll and put it in my handbag, thinking I'd chuck it at the first opportunity when we went out. Of course he went and looked in my handbag for matches in the pub while I was talking to someone else. And found a turd in his girlfriend's handbag.'

'Did you explain it?'

'Didn' get a chance. An' of course he told everyone.' Fairfield had begun to slur her words. 'I think the thing quite disturbed him. See? I'm crap at relashionships.' She had drained the entire pint while relating the story. 'An' I do believe

I'm finally utterly pissed. Be a gennelman an' cab me a call. Call me a cab.'

McLusky offered to drive her home but was glad when Fairfield insisted on a taxi and he had eventually waved her off from the end of Boyces Avenue. When the cab had turned the corner he became very aware that he was standing two minutes' walk from Louise's flat; Louise who was now no longer seeing Fairfield.

Probably, he thought. Then he walked to his car and drove home.

Twelve

'Come!' By now McLusky recognized Austin's knock, which meant he did not need to hide his cigarette. Austin closed the door and seductively waved a piece of notepaper. 'This is my first mug of coffee of the day,' McLusky told him. 'If you have come to spoil it with whatever you have written down on that nasty piece of paper you are holding I will have to push you out of the window. In fact, don't read it to me for five minutes, that's all I ask.'

'And how are you this morning, sir?'

'Not too bad, though I did have a few beers last night. And you'll never guess who with.'

'I shan't try then.'

'Kat. Bumped into her last night in Clifton Village and we had a couple of beers together. I think the ice is definitely broken.'

'Really?'

'Yeah. We even talked about the Louise thing. Apparently it's all over between them anyway. That should normalize relations a bit.'

'Oh aye, totally normal. I saw Kat hide behind the drinks machine until you had crossed the corridor with that mug of coffee.'

'Really? Ah. Yes, well . . . she did tell me one or two things she might not have done in the sober light of day. I was hoping she was too drunk to remember.'

170

'Looks like she remembers all too well. Do tell,' Austin said conspiratorially.

'Nah. If I tell you then I won't be able to blackmail her with it.' He checked that no one stood below before flicking his cigarette butt through the window. He drained his mug of coffee. 'Right, I'm ready to receive your earth-shattering news.'

'The boffins have wrung out Barbara Steadman's shagging phone.'

'Now he tells me.' He snatched the paper from Austin's hand.

'And she only ever used it to call two numbers. Her driver, Lisa Burns, and someone called Marcus Catlin.'

McLusky was already putting on his jacket. 'And who is he when he's at home?'

'Don't know. But when he's not at home he's a vet.'

At Marcus Catlin's veterinary practice on the outskirts of Keynsham, a small town southwest of the city, his elderly receptionist chided them. 'You really should have called ahead, Mr Catlin is very busy and he has three appointments this morning alone.'

'Perhaps we could talk to him between appointments,' McLusky suggested.

'You could try and catch him in between, yes, I suppose so.'

'Well, would you let him know we are here, now,' he said, becoming impatient.

'You being here is just the problem, because he isn't.'

'Why didn't you say so in the first place?'

171

'I told you he had three appointments this morning. His first was at Broadacre Farm, but that was just vaccination, he'll be finished there now, I expect. You could try and catch him at Wychslade Farm. I'll write down the postcode for you, and his next appointment, too, just in case. I can send him a voicemail or text if you tell me what it's about. He keeps his mobile turned off, it scares the animals when it goes off, but he checks for messages in between appointments.'

'He could set it to vibrate,' Austin said helpfully.

'Oh no, it always makes him jump, he says, and that wouldn't do at all. There you are then.' She handed over the paper with a worried smile. 'Everything is all right, isn't it? He hasn't . . . *done* anything, I mean.'

'Not that we're aware of,' McLusky said. 'Nothing to worry about. But please don't contact him, we would like to speak to him first.' Outside he studied the addresses, then looked up and sniffed the air; it was just beginning to rain. 'He's *that* kind of vet. I thought cats and hamsters, but he's probably got his arm up a cow's arse right now. No wonder he doesn't want to answer his phone.'

Back behind the wheel he still mused about it. 'I wonder what the attraction is. I mean, if you could choose between a well-appointed surgery treating gerbils for hiccoughs or whatever and standing in a smelly shed up to your ankles in cow shit, why would you choose the cow shit?'

Austin didn't have to think long. 'Probably for

172

the same reason you would never choose a desk job over real policing. You wouldn't be happy as a CONGO.' CONGO was Austin's acronym for desk jobbers: Clock On, Never Go Out.

'Too right.' He handed the note to Austin. He hadn't got around to fitting sat nav in the Mercedes yet. 'Stick that in your phone and get us to the first one.'

Austin took out his iPhone. 'As long as you're sure. You might get your new car muddy. Take you hours to get that shine back.' The Mercedes was already as dirty as every other McLusky-owned car had been.

It rained all the way. Wychslade Farm looked to McLusky like a mudpack thrown against the side of the hill. The farm gate, the farmhouse and the massive sheds appeared to stand on the slant. McLusky parked his mud-streaked car in the concrete yard next to an even muddier pair of Land Rovers, 'I haven't opened the door yet and I can smell it. This place stinks bad.'

'Pig farm,' said Austin cheerfully. 'They all smell like that.'

'Again, Jane, if you had the choice between growing sweet smelling peas or whatever and living with the smell of pig shit all your life, who would choose this stench?'

'Pigs are very intelligent. More intelligent than dogs. Just not cuddly. We shouldn't really eat them.'

'I'm surprised farmers can eat at all with this smell around,' McLusky grumbled and got out of the car. A pale, grey-haired man in rubber boots, waterproof overall, plastic bib and black

173

rubber gloves had appeared from one of the sheds, frowning across the dripping yard at them. McLusky showed him his ID. 'We're looking for Mr Catlin,' he said. 'We need to speak to him urgently.'

'Urgent, is it? I'll tell him.' IIe turned and disappeared back into the concrete shed. McLusky was convinced it was at the centre of all the evil smells in the world.

It was several minutes before another man emerged from the broad metal doors. He was younger than the first man, in his thirties, with bright blue eyes and fair hair, and his overall was made from blue cotton. He nodded across to them before divesting himself of his plastic bib. He hosed down his black rubber boots at a tap outside the door before unhurriedly walking over to them. 'Gentlemen? What can I do for you,' he said in a jovial voice while raising a quick eyebrow at the muddy black Mercedes blocking the farm exit.

'Are you Marcus Catlin?' The man confirmed it. 'I'm DI McLusky, this is Detective Sergeant Austin. We have reason to believe that you were acquainted with the late Barbara Steadman.'

Catlin shook his head. 'Barbara Steadman? The woman that was killed? I read about that in the *Herald*. What makes you think I knew her?'

McLusky dug his hand into his trouser pockets. 'Ah. Interesting. OK. While my sergeant here is quite happy to stand in the rain breathing pig shit all day, personally I prefer the smell of Interview Room Two at Albany Road Station where I'll begin by charging you with obstructing a murder investigation. Austin, caution the man.'

'All right, all right.' Catlin lifted his hands in a calming gesture. 'What do you want to know?'

The rain was beginning to annoy McLusky yet rinsed wellies or not, there was no way he wanted the man in his car; they all climbed into the vet's Land Rover instead. The back seats were cluttered with small boxes and equipment of some kind but Austin squeezed himself amongst it. McLusky now convinced himself that the interior of the Land Rover also smelled of excrement. His stomach gurgled; he felt hungry and revolted at the same time.

'I thought I could keep completely out of it. She was married, after all. And we had split up a few days earlier, so strictly speaking we were ex-lovers. You see? Much easier for all concerned, I thought. Especially the husband.' Catlin spoke as though he was explaining a veterinary procedure to a nervous client.

McLusky gave an irritated nod. 'Your concern is touching. How long had you known Mrs Steadman?'

'About six weeks.'

'Not very long. Which one of you ended it?'

'I did.'

'You sure?'

'Yes, Inspector, I have a very good memory.'

'Perhaps she dumped you and you could not forgive her?'

'You're not listening.'

'Why did you finish it?'

'We were completely unsuited to each other, our lives were different, our expectations. Barbara was . . . a typical city person, I suppose. When I told her I was a vet she immediately assumed I looked after cats, dogs and hamsters from nine to five.'

'*Really.*'

'I do very little of that, it doesn't interest me in the slightest. I grew up in a farming community and Barbara, it was like she had never set foot outside a town. I swear until she met me her shoes had never left tarmac. My idea of a good time is to take long walks.'

'And hers?'

'Driving her car – she talked a lot about her car – and sitting in bars and restaurants and drinking too much.'

'How did you meet her?'

'She ran into me in Bristol and dropped her shopping. She told me later that she had done it on purpose. She'd seen me, fancied me, and staged the thing. *And* she had done it before, how corny can you get?'

'How was the sex?' McLusky asked.

'The sex was good.'

'Your place?'

'My place.'

'But you decided you'd had enough good sex.'

'I think, Inspector, it's because I'm still dreaming of meeting the future Mrs Catlin. The vet's wife. Barbara was not it. She had no intention of becoming my wife, either.'

'Did you have rows?'

'Not about that.'

'Where did you tell her it was over?'

'Not in a lay-by.'

176

'Where then?'

'We were going for a walk at the time.'

'Where?'

'Along the canal. But not *that* canal. Along the Kennet & Avon near Bath. It was her idea. If we had to walk then at least it was flat.' Catlin sighed at the memory. 'She told me her feet hurt after eight minutes. I timed it. I decided there and then it was never going to work.'

'OK. Lisa Burns.'

'Who?'

'Come on, now, you were doing so well there. Her driver. How much did you pay her to say she didn't know what you looked like?'

He paused, exasperated. 'Five hundred.'

'Waste of money.'

'It appears so.'

'Did she ask you for it?'

'No, I went to see her at her new job when I heard about Barbara.'

McLusky opened the passenger door. 'Thank you, Mr Catlin. I would like you to come to Albany Road station within the next twenty-four hours to make a full statement and give a DNA sample.'

'Is that really necessary?'

'Yes, *really*. We can of course send someone round to your practice. Shall I arrange it through your receptionist?'

'I'll come to the station.'

McLusky got out and slammed the door. 'Thought you might.' Back behind the wheel of his own car he couldn't decide what to do first, have a cigarette or chomp on a chocolate bar.

First, he decided, he would drive and leave the bad smell behind.

In the canteen at Albany Road he mulled it over with Austin over a plate of plaice, peas and chips.

'I see you went for the safe option,' Austin commented. 'Wish I had.' His Mediterranean-style fritters appeared to consist mainly of bread-crumbs and dried herbes de Provence. 'Was it safe to let the vet go?'

'Not sure.' In retrospect, and with no other suspect in sight, it may have been premature. He even suspected himself of having done it so he could get away from the nauseating smell, though he had to admit to himself that it was less nause-ating than the smell of a decomposing corpse. But only just, he decided. 'We'll have to talk to Lisa Burns again, see what else she was paid not to reveal.'

'Are we paying her another visit?'

'Lord, no, bring her in, charge her with obstructing a police investigation.' He squeezed tartare sauce from a couple of sachets over his peas and began shovelling them into his mouth. 'Do you ever get tired of being lied to, Jane?'

Austin pulled a dismissive face. 'I expect to be lied to, everyone lies to the police.'

McLusky put down his fork and sat back in his chair. 'Doesn't that bother you? That every-thing you hear is probably a lie? And that you expect it as soon as someone opens their mouth?'

'Not really.' He washed down his dusty fritters with a few gulps from a glass of milk. 'It's a challenge, that's how I see it.'

178

'I'm rapidly losing patience,' said McLusky. He returned to his food and stabbed viciously at his fries.

'I've just heard we have a thief in the station,' said Austin.

'One of ours, you mean?'

'Canteen staff did a stocktake and they're convinced someone is helping themselves without paying. Mostly chocolate bars, apparently.'

'Fiendish behaviour,' said McLusky and stuffed some more fries in his mouth.

Michael Leslie was angry. He was angry with his brother and angry with himself. But he had to admit that he had never before enjoyed himself so much while being absolutely livid. It was getting dark and the headlights had come on automatically. It had made him laugh; an angry laugh. He was hungry now. Lunch was a long time ago. But in a car like this it was easy to forget everything else. The automatic gearbox on this thing was so smooth you forgot it had gears at all. The Jaguar XJ was a point-and-squirt car; you pointed it at where you wanted to be and put your foot down and it didn't drive you there, it catapulted you there. That was how the day had felt: he had a machine that obediently zoomed him to wherever he wanted to be, effortlessly, almost magically. *Set the controls to the heart of the sun* was the line from the song; Pink Floyd, wasn't it? He had played no music at all today even though the sound system was probably as good as the rest of the car. He needed headspace. He needed to come to some kind of decision about his life and after all the arguing he and his brother had done over the last couple of days he was still sure that his brother was wrong. Only now he was equally sure that they had both been wrong. About what it all meant. About what was important. About money. And this car made the point perfectly, that's why Rick had leant it to him, *challenged* him to drive the car and then come back and tell him that material possessions were unimportant. Rick probably hadn't meant him to go on a ten-hour drive, but so what? His brother had so much money he owned a Range Rover as well as the Jaguar. *Matthew 19.24* he had quoted at his brother, about camels and rich men going to heaven, about the first being last and the everlasting question: 'Who then can be saved?'

He realized now that it had been his own spiritual crisis that had made him react so fiercely; it wasn't his brother he had been trying to convince that the bible was more important than the bank statement, it had been himself. And since he was living entirely on his brother's charity right now, attacking his riches as immoral had been a silly and ungrateful thing to do.

He smiled grimly at the thought of handing back this car and getting back on the bicycle he had praised so much to Rick as being eco-friendly, democratic, cheap and honest. But you didn't zoom on a bicycle. Nearly there, he thought, and felt his heart sink as he recognized the country lane that ran past his brother's 'rural retreat', as Rick liked to call it. But it was time to be brave and face up to it honestly. Perhaps they should both for once compromise? Jesus!

He stood on the brakes yet the Jaguar only just managed to stop before crashing into the white van that had stupidly pulled out from the side of the lane. How could the moron not have seen his headlights approach on an unlit road? He gave a retaliatory blast on the horn. Now the van jerked forwards a couple of times and stopped. Must have stalled the engine. Great. You see? On a bicycle you'd have squeezed past that thing but now you're at the mercy of that idiot van driver. As if in answer the driver's door opened and a man climbed down into the road, making apologetic gestures and shrugging his shoulders. 'Oh no, don't come and tell me you've broken down', he said to himself as he let down the window. The driver walked up to it. 'Having a problem?' he asked him.

The man bent down to bring his face closer, laying one hand on to the roof of the car. 'Mr Leslie?' he asked.

'It is, but . . .'

As if out of nowhere a shiny semi-automatic pointed straight at his nose. 'Then shut the fuck up or I'll shoot you right here.'

Thirteen

The boat that had most likely been used to transport Barbara Steadman to the site where she had been murdered had belatedly been reported stolen by the owner. Before it disappeared it had been tied up to a larger boat near the Nova Scotia pub. 'The owner is a well-to-do plumber,' Austin said, looking at the report.

'They're all well-to-do,' McLusky said without a flicker of interest. The boat itself had been handed over to forensics where it had apparently sunk without a trace and McLusky did not expect to hear back from them until long after the killer was in custody.

'There's nothing to connect him at all and naturally his DNA and prints will be all over the boat,' Austin added.

'Yes,' McLusky said, disgust in his voice. 'Let's get some coffees.' He gathered up a colourful bouquet of dirty mugs and led the way.

In the CID room DI Fairfield was standing next to the seated Sorbic, tapping his monitor to draw his attention to something. She looked up, nodded a greeting at McLusky and quickly ducked her head down again. While the kettle heated McLusky stood in front of the large scale map of Bristol on the wall. 'And where was it found again?'

'It was drifting past the SS Great Britain site,'

182

Austin said, spooning coffee granules. 'The harbour ferry people reported it and we got the water rats to bomb out and pick it up.'

'He's not stupid then. Letting it go was the best thing to do, really, now we have no idea where he came ashore.'

'Surely the best thing to do would have been to scuttle the thing?'

McLusky narrowed his eyes. 'Yyyes.'

'You mean no,' Austin told him. 'You usually mean no when you say yyyes.'

'Do I? No wonder I'm confused. It's just a feeling I get about the man. He's only interested in one thing, killing his victims. He doesn't think "I'll have that iPhone and that Gucci watch off her" for instance.' He glanced at his own watch and compared the time with the clock on the wall. Ten past four. His Rolex kept perfect time. 'He didn't rob his victims. He even put Bothwick's jacket back on him after he had killed him. He had no possessions removed from him.'

'Apart from his life.'

'Precisely. Our killer has an agenda and nothing beyond that agenda. He took the boat because he needed it for his plan but he didn't want to destroy it. He had just borrowed it.'

'Should have returned it then.'

'Too risky.'

'So what you're saying is that this is a decent man with a good sense of right and wrong?'

'Yes. Apart from being a psychotic killer and a sadistic swine, of course.'

The kettle boiled and Austin splashed water

183

into a couple of mugs. 'That man you saw at both sites, did you get any idea how old he was?'

'From his shape and the way he moved I'd say he was between eighteen and forty, but it's just a feeling, he could equally be a fifty-five year old who keeps fit. And there's still a possibility that he's a she. Is there nothing at all to connect the boat chap? What's his name?'

'Timothy Burr.'

'Timber!'

'Oh yeah,' said Austin, brightening up. 'Here.' He handed McLusky a mug of instant. 'Absolutely nothing we can find. And he was at home with the missus at the time.'

'That, as ever, is not an alibi. But it's not him. Not a plumber.'

'There's that radiator. He'd have easy access to those.'

'It's not a plumber,' McLusky insisted as they left the room with their coffees.

Sorbie lent back in his chair and threw his plastic biro on his desk in disgust. 'There you have it: the killer is not a plumber because McLusky says so.'

'Let it go, Jack.'

'Have you seen his new car, Kat?'

'Yes, I have.' She really didn't want to think about McLusky and that drunken evening. It had haunted her. She remembered telling him some things she'd never told anyone. How did that happen? She only had a hazy memory of how she had got home. What else had she told him?

'It's a five litre Merc, for God's sake. And have you seen his watch?'

184

'What's wrong with his watch?'

'It's a Rolex.'

'Yeah, but it's hardly going to be a real one. You can buy those for fifty quid on holiday.'

'That's a real Rolex, trust me. It's a 1940s perpetual motion gold Rolex, you can't get fakes of those.'

Fairfield was getting tired of this. 'What are you saying, Jack?' she murmured. 'That he's on the take? Perhaps he inherited it. Leave it alone, Jack.'

'And have you heard about our chocolate bar thief?' Sorbie continued undeterred. 'A girl from the canteen told me they are setting a trap for him. It wouldn't surprise me if that was him as well.'

Back in his office McLusky had only just sat down opposite Austin when his phone went. He snatched it up. At the other end was Lynn Tiery. 'DSI Denkhaus wants to see you in his office for a progress report.'

Upstairs Tiery never met his eyes, simply announced his arrival on the intercom and returned to her work at her computer. He stood and waited while the secretary hammered at her noisy grey keyboard with unnecessary force, as McLusky thought. After a long while he heard the superintendent's voice squawk on the intercom and Tiery motioned him into the office, which he entered with the usual feeling of foreboding.

For once his feelings were unjustified. Denkhaus distracted face travelled from grave via neutral to benign. 'Take a seat, McLusky. Any progress on the Steadman murder?'

185

'The boat he used has been found but you're aware of that. I've had a couple of thoughts about that . . .'

While he enlarged on his theory on what kind of man – if a man at all – the killer was, Denkhaus swivelled in his chair and played with his gold fountain pen, then cut across him. 'Interesting,' he said, now inexplicably in a good mood. 'You are of course aware of the fact that usually about fifty per cent of your hunches are way off the mark?'

McLusky shrugged. 'Fifty-fifty isn't *that* bad a ratio.'

'Nonsense. It's no better than flipping a coin.'

'I shall try and improve my odds, sir.'

'Yes, it's called police work. All right, good work, carry on. Oh, there is one more thing. That new car of yours . . .'

'Yes, sir?'

Denkhaus hesitated. 'How can I put it politely? It's *monstrous*.'

McLusky was already standing. 'It is quite big, yes.'

'It's not really the kind of car people expect a DI to arrive in.'

'But unlike my last one, it won't bring the force into disrepute.'

'I expect not.' Denkhaus knitted his brow. 'Is that what you spent your compensation money on?'

'Oh no. The car's twenty years old, it was really quite cheap, considering. Of course if it ever needs a new set of brakes or, God forbid, the tank needs filling, it will probably bankrupt me.'

Back downstairs McLusky slammed into his office. Three things needed his immediate attention. The mug of instant on his desk had gone cold, he had a definite chocolate craving and he needed a cigarette. He ignored the cold coffee, turned around and clattered downstairs to the canteen where he bought a real coffee and filled his jacket pockets with his favourite chocolate bars. He was definitely becoming too much of a connoisseur, he thought, three weeks ago he wouldn't have been able to name more than three, now he was an expert. He covered the cup with the saucer and climbed up the stairs. Back in his office he squeezed behind his desk, uncovered the cup, and sniffed at a dark chocolate Bounty bar before devouring half of it. 'You'll get fat,' he told himself aloud. 'And you'll fail the next fitness test, too,' he added as he lit a cigarette. A knock on the door. McLusky sighed, opened the window behind his chair a crack and balanced his cigarette out of sight on the windowsill before admitting his visitor.

It was DC French. 'Just to say Jane has—' she consulted the yellow Post-it note in her hand – 'Lisa Burns in IR One.'

'Ta muchly. I'll look in on them in a minute.' French stuck the Post-it note on the light switch and left. 'Cheeky!' he called after her. When he turned to fetch his cigarette he was just in time to watch the wind twirl it off the windowsill and carry it away. He lit a fresh one and smoked it while trying to convince himself that the canteen coffee was a definite improvement on instant. Then he popped the other half of the chocolate bar in his mouth and went to find Austin in Interview Room One.

'DI McLusky entering the room,' Austin said for the benefit of the tape. 'No, you are not under arrest, Ms Burns,' he continued.

Lisa Burns looked defiant. 'I don't see what the big deal is. Everyone tells lies once in a while.'

'You know, we've long suspected that,' McLusky said as he sat down. 'That's why we are taking time off from a hectic schedule in this murder investigation to try and explain to you that when a suspect lies to us and we find out about it the judge will take that into consideration when he passes sentence.'

'But I'm not a suspect, am I?' Burns objected.

'When a *witness* lies to us however,' McLusky said, continuing with audibly strained patience, 'that constitutes "obstructing a police investigation" and the judge doesn't like that at all. If as a result of a false witness statement the wrong person gets convicted or the perpetrator goes free it is called "perverting the course of justice" and that carries a *mandatory custodial sentence*.'

'Prison?' Burns' eyes and mouth were round.

'How much money did Marcus Catlin pay you to say you had never heard of him?'

'Five hundred.'

'Generous.'

'Well, actually, no. He started by offering me two hundred.'

'I see. But you haggled.'

'Too right, two hundred is nothing. I'd just lost a good job.'

188

McLusky folded his hands and tilted his head in a dearly beloved pose and smiled thinly. 'You see, again, if he offers you two hundred and you take it, that's bribery and since you are not in public office and he is not on trial yet that is not an offence. On his part. But if you say: "I won't do it unless you give me five hundred", that turns it into blackmail. And guess what, Ms Burns.'

Burns swallowed. 'Prison?' McLusky nodded with exaggerated slowness. Her hand shot to her mouth. 'But I honestly had no idea.'

'It appears not. Have you heard the phrase *ignorance of the law is not an excuse*?' He was interrupted by a text alert on his mobile, which he had set to vibrate. He glanced at it. It was from DC French and looked more interesting than greedy Ms Burns. He stood up. 'OK. Today, Ms Burns, you find us full of the milk of human kindness and since there are never enough cabs in the city anyway DS Austin will arrange for you to receive an official police caution which will go on your record.'

'DI McLusky leaving the room,' Austin said for the tape as McLusky swept through the door.

Standing in the bleak corridor outside the interview room McLusky admitted to himself that he had reached a state of permanent, growling short temper, which no amount of cigarettes or chocolate bars was likely to alleviate. He called French on his mobile. 'What's this about an abandoned Jag?'

DI Fairfield had managed it at last: to get home at a reasonable time, with all her shopping done,

189

without feeling drained and down and in a foul mood. She had bought a carton of wine and rented the box set of Downton Abbey, for the telly and DVD player she had the previous night freed from their prison in the cupboard under the stairs and restored to pride of place in the sitting room. It was time to do some catching up. Could her good mood really be that easily explained? A couple of supermarket *Finest* ready meals, a box set of slushy stuff and all the wine you could want to drink while watching it. 'You're a simple soul, really,' she told herself cheerfully. She even managed to get into the house without putting her shopping down. As she gratefully pushed the door shut with her behind she spotted it. Across the threshold of her front door lay a single red rose. She unlocked the door to her maisonette and stepped across without picking it up. 'Oh no, Dr Rennie, you'll have to do a lot better than that.'

Norton Malreward. At first McLusky had thought French had made the place up. It sounded more like the name of a villain in a tacky period drama than that of a village. There were several Nortons around but this one was new to him. The Jaguar had been found in a lane leading up to the village, blocking it completely, and had turned out to be abandoned. A driver who had come across it blocking his way had called the police. Had he reversed away and used an alternative route he would have been home twenty minutes later. As it was he was still there two hours after making the call and was bitterly regretting his helpfulness. Now the road was truly blocked, choked with police cars and a large forensics van. Uniformed police were at last arranging for the civilian to leave, which involved a lot of reversing which the man was very bad at; McLusky shook his head as he watched him zigzag away.

'Keys in the ignition,' said the SOCO team leader with the walrus moustache. 'Nothing in the boot apart from the spare and an empty wine crate. No sign of a struggle.'

'What does that remind you of?' McLusky muttered.

'Thinking of having a look in the canal for him?' the SOCO asked.

'Let's not go there.' He turned to a uniformed police sergeant with very pale skin and almost white eyebrows under his cap. 'And we're looking for . . .?'

The sergeant read from his notebook. 'The car is registered to a Richard Leslie, fifty-nine years of age. He lives less than a mile from here if our information is correct, in Norton Malreward. But actually Richard Leslie isn't missing. It's his brother who borrowed the car. Borrowed it this morning, apparently. Didn't show up when he was expected to.'

'Right. And presumably we've already been all over these fields?' McLusky stretched out his arms to encompass the surroundings.

'Yes. I still have a few of my officers out there, you can see their torches moving over there.'

'It's unlikely, isn't it? Unless he's got dementia or fought his way through one of these hedgerows.

191

The next access to these fields is nowhere near the car. No, this smells of abduction.'

'No sign of a struggle again,' the SOCO offered.

'Any marks on the car?'

'Not to the naked eye.'

McLusky called Austin at Albany Road and forty minutes later the DS joined him.

'I was about to clock off,' Austin said matter-of-factly. He looked up and down the lane which was now crowded but he could imagine it empty, with only the lone Jaguar, driver door open. 'It's spooky somehow, abandoned cars, don't you think?' Austin said. 'If this one turns up floating in the canal we'll wait for the water boys to pull her out. I still get the shivers thinking about pulling on that chain.'

'I'll bear that in mind,' McLusky promised.

It turned out McLusky had driven past the Leslie residence on the way to the abandoned car; it was a very large post-war house set in acres of gardens just outside the village proper. To McLusky's eyes it managed to look ostentatious and bland at the same time. Lights showed at every window but the drive and the outside of the house lay in darkness. The bright red convertible parked outside was dwarfed by the dark Range Rover beside it.

The door was opened by a man in his late-fifties, his immaculate grooming marred only by a braided gold chain, gold bracelet, watch and signet ring. He was tall but stood with a stoop as though offering his receding grey hair for inspection. He introduced himself as Richard Leslie. 'Any news of my brother?'

'Not yet, I'm afraid,' McLusky admitted.

The man grunted and led the way into a vast reception room. Three enormous cream leather sofas were grouped around a square glass and wrought-iron coffee table. Everything in the room looked oversized. One wall was given over to a monstrous fireplace that appeared to be built of local freestone. There was a four-foot-tall white-and-gold porcelain Buddha sitting on the floor, being kept company by a multicoloured three-foot statue of the Hindu elephant god, on a carved wooden pedestal. Almost dwarfed by the religious icons was the slender woman in one corner of the furthest sofa, wearing a pink dress and white glasses with her straw-coloured hair in a ponytail. She looked to be of the same age as Richard Leslie and was clutching a cut-glass tumbler of amber liquid. 'My wife, Pauline. Police inspectors,' he added for her benefit. Introductions made, she nodded at them and set her glass on the table.

Richard Leslie motioned them to sit and McLusky and Austin took possession of one sofa while husband and wife occupied a sofa each. McLusky thought that now all three parties, wife, husband and police, were as far from each other as was possible without standing in the far corners of the room. Leslie sipped from a stemmed glass of German lager. 'I won't offer you a drink since you are on duty but I'm sure we could stretch to tea or coffee.'

'We're fine,' McLusky said without consulting Austin who would have welcomed a cup of tea. 'We understand that your brother was driving the Jaguar.'

'That's right.'

'You lent it to him.'

'Yes.'

'And what did he borrow the car for? To go where?'

'Well . . .' Leslie took a swig from his glass. McLusky got the impression that Leslie had drunk a few glasses already. 'He didn't want to borrow the car. That's just it.'

'Please explain.'

Pauline Leslie reached for her glass and without looking at anyone said: 'Michael's a Luddite.'

'My brother,' Leslie continued, 'is not anti-car per se, I think, although he rides a bicycle. It was really about money, a stupid argument we had.'

Pauline Leslie inclined her head towards McLusky and Austin but without actually looking at them. 'One of many stupid arguments Michael started, attacking my husband's life-style choices. And by extension, mine, naturally. If Michael has decided to leave the car and walk to Africa to help the starving then let us all be grateful.'

'Please, Pauline,' Leslie said. 'You have to understand, Inspector, my brother is a very religious person. To him even the simplest things have a moral dimension. And he disapproves of luxury.'

'He doesn't mind living off our generosity though, does he?' his wife interjected.

He shook his head. 'He has suffered some kind of breakdown. He converted to Catholicism and became very active in the Catholic church. We grew up C of E. He said he wanted to go to Africa as a missionary. But he became a bit hyper.

194

He's not been so bad these last few days, I thought he was calming down. I was hoping he would make new plans. More worldly plans.'

'And he lives here with you?'

'Only for the last two weeks or so.'

'Sixteen long days,' supplied his wife.

'He was up in Bradford before that but he lost his job and got thrown out of his flat and turned up here. He cycled all the way, too. Was half starved when he found us.' He shrugged, looking at McLusky as though for support. 'You can't turn your own brother away from your door, can you? However much he annoys you. And this morning we had this argument again about possessions and money and I got so pissed off with him I threw my car keys at him, the ones for the Jag, and told him to take that for a spin and then come back and say that money is not important, that money doesn't make a difference to your happiness. Because it does. And I deserve it. It's not as if I didn't work hard for my money.'

'What is it you do, Mr Leslie?' Austin asked.

'I own an independent supermarket, with six branches, all of which I built up from nothing, I might add. I'm doing good business and I enjoy what the money buys.'

'We're supposed to give all of it to the poor,' Pauline Leslie said. 'It's not like we're giving *nothing* to charity.'

'So you gave your brother the keys to your car,' McLusky said. 'When was that?'

'Early this morning. We argued over breakfast.'

'Did your brother have any money at all? We're

195

trying to establish where he has been, how far he may have driven the car.'

'I gave him the odd fifty now and then. The car had a full tank.'

'We'll check. You don't keep track of mileage?'

'Life's too short.'

McLusky silently agreed. 'Would your brother have offered a lift to a hitchhiker?'

'Here, that's a thought. Almost certainly, being charitable.'

McLusky let a pause develop, then said: 'We have to entertain the possibility that your brother was abducted. I want to arrange for a police officer to stay here. In case you are contacted.'

Leslie looked at him hard. 'Do you really think it could be a kidnapping?'

'It is best to be prepared for all eventualities.'

'Michael getting himself kidnapped!' Pauline scoffed. 'That would be the last straw. If we'd have to pay to get him *back*! Now I really *do* need another drink, darling,' she said as though they had discussed it earlier. She held out her empty glass and her husband stood up and took it absentmindedly.

As they were being let out at the front door Austin asked: 'And your brother has no friends in the area?'

'None that he mentioned. We didn't grow up around here, we grew up in Swindon.'

'We'll keep you informed, obviously,' McLusky said, just as DC French arrived in her grey Polo to stay overnight with the Leslies in case they were contacted. After a short briefing they let her go inside.

196

'Do you believe in abduction and ransom?' Austin asked.

McLusky looked over his shoulder to check the door had closed before saying: 'No. I believe in abduction and murder.'

'Then God help Michael Leslie.'

Christine Rainer thought that hoping for a lot of things and being full of hope were such different states of being that they ought to invent separate words for it. She hoped the education secretary would fall down a manhole. She hoped her teenage students, many of whom she had occasion to berate about smoking, never found out that she herself smoked fifteen a day when at home. She blew smoke from her filterless Egyptian cigarette into the pool of light from her brass desk lamp that provided the only illumination to the room apart from the dimming glow of the fire. Christine Rainer hoped spring would get a move on so she could leave the French windows open in the study. It was this room that had sold the house to her; she had seen it immediately: the French windows into the garden wide open, a desk to work on with the little Edwardian fireplace at her back and a comfortable armchair and reading lamp by the bookcases. Being a spinster schoolmistress really did have its compensations. But tonight her French windows remained closed against the cold April night and she yearned for milder evenings when they would stay open late and her cat, Mackerel, could wander in at will and release half-dead mice into her study which she

197

would then spend hours trying to recapture. Happy days.

There was a muffled thump upstairs which could only mean that the cat was up to no good in her bedroom. She thought she had closed the door earlier but sometimes she suspected that Mackerel had somehow learnt to turn doorknobs. She yawned, drained her cup of Lapsang Souchong; it had gone cold and hadn't had the desired effect. She was just too tired to keep writing endless polite variations of 'could do better'. She shut down her laptop and stubbed out her cigarette, then emptied the entire ashtray into the fireplace. As she raked the embers to make the cigarette butts disappear, Mackerel turned up by her side. 'There you are, what have you been up to? If you've knocked the big yucca over again then you'll be banned from the bedroom forever. I *mean* it,' she said, not meaning it. She petted him affectionately, knowing that exhortations were entirely wasted on cats, then went and closed the curtains. With the desk lamp switched off she crossed the dark room by the light of the tiny glow left in the fireplace and walked into the hall where she stopped. It was really quite cold here as though she had left a window open somewhere, and there was an odd smell, like WD 40 or something like that. Mackerel followed her into the kitchen where Christine switched on the downlights above the worktop, less bright than the ceiling lights, and squeezed slippery cat food from a pouch into Mackerel's bowl; still the best insurance against being woken by him mewling in front of the bedroom door in the middle of the night. She turned off the lights while the cat approached her food bowl unhurriedly. Christine went upstairs yawning, then stopped and frowned. There was that smell again; very faint. More like deodorant, she decided. Strange. Had the cat knocked something over in the bathroom? She walked on to the top of the stairs then halted again, surprised: the bedroom door was closed. She wondered what could have fallen over to have made the earlier noise. She opened the door wide. No, the yucca Mackerel enjoyed pushing over was standing on its tripod stool and nothing else seemed to be out of order. There was a draught somewhere; Christine pushed the bedroom door closed and began to undress by the pinkish glow of the bedside lamp, dropping her tights and knickers into the decorative laundry basket beside the built-in wardrobe with the louvered doors, then put on her pyjamas. What she really enjoyed was to read in bed but she had left writing the reports to the last minute and was now too tired. And she had forgotten to get her glass of water. Kitchen water of course, never bathroom water. She took the empty glass from the bedside cabinet and went to fetch water from downstairs. She would do it without the benefit of lights or it would convince Mackerel that it was not yet time for bed after all. The cat was nowhere to be seen. It was definitely draughty down here; she felt it on her bare feet as she padded across the vinyl floor. Water glass recharged, she concentrated hard on not spilling anything from the brimful glass on to the carpeted stairs. She knew she always stuck her tongue out a tiny bit when she concentrated and was doing it now; it made her smile but she did not retract it. That's the way I am, she thought, a silly woman who can't drink bathroom water and must carry kitchen water with her tongue sticking out. The silhouette of the man at the top of the stairs loomed over her like a malevolent shadow from a fairy tale, backlit by the feeble glow coming from the bedroom, and he advanced on her. She threw the glass at him in a feeble attempt to fight him off but it did not stop him. He slammed into her on the narrow stairs and she fell backwards with nothing to hold on to as he barged past her down the stairs. Christine tumbled head first, arms flailing, rolling over until her head smashed against the newel post at the bottom and everything went black.

'I told you this sort of thing always escalates,' Fairfield said to Sorbie. 'Now we have a woman in hospital. It was only a matter of time.' They had visited Christine Rainer in hospital. She had suffered concussion, a broken collarbone, and she was traumatized.

'We don't know that it has escalated yet,' Sorbie said flatly. He could barely manage his anger. DS Austin was working with McLusky on the murder investigation while he was hunting the great underpants thief with Fairfield. 'Could have been an accident.'

'He wasn't in her house by accident though. I think he started off by pinching underwear off the line and now he breaks into people's houses. It's only a matter of time before something much worse happens. He hid in her wardrobe, Jack,' Fairfield said as they drove off. 'He watched her undress, then stole the underwear she had just put into the laundry basket. If that isn't escalation then what more do you require?'

'Yeah, that's quite creepy, I admit.' He thought for a moment. 'The peeping Tom thing I understand. Who doesn't enjoy watching women undress? But stealing underwear that's the weirdo bit. Do you think he wears them to work?'

Fourteen

'It'll be a complete waste of time of course,' McLusky said without even looking up from the mess on his desk.

Austin, who was standing just inside the door had come to tell him that DNA samples had been taken from absolutely anyone who had ever been inside the abandoned Jaguar. 'Apparently the Leslies were not at all happy about giving DNA samples.'

'Why on earth not? Their DNA will be all over the bloody car, I'm sure even they can make out that we need to eliminate them.'

'Mr Leslie thought that someone scraping around in his mouth with a cotton bud invaded his privacy.'

'Yeah? I'd like to go round there and invade his privacy with a six foot cotton bud sometime,' McLusky growled.

'Yeah, like they used on *Gladiators*.'

'If you say so, Jane,' McLusky said irritably. He was still picking up bits of paper, scribbled notes and chocolate wrappers and dropping them again with a look of disgust on his face. McLusky frequently felt disgusted by the mess in his life, from the chaos in his office to the daily palaver of hunting for underwear and matching socks in the morning. Which reminded him: a bin liner full of dirty laundry had been sitting in the boot of his car for a couple of days now; if he didn't get it done today he would have to go commando tomorrow.

'What are you looking for?' Austin asked.

'The super sent me a self-assessment thing to fill out. As though I didn't have enough to do.'

'Ah.'

McLusky stopped abruptly and looked up. 'I know that "ah". It always means you are going to disappoint me. Not personally of course. Just in general.'

'Oh, aye, you're going to absolutely love this one.'

McLusky recognized all the warning signs of procedural nuisance and called: 'Wait!' He fumbled a cigarette from his pack, lit it and leant back in his chair with his arms crossed in front of his chest. 'OK, I'm calm,' he said, the cigarette dancing on his lips as he spoke.

'You've been cordially invited to attend a day of seminars, held at Trinity Road.'

'On . . .?'

'All sorts. Appraisal systems and personal development review for one.'

'Personally I think I'm coming along fine so I think I'll skip it, if it's all the same to you.'

'To me, yes, to Denkhaus, no. Compulsory from DCI downwards. We're all going, and the message from Denkhaus is that only hospitalization will be accepted as an excuse.'

'OK, can you arrange that for me, please? Something less painful than a bloody seminar, of course, say a broken pelvis.'

'And do you know what the whole thing is called?'

McLusky had resumed his haphazard search among the office chaos. 'How to waste a day in the life of DI McLusky?' he growled.

'Meeting the Challenges of the New Performance Landscape.'

McLusky could practically hear the capital letters. 'Marvellous. Look forward to it. Any more cheery news, Jane?'

For a while after Austin had left he sat, smoked and stared morosely at the mountainous land-scape on and around his desk. His office was so small that a lot of files and reports ended up in piles on the floor where he frequently sent them skidding or tumbling trying to get past. His eyes had slid from the disorder on his desk to the metal wastepaper bin, which was in need of emptying, when he espied the corner of a thick wad of A4 paper with the Avon and Somerset Constabulary crest at the top sticking out from the rubbish. With difficulty he dislodged it from the bin, then proceeded to free it from an encrus-tation of dried-on teabags and black, shrivelled banana skins. So that's where the self-assessment forms were hiding. He flopped the damp and curling forms on top of the mess on his desk. 'Result!'

McLusky spent half an hour looking through the questionnaire, then put it aside to do more paperwork, then pulled it towards him again with a stony heart and scribbled down a few ideas on a notepad. McLusky hated the convo-luted police speak they had all been taught to use. It was meant to be precise and elevate their speech from the conversational but it grated on him. He was quite good at it, though he had to constantly check that he did not drift into parody; his superiors were not big on irony and he needed to appear as normal as possible for a while. McLusky was pretty convinced that he wasn't, or at least that he was not really ideal DI material. Only grown-ups should be allowed to do this job and he had long admitted to himself that he possessed a wide, ineradicable juvenile streak. It had driven Laura to distraction and together with the erosion of his private life by the demands of his job it had cost him that relationship. From time to time he could give quite a good imitation of a mature thirty-something, enough for his employers to give him the benefit of the doubt, but it was threadbare and would inevitably come apart at the seams sooner or later.

He caught up with all the emails and updated reports on the system, checked the time on his immaculately performing Rolex and logged off. They were now awaiting forensics reports on almost everything to do with the killings and now the abandoned Jaguar too. There had been no news about Michael Leslie's disappearance; no contact had been made, no demands. McLusky was pretty sure there never would be; sooner or later someone would stumble over the man's body. So far there was nothing to connect the disappearance of the devout brother with the killings but as soon as he had seen the car in the lane McLusky had known there was one, only

205

none of them could see it yet and that, sadly, included himself.

This kind of morose speculation did not require him to sit in his claustrophobic office, he could just as well do it sitting in the launderette. At the newsagent's in Albany Road he stocked up on cigarettes, checked his change, then tried to sweet-talk the woman behind the counter into giving him some twenty-pence pieces he would need for the washing machine and dryer. She told him that they never had enough as it was and that the banks charged them for providing bags of change. He bought a couple of chocolate bars with a ten-pound note and she shook her head, sighed and let him have a few twenty-pence pieces in the change because she had decided he had nice eyes.

At the launderette McLusky stuffed all of his washing unsorted straight into the machine, chose 'hot', fed the coin slot and watched the machine start. He would now have forty minutes to fill and since he'd had enough of sitting under humming neon lights he went outside. It was pretty cold again and his own place would be unheated and badly stocked. Picton Street was only a few minutes' walk away and at the top of it was the excellent *Bristolian*, one of his favourite cafés in town for two reasons: it was the first café he had entered when he came to Bristol and the name seemed appropriate then. It also happened to be the only café he knew Laura frequented. He was not sure whether he went there because he knew he might see Laura or whether Laura went there because she knew she might see him but whatever the truth, both continued to go there. Laura, admittedly, was usually accompanied by one or more of her college friends.

Even though he had been hoping she might be there or drop in, when he entered the café and was immediately faced with her sitting there and smiling up at him it felt like a physical blow to his body. She was with the chap he had last seen her with, a young Canadian whose name he would pretend to have forgotten.

'It's Ethan,' Laura said when he expressed regret about not remembering.

'I'm not usually good with names either,' said Ethan, 'but I never forget a policeman.' Ethan made room so he could get to a chair.

McLusky immediately had to get up again to order at the counter. He asked for a cappuccino, which he knew would be excellent but was told he was too late for the all-day breakfast. He opened his mouth to say something pithy but ordered a burger with everything instead. When he had balanced his cup of coffee back to the table his arrival extinguished a conversation between Laura and Ethan. McLusky decided he hated young men with long hair, especially when it suited them. 'I can sit somewhere else if I'm interrupting something,' he said as he sat down.

'No, don't be silly. We'll have to go in a minute anyway. We've already eaten. We had the tapas. The patatas bravas here are excellent, you should try them.'

'Yes,' said Ethan, 'they're triple cooked. Very authentic.'

207

'I've ordered a burger.'

'You old adventurer,' said Laura.

'How was your dig?' McLusky asked. 'Stonehenge, wasn't it?'

'It was good. Close to Stonehenge. We think it's the site where the actual workmen who built it were housed. Of course it tipped down for the last two days. I ended up kipping in Ethan's van.'

'Ah, the handy van.' McLusky immediately suspected that Ethan had only bought it so he could entice female first-year students to shelter in it.

'It's all right, I had Val with me to protect my modesty.'

'I'm glad.'

Ethan drained his orange juice and rose. 'Look, I'll leave you two to catch up. I'll be in the library,' he said to Laura, nodded at Liam and left the café.

Laura had made no polite attempt to stop Ethan and didn't seem to be in a hurry to rush off herself. McLusky sniffed after Ethan like a rabbit. 'Does he wear perfume?'

Laura gave a Gallic shrug and pulled a face. 'Body spray. I did mention to him that if you can smell it from across the room you're overdoing it but it's his signature smell. Minx *Fatal Attraction* for men. I seem to remember you were using some foul deodorant when we first met.'

'Oh, but mine was nice.'

'Yeh, right.'

'So, archaeology one-oh-one. Is it all you dreamt it would be?'

'It is. It's frightening, everything about it is

208

brilliant. Everything I did before archaeology was a waste of time.'

'I see.' McLusky was tempted to ask if that included their relationship but stopped himself in time.

'I was prepared for a lot of stuff I would find hard or boring but I love all of it, the science, the history, the endless grid-drawings, the computer stuff, the surveying, finds recording, the lot. This really is what I want to be doing for the rest of my life. Problem is I'll be competing with thousands for a job at the end of it. It's the bloody telly, everyone wants to be a field archaeologist and because we're queuing up to do it they can afford to pay us next to nothing if they do give us a job.'

'I'm sure you'll find work at the end.'

'It's years away, I don't really want to think about it yet. How's yours? Caught him yet?' She smiled. It was something she had asked Liam every day by way of greeting in the early days, before the reality of his job had bitten, before she had begun to hate it. Yet for some reason a wave of unwanted nostalgia threatened her and she kept smiling. The arrival of McLusky's burger broke the mood. 'See, it comes with patatas bravas, so no need to feel left out.'

'Who says I was feeling left out?'

'And? Have you?'

'What?'

'Caught him yet.'

'I thought that was rhetorical. No. And I think he has just managed to bag another victim. A bloke disappeared from his car, just like the woman.'

'Did they know each other?'

'Not that I can see, no,' he said with his mouth full. 'Spicy potatoes, not bad,' was his verdict on patatas bravas. He started attacking his burger and stuffed enough of it in his mouth to be able to quietly look at Laura for a minute. She looked more beautiful than ever. Happier, too, somehow. Was it because she was no longer stuck in a dead-end job or because she was no longer living with him? It was the uni, he decided. He had enjoyed it too. And then some kind of madness had gripped him after graduation and he had gone straight on to police college.

'How are you keeping now? Have you done anything about your flat yet?'

'Some. Bought some stuff. Got a fridge.'

'Heating?'

'Sure.' Since there was no heating in his flat he had gone to the junk shop down the road and bought a two-bar electric heater with backlit plastic logs at the bottom. It heated mainly itself so he used the gas oven for extra heat. He'd sort it out before the next winter. Laura knew that 'sure' from McLusky's mouth almost certainly meant 'not quite' and she opened her mouth to say so when McLusky's mobile rang.

He semaphored regret and apology as he fished it from his jacket. It was Austin. 'You're not going to believe this,' he heard him say.

'Yes I will, Jane, because I know you wouldn't lie to me.'

'Michael Leslie has turned up.'

McLusky sat up straighter, absentmindedly spearing potatoes with his fork. 'Alive?'

210

The connection was crackling and noisy. 'Yes, at his brother's house. DC French was there when he turned up. In a taxi. Leslie claims he just left the Jaguar and went walkabouts but according to French he looked in a bad way. Whatever, he's at his brother's, he's alive and off our hands.'

'Jane, "whatever" is not part of my vocabulary.'

'I've noticed, sir. There's something weird going on there. I mean with the Leslies. Oh, and Richard Leslie wants his car back and his DNA samples destroyed.'

McLusky had stuffed his mouth full of food while he listened. Now he swallowed hard and angrily before saying: 'Not a snowball's! Forensics have got the car and he can have it when they're through with it. Are you still at Albany?'

'Driving home. Why?'

'I'm thinking.' He picked up the burger one-handed and messily nibbled on it. 'I need to talk to that man. But you go on home. I'll drive out there now and have a chat.'

'Good news?' asked Laura when he had put his mobile away. 'I managed to pick out the word "alive" from all that.'

'Yes.' McLusky frowned at the remains of his massacred burger. He had no recollection of having eaten any of it and was still hungry 'The bloke we thought had been abducted by our killer turned up alive. Says he just went walkabout.'

'You don't sound terribly pleased,' she observed correctly.

McLusky wiped his hands on a paper napkin

then dropped it on to his plate. 'I'm not, damn it. That man was abducted, I just know it.'

'And let go? Do you think a ransom was paid?'

McLusky froze for a moment, his eyes staring into the middle distance while he thought about it, then he shook his head. 'No. Too quick. Anyway, we had left a police officer there with a digital recorder in case his brother was called. Even if he dodged French I don't believe he could have arranged to pay a kidnapper without us noticing. Though I will test this theory.'

'Then what did happen?'

'I don't know,' he said getting up. 'But I'm going to find out, aren't I?'

Through the café window Laura watched him walk out of sight down Picton Street. In small doses Liam was good to be with but the last half hour had once more proved her point: as long as he was working on a murder investigation half of him was always out there, stalking the streets, even when the other half sat opposite you wolfing down burgers.

McLusky got in his car and drove to Norton Malreward. He resented Michael Leslie for re-appearing; it did not fit. The man was supposed to be dead. His continued existence contradicted all of McLusky's predictions. So what? As the super had said, with him it was fifty-fifty. But Michael Leslie was in the wrong fifty. If he wasn't dead then he certainly had some explaining to do.

When he got to the house it looked shuttered, all the curtains were drawn and the security lights were on. 'It's all fine, it's all resolved. Really,' said Richard Leslie. He was reluctant to let him cross the threshold but McLusky ignored it and walked in. Leslie went into confidential mode, lowering his voice. 'I'm sure, Inspector, it's to do with his breakdown, I think he just wandered off and fell down a hole or something and hurt himself. He doesn't want to talk about it, understandable, really.'

'Very. Where is he?'

'He's in the drawing room,' he said, pointing towards the white double doors, which were closed. 'But he's had a few drinks now and I really think it's best if he goes to bed soon and sleeps it off.'

'I'll just have a quick word, then. Is DC French still here, by the way?'

'No, she was called away. No reason for her to stay, was there? Look, can't it wait until he has recovered? He is still very shaken by the whole affair. We all are.'

'Through here, you said?' McLusky broke eye contact, strode past him and walked through the door.

The pitiful figure of Michael Leslie huddled near the Buddha statue, wrapped in a blue dressing gown and folded into a corner of one of the white sofas. His hair looked damp. He looked up, frowning at him as McLusky came through the door. Frowning must have hurt him since his eyebrows were both split open and scabbing over. His face was puffed up with colourful bruises, one of his eyes was completely shut from the swelling and his lips were swollen. His nose looked broken. His left hand was inexpertly bandaged. Michael Leslie was alive but

213

found it a painful experience. It was apparent that even lifting his wine glass caused him pain.

'Have you seen a doctor?' McLusky asked.

There was a pause during which Michael Leslie drained his glass, then, with painful effort, refilled it. 'Who are you?' he asked croakily.

He showed his ID. 'Detective Inspector McLusky. I strongly suggest you see a doctor whether you think you need one or not. What happened to you?'

'I don't need a policeman either. We are OK now. Everything will be fine.'

'I am glad you think so. What happened to you?'

'Nothing for you to concern yourself with.' Speaking too seemed to cause him pain. He spoke as though through loose teeth.

'You just left the car, not parked up but in the middle of the lane, blocking it, left the keys in the ignition, and then what?'

'Yes, I'm sorry about that. I just had a weird moment there and ran off into the blue.'

'Which blue was that? Where did you go?'

'I have no idea.'

'Nobody saw you?'

He half completed an arm gesture, winced. 'I walked across the fields, Inspector.'

'How did you get injured?'

'I fell down a steep bank somewhere and hit my face on a tree.' He pulled a grimace of pain and drank more wine.

Definitely loose teeth, thought McLusky. Definitely lying, too. As a police officer he had lots of opportunity to see the aftermath of fights

214

and this looked like the man had been beaten, and beaten savagely.

'Look,' said Richard Leslie who stood behind McLusky. 'Can't you see my brother is in pain, Inspector? Go up to bed, Mikey. Take the bottle with you, if you like.'

'OK, gentlemen,' McLusky said quietly. 'We'll leave it there.' He gave Richard Leslie a friendly nod. 'For the moment.' He turned to the injured brother. 'We'll take a detailed statement as soon as it is convenient. I wish you a speedy recovery, sir.'

In the hall, Richard Leslie firmly closed the double doors to the drawing room behind him before asking: 'When can I expect my car back?'

'No idea,' McLusky said cheerfully. 'Whenever forensics are finished with it. They're very slow. Not like the telly at all. You'll be informed.'

'What can forensics still want with it? I told you my brother was not very well, he's had a breakdown. He just had a strange . . . *moment* and went walkabout.'

'Is that what he told you or is that what you want me to believe?'

Leslie looked at him for a moment, working on his anger. 'I don't know what you are trying to say, Inspector, but I really think you should leave now.'

McLusky thought so too. Leslie closed the door heavily behind him. By contrast McLusky pulled the driver door of his car shut so slowly and distractedly that he had to open and shut it again to close it properly. For a moment he sat behind the wheel in the drive of the Leslies' bland house, with the security lights bathing everything in unnatural brightness. The sun had set far beyond McLusky's yardarm and he craved a drink. He started the engine and drove, away from Norton Malreward, towards Bristol, towards the pub. Yes, the pub would be a good place tonight. He wanted to stop thinking about the corpse floating in the Feeder Canal, about the body by the railway line and about the Leslies. Tonight, he wanted to drink a few beers and think about Laura.

One hour and two pints later, standing at the bar of the Barge Inn and waiting for his third pint of Guinness to be poured, he still hadn't managed it. His thoughts came back to the sight of Michael Leslie's face. When he had reached for his glass of wine he had moved like a man with broken ribs. McLusky remembered broken ribs well, could still feel the pain of breathing in, of reaching for a glass of water on the hospital beside table. That man had been worked over. By his brother on his return? No, the atmosphere was different. McLusky always ended up back at his original premise: Michael Leslie had been abducted. And let go again. Why? *Because whoever dragged him from the car thought he was Richard Leslie.* How was the kidnapper to know that the man driving the Jaguar was his brother Michael? Did Michael know his brother had been the target? Did he tell Richard? If Richard knew then why lie about it? Why not scream for police protection? After all, drawing your curtains and turning on your security lights wasn't going to scare off a killer. Which reminded him: had it been checked whether Leslie had a

216

firearm's licence? He couldn't remember.

Back at his table he dialled the Albany Road number. He got through to the duty officer and told him what he wanted: two officers parked outside the Leslie residence until further notice. Or until the super blew his top. He would sort out the paperwork for it tomorrow, he promised. Then McLusky picked up his pint, stopped working, and drank.

'Oh, pants!' It hit him like a hammer blow. Still dripping from the shower McLusky dropped his towel on the floor and stomped into his freezing cold bedroom. 'Bugger!' How could he have forgotten all about his laundry? He had never gone back there, had just left it sitting in the machine at the launderette! He had to get there pronto this morning and shove it in the drier. Meanwhile there was no way he was going to wear the same pair of underpants again, the very thought made him shiver. He slipped into his suit trousers, put on a nearly ironed shirt. There were no clean socks, either, he discovered.

Sockless in his shoes he noticed gratefully that the weather had changed once more and was now mild but windy, with warm air blowing in from the south. At the launderette the machine he had stuffed his clothes into the night before was empty. There were only two customers here this early, both black women in their forties who looked like sisters, sitting very close to each other and reading age-old magazines from the pile in the corner. Had they noticed what had happened to his washing?

217

'No, love, they was all empty when we came,' said one. 'Best ring them up, perhaps they put it by somewhere safe for you.'

He rang the contact number on the laminated printout on the wall and was told categorically: 'There was no washing left when I locked up last night. That was a silly thing to do, leave all your washing behind. You have to keep an eye on things around here. You know what it's like, if it's not nailed down . . .'

McLusky, wondering how you might successfully nail down a carrier bag full of wet washing, hung up disconsolately. All his socks, all his underwear, some shirts and tee-shirts, his favourite pair of jeans and his second favourite pair. He felt bereft.

'No luck, love?' commiserated one of the sisters. 'Aah, that's a blow. But you really have to keep an eye on your things around here, you know?'

McLusky did. The crime figures for his neighbourhood made interesting reading. He also knew that now he would have to engage in his least favourite of tasks: shopping. Naturally he would put that off until the last possible moment.

The day dragged on through meetings, past lunchtime (where he skilfully dodged the *Pasta and Broccoli Bake*, now relaunched as *Macaroni and Calabrese au Gratin*) and through an afternoon filled with report sifting, reading of witness statements and the dreaded progress report to DSI Denkhaus.

Denkhaus, however, was unexpectedly on McLusky's side when it came to the Leslies.

218

'This could be one of your better hunches,' he said, swivelling his chair so he could throw a glance out of the window, which he did whenever he was mulling things over. 'The wrong brother. Entirely possible. Always assuming that there really is a connection between Michael Leslie's temporary disappearance and our two murders. What is the connection between them other than an abandoned car?'

'I haven't found it yet.'

'But naturally you remain stubbornly confident that there is one.'

'Yes, sir.'

Denkhaus swivelled some more. 'The Leslies haven't asked for police protection. If they have a mind to complain about a police car parked in front of their house we will have to withdraw it, you know that. No crimes have been committed or at least none reported.'

'But until they complain we'll keep an eye on them?'

'Yes. I can let you have one officer to keep out there. When can you interview the injured brother?'

'He reluctantly agreed to talk to me at his brother's house tomorrow.'

'We'll discuss it again after you have taken his statement. But if he is mentally a bit wobbly, tread softly. Don't press him too hard.'

'Wouldn't dream of it.'

An hour later he found himself in the men's clothing department of Marks & Spencer's. Clothes shopping was McLusky's worst nightmare; he

219

genuinely thought he preferred autopsies to having to select and try on clothes, then queue at the till to pay for them. To him it seemed to drag on forever when in reality he had spent no more than fifteen minutes in the shop and found more or less everything hc needed immediately. To avoid having to do it again this decade he had nearly depleted the shop's supplies on men's underwear and socks, had added several shirts, an armful of tee-shirts, two black sweaters and three pairs of black jeans to the pile he now carried in his arms and could barely see over.

It was as he made his way to the nearest till that Fairfield, herself there to buy a bath towel, espied him from the other side of the escalators. Fairfield enjoyed shopping; for a start, shopping meant that she had money to spend. But even to her the pile of clothes in McLusky's arm looked like conspicuous consumption for a DI. Had he not just bought a huge Mercedes as well? And then she remembered what Sorbie had said about his antique Rolex: you couldn't buy replicas of those. She shrugged and told herself to take her own advice: let it go. Perhaps he really had inherited.

The next day started mild and windy, with the firm promise of showers later. McLusky, wearing new clothes all over, drove out to Norton Malreward. Now that he had got over the shock of having lost half his wardrobe he felt quite good in his new black jeans and sweater and virginal underwear. Taking all the labels, stickers and tags off his new wardrobe had taken longer than buying them.

Even though he had made an appointment it took a long time before the front door was opened, reluctantly, by Richard Leslie. 'I don't seem to be able to find my brother,' he said by way of greeting.

'Oh?' McLusky stepped past him. 'Has he disappeared again?'

'I couldn't say,' said Leslie. 'But he was here not long ago.'

Leslie's wife Pauline could be heard from the living room. 'He's hiding in the garden, the stupid childish man.'

Leslie nodded heavily and sighed, acknowledging that he had known. 'Look, he really doesn't want to talk to you.'

'I'm afraid he doesn't have a choice. Which way to the garden?'

McLusky liked the garden even less than the house. It was large and cluttered with an accumulation of features like off-the-peg statuary of the bare-breasted maiden type, pastel-coloured gazebos, clogged-up water features, sad island beds, wrought-iron arbours and uninviting cast-iron benches.

'He's hiding in the shed. We had one at home,' said Leslie. 'It was his favourite hiding place even then.' He began to lead the way to the shed, which was half hidden behind a pond fringed with frazzled pampas grass, but McLusky waved him off.

'It's OK, I'll find him. I need to speak to him alone.'

Richard Leslie seemed unhappy at the prospect and only reluctantly turned back towards the

221

house. McLusky took his time approaching the shed. Diplomacy had never been his strong point but DI Denkhaus was probably right about treading gently. He peered into a half-blind plastic window but could see only dark shapes that could have been anything at all. He did not knock but stood in front of the door, listening for a moment; all was quiet. 'Mr Leslie? Hello?' No answer. 'I'm Detective Inspector McLusky, we've briefly met before.' He could hear small noises inside now but no answer. 'How are your ribs? Does it still hurt when you breathe in?'

After a moment's pause the door was opened as though by a very ancient person. Michael Leslie did not look at him but shuffled away again to sit on a stool in the furthest corner in front of a potting bench. The shed was well stocked and almost pathologically tidy, with all the tools in their place and a large lawnmower taking up much space. The place smelled darkly of vegetative growth, with a hint of petrol fumes from the mower.

McLusky closed the door behind him. 'Do you mind if I smoke?' he asked. Leslie shrugged which McLusky decided to take as consent and lit up. 'I don't want to make you cough, I know what cracked ribs feel like, the last thing you want to do is cough.' Leslie looked as though he wanted to respond but changed his mind. 'Have your teeth stopped feeling shaky?'

Leslie nodded. 'Yeah.'

McLusky took his time, lit his cigarette and exhaled smoke away from the hunched man. 'I like sheds. They say every man over forty should have a shed. That leaves me a bit of time to find one. And a place to put it, of course,' he added almost to himself He let a pause develop before he said: 'You were extremely lucky, Michael.' Leslie looked up at the use of his name but made no answer. 'He could have killed you. He has killed before.' Leslie stirred on his seat but looked straight ahead at the stacks of black plastic flowerpots under the bench. 'How long before he recognized his mistake?' Leslie seemed to squirm under some kind of internal pressure, either to tell or to contradict him, but he remained silent. 'It was your brother he really wanted but there's a strong family resemblance and of course you were driving his Jaguar. Did he even know Richard had a brother? No, you're right, how could he have known, you are not part of this set, are you? You despise riches. You would give it all to charity. But there you were, driving a luxurious sports car and got mistaken for your filthy-rich brother. Did you tell him straight away? Or only when you knew he was going to kill you whatever you did.'

Leslie's voice was small and worn rough from crying. 'When I knew it was not a ransom thing. When I knew he meant to kill me. That's when I told him.'

'And you denounced your brother, you disowned him.' Leslie's eyes welled up and he gave tiny nods of his head, his hands clamped to the sides of his seat. 'You told him you despised his wealth. You told him why you had been driving the car.' Leslie still nodded. 'And he let you go. Where had he taken you?'

'I don't know, it was dark in the van and he put a bag over my head and tied my hands. I screamed for help but he hit me until I stopped.'

'What kind of van was it?'

'I don't know, I don't remember that. All I remember seeing is the gun.'

'What kind of a gun?'

'A big silver thing. Like an automatic.'

'Did you get to see his face?' When no answer was forthcoming McLusky almost blurted the next, the all-important question. 'Why did he want to kill you? Or your brother? Did he say *why*? You must have asked!'

Leslie's nostrils flared, in anger at the questions or at the memory of it all. 'I can't tell you anything. Don't you see?' He suddenly looked up at McLusky. 'I had to promise!'

'He is a killer. And he wants to kill your brother. Surely a promise to a man like that does not have to be honoured.'

'He won't kill my brother now. Not unless . . .'

'Not unless you talk to the police.'

'Yes. But I'm not telling you anything, I can't tell you anything that will help you catch him. I want you to go away. Please go away. What if he finds out I'm talking to you?'

'Do you know anything that would help us catch him?' Michael remained silent. 'Surely you must want to help us put him away. We can protect your brother. And you. And once we have the killer in custody your brother will be safe, everyone will be safe.' McLusky wanted to shake the man by the shoulders, shake the answers out of him but instead sucked

224

so furiously at his cigarette that it made him cough. He nearly missed the next thing Michael said.

'I cannot break my promise. Don't you see?' He looked up and sought McLusky's eyes. 'If I broke my promise then I would have bought my life with a lie.'

'Sometimes it is necessary to lie in order to deceive the enemy and win the war.'

'I am not at war with him. And I did do more than just make a promise.' Leslie's head sank down almost to his chest, crushed.

'You did what?'

It took him a long time to answer while his face worked with the difficulty of the next sentence. 'I swore on the bible. *That* bible.' He nodded towards a book on the workbench, a pocket edition of the bible with a worn leather cover. 'If I hadn't had it in my pocket I don't think I would be alive now.' With a sudden burst of energy he stood up, no longer crumpled, grabbed the bible and stuffed it in his back pocket. He spoke with a clearer, stronger voice now. 'I swore on the bible and that's an oath I cannot break. And he accepted that. So there is no point talking to me. You'll have to find another way of catching him. Excuse me.' He squeezed past and out of the door.

McLusky watched him walk awkwardly across the lawn, hands deep in the pockets of his trousers, his little bible clearly outlined in his back pocket. All the answers to your life in your back pocket, McLusky thought. All you'll ever need to know, all your protection against the evils of

225

the world in a handy pocket edition. He flicked his cigarette end into the lawn. 'Marvellous.'

At last. This was it, she could feel it. Tonight was the tipping point, she was sure of it, both for her mood and the season. Every winter her mood took a dive, she wouldn't quite call it depression, didn't want to call it that, the word scared her, oppressed her, but her mood definitely took a dive around November and would not lift until spring was in full swing. Lindsey Goodall stuck her arm out of the window to feel the rain that was falling in the darkness on to her little urban garden, the earthly paradise attached to her ground-floor flat that made all the difference between balance and health, being connected with the seasons, and going stark raving mad staring at the wall or a TV screen. Spring was here, it had deceived them with false starts but this was genuine spring rain, it came from far south, you could almost smell it, all the way from the Azores and you could not possibly resent it like winter rain, which was hateful and hideous and made you want to do nothing, nothing, nothing, not even work, and Lindsey loved her job at the university.

From now until the arrival of the next dreadful November she could sleep with the window open again. She had mentioned it in the refectory today and it turned out it was nearly fifty-fifty, straight down the middle: half slept with the window open and half with the window closed. Closed? But how could you? With the window closed she felt as though she was slowly being suffocated,

226

separated from the world of nature, the smells and sounds cut off by double-glazing.

One of her colleagues had looked at her as though she were babbling mystical nonsense. But then Lindsey knew she lived in a fourth-floor flat that had plug-in air fresheners in every room so she would never have to open her windows at all. It still made her smile even now as she got ready to go to bed, how two people, working beside each other in the same library, could have such completely different ideas about what was important. She turned out the main light and undressed by the rosy glow of her bedside lamp; no one could really see in, the big tree and the laurel at the bottom of the garden took care of that. It was true, the place would be much warmer if she kept all her windows shut but she was no wimp. Naked, she padded to the bathroom, stuffed her hair under a shower cap and turned on the water. Lindsey made herself step under the shower even before it had warmed up. I'm not a city softie yet, she told herself, but she was grateful when the short burst of cold was replaced by beautifully hot water, sluicing away the cares of the day. Her late-night showers were to her like the crossing of a river, from which she emerged on the other side cleansed, with the day that had just passed left behind her on the other shore. As she replaced the soap bar on to its ceramic shelf she thought she saw a flash through the half-open door, like lightning, yet there was no thunder following it.

She towelled herself dry and shook her dark hair from the shower cap. No more jim-jams either; from tonight, she would sleep in the nude again, between clean crisp sheets. She sniffed: a strange smell in the air. Almost like one of her colleague's synthetic air fresheners. Could it be the new soap she put out earlier? She hoped not.

She knew he was in the room even before she turned around; there was a strangled sound coming from behind the door as she entered the bedroom. There he was, tall, menacing, his face distorted by the dark stocking he wore over his head. She screamed. 'No!' Her scream was not directed at him, it was directed at her life. '*No*!' This was not allowed to happen in her life. He lunged at her, grabbing at her breasts, but in a fumbling, uncertain way, like an afterthought. She slapped his hands away and kicked out at him. 'Go away, you creep!' she yelled at him.

And he did. Turned and fled, climbed out through the window and again he made that strange strangled sound, almost as though he was trying not to cry as he dropped down into the garden and disappeared into the dark. Lindsey closed the window, drew the curtains and ran back into the shower, letting the hot water run all over her again. Wash it away, wash it away, wash it away, please just wash it all away.

Fifteen

'Incompetent?'

'Inept. A bungler.' McLusky had just watched DSI Denkhaus ruin his coffee with too much sugar and cream but it still smelled enticing. 'Apart from being a sadistic murderous swine, naturally.'

'You're not going to say that!' Denkhaus protested.

'Of course not. But a bungling idiot. And I'll mention that Michael Leslie, a devout Christian, is honour-bound not to give us any information. That might help keep him and his brother safe.'

'Are you absolutely sure we can't get him to talk?'

'Not without putting extreme pressure on him. And he is a victim, in all senses of the word. I'd like to try the fake interview first.'

Denkhaus swivelled in his chair and squinted out of the window. It was raining but just then a ray of sunshine pierced the greyness and glittered through the wet city. 'Do you not think Michael Leslie might change his mind in time? No? Nevertheless, we can't afford to give up on him. Give it a few days then work on him again. On Richard Leslie, too, perhaps he can persuade him. Or perhaps Michael already told him and *he* can be persuaded to pass it on.'

'And the interview? Phil Warren would be

delighted to set it up for us. The *Bristol Herald* would give someone's right arm for it.'

'Provoking him could backfire, you know?' Denkhaus was leaning forward on his desk now, playing with his gold pen, tapping it against a notepad as he spoke. 'There's no guarantee he'll contact you, or anyone else.'

'I'm sure I've seen him twice, now. He went back to the canal and went back to the railway cutting. He is chewing on it, whether it's his conscience or whatever it is, he's knee-deep in it. It's all that matters to him. He works alone and he's lonely. He cannot talk about it to anyone. Each time I saw him I thought he was making a rude gesture, giving me the finger, or two fingers but he wasn't making rude gestures, he was counting on his fingers. Number one, number two. He is communicating already, and calling him an eejit in public would make him want to justify himself somehow. He has some kind of a set of morals or he would have just killed the wrong brother and be done with it. He thinks of himself as a moral being, he thinks he has standards. Letting Michael live was taking a big risk.'

'Yes. So was drowning the woman in the middle of the canal. That was quite daring or insanely stupid, depending on your point of view. And therefore it must have been important.' Denkhaus hesitated again. 'Number one, number two . . . there'll be a number three, won't there? I'll put it to the ACC. Even so, you do realize that I will have to be seen to haul you over the coals for this? It will have to be your personal opinion that's expressed in that interview and I'll be dragging you in here threatening disciplinary action etcetera to make it convincing.'

'Does that mean we're not telling the *Herald* either?'

'No, no, of course not, they can't be trusted. You know Phil Warren well enough now, go for a drink with her, unburden yourself and she'll do the usual and print every word of it and invent some more. She's a menace that woman but a predictable one. Exploit her. She'll get her story, that's enough. Use them. Lie all you like to them but don't bring the force into disrepute.'

'Try not to, sir.'

'Try hard, McLusky, try very hard. I can't shield you if you go overboard.'

They met at The Eldon House. It had been Phillipa Warren's choice and McLusky's first impression was that it was yet another gastro pub he was going to hate. But he changed his mind when he saw the array of real ales on draught. McLusky liked traditional pubs but found that increasingly they only sold indifferent mass-produced beers and lagers while the new breed of pub often served carefully selected beers, like this Bath ale he was now sipping with his back to an enormous potted palm. Phil Warren, who like him had arrived by cab, was also gulping beer from a slender pint glass. Her hundred-millimetre cigarettes were on the table and he knew from experience that she would nip outside four times an hour to smoke, come rain or shine.

Warren was forty, had wiry hair dyed an absurd shade of brown and spoke with a permanently hoarse voice. She was not beautiful but possessed

231

of a strong sexual aura and was aware of it. Tonight she was wearing a short black skirt, patterned purple tights and a purple top with a deep lace neckline showing the swelling tops of her breasts. 'You did say you wanted off the beaten track,' she growled, 'and I can promise you I have never seen a copper in here, so you can stop scowling at my breasts.'

'No, it's fine,' said McLusky, rearranging his face. He had been unaware that he had been scowling or staring at Phil's breasts. He let his eyes travel elsewhere and told himself that he really liked the wooden floorboards. And the tables. Though skylights and palm trees in pubs were not really his thing. He leant back out of the orbit of her breasts. 'Never seen a copper in here? You know them all, then?

'CID? Pretty much, yeah.' She smiled sagely. 'It's usually me chasing you.' It had taken McLusky two days to get hold of her. 'So what's up?'

McLusky gave her a harmless look. 'Just beers, I thought. Cheers.'

'I would actually be quite pleased if I believed a word of it. Have it your way. You'll tell me eventually, I expect.'

They drank, talked, drank. To make an unburdening of the heart even remotely plausible he would have to appear to be quite far gone, which was why he pretended to have had a few already and now drank quickly. When Warren excused herself to go to the 'little girl's room' he managed to feed nearly a whole pint to the potted palm behind him. McLusky had packaged his story inside a general rant about work, everything from the relentless cuts, and constant restructuring to tedious paperwork. He flowed straight on into the case. 'The man is a complete idiot. He is completely out of his depth and has no idea what he is doing. A fumbling bungler. He snatched the wrong man from a car simply assuming that the driver was the owner. In fact it was his brother. He nearly killed him before he let him go. We're protecting the brother now, of course.' McLusky kept working the idiot angle. 'Our killer is an incompetent twit.'

'Bloody hell,' said Phil appreciatively and surreptitiously nudged her phone a bit further across the table. McLusky was pretty sure she was using it to record the conversation, which was not good because it meant she could prove he had really said it all, but he did not want to spoil the mood by challenging her. 'So do we have a description at last?' she asked.

'I'm afraid not. The brother did not see him clearly and anyway is refusing to cooperate. He promised, you see? He's very religious and he swore an unbreakable oath.'

'There's no such thing as an unbreakable oath.' Phil scoffed and gulped more beer.

They argued about that for a while. It was pretty clear that Warren's morals were even more flexible than his own. 'Are you telling me,' he asked, 'that there is nothing in your world that would make a promise from you unbreakable?'

Phil pulled a face, briefly glanced up at the darkening skylight for inspiration, then shook her head. 'No, nothing. Oh, fear of prosecution, of course. I'd probably tell the truth under oath. Then again I might want to tell the truth anyway. But if lying to someone gets me what I need then I'll lie, cheat, break promises, sneak and cajole.'

'You mean threaten.'

'Lean on someone. Look, I'm a journalist. You don't get a good story by asking nicely. Without investigative journalists who would expose the scandals? You'd all be eating horsemeat sandwiches if it weren't for the likes of us.'

'Nothing wrong with horsemeat.'

'That depends on the drugs the beast had inside it, but you're welcome to it, I'm a vegetarian myself.' She impatiently waggled her glass at him. It's your round. Get them in while I nip out for a quick fag. Back before you know it.' She grabbed her cigarettes and crossed the bar room, several pairs of male eyes following her figure to the door.

McLusky picked up Warren's phone, found the recording app, stopped the recording and deleted it, then returned the phone to where it had been and went to get more beers.

The next morning McLusky felt that he had overdone verisimilitude by at least two pints and for the first three hours he worked at half speed, feeling irritable. More irritable even than he had already been these last few weeks. This morning he had begun to slam doors and ram drawers open and shut and hammering at his keyboard like a demented mechanical toy. He scratched his head, puffed up his cheeks. He drank too much canteen coffee, smoked by the window, ate diabetic amounts of chocolate bars.

Last night in their shared cab Phil had made an ironic attempt at asking him up for coffee but McLusky had taken a lonely taxi home instead. It was not that he was immune to Phillipa Warren's charm, a great deal of which was by then on display, but he had recently been thinking more and more of Laura, to the point where he was wondering if her being in Bristol should not be taken as an omen that perhaps they might yet get back together again. What spoke against it was that Laura had still not told him where she lived and he did not want to ask in case she refused to say. A sudden thought turned his stomach sour: what else was she not telling him? For all he knew she could be living with someone and prefer him not to know about it. Could he really expect her not to be sleeping with anyone? He himself had not exactly been celibate.

He forced himself to concentrate, paused for a burp that tasted of chocolate, coffee and hazelnuts, then grabbed the phone and made the first of many ill-tempered phone calls to all and sundry that took him all day and by the end of it left him in no doubt that the investigation was bogging down.

'He's getting better at breaking into houses. He no longer breaks window glass, he's invested in a glass cutter and he's learnt to jimmy open sash windows by releasing the catch from the outside.'

'Progress of sorts,' Sorbie said.

'We now have definite fingerprints too, same ones we lifted from the last place.

'But he's not on file, is he?' Sorbie said petulantly.

'It *means*,' said Fairfield irritably without looking up from her file, 'we'll almost certainly get a conviction.'

'We'll have to get him first,' Sorbie said quietly to himself as he went to make his eighth mug of instant coffee that day. He checked his wrist-watch, a sports watch with a satisfying amount of buttons of which he had been quite proud until he had seen McLusky's classic Rolex. It was nearly six o'clock. He shot the cuff of his shirt to cover up his watch and clattered crockery and spoons and shrugged his shoulders impatiently.

Fairfield read the transcript of the latest victim's recorded statement for the second time.

Next thing I know the door bursts wide and he jumps on me, throwing me back on to the bed. He had a black stocking over his head and was holding a knife, like a small kitchen knife. He had a stocking wrapped around the grip of it, that's what it looked like. And he let himself fall on top of me. But he didn't do *anything, he didn't try to rape me he just pawed at me and groaned while he was doing it. He wasn't putting the knife to my throat or threatening me with it either. It was almost as though he'd forgotten he had it, he was too busy groping me. I screamed and he put a hand over my mouth but again quite feebly. I knocked his hand away and screamed some more and he didn't try it again, he rolled off me and I kicked him hard several times and he shot up and out of the room. I doubt I did much damage though, only caught him on the thigh. I heard*

236

*him running down the stairs and I felt like running
after him and hitting him with something heavy,
but of course I didn't. I had trouble dialling 999
because I was shaking badly by then. It was all
so hideous, it really was like a nightmare where
one minute you're fine, the next minute terrible
things are happening. I don't think I can ever go
to bed again without checking the wardrobe and
under the bed first.*

Fairfield drummed her fingers on the file. 'He's
working up to it,' she said in Sorbie's
direction.

'Up to what?' said Sorbie without taking his
eyes of his monitor.

'Rape. Otherwise why the knife? He didn't use
a knife before. He's going to rape someone, Jack.'

It was Thursday lunchtime and McLusky was
seconds away from leaving for the canteen when
Austin knocked on his door, bearing a copy of
the Bristol Herald, fresh off the press. 'They
printed it,' he said, but his voice sounded
doubtful. 'Warren peppered the article with your
name. Did you really say all that?' He handed
McLusky the paper. The story had made the
front page. Below the headline *Police Brand
Killer Inept* he read: *Yet no new leads in murder
probe.*

'Murder probe!' McLusky scoffed. 'I don't
think I have ever *probed* a murder, have you?
Where do they get their language from?' He
scanned the article. '"Complete idiot", check . . .
"fumbling bungler", check . . . "incompetent
twit", check. Yup, it's all there. Looks like Warren

237

is riding her hobby horse though, incompetent police and, ah yes, *clueless*, we're always clueless.'

The phone rang; Austin snatched up the receiver. 'DI McLusky's office.' He listened briefly. 'He's on his way up.' He dropped the receiver on to the cradle. 'His nibs wants a word.'

'Hardly unexpected.'

Lynn Tiery waved him straight through. Denkhaus did not look happy. He was holding the same edition of the Herald as McLusky. 'Phil Warren has some sort of grudge against us.'

'I haven't had time to read the article properly yet, sir.'

Denkhaus grunted. 'You managed to plant your insults, at least. Let's hope he reacts the way you imagined it. You are running quite a risk provoking him. The ACC was impressed, it shows dedication, but he also voiced concern for your safety. Of course if it backfires it'll all be your fault, there's no way we can admit to having authorized this. Shame Warren had to lace her article with the usual criticisms and horror statistics. It's an even greater shame that most of them are true. Those are official figures. We are now having to ignore nearly fifty per cent of all reported crime, we just don't have the time, money and resources, even if we did have the personnel.' As the DCI warmed to his theme his gaze slid from McLusky's face and he swivelled his chair so he could look out over the harbour area. 'And as ever Warren refuses to see that it's hardly our fault. Even if the service hadn't been pared to the bone, even if we had all the officers we wanted, there's no

238

point in pursuing inquiries if we know the CPI won't prosecute because there's no chance of a conviction. Most of our crime is drug related anyway. The vast majority of burglaries and street crime are committed by drug addicts. We pick them up, the courts let them go because they promise to turn over a new leaf. And off they go to commit more crime, some on a daily basis. If we rounded up all drug addicts and kept them off the streets our crime figures would look like we're back in nineteen fifty-eight.' He silently mused for a moment, then snapped his attention back into the room and swivelled around to face McLusky. 'I read this war memoir, by a Bristol man, about what it was like during the Blitz. He had an allotment and one morning he found someone had stolen three of his leeks during the night. He called the police. They came and investigated, found a boot print and took a plaster cast of it. They later matched it to the boot of a soldier who was manning a nearby anti-aircraft battery. Went to court, fined ten bob. Can you imagine what would happen if you reported three leeks stolen from your allotment today?'

'Vividly.'

'That's a lost world, McLusky.' He snapped out of his nostalgic reverie. 'Mind you, lots of crimes committed during the blackout and the black market were shocking, spivs everywhere. All right, let's wait and see if you've stirred up your man. And let's hope he's stupid enough to call from his home phone.'

McLusky rose. 'I think that may be asking too much.'

'I expect so. But, McLusky, he knows your name. That means he can find you. Be extra careful out there, won't you?'

Fairfield broke the seal on a tin of twenty Café Crème cigars, pceled back the paper and sniffed the aroma. Not only had cartons of supermarket red made a comeback on her kitchen counter, tonight she was going back to smoking cheap cigars from the newsagent's. In the middle of the table lay another red rose, left without comment in front of her door. It had very little fragrance and she decided that she preferred even the aroma of cheap cigars to florist's roses. She sat for a while without lighting up, then got to her feet, filled a glass with water and dropped the thornless, odourless rose into it. Why take it out on the flower?

Triandáphila, thirty petals, they were called in Greek, but she had never bothered to count them to see if it was true. Why should she? *Stubborn.* Her father had always said she was stubborn. It was a good thing to be in her job, but was it equally good in relationships? She missed Louise but she could not see it working; Dr Rennie was simply out of her league and Fairfield suspected that she took a secret pleasure in demonstrating her superior education and background. At first Louise and her beautiful Clifton flat had been like a haven, had given her the feeling that she had escaped into another, better world than her own, brighter, clearer, more sophisticated, infinitely more pleasurable and exciting. But soon it began to make her feel inferior, gauche even.

240

She lit one of the cigars and blew a cloud of smoke towards the rose. These were honest little cigars and she wouldn't have to worry about bankrupting herself by smoking them. And drinking the Californian red from the carton was no hardship either. No, she had made up her mind, she would ask for her keys back. Not that Louise had used them often. She had surprised her with breakfast one Sunday morning and on one occasion Fairfield had walked into her kitchen to find a bottle of wine, a bouquet of flowers and a card whose message had made her blush. Still made her blush. But Louise preferred to spend time at her own place and neighbourhood and she had never reciprocated by offering her the keys to her Clifton flat. Now she was letting herself into the communal hall to leave roses on her doorstep. It's your move, they seemed to say, give in, come back. But she had made up her mind. She would call her and ask for her keys back. She refilled her glass from the tap on the carton. But not tonight, she was on her fourth glass and she found Louise's voice hard enough to resist when she was sober.

McLusky was walking towards his office when an excited Dearlove came skidding around the corner. 'Sir, the desk have someone on the phone for you, they think it's him.'

McLusky sprinted to his office, snatched up the receiver and called down to the desk. 'McLusky. Put him on.'

Sergeant Hayes was apologetic. 'He's gone, sir. Hung up. It took too long, I expect, and he got suspicious. We tried everywhere for you, your office, incident room, your mobile and your radio. Where were you?'

'A man must be allowed to occasionally visit the toilet.'

'Well, perhaps you should have, you know, told us.'

'You want me to announce my bowel movements to the front desk? If it was him he'll call back.' He put the receiver down but secretly he was not so sure. Had he messed up his one chance to make contact with the killer?

From then on McLusky expected the phone to ring at any moment and carried his radio and phone with him even when all he was doing was to go across to the incident room or to make himself coffee at the CID room kettle. He found it hard to concentrate and when the phone in his office shrilled in his ears it actually made him start. He snatched up the receiver. 'McLusky.'

'Hayes. He's back.'

'Put him on.'

Sixteen

'Putting you through now,' said Sgt Hayes in a level tone as though he was connecting killers with CID every day.

When McLusky heard the line open with a lot of background noise he identified himself. 'Detective Inspector McLusky, who is that?'

'Very funny, Inspector.' McLusky's mind started to analyze the sounds in his ear: mobile phone, traffic noise, male voice, thirties/forties/fifties, British, possibly white, possibly local. 'I expect you are recording this?'

'Not at the moment, would you like me to?'

'You really are a clown, then.' The voice sounded aggrieved. 'I have things to tell you. I want to set the record straight. But not like this.' A car horn blared. 'I'm sure the whole police station is listening in and you'll be trying to trace the call. Give me your mobile number.'

'You want my mobile number?' asked McLusky inanely. He was trying to stall him until he had a better idea but none came.

'Yes, you arse, your mobile number. Hurry up with it.'

McLusky thought he could hear the man sucking on a cigarette. 'Hang on, I don't know it by heart,' he told him and spooled through his mobile's display until he found it. He read the eleven-digit number out.

243

'Got that,' said the voice, now almost bored. 'Got to go now. But I'll call you.' The line went dead.

Hayes' line opened up again. 'Did you get all that?' McLusky asked him.

'It's logged and recorded if you need it.'

'I doubt it, he didn't give much away.' Then he called Denkhaus. 'He took me by surprise, he wants to talk to me on my mobile.'

'Yes, I just listened to the recording. He sounds local. Not enough to analyze the voice yet. Also sounds like he was outside, there was a lot of traffic. OK, go straight to Technical Support and get them to set up your mobile to record all conversations and *make sure you keep the thing charged*.' Flat mobile batteries, like mysterious Airwave malfunctions, were the standard excuses when officers did not want to be found.

At Technical Support a technician with surfer looks and earrings listened to McLusky's request, nodded and took charge of his phone. He opened up the back, plugged it into a laptop and started hammering on the computer's keyboard, each time hitting the enter key with a flourish. Then he exchanged SD cards, replaced the back on the mobile and handed it back to McLusky, together with a micro SD card. 'I took all your personal stuff off and put it on there. You'll need to get yourself a new mobile for your private business.'

'Oh, marvellous.'

'Just a tick,' said the technician. He dived down into a blue plastic stacking crate full of cables and phone parts and came back with a pay-as-you-go phone and charger. 'It's crap but it's on the house.'

'It's also bright pink.'

'There is that. You get what you pay for. The sooner you catch your man the sooner you'll have your nice phone to yourself again.'

McLusky would have thought it impossible that his mood could sink lower or his fuse shorten further, yet as he left Technical Support he felt as though his energy was draining from him with every step he took. In his jacket pocket the modified phone, now for the sole use of the killer, seemed heavy with malice, weighing him down. Would he call again? When would he call again? As he haunted the corridors of Albany Road Station, McLusky felt like an unexploded bomb, a bomb whose fuse was set to go off when he reached maximum tiredness and frustration.

The Leslie house was still being watched and it appeared all three of the inmates were staying at home and out of sight. McLusky was itching to have another go at Michael Leslie to get him to cooperate but in his present mood he could not see himself charming the man into it. Wherever he went colleagues asked or just raised questioning eyebrows: had he called yet? He thought it quite as irritating as the wait itself.

McLusky knew what he needed and he knew where to get it. He swung himself into his car and zoomed down to Picton Street. He parked on the double yellow in front of the Bristolian, let the counter staff furnish him with a fragrant cappuccino, then took it outside. He sniffed the coffee, sipped froth, then lit a cigarette and inhaled deeply. He could feel the knot in his stomach begin to unravel after his second sip of real coffee.

When his mobile chimed he nearly spilled his coffee in his haste to get to it. 'DI McLusky.'

'Are you alone?' asked the voice. There was traffic noise as before but this time it sounded like he was speaking from a moving vehicle.

'I'm alone.' He looked around him. There was no one too close to him. 'You know you shouldn't talk on a mobile while driving.'

He ignored the remark. 'You're in your office?'

'No, I'm sitting outside a café.'

'Café? You don't have time to hang out in cafés, not with all these murders happening.' A joyless chuckle.

Just a mobile phone voice, he could be anyone, anywhere. 'How do I know you are who you say you are? You could be just another crank. We always get them. Already two people have called us to say they killed Steadman and Bothwick. Tell me about Michael Leslie.'

'You leave Michael Leslie alone. He is a good man, a God-fearing charitable man. He swore not to help you. And he forgave me.'

'And you took his word?'

'He swore on the bible.'

'Your bible?'

'His little bible.'

'OK, I believe you.'

'That's big of you.'

He thought he could hear the man at the other end inhaling smoke. 'Now tell me, why?'

246

'You really do think I'm stupid. I can't tell you that now; that would immediately give it away. If you knew why, you would soon find out who I am and I can't allow that, not until I'm finished with the wankers.'

'Finished? You mean you will kill again?'

'You'll have to wait and see, won't you.'

'Why did you let Michael Leslie go?'

'I wanted his bloody brother, not him. And I couldn't bear to make the same mistake twice. I make mistakes, I admit it. But I'm not a bloody moron, I'll prove it to you. For a start, don't bother trying to trace this mobile. It's nicked. I'm good at nicking mobiles so I can afford to chuck them away when I'm done talking. Well, I hope you're learning something, Inspector.'

'Like what?' McLusky asked but the line went dead.

Angrily he shoved the phone back in his pocket. He had learnt nothing, he had got no nearer to discovering his identity. He was no further toward knowing what connected Bothwick, Steadman and Leslie. He had messed it up 'What?' He dug out the mobile and fumbled until he got to the recording app, and played the conversation back. Out here in the open it sounded tinny, far away, improbable even. There it was. *And I couldn't bear to make the same mistake twice. I make mistakes, I admit it. But I'm not a bloody moron.*

He thumbed for the directory before realizing that all numbers had been taken off. His pink mobile showed no bars. McLusky dived into his car, started the engine and turned the big Mercedes around one-handed while thumbing his airwave radio. 'Alpha nine, can I come in please . . .?' When he was through to control he burbled away into his radio while spinning the wheel and bullying his way into the traffic on Stoke's Croft. 'I want every available unit to go to the David Lamb residence and his office. Lamb, the councillor. Contact him on mobile, landline, email. And send armed response, too. I believe there is an immediate threat to his life. Find him wherever he is and sit on him. I'm on my way to his house.' He dropped the radio on the passenger seat and impatiently stomped on the accelerator. 'Come on, come on!'

He was still several miles from Barrow Gurney and the Lamb residence when he was told over the radio that the councillor was neither at his offices nor at home but had taken the rest of the day off and gone out, taking his car, without saying where. 'Circulate description and vehicle details and keep looking.' He saw that his mobile had coverage now, terminated the transmission and called Austin. 'He called me. Bothwick was not the intended victim.'

'Did he tell you that?'

'Indirectly. He said he let Michael Leslie go because he could not bear to make the same mistake twice. Bothwick was a mistake.'

'We checked Lamb's house and offices and called his mobile but it's switched off. I sent a car round to Bothwick's flat in case he went there to grieve but no reply. You think he's going after him next?'

'I'm pretty sure of it or he would not have mentioned that he made a mistake.'

'If we can't find him perhaps he might not be able to find him either,' argued Austin.

McLusky slowed down in the lane towards Lamb's house and let the car roll to a stop before answering. 'I have a feeling he does know,' he said at length. 'He was driving while he spoke to me. I think he was following him in a van.'

'Shit.' Austin had also been at the autopsy and remembered the state of Stephen Bothwick's corpse. 'If what he did to Bothwick was meant for Lamb then something quite awful is about to happen.'

McLusky drove up to the Lamb residence where a patrol car was parked across the drive. Two uniformed officers stood by their car, having been told to stay at the address for the time being.

McLusky asked: 'Has anyone checked his love nest down the road?'

'Don't know anything about that, sir,' admitted one of them.

McLusky turned back to his car. 'That's what I love about being on the force, the team work.' He raced down the narrowing lane from the house towards the cottage Lamb and Bothwick had used for their regular S&M sessions. He tried hard not to imagine them. He tried hard not to dislike Lamb to the point of not caring what happened to him. He had tried to see catching the killer as a job, a task, something Avon & Somerset constabulary were collectively engaged in as an agency but found it impossible. However he thought about it the thing always ended up back

249

at his own feet. It had always been personal to McLusky, from the moment he had seen Barbara Steadman's body emerge from the canal. The super had made it clear enough that he too thought it a test of his capabilities, that the ACC would be watching his performance closely. Now McLusky had spoken to the killer he had lost all distance from him. How could he maintain a distance when he had given the killer a private line to him?

He was driving so fast he nearly missed the cottage, braked, reversed and stepped out into the lane. Lamb's Lexus was not there. It was quiet apart from the nearby A-road soughing like wind in the trees. He deflated. The great urgency he had felt earlier evaporated. They were too late. Lamb was gone, his mobile was turned off and in his mind's eye McLusky could see the Lexus standing abandoned, with the keys in the ignition and not a trace of foreign DNA anywhere on it. McLusky did not himself watch television but had been assured by his colleagues that on telly it was now forensic science that solved the crimes, usually within ninety minutes. He had yet to work on a single case where an unknown killer had been found through forensic work. Convicted, yes, found, never.

There were a few more flowers coming up in the garden now. The mournful rotary drier still stood in a corner of the lawn like a leafless tree. He tried all windows, rattled back and front door. He lit a cigarette and smoked it, doing two rounds of the garden. He kicked a stray plastic flowerpot but found it too flimsy to satisfy his anger. He

250

let his shoulders drop and strode back to the car in time to answer his radio. DSI Denkhaus wanted him urgently.

David Lamb pulled his shoulders up to his ears and let them fall again as though he could shake off everything he had left behind him in Bristol as he crossed the city limits. He had left the office early and headed out of town into the Chew Valley. He needed breathing space, thinking space, grieving space, away from it all. Of course there were plenty of green spaces in Bristol where a man could walk and feel sorry for himself, but he would still feel surrounded by it all. And Chew Valley was different. Early in their relationship, before the cottage and before the flat in Clifton, he had come here with Stephen, walking by the lake, sitting by the lake, drinking tea and pretending they were far away and did not need to head back to work and reality. That was why he needed to go back here at the end. To get some kind of perspective on where it left him now. To tie up all the loose ends and all that would forever remain unfinished, undone and unsaid. Before Stephen he had had only casual relationships with men. Stephen had been special. And in the beginning, before the arguments had started, soft, yielding, attentive, adoring. Lamb had thought of it as permanent even, running parallel to his marriage routine, and there perhaps he had made his mistake, had begun to take him for granted, and Stephen had become resentful. Had he really been thinking of leaving him? He would probably never find out now.

His speed crept up without his noticing. Why had Stephen been killed? And where? By whom? Those stupid police officers had seriously thought that he had killed Stephen himself, without a shred of evidence and never mind that he had no real motive. You didn't go around killing people just because you thought they were about to ditch you or there would be carnage across the land.

The lake lay on his right as he drove, glimpsed here and there through the trees. He found the entrance to the visitor centre, a single-track lane through the trees, easily missed, almost secret. In the summer the place often teemed with people, now there were only two cars in the car park and no one to be seen. It was about to rain, which would suit his mood. He stood for a moment looking out over the lake that lay dark under a darkening sky now; further to the south side three sailing dinghies made good speed in the strengthening wind. None of the tables outside the café was occupied and inside only one elderly couple sat writing postcards, not looking up. He took his coffee to a table outside despite the wind and the threatening rain. This view, this air, this mediocre coffee drunk at this damp picnic table reminded him more of Stephen and how he had felt about him than the cottage did where they had met many more times. It was here that he seemed to rediscover the emotions that had carried them along in those early days. It wasn't the Italian lakes but he thought of it as their place and the memories of those days together rolled over him now, threatening to bring tears to his eyes again. He breathed in deeply and sat up straight. No, he was going to find something good in this somewhere, some kind of legacy, or even residue, that Stephen had left behind, that could enrich his life, not darken it. Only, until his murderer was found and his murder explained that would remain an impossibly hard task.

A raindrop fell on to the table, then another. He drained his cup and rose. No, he was not going to walk melodramatically in the rain. He would take the resurfaced memories back with him and get on with his life and work. Especially, and more than ever now, his work. He returned the cup to the café and by the time he stepped outside again rain fell steadily. He jogged to his car but by the time he managed to slip inside his clothes were damp. For a moment he sat and looked through the windscreen at the reed beds and the lake. The dinghies had disappeared from view. No, he would not come to this place again. He would leave it all here. Lamb started the engine and drove up to the exit, another narrow one-way track through the trees. Half way to the road a van that had been stationary on the track suddenly reversed towards him. Lamb parped his horn to alert the driver that he was behind him. The van came to a stop only a foot from his front bumper. What was the idiot playing at? The door opened and a man in a dark jacket jumped out, a blue baseball cap pulled down deep into his face against the rain. He was carrying some sort of sack as he walked up to his window. Lamb let it down and opened his mouth to speak when the sight of the gun momentarily struck him dumb. The man shoved it through the open window straight in his face. His first impulse was to try and close the window again but it was too late. When at last he found his voice all he managed to say was: 'Oh, no, no, please.'

The man hissed at him. 'Shut the fuck up and get out or I'll shoot you right here.'

'He could still turn up, of course.' Denkhaus said without conviction.

McLusky pushed out his bottom lip and shook his head. He tried not to imagine what might be being done to Lamb at this very moment by thinking of him as dead already. 'No, Lamb was the killer's target all along. The night Stephen Bothwick was taken and killed he had come with Lamb in his Lexus to his place in Barrow Gurney. But they argued. Not having his own car there and wanting to spite Lamb, Bothwick drove off in Lamb's car. He had dyed his hair grey to annoy Lamb who had wanted him to make himself look younger. That's what got him mistaken for Lamb and abducted. Once the killer realized his mistake he did away with him anyway.'

'Bothwick is much younger than Lamb, though.'

'True. But it was dark and in the heat of the moment it may not have sunk in. Only when he got him back to wherever he took him might he have realized his mistake. He killed Bothwick only to avoid being identified. That explains the way in which he was dumped. Our man has an agenda, that's why he killed Barbara Steadman in the way he did and hence the elaborate way in which she was left for us to be found. Bothwick didn't matter which is why he was dumped like garbage.'

'Yes, I'll accept that.'

'If I'm right and Lamb is his next victim then we can expect to find his body in a public place again, like the canal.'

They had both listened several times to the recording of the phone call and had earlier sent a copy across to digital forensics. 'He's definitely a local man,' Denkhaus said. 'He may be trying to disguise it or has had it educated out of him but it's there in the background.'

'Or he has moved here and his accent has taken on local colour. Neither gets us much further. And I'll bet you a fiver, sir, that digi forensics will sit on the recording for a week and then come to the same conclusion.'

'Oh, absolutely. And not only that but they'll charge us a fortune for it.'

His plastic intercom squawked with the tinny voice of Lynn Tiery. 'Traffic division have found Mr Lamb's car. Abandoned, keys in the ignition.'

Denkhaus gave him a hard, unfriendly stare.

McLusky shrugged. 'It was only a hunch.'

McLusky and Austin took separate cars. This was not always a foregone conclusion but McLusky had barely looked at him and seemed to be keeping down a boiling fury as he strode across the station's car park. Once outside the city the DS struggled to keep up with the inspector's car on the damp roads and once, on a straight bit of empty A-road, the Mercedes pulled away from him so fast he guessed McLusky must be doing well over a hundred. When he caught up with him at the entrance to the visitor centre

McLusky was reversing towards him since he had overshot, going too fast to stop in time. Even with the windows closed he could hear some kind of rock music pumping from the Mercedes as it stopped, turned, and shot forwards under the trees past a uniformed officer who took a step backwards. Austin was very glad to be driving his little baby-blue Micra. When he parked next to the inspector's car, McLusky was already walking stony-faced towards the trees but then stopped, lit a cigarette and waited for him.

'What was Lamb doing out here, I wonder?' Austin said.

'Feeding the bloody ducks, I expect.' Two cars with local police from Chew Magna had arrived before them and a forensics van was now rolling into the car park. McLusky had driven here on a wave of fury but as soon as he arrived a flat feeling of futility had taken its place. Officers were fluttering police tape between trees now, stopping any more visitors from entering the place. He turned his back on it all and looked out over the wind-rippled lake, a fresh breeze snatching away his tobacco smoke.

'Do you think he could have been lured here?' Austin asked. 'It seems an odd place to go, especially for a busy man on a work day.'

'On the contrary, I think it's perfect, though a bit of a drive. But yes, of course, it's possible he was lured here. Check with the family if the place has any significance that they know of.' He flicked his cigarette end into the wind. 'Right. Witnesses . . .'

The young woman who at this time of the year

256

was running the café single-handed confirmed that Lamb had been on his own. She had seen him through the café windows drinking his coffee at a table outside. 'And he brought his tray back in and said "thank you", not like most people who just walk off, leaving it for me to clear up. What could have happened to him?'

The only other witnesses were an elderly couple who had found the Lexus blocking the exit road. They had confirmed that they had not touched the car and were allowed to leave via the entrance road. McLusky was not in the mood to don a scene suit so kept his distance from the forensics team, eating a chocolate bar and following it with another cigarette, with Austin standing impatiently beside him. 'They're wasting their time,' McLusky told him. 'We're wasting ours. There's nothing here, there won't be a speck of DNA to find. Lamb had enough of the lake but on his way out found his road blocked by a van, just like Michael Leslie had. Our man walked up to him, pointed a gun at him and invited him to step out of the car and into the back of the van.'

'I'd rather be shot in my car than get into the van, knowing what's going to happen next.'

'Ah, but we didn't tell Lamb how Bothwick died. We didn't tell him about the botched electrocution and the beatings. We told him "head wound". Hope springs eternal and if you have the choice of dying now or later you choose later, it's instinct.'

'You've given it some thought, then?'

'Yes, plenty.'

SOCO thought they had found tyre tracks on

the damp ground that might give a clue to the type of vehicle used and took imprints of them. McLusky mumbled that they would probably tell them that they belonged to a van. It was getting dark by the time the operation was wound up, forensics had gone and the Lexus been taken away on the back of a police transporter. McLusky waved at Austin as he left in his Micra and had another look around when everything had gone quiet. He walked along the path, across the car park, looked out over the darkening lake.

Nothing, he thought. *Another one gone and nothing left at all. I hope it's a short list you've got, you bastard.*

The atmosphere at Albany Road became tense, as though the entire station had taken its cue from McLusky's mood. Extra civilian staff had already been brought in to expedite background checks and collation of the information McLusky demanded. Dearlove, who had an accurate premonition of what was coming had hastily stocked up on crisps and mushroom soup.

McLusky was thinking likewise. In the canteen he stuffed his pockets with chocolate bars and balanced a cup of coffee upstairs, grunted at anyone acknowledging him and then steamed into the incident room.

'I want all communications Lamb has had in the past three days, in case he really was lured there, including Post-it notes and writings in the sand. I want every scrap of information on Lamb on my desk by tomorrow morning. How he made his original money, how he got appointed, what rivals he had, any lawsuits and disputes, reported threats or pub brawls going back to his teens. Who did he piss off? If he gave verbal to a traffic warden or said boo to a goose, I want to know about it.'

McLusky knew he was asking the impossible. A Deputy County Councillor could in one stroke alienate thousands of people or whole sections of society, that was the nature of politics. He thought he himself would probably never make it into the realms beyond DI where police politics took up most of your working life. He left his office door ajar so people could come in and out without formalities. During his agitated speech a lot of his coffee had spilled and he greedily sucked it up from the saucer now. It was tepid and flavourless but McLusky barely noticed.

It was not until the next morning that footage arrived from the protest marches against the cuts which, each time, had ended in chaos around the council offices and on College Green. McLusky and Austin watched it together at Austin's desk in the CID room since it would have been impossible to fit both of them behind McLusky's desk. They were both unshaven but while McLusky simply looked overworked, Austin's dark stubble gave him a piratical look. They were eating jam doughnuts from down the road since mysteriously there had been no staff in the canteen when they went down to look for breakfast. Rumours of a strike were making the rounds, sending waves of anxiety through the ranks of the coffee, sugar and sandwich addicts in the station.

The footage was of wildly differing quality, having been collated from various sources, TV stations, police surveillance, CCTV and mobile phones. 'This is the second protest march and it was a lot more lively than the first,' Austin said, tapping the screen with a sugary finger. 'Although the hard-core trouble-makers only started up after dark when most people had dispersed.'

'But this is when the wing nut thing happened?' McLusky took a large bite from his doughnut, could feel jam escaping and leant forward to save his shirt, dripping bright red jam into Austin's keyboard instead.

Austin did not notice. 'Yes. Lamb comes out to make a statement, hoping to calm things down. There he is, this is the bit you wanted.'

This was footage from BBC Bristol and consequently of good quality. The council had previously announced that Lamb would address the protesters in front of the colonnaded council offices, in what the *Bristol Herald* later called a 'monumental miscalculation of the public's mood'. A crowd of over a thousand protesters, many carrying placards denouncing the draconian cuts to services, was gathered in front of the council offices and the green. Lamb stepped up to the public address system, soberly attired in suit and tie. He made calming hand gestures that had no effect on the noise levels. Against a continuous cacophony of jeers, taunts and chants from the crowd he launched into a speech that, according to the *Herald*, was low on content and high on platitudes. It was only three minutes into the speech, when Lamb suggested that 'we will all have to make sacrifices', when the noise of the angry crowd began to drown out his voice

260

completely. A moment later the councillor recoiled as the wing nut hit him in the face.

'Ouch,' said Austin. 'Just missed his eye, that. It was done with a catapult but from the back of the crowd so it did no lasting damage. We never caught the guy who did it. You'll see him in a minute.'

Lamb was now out of sight behind the crowd as he crouched down in pain. The camera zoomed in first to search in vain for more detail, then pulled back to take in the crowd. Austin paused the footage and tapped the monitor. 'Here, it's that bloke there.' A figure in a blue hooded top and what looked like jeans was loping away at the edge of the crowd. When Austin restarted the recording the figure disappeared after less than two seconds in shot. 'The CCTV shows him actually using the catapult.' He found the footage and ran it, one finger poised to pause when necessary. The footage was in black and white and grainy.

'I see him,' said McLusky. The same figure, now in shades of grey, his face hidden by the hood of his top. He seemed to be balancing on the balls of his feet, his arms stretched out in front of him. He half raised them, then lowered them again. A moment later he took a step back and raised his arms and the catapult became visible. He pulled back on the elastic and shot over the heads of the crowd, though the projectile, a weighty metal wing nut, was almost impossible to see. Immediately after the shot the man hid the catapult and began to move away but he turned once more, flung an arm out towards the

261

place where Lamb had stood and shouted. For a brief moment the lower part of his face was visible under the hood before he turned his back on the camera and jogged out of sight. 'Did you see that?' McLusky asked. 'He was shouting something. Go back.' Austin obliged and they watched it again. 'There. You can clearly see his mouth.'

'Clearly is not a word that springs to mind,' Austin objected.

'What is he saying?'

Austin ran the clip again. And again. And one more time. 'Nah, that could be absolutely anything, it's too indistinct.' He adjusted brightness and contrast but it made no difference to the clarity of the clip. 'I can't get it any clearer.'

'But I know a man who might,' said McLusky.

Austin stared at the frozen image. 'You really think this might be our killer?'

McLusky drummed a nervous tattoo on the desktop. 'That's him.'

'But he's using a catapult, that's kid's stuff. Michael Leslie said he had a gun.'

'Violent people always escalate. He graduated from catapult to gun. As a kid he probably chucked stones at cats. Now he's got himself a gun and thinks he is someone. Dispensing justice. You can't coerce someone with a catapult but a gun always does the trick. Anyway, we don't know that it's a real gun, could be an air gun or a replica. None of the victims were shot, not even Bothwick who he snatched by mistake.'

'Guns make noise.'

'So do people if you connect their extremities

262

to the national grid.' McLusky stood up. 'Whoever he is he has a place where he can kill at leisure.' He tapped the screen. 'That's our man and I'm going to get him. Give me that footage, I'll get it cleaned up.'

At Technical Support he handed it over to a perma-tanned technician in his twenties. At a messy workstation covered in empty crisp packets and drinks cans he showed the man the clip and the face of the suspect. 'I need to know what he is shouting.'

'Righty-ho. Leave it with us.'

'I need it done yesterday. We think he might be our killer.'

'I'll send it across as soon as it's done.'

McLusky, whose technical expertise did not stretch much beyond on and off buttons, liked Technical Support.

Seventeen

Fairfield knew it was nonsense and cost silly money, money that would better be put towards a new car or a holiday but retail therapy really did work. All her favourite shops were here in this mall, it could have been built for her. It was a terribly girly thing to do, too, or so Louise had kept telling her. Naturally, master chef and brain-of-Britain Dr Rennie would not consider spending a few hundred pounds in the cook shop, or the bookshop for that matter. It was the frivolous things Fairfield bought that had always attracted ridicule: bath bombs, lotions, skimpy tops, trinkets, novelty egg timers and place mats with pictures of songbirds on them. Louise had taken the joy out of that kind of senseless shopping. Acquiring things merely to cheer yourself up was considered bad form and vulgar. *Merely*! There was nothing 'merely' about cheerfulness; it was a rare commodity. University lecturers didn't need cheering up as much as detective inspectors, that was clear. While she was seeing Louise she had tried not to indulge in any of it and now that she had stopped seeing her Louise still managed to ruin it. *Of course, it's me ruining it, by constantly wondering what Louise would have to say about it*. It was over and it had to stop but as long as Lou still had keys to her house and left roses on her doorstep it would never be completely finished. So why hadn't she called her to demand them back?

She walked up to a quartet of benches surrounding a giant planter full of spring flowers and set down her bags. Why put it off any longer? She checked her watch: half past six, she might well be home by now. Fairfield swallowed hard as she pulled out her mobile, noticed that she had swallowed and said out loud: 'You're a detective inspector, Kat, be brave.' A split second before pressing the button to call Louise Rennie, something in her peripheral vision made her look up; her thumb froze above the green button. She would not have to call Louise after all. She was right there, ambling towards her in her designer jeans and jacket, casting a lazy glance over the window displays. Fairfield stood like a rabbit mesmerized by car headlamps. Louise's name was on her lips but the courage began to fail her and she simply stood very still and stared. Louise drew level with her and just when it seemed she might pass without noticing her she looked across and their eyes met. Rennie curved towards her as though reeled in by a lasso. She came very close before speaking to her. 'Hello, Katkins.'

'Lou.'

'You weren't going to stop me, were you? You weren't going to say anything, you were just waiting for me to pass without noticing.'

Fairfield's resolve crumbled. 'No, no of course not. You just took me by surprise. It was only the coincidence that made me hesitate for a second.'

265

'What, the amazing coincidence that we both went shopping on the same day?'

'No, because I was just this minute going to call you.' She held up her phone in evidence, which showed Louise's number and smiling photograph.

Louise reached out and cupped her hand in hers, gently turned it and kissed her wrist. 'Speak to me then,' she said gently. 'Or would you prefer me to stand over there somewhere so you can call me? What was it you were going to say?'

Despite the knee-weakening effect of Louise's closeness and perfume Fairfield at last found her courage and blurted out: 'Actually I was going to ask you to stop leaving roses on my doorstep and to give me my keys back.'

Rennie's eyes widened. 'Roses! Your keys you can certainly have, I have them here.' She produced a large bunch from her handbag and slid the two Yale keys off the split ring. She handed them over. 'There you are, free at last. Only I didn't leave any roses. What colour were they?'

'Red,' said Fairfield thoughtfully.

'That should have told you it wasn't me. Tacky language-of-flowers rubbish. I'd have left you an orchid.'

'What do they signify?'

'Nothing at all, with any luck. Looks like you have another admirer. It'll be a chap, though,' she said and turned away. 'I'd be wary of him,' she added over her shoulder, 'bound to have limited imagination.' Rennie strolled away and resumed her window-shopping, with Fairfield

266

watching her, keys in her fist, until Rennie drifted from sight.

If the rest of the team thought McLusky was walking around like an unexploded bomb it was nothing to how McLusky felt about the mobile phone he had given over for the exclusive use of the killer. He would sit and stare at it, willing it to ring. He had developed an obsession with checking the status of the signal strength and the battery, peering at it at every half hour or so and feeling for its presence in his jacket pocket whenever he was on the move.

It came as a relief when the cleaned-up footage arrived. The note accompanying it, however, was not encouraging. It read: 'Best we could do. None of us can make it out, though.' It was signed 'F'. McLusky had no idea what it stood for and didn't care. He found Austin who had just connected a different keyboard to his computer, complaining that the old one had developed sticky keys. Together they watched the footage, staring at the movement of the mouth, rewinding, repeating.

McLusky was unimpressed. 'This is an improvement?' He had pinned a lot of hope on the clip. 'Play it again . . . there, it looks like three separate sentences he's saying there.'

Austin scratched the tip of his nose and squinted as the footage ran again. 'I've got it, it's agadoo, doo doo, push pineapple . . .'

'Very funny, Jane. We might be looking at the bloody key to it all. OK,' he said lightly, 'if we can't do it then what we need is a forensic lip-reader.'

267

However, after having convinced Denkhaus of the necessity of bringing in a lip-reader he soon found that forensically trained ones were thin on the ground. When he found one who might be available he realized that picking up the phone was not an option since the lip-reader was deaf herself.

There was a whole day's delay before she arrived at Albany Road, escorted up to McLusky's floor like an invalid by Sergeant Hayes. He knocked on the inspector's door and when he heard McLusky's ill-tempered 'yes'. Hayes opened the door for her and shouted: 'There you are, Miss, you can go in!'

McLusky apologized for Hayes and offered her a chair. 'Sorry about that, that's how he talks to people who don't speak English, too, *loud and slow.*'

She shook her head. It didn't matter, she was used to it. McLusky looked at her and found himself thinking 'She can't be deaf, how can she be deaf?' and even while thinking it realized the absurdity of the thought. He had simply responded to the woman's extraordinary beauty. She was in her early thirties and everything about her seemed perfect, her features, gas-blue eyes, a heart-warming smile revealing perfect teeth and very blond hair. How could someone this perfect be deaf?

'You're Inspector McLusky? I'm Claire Henderson. I believe you have some video footage you want me to analyze?' Her voice, to McLusky's ears, had a curious pitch, almost foreign, and even that he found disturbingly attractive.

268

'Yes,' he said, 'erm, we'd better go to the incident room, it's a bit cramped in here.'

'Yes, it is a bit on the cosy side. My bathroom is bigger than this.'

'Then you won't mind coming next door.'

'Will there be other people?'

'Yes, it'll be full of people but we'll borrow someone's desk.'

'Then I'd rather we made do in here, I'm not completely deaf but rooms full of people all talking becomes confusing to me. Background noise, that sort of thing. Perhaps we could manage in here after all?'

'Yes, sure, if you prefer, erm . . .' He pushed his chair to the side to make room behind his desk.

'Perhaps it would be an idea if you turned the monitor around and came out from behind there, there's more space in front than behind your desk, Inspector.'

'You're right, of course.'

Henderson stood up and gave McLusky room to fluster and clatter about until he had set it up. 'That's more like it,' said Henderson. 'Let's make a start.'

McLusky found the way that Henderson never took her eyes off his face vaguely unnerving. 'Can I get you anything? Watery tea, economy instant?'

'You make it sound very tempting but let's just get started.'

He ran the footage and for the first time her eyes left his face as she scrutinized the images on the screen. 'The resolution is rubbish,' she said. 'There

269

goes the catapult. He must be a good shot.' The footage ran on, the shooter turned, gestured and shouted. 'How do I control this?' McLusky surrendered the mouse and Henderson spooled back to the beginning of the sequence with the suspect turning back towards the camera. 'Shouting is usually easier than talking,' she told him, 'people enunciate more clearly, the mouth gestures are more pronounced but this is very unclear. 'The first bit is "I'll" . . . yes, it's "I'll get you".'

'Makes sense.'

'He's taking a breath and then it's "I'll get" again. "All over"? No, "all of". "I'll get all of you."'

McLusky's scalp tingled. 'Makes even more sense.'

'You wanker.'

'Pardon?'

'He says "you wanker" and that's all.' She gave him a blue-eyed smile. 'Economy instant, please.'

It was while he walked Claire Henderson towards the canteen in the hope of finding better coffee than the CID room instant that his phone chimed and buzzed in his jacket. McLusky gave a start, scrabbled it out of his pocket and blurted: 'I've got to take this,' before answering it. 'McLusky.'

Traffic noise, not inside his van, but rather standing or walking by the side of the road. McLusky registered it even before the killer spoke. 'You got some more fresh air at last, down by the lake. Nice down there, I must go back soon, have another look around. You don't get enough fresh air, the furthest you ever seem to walk is the pub opposite your house.'

McLusky went cold. He had been followed. It was easy, he was on the electoral register, his name had been in the paper. He felt the balance of power threatening to shift and had to fight the urge to tell him about the CCTV footage. He needed the killer comfortable, needed him to feel safe, blasé even, superior. Then he would make mistakes. *Keep calm and play stupid.* 'What have you done with Mr Lamb?'

'Oh, he's a temporary guest with me at the moment.'

'Temporary? You mean you'll let him go?'

'To a better place. I don't think he'll last much longer, he's in quite a bit of discomfort at the moment.'

McLusky turned his face away from Henderson and took a few paces down the corridor. 'You're a sadistic swine as well as a moron.'

The voice remained unmoved. 'Why upset yourself about him? He's not a friend of yours, is he? He's just a rich wanker, I don't think even his family will miss him. Got to go now. I'll deliver his remains to you soon.' The line went dead. Quickly he checked that the call had been recorded, then turned to Henderson.

'Bad news?' she asked.

'Yes. No, just something I need to deal with. One moment.' He jogged back to the incident room and handed the phone to Austin. 'Get the last recording analyzed and get it back to me as soon as possible. If it rings do not answer it. I'll be having a quick coffee with the lip-reader in the canteen.'

But he did not. When McLusky and Henderson entered the canteen it was deserted and the counter unmanned. A stark placard in black on white explained it: the canteen staff were ON STRIKE.

Despite the pressure on housing and workshop space there remained a surprising number of empty properties in the greater Bristol area; officers visited them all, looking for signs of break-ins, trying to find the place where Lamb was being held, but to no avail. 'It's not completely fruitless,' said Austin in an attempt to cheer up McLusky, 'uniform turned up a cannabis factory. They were stealing their leccy from the repair workshop next door.'

McLusky did not even look up from his paperwork. 'Any arrests?'

'Scared them off.'

'Marvellous.'

When it arrived they eagerly studied the analysis of the last phone call. The background noises had been enhanced and the Digital Forensics had drawn attention to a public address announcement in the far background, but it was too faint to make out any words. It was further suggested that the phone call was made from a roadside with busy multi-lane traffic. 'We are creeping towards the bastard,' McLusky said grimly.

The canteen strike over a change in pay and conditions meant that Albany Road station had to cast about for alternative sources of nourishment. McLusky revived an earlier tradition: living over Rossi's, the Italian grocer's, meant he could stock up on sticky pastries on his way out.

Additionally he would then buy fistfuls of chocolate bars at the newsagent's around the corner before driving to work. The crisp- and soup-vending machines emptied in a single day. The rubbish bins at Albany bore witness to the sad fact that the nutrition of most officers now lay in the dubious care of the Cup-a-Soup and Pot Noodle companies while hundreds of triangular sandwich boxes attested to the popularity of the double ham-and-cheese combo. An opportunistic sandwich seller with her wares in a basket somehow found her way into the station and nearly sold out before getting arrested by her customers for not having a trading licence or health certificate; the arresting officer ate the evidence and she was released without charge. It wasn't long before pizza smells began to waft through the station. 'You can smell pizza everywhere,' complained Austin. 'The prisoners in the cells can smell it all day long and they're not getting any. They say it amounts to torture and they're going to sue.'

McLusky just nodded. 'I should think so too.'

Denkhaus however put a stop to pizza boys dumping their deliveries at the front desk since Sergeant Hayes could not get any police work done while having to sort out whose was the *meat feast* with extra chilli and who had ordered the *ham-and-pineapple*. McLusky didn't care. He hardly noticed what he was eating these days; more than once he surprised himself by finishing a chocolate bar while working and only realizing it when it was gone, then having to uncrumple the wrapper to find out what kind it had been.

273

Being a detective inspector was a stressful job at the best of times; with the canteen stubbornly closed, endless cups of instant coffee and his bloodstream racing with sugar it became a physical challenge as well. He had developed a cough, his body felt itchy as soon as he stepped from the shower, he had given himself a shaving rash and half of the time felt like throwing things at the wall, in particular his mobile, which stubbornly refused to ring.

He was at the newsagent's buying more cigarettes and chocolate bars when at last it did. He ran out of the shop before answering it, with the girl calling after him from behind the counter: 'You've left your change! And your Mars bars!'

McLusky stuck a finger in one ear to shut out the noise and hear what was being said. 'Well, you've wanted to know what happened to the lamb in wolf's clothing, you've got him back.' Street noises at the other end, street noises at McLusky's end too as a noisy scooter prattled past him.

'Did you kill him?' McLusky asked in a matter of fact voice.

'He expired last night. I take it you haven't found him yet. Get a move on or you'll start lagging behind.'

'Behind what?'

'Behind me, Inspector.'

'What have you done with his body?' Even to himself his voice sounded tired.

'I'm not telling you that, you need to have something to do, can't expect to get everything handed to you on a plate. You're going to find

274

him soon enough, I expect.' McLusky thought he could hear the sound of his adversary taking a drag on a cigarette and exhaling. 'I'm making it easy for you as it is, I could have buried them all six foot under and you'd never find them. But I want you to find them.'

'Why?'

'So everyone knows you can't get away with this shit forever. Right, got to go.' The line went dead. McLusky used his airwave to tell control that he had been contacted and that there was one more dead body to be found somewhere in the city.

Another day, another body. McLusky tried to feel some kind of compassion for the dead councillor but all he could find in his heart was loathing for the killer.

'He's bound to be mental,' Austin said. 'Does he sound mental?'

'They are all mental. The question isn't "is the killer mental" but "does he know it's currently against the law to kill people who have offended you" and I'd say he knows that well but doesn't care. So spare me the mental-health angle.'

'Yeah, all right, I wasn't making a case for leniency, you know?'

'Good. Now get on with something. Go and harass forensics. Or go and find Lamb's carcass.'

Austin left McLusky's office swiftly and closed the door noisily. McLusky sat back in his chair and silently fumed for a moment, then realized that his hated mobile was still at Technical Support and took a deep breath and exhaled noisily. The absence of the phone's evil presence soothed him a little. He opened his desk drawer and chose a sticky almond Danish from the bag of six assorted ones he had bought at Rossi's on his way out, sank his grateful teeth into it and started work. The morning passed without Lamb's body being found and McLusky began to worry. The body was the only true connection they had to the killer. The phone calls were too short to fix a location, the phones stolen and the connections between the victims tenuous. Without the body, progress would grind to a crawl. Back in Southampton, as a DC, McLusky had been part of a failed murder investigation and he never wanted to repeat the experience. Naturally no one spoke in terms of failure; unsolved murders were never forgotten, cases never shelved but regularly reviewed. All detectives dreaded those cases that might come back to haunt them in the future, often revealing omissions or mistakes made by the original investigators.

By lunchtime McLusky felt queasy from worry and too much sugar. He knew the only answer to that was to eat real food. He left the station and made for the Bristolian. There were other places closer to the station but not only did he like the place and liked the food, he knew that there was at least a faint chance of finding Laura there.

He didn't. He did spot Ethan, the long-haired second-year student he had twice seen her with. He was sitting with two other men of a similar age, talking animatedly over open notebooks, iPads and coffee cups; there was always the possibility that Laura might join them. He could tell

Ethan had noticed him but had chosen to ignore him. McLusky ordered the big breakfast platter that, besides all the cholesterol a police officer could ask for, comprised a blob of 'sesame infused spinach' which he frowned at as an alien invader in the land of the full English but wolfed down anyway. Laura did not make an appearance. He would have to be grown-up about it and call her. But not today, not until the investigation had borne fruit.

The *Bristol Herald* printed a special edition almost entirely devoted to the case. The tone was becoming hysterical; no one was safe. The police were unable to protect the citizens. And, naturally, they were 'clueless'. Phil Warren continued her theme of the 'bungler' and posed the question of whether the killer had abducted the right victim. It sailed perilously close to unacceptably bad taste but the edition sold out within two hours. A profile of the councillor took up a double spread, with photographs of the family and the house. A photograph of McLusky with the caption *Detective Inspector Liam McLusky speaking to investigative journalist Phillipa Warren* surprised him. 'The devious cow,' he muttered when he realized that Phil had secretly brought a photographer with her to the Eldon House meeting. McLusky recognized the potted palm behind him; the photograph had been cropped and the drinks on the table photoshopped out. The *Herald* had made an official request for a second interview with McLusky as the investigating officer, which had been refused. DSI Denkhaus also refused to hold a press conference but made a short statement to the press on the crumbling concrete steps of the station. He made reassuring noises for precisely ninety seconds and took no questions. McLusky's shift ended without Lamb's body having been discovered; he went home via a convenience store where he bought a 'Hot & Spicy' Indian ready meal. When he unpacked it in his kitchen he realized it was a meal for two. Undeterred, he heated it up and had a good stab at eating all of it. He groaned as he walked wearily across the street to the Barge Inn where he sat at the bar and let Paul the landlord refill his pint glass until closing time.

It was two in the morning when he woke to the unfamiliar bleeping of his pink plastic mobile. Blindly he groped around for it and when he found it had to prise his eyes open to find the right button. He grunted something only an experienced DS like Austin could interpret as 'McLusky'.

'Your airwave is off and you didn't give control your new mobile number,' McLusky heard him say. 'Lamb's body has been found. It's in Mina Road Park.'

'Is that where you are?'

'Yes.'

'OK. On my way.'

For a long moment McLusky was not on his way anywhere. Eventually, knowing he would lose the fight to stay awake if he tarried much longer, he pushed himself upright on the mattress. Nausea swept over him and half of his brain seemed to have refused to come up with him. He was still drunk and his insides churned with

278

Indian spices and beer. Having shuffled to the bathroom it took him twenty minutes to come out again, considerably lighter, feeling less sick but slow-witted and deeply unhappy with his lot.

While he brewed coffee his mobile bleeped. 'Denkhaus has just pulled up, where are you?'

'Logistical problems,' he managed to get out. 'Practically on my way.' The pain he felt as the coffee hit his stomach did more to wake him up than the caffeine. He added two antacid tablets to the breakfast menu and drove out to St Werburghs.

Mina Road Park did not look at its best at three o'clock in the morning, swamped by police officers and dissected by police tape. McLusky's Mercedes was the last of over a dozen police vehicles to arrive at the little park. The trees were still bare; flower beds and grass looked grey under the glare of generator-powered lights. Austin, who had looked out for his arrival filled him in as quickly as possible. 'Body was found by a Keith Barren. He's a chef and was on his way back from work.'

'Works late.'

'Had a few beers afterwards. He remembers seeing the figure of a man asleep on that bench when he went to work and didn't think anything of it.' Austin gestured at the cluster of white-suited investigators around the bench. Behind it McLusky could make out the signature feature of the park, a restored Victorian urinal. 'The body was rolled in that filthy blanket so he assumed it was a homeless bloke but when he saw him again on his way back from work and he didn't seem to have moved he decided he'd see if he was all right. Gave him quite a shock.'

McLusky's voice betrayed little enthusiasm. 'Is it bad?'

'Quite bad, yes. Worse than Bothwick. You look a bit under the weather if you don't mind me mentioning it.'

McLusky crossed the grass to the deposition sight. 'I'm fine, it's just the lighting, Jane, arc lights don't suit my complexion.'

Denkhaus looked wide awake. 'I hope you have a strong stomach, McLusky, it's not pretty, first thing in the morning. You did take your time getting here.' Waving away an attempt to excuse his late arrival he kept talking while McLusky suited up. 'This is a high-profile case, Deputy Chief Exec abducted and killed. The press will have a field day if they find out that you spoke to the killer moments before Lamb was snatched from his car. It's already beginning to look like they're right when they accuse us of being unable to protect people. We're playing catch-up, we're just mopping up after the killer.'

'What about Richard Leslie? Can we arrange closer police protection for him?'

'He's refusing. We still have a couple of uniforms outside his house but he complained when they followed him to work. He feels he has no more to fear from the killer after his brother and his bible intervened. You must have another stab at interviewing Michael Leslie. Surely he can be made to see that the living are more important than a bloody oath on the bible.'

'That's pretty unorthodox talk for a CID officer, sir, if you don't mind me saying so.'

Denkhaus tutted irritably. 'It's different in a court of law.'

'I'm not sure he'll see it that way but I'll have another go. I had planned to all along, I'm hoping a few days without questions have calmed him down a bit. I'm not holding my breath though.'

McLusky unconsciously held his breath, however, as he bent over the corpse on the bench, then let it out audibly when he saw the extent of damage done to David Lamb's face.

'Inspector.' Dr Coulthart greeted him softly and scrutinized McLusky's face while he scrutinized Lamb's. 'If you don't mind me saying . . .'

'I don't look well,' McLusky forestalled his solicitude. 'It's called a hangover.'

'That, indeed, would have been my diagnosis.'

Lamb's face was distorted in death agony, his mouth open, revealing his front teeth had been broken. The inside of his mouth was black with dried blood, his skin exploded around the closed eyes, the nose destroyed. 'Did he fry him?'

'Electrocution? Yes. I'll have yet to establish if that is what killed him, though.'

'It's what he had planned for him. He did it to Bothwick by mistake. Though right now I don't really give a shit whether he died from electric shock or had his head caved in or you find a knife in his back.'

Coulthart was taken aback and looked at him quizzically. 'But surely you should, Inspector.'

'I know, I should, but this morning I really

don't.' The pain in McLusky's stomach had receded to a dull ache. The headache that sat above his eyes throbbed whenever he bent down or moved his head from side to side. His chest felt raw from smoking too much yet he craved a cigarette even while suspecting it would make him throw up.

'I will try and fit in Mr Lamb's autopsy this morning. Will it be you attending?' Coulthart asked doubtfully.

'Yes, it'll be me.'

'Then we'll make it late morning, give you time to recover first.'

'I'd appreciate it.' McLusky quickly put distance between himself and the corpse.

A fingertip search of the entire park was well under way even though nobody expected to find anything useful. 'He stopped his van over there, I expect, closest point.' Austin waved an arm towards the road. 'He carried him. SOCOs identified a couple of places where he put him down or dropped him.'

'Lamb was quite heavy,' McLusky agreed. 'And again, he could have just dumped him close to the road and driven off. Carrying him all the way to the bench was a considerable risk, he could easily have been seen. But he wanted him on that bench, he wanted him to look like a rough sleeper. It was important. No CCTV anywhere?'

'No. Carefully chosen, like the other deposition sites.'

They both stood, with their hands in their pockets, studying the scene, thinking.

'There'll be more,' McLusky said eventually. 'But how many?'

'And why?'

'If we knew that. I asked him that and he wouldn't reveal it. But how many more and who? It drives me up the wall.'

'Next time he calls, ask him?' Austin suggested.

'Yes, DS Austin, I will.' He would get the phone back later this morning and hated the thought of it. 'The papers are right, we can't stop him.'

It was a few minutes before noon when McLusky found himself in Barrow Gurney in the viewing suite of the autopsy room. 'You look almost human,' Coulthart greeted him.

McLusky had recovered to the extent that he now thought of himself as at least eighty per cent human. He had smoked, coughed, sipped strong tea – a drink he reserved for the times when his stomach refused to hold down coffee – and around mid-morning had forced himself to eat a day-old Danish pastry from his desk drawer. 'Can we just get on with it?' McLusky snapped.

'Perhaps I'm mistaken,' Coulthart said softly. 'By all means, let us proceed.'

This was the point when McLusky usually unfocussed his eyes to spare himself the details of the procedure, unless the pathologist drew his attention to particular features. Today, however, McLusky paid close attention. He was angry with himself for having drunk too much the night before and was punishing himself, yet he found that far from making him feel worse it managed to divert his attention from the precarious work-ings of his insides.

'Mr Lamb was severely beaten.'

'I can see that. What with?'

'All sorts. Fists, I believe, the size of the bruises around his eyes and cheeks are consistent with that, but also instruments, perhaps a broomstick or a piece of pipe. And I believe he was kicked, too, probably while lying on the ground. All his ribs are broken on his left side, one pierced his lung.' Coulthart indicated the X-ray displayed on one of the monitors. 'And his elbow was probably broken at the same time. He has a shattered cheekbone too. Quite a frenzied attack.'

'What killed him?'

Coulthart looked up and gave him a benign smile. 'I am glad you have recovered from the world-weariness that ailed you earlier this morning. It was heart failure, brought on by electrocution. I'd say he died late yesterday evening. As you saw this morning he was dressed, though his shoes are missing. The blanket has gone to forensics. Synthetic, faded blue, probably had been washed several times in the past or bleached by sunlight. It was liberally stained from various sources so forensics might make you a happy man soon.'

'That'll be a first,' McLusky said automatically, though quietly he kept his fingers crossed that the blanket would have a story to tell, unlike the radiator, which probably came from a skip, the clothesline, which was too ubiquitous, and the buoy, which had been stolen along with the dinghy.

Curiously, when McLusky left the mortuary building after the autopsy he stepped into a ray

284

of sunshine that seemed inexplicably to lighten his mood. He lit a cigarette and stood for a while, eyes closed, his face turned towards the sun, sensing its brightness through his closed eyelids, trying to absorb it. He would go and find something proper to eat and then go and nail the bastard.

The ringing of the phone shocked him out of it. 'I see you found him then. I'm glad I got him off my list at last.' Traffic noise, as before. A particularly loud engine came past, forcing the voice to pause.

McLusky almost shouted. 'How long is your bloody list?'

'Well, that's the thing. The more I think about it the longer it gets. After what you said to the press about me I'm wondering if you shouldn't be on it.'

'That's been tried before, you sadistic arsehole, and I'm still here.'

There was a pause. 'You shouldn't have said that. You really shouldn't have said that.' The line went dead.

McLusky got into his car and drove to Technical Support.

Fairfield slammed the front door of her building, unlocked the door to her mezzanine and slammed that door behind her. The bulky bag and roll of paper she'd been carrying dropped heavily on to the sitting room floor, followed by her shoes. She needed a drink. In the kitchen she poured herself a glass of wine and drained it. *I needed that. I wanted that drink two hours ago.* Fairfield told

285

herself that if things progressed the way they were going at the moment she'd probably end up sipping from a hip flask at unobserved moments.

She had meant today to be about a new beginning, a new post-Louise era. Shc would no longer live to please others, she could be cultured in her own right. Tonight she had gone back to her life drawing classes, which she had neglected for two whole terms. Snapping off the rubber band that held the charcoal sketches from tonight's class she smoothed them out on the floor. Fairfield gave a tired dismissive groan. She had lost the knack. Last year she had kidded herself that she had become quite good at it, tonight she had drawn as though she had never held a piece of charcoal before. It was like a muscle, her tutor had said, you had to exercise it to keep the skill. But she had also promised that Fairfield would get it back if she stuck with it. Last year she had sometimes pinned her drawing up so she could enjoy looking at them for a day or so, this time she let the drawings curl back into a roll and stuffed them into the recycling box in the kitchen. Another glass of wine at the kitchen table and yet another small cigar. Smoking so many now, her hair smelled of cigar smoke. Was she destined to become a cranky eccentric spinster? Was it time to get a few cats? In the centre stood the glass holding the single rose, looking unchanged. There was always the mysterious admirer leaving petrol station flowers on her doorstep. An admirer with limited imagination, Louise had scoffed. Red roses. *Triandáphila*. A sudden impulse made her grab the thornless rose and yank its flower head off. Ripping it apart she counted the petals. 'Well, I never,' she said out loud. She swept up stalk and petals and dumped them in the dustbin. The fingernails on her right hand were rimmed black with charcoal dust. In the upstairs bathroom she turned on the shower and closed the door to warm up the room – she hated showering in cold bathrooms – then scrubbed at her nails until her finger tips felt raw and wondered if she could get away with wearing dark nail varnish and not bother about charcoal dust. She dropped the dark clothes she wore to her classes on the floor and stepped into the shower cubicle. Sometimes she thought this was perhaps the finest moment of the day, warmth, cleanliness, the smell of soap and shampoo, and the day having ceased its demands on her to be this thing or that person. The role play finished, sleep beckoning. Wrapped in a towel she scooted across into her bedroom where a sensible, grown-up Kat had already laid out on a chair the clothes to wear to work tomorrow. Except for her tights.

She knew he was here even before she saw the rose on the bed, smelled the aggressive perfume of his body spray and felt him advance from behind the door. Too late did she try and turn, the knife was at her throat, his body slammed into hers from behind and pushed her forwards, both attacker and victim staggering into the space between the bed and the wardrobe while he ripped the towel off her. It came away all too easily. Pushing her against the wall by her bedside table he breathed hard while he fumbled for her breasts. An almost childish groan escaped him as he ran his hand down her flank and into her pubic hair. Fairfield felt her muscles go taut throughout her body as he tried to force his hand between her legs. Another groan. She felt the pressure of the blade disappearing from her throat. In one swift movement she had turned, picked up the bedside lamp and smashed it into his stocking-covered face. He staggered backwards, caught himself and brandished the knife. Fairfield drew herself up to her full height and bellowed: 'You fucking *bastard*. You'd better be good with that knife because otherwise *I'll tear your fucking head off*!' She knew it was a stupid thing to do even while she advanced on him. He slashed the knife through the air in a wild gesture to stop her advancing, without connecting with her skin but then, after only a second's pause while he seemed beset by doubt, he turned and ran out of the door and down the stairs. She followed him to the top of the stairs and saw him disappear left out of sight. She heard the door to the garden being opened. A moment later the fresh air rushing up from the open door covered her entire body in goose bumps. Fairfield grabbed her dressing gown and hammered down the stairs. She aimed a kick at the door so it flew shut and turned the key to lock it. The glass pane above it had been cut. She yanked out the key and flung it down the corridor. Her airwave radio trembled in her hand while she prepared to call it in. She stared at it, at her hands, then slowly,

slowly sank to the ground until she sat on the cold dark kitchen floor. She put down the radio and started crying, howling like a lost animal in the dark.

Eighteen

'Not the call he made immediately before Lamb's abduction,' said the technician. 'That one was made on the move from a moving vehicle, definitely a van. You can tell from the engine revs and the gear changes.'

McLusky sat impatiently in front of a couple of monitors at a long desk at the Digital Forensics department. 'But the others were all made from the same place?' he asked hopefully.

'They were, and we can nail down the place, too, within reason, of course,' said the technician. He was familiar with McLusky and knew he was difficult to impress but he could sense the man's excitement and savoured it.

'Well? Out with it.' McLusky felt like shaking the man.

'Listen to this, Inspector.' He clicked on a file on the left monitor. Along with the sound from the speakers a multicoloured graph sprang into life on the second monitor. He heard his own conversation with the killer, slightly distorted. The background noises had been enhanced and there was much hissing and crackling. 'There it is. Did you catch it?'

'No, what is that? A public address system?'

'It is. I'll play it again. Listen out for the word "Neptune". Here it comes.'

McLusky nearly crawled into the loudspeaker.

'Again!' he demanded. The technician obliged. 'And again.' At last he straightened up, his expression beatific. 'And that's on two of the recordings?'

'Yup.'

'You're a bloody genius. Can you put that on disk for me?' The technician waggled a CD in a sleeve at him. McLusky grabbed it and practically ran from the building.

In the incident room at Albany Road he scooped up Austin. 'It's quieter in my office,' he said, waving the CD. 'Close the door.' He flicked on his computer and inserted the CD. 'The bastard has a job and I know where, Jane.'

'Where?' asked Austin, astonished.

'You'll hear it in a second. There.' He played the first recording. 'Listen to the background noise, the techies enhanced it for us.'

Austin leant in. 'Oh, aye, it's a tannoy. Oh, I know what that is, it's the bloody open-top tourist buses you get stuck behind. What's he saying?'

'Can't make it all out but he's talking about the statue of Neptune in St Augustine's Parade. That bus is going past the statue with a tour guide commenting on it while the bastard is standing in the street, having a fag break and calling me.'

'There's plenty of CCTV, we have the times of the calls logged. We've got him.'

Three hours later McLusky and Austin sat side by side in front of a monitor, looking deflated. McLusky rubbed his eyes, thinking he had never stared so hard at things that weren't there.

The operative who had run the CCTV recordings for them gave a slow apologetic shrug. 'I'm

291

sorry, gentlemen, but that's all there is.' Again and again they had excitedly tapped the screen when they spotted male pedestrians using mobile phones at the right time but none of them matched the length of the phone call or the rhythm of the conversation. At any one time, it sccmed, there were dozens of people wandering through the area while talking on the phone. 'There are several side streets,' the operative said. From the vantage point of the cameras we can't look into every doorway. He could also be standing inside a building by an open window.'

'No matter, no matter.' McLusky tried to sound an upbeat note as they got into his car. 'We know the area. Two phone calls from the same area. He's got a job there, I'm sure of it, it's just a matter of elimination.'

'There's an awful lot of people working in that area. Could be thousands.'

'Yes, yes, yes. Half of them are women. And we know he's white, so that's another slice of the population ruled out.'

Austin, instead of putting his seatbelt on leant back against the passenger door to face McLusky. 'You think he's on a fag break?'

'The bastard works in St Augustine's Parade and steps out for a fag break. You heard the bus announcement, they always spout the same stuff at the same place. He was near the statue of Neptune each time.'

'There are also newsagents in St Augustine's, and sandwich bars. He could be working a few minutes' walk from there and only go there to buy fags or a pasty.'

Without a word McLusky started the engine and drove off with squealing tyres, throwing Austin back in his seat and creating an avalanche of loose cassette tapes.

The DS scrabbled for his seatbelt. 'Liam . . .'

But McLusky had already slowed down to normal speed as they became snarled up in late afternoon traffic. 'No matter,' McLusky said. 'I'll get him. By Neptune, I'll get him. If not today, then tomorrow.'

'You won't get him tomorrow. It's the seminar tomorrow, all day.'

'Marvellous. In the middle of a murder investigation. Bloody marvellous.'

She would be late but she didn't care. She had to do it now while she felt angry enough. At least Fairfield did expect her anger to subside but who knew, perhaps she'd stay angry, hang on to this fistful of hate she'd felt through her entire life. Her nasal passages were beginning to feel numb; she blew her nose on a crumpled tissue, picked up the next bottle of deodorant, wrenched the cap off and released a stream of sickly alcoholic spray. No, not that one either. She put the cap on and picked up the next. There had been one possible contender early on in her search but now she was no longer sure. She thought she would know it instantly, his smell had been cloyingly rich, as though all his clothes had absorbed the fragrance too. She had opened the windows wide. Then she had nailed her breadboard over the little pane of glass he had broken to reach the key in the lock. Leaving a key in the lock was asking to be burgled. How had she become so complacent? She had decided not to call it in at all. There was no significant DNA anywhere and it wasn't worth it. She didn't want it on her record, she didn't want people to look at her and know that this had happened to her. It would stick to her forever if she made it public, she would forever be the one who had been assaulted by the bastard in her own bedroom. Another spray, another squirt. 'God, that's awful,' she said out loud. She checked the label: *Xtreme Temptation*. 'Really?' She felt a presence next to her and looked up. A young woman wearing the shop's livery was closely backed up by a store security guard.

'Good morning Madam. You have been trying a lot of body sprays, the whole shop is beginning to smell of it. We don't mind you using the tester bottles but it looks like you have tried all those. These are not tester bottles.' She indicated the row of expensive brands of fragrances Fairfield had been tackling.

Fairfield listened patiently, then held out her ID. 'I am trying to identify the smell of a deodorant a suspect was wearing. It might help us in identifying him.'

The woman's demeanour changed and she nodded at the security guard who left wordlessly. 'That is different. But I wish you had told us about it, we'd be only too glad to help.'

'I had no idea there were so many of them.'

'Oh yes, men have quite the same amount of choice as women now when it comes to toiletries, and men are much more conscious of it.'

'And it saves on soap and water, I expect. You're OK with me going through these last few ones? If you don't mind me saying so, half of these smell disgusting, I think I'd prefer sweat.'

The woman smiled uncertainly. 'I'll leave you to it.' She walked away down the aisle, straightening a few bottles as she went.

With a sigh Fairfield picked up the next spray and released a small puff, waving it towards her. 'Jesus!' She said it loud enough for the shop assistant to turn around and give her a quizzical look. Fairfield waved the bottle of *Fatal Attraction*. 'I found the bastard!' She rushed to the nearest till with it, earning her a thin smile from the shop assistant as she passed her. Fairfield checked her watch. Yes, the seminar was just starting but Trinity Road nick wasn't that far, she could get there in minutes.

Austin nudged McLusky's arm when the side door of the conference room opened and DI Fairfield slid inside, making apologetic gestures to the speaker who interrupted his endless welcome speech and preamble ungraciously and told Fairfield to come and pick up an information pack from the desk at the front. Fairfield did so and then disappeared to the back of the room.

'Looks peaky,' remarked Austin.

'She's lucky Gaunt is still in hospital, punctuality is his hobby. Other people's, naturally.'

The speaker resumed his delivery, repeating the last three sentences of his preamble to *Meeting the Challenges of the New Performance Landscape* verbatim and with identical intonation, like a recorded message. McLusky slid deeper on his uncomfortable chair and closed his eyes. The drone of the speaker soon threatened to send him to sleep. The PowerPoint presentation that followed eventually did. He woke with a start, sat up straight and found to his disappointment that he had only been asleep for an instant.

By the time the lunch break arrived McLusky felt he was at breaking point. He knew of course that Denkhaus and civilian staff were holding the fort and that any developments would immediately be communicated to him but his impatience had grown with every dragging minute. Since the canteen staff of Trinity Road was also on strike, outside caterers had supplied a cold buffet which as far as McLusky could see consisted of several types of sandwiches cut into the dreaded triangles, Clingfilm-covered plates of anaemic-looking salads and a selection of crisps.

McLusky would not go near it and pulled Austin away with him. 'Let's get out of here and get some real food. We've got an hour.'

Austin did not have to ask what the inspector meant by 'real food' in theory anything that wasn't triangular but in practice it meant fish and chips from Pellegrino's. The weather had turned grey and was threatening rain. They got back into the car with their food parcels but instead of eating his straight away, as Austin was trying to do while being shoogled about, McLusky drove like a man possessed to St Augustine's Parade. He pulled into a bus stop near the enormous statue of Neptune, turned off the engine and absentmindedly opened his take-away while looking around him as though he had never seen the place before. From here he could overlook a good portion of the parade, the march of nonsensical columns, the repetitive arcs of the fountains. It looked soulless and pompous to him and made him feel desolate. He liked fountains, but this looked more like sewage treatment to him.

'You think he'll call again from here and you'll be able to spot him when he does,' Austin said, nodding, and stuffed three chips in his mouth. 'Worth a try.'

'Yup, s'what I thought.'

'The place is far too big, though. You can't see all of it. You'd have to be extremely lucky.'

McLusky attacked his portion of cod with a stab of his wooden fork. 'You don't play, you can't win.'

'In that case perhaps we should pitch camp at the CCTV hub.'

'I thought about it but I don't want to see footage of the bastard, I want to grab him there and then. We'd have to flood the place with police and there's no guarantee he'll do anything anytime soon. I'd never get it past Denkhaus.'

'Overtime.'

'Precisely, not in the budget. In the new performance landscape we'll have to catch murderers in a more cost-effective way.'

'Oh aye, it'll be two for the price of one next.'

McLusky scrunched up his depleted take-away parcel and lobbed it over his shoulder on to the back seat. He reached for the ignition, took one long angry look at the lunchtime crowd, then started the car and drove off just as a traffic warden approached.

Back in the conference room McLusky struggled to contain his anger. He no longer tried to get Austin to laugh by making whispered sarcastic comments; he sighed and fidgeted. The second half of the training day was entitled *Appraisal Systems in Personal Development Reviews* and to McLusky the title alone summed up much that was wrong with how they were now supposed to use their time. Two hours into the second half he noticed that he was not the only one fidgeting. First one, then another of the officers excused themselves and left the room. He saw DS Sorbie leave the room as though he had been urgently called away. Several more officers left in a hurry and he heard murmurs of 'not feeling well'.

'What's going on?' asked Austin.

Just then the speaker, who had droned on robotically like an unstoppable mechanism for the last hour, faltered, lost his thread and then stuttered. 'I'm afraid I'm . . . not feeling . . . all that well. I think we will have to postpone . . . excuse me.' He left the room hurriedly, leaving his laptop and projector running. McLusky looked around. There were many pale faces and the room emptied rapidly. He saw Fairfield slinking away and called after her but she either did not hear or ignored him. Soon all one hundred and eighteen CID officers had disappeared, most to find the toilets.

'And then there were none,' McLusky said, lit a cigarette in the corridor and strode from the building.

At a very quiet Albany Road station Sergeant Hayes looked mystified at Austin and McLusky. 'How come you sirs aren't affected?

298

Austin nodded his head towards McLusky. 'Triangular food. The inspector doesn't believe in it.'

'It's not natural,' McLusky said, shaking his head lugubriously.

'We went out for fish and chips.'

'Food poisoning!' Hayes marvelled. 'Every CID officer for miles around is now off sick? For how long?'

McLusky threw up his arms. 'Who knows? But until they recover it'll be me, Jane here and the super, I suppose.'

Hayes shook his head slowly. 'Denkhaus has been taken ill as well.'

'How? He wasn't at the seminar.'

'It was him who organized the caterers to come in. Ordered a couple of rounds of prawn sandwiches for himself and his secretary. Both taken ill.'

'Marvellous. Bloody marvellous.'

Hayes beamed at them. 'I had a Pot Noodle.'

Fairfield thought she had never heard so much retching or seen so much puke in her life. Every time she thought it was safe to leave the cubicle her innards convinced her otherwise. She felt she had been in here for hours and felt utterly wretched and continuously sick. For a long while the cubicles to either side of her had been occupied by other vomiting wretches but it had gone quieter now. Two obviously unaffected women were chatting at the wash basins, uniform or civilians, Fairfield surmised. She paid little attention to what was being said until she heard one of them say something that electrified her. Already on the way out of the toilets one of the women said: 'But I did something out of the ordinary today, I gave my tights to a complete stranger. His van had broken down.' The door closed behind the women and she heard no more.

Fairfield struggled out of her cubicle and ran after them as fast as her stomach cramps and nausea allowed. 'Wait!' she called after the two who were already disappearing around a corner in the corridor. The women looked back, stopped and gave her a quizzical look. Both were civilian staff. Fairfield leant weakly against the wall and waved them back.

'You do look terrible,' said the older one. 'Is it the food poisoning? Do you need help?'

Fairfield weakly shook her head. 'It's not that. I heard you talking. Giving your tights to a stranger . . .'

'Yes, that was me,' said the younger one. 'On my way to work this morning. He flagged me down. His van had broken down, the fan belt. He offered to buy my tights off me.'

'Camper van?'

'Yes, old-fashioned one.'

'Twenties, shoulder-length hair? American accent?'

'Canadian, actually. My sister-in-law is Canadian, I can tell the difference.'

'Bastard.'

'What?'

'Nothing. Can you remember anything else about him?'

'Nice van, cosy. He let me take my tights off

300

inside, there was traffic about. Smelled a bit strong but nice.'

Fairfield found talking difficult; she felt faint and thirsty. 'Smelled of what?'

'All sorts. Cooking. And deodorant.'

Fairfield dug around in her handbag and withdrew the body spray. She squirted a jet of it into the corridor. 'This one?'

'Yes, that's the one, a bit nauseating, don't you think?'

Fairfield nodded weakly and swayed back to the toilets, heaving.

McLusky stood in the CID room, staring at the empty desks.

He had found two civilian operators keeping their heads down at their computer terminals, counting their blessings and the minutes until their shifts ended. It was preternaturally quiet on the entire floor.

Austin stood a little forlorn, scratching the tip of his nose. He tried to strike a positive note. 'They'll all be right as rain tomorrow, I expect.'

'They had better be, because right now Bristol CID is more or less you and me!'

His mobile chimed. He answered it. 'Hi Kat, are you all right? Sorry to hear that. That bad?' He listened for a while, then said: 'Hang on, I'll write all that down.' He grabbed a pen and note pad. 'Shoot.' He took notes for what seemed an age to McLusky, then said: 'We'll look into it as soon as poss. Get well soon, OK?'

'Was that Kat? What does she want?'

'Mainly she wants to stop puking. She's got

the bug bad and she says she can't raise Sorbie. But she thinks she has just got a lead on the tights man they've been chasing, don't ask me how. Here.' He handed McLusky the note pad.

The inspector took one look at it and handed it back without interest. 'I can't read your writing anyway. Underwear thieves can wait, we've got our hands full.'

Austin read from his notes. 'She has a description at last. Shoulder-length fair hair, drives a classic VW camper van, wears lots of body spray called *Fatal Attraction*, and he's Canadian.'

'Bugger me!' McLusky shot out of his chair.

Austin looked over his shoulder. 'What?'

'I think I've met the bastard.'

Neil Shand was angry. He gripped the steering wheel of his Range Rover as though he were trying to strangle it and accelerated hard, the growl of the four-litre engine expressing well what he felt. Bloody tenants! When the agent had told him about the state of the flat he had to go and see for himself because the house in Filton was where it had all started, the first property he had bought, and the flat in question was the very place he had occupied as a live-in landlord, twenty-five years ago. And the bastards had wrecked it. They had walked off with the copper from the immersion heater and had stolen the electric cooker. They had even taken up half the floorboards and pinched those too, God knew what for, the wash basin in the bathroom hung off the wall and the toilet bowl was cracked. How did you crack a toilet bowl? What did these people eat, rocks? After that he had knocked on the other doors in the building and asked questions, angry questions: hadn't they noticed the bastards were stripping the flat? He had demanded to look around their flats and found disgusting mess in most of them. Why did people want to live like that?

Shand was glad when he left Filton behind. It was dark and a fine rain was falling and he found it all depressing rather than nostalgic. He was secretly proud of his humble roots and his achievements: twenty-eight properties in the area now and he had recently moved into one of the finest harbourside penthouses money could buy. Elaine was no longer with him, which meant he had no one to share it with, yet still, quite an achievement.

But those idiots. They didn't ventilate the place properly to save on heating and let sooty black mould spread around the kitchen and bathroom. That was the problem with letting to people on benefits, they couldn't afford to look after a place properly and now with the changes in benefits he had twice as many people behind with the rent. It was more hassle than it was worth and his mind was made up, he would give all of them notice.

Shand breathed a sigh of relief as he drove slowly along Anchor Road. His new home. This is where he belonged now. He had calmed down at last, his decision made. No more tenants on benefits, ever. Get rid of them. He would be fair, he'd give them fair notice, but from now on it was working people only. He indicated to turn into the entrance of the car park. A shabby van had at that very moment decided to pull away from the kerb and he waited for it to pass. But the idiot driver suddenly turned the thing towards him as though trying to execute a U-turn just there. Shand worked his horn but the van did not stop until it was no more than a few inches from his front bumper. He gave a low growl of frustration and anger. The world really was full of idiots. The door of the van opened and a man climbed out. 'Don't get out, move away from there,' Shand muttered to himself as the driver, who had the hood of his top up against the rain, came to his driver window. 'What now?' Shand let down the window. 'What do you think you're playing at?' he barked at the man.

He had expected an argument but not the gun. He had never in his life seen a real handgun and the unreality of the situation held his fear at bay for a few seconds. 'There's no need for that, take the bloody car!' He had always thought that resisting in a robbery was a stupid thing to do. He slid off the seatbelt and got out.

The man jabbed the gun hard under his chin and Shand felt himself go rigid with fear. The man brought his face close to his. 'I don't want your fucking car you wanker. Make one noise and I'll blow your fucking brains out. Get into the van. Lie on the floor.' Shand did as he was asked, his heart hammering, his mind racing as the door slid noisily shut behind him. What could he want? His abductor was breathing loudly near his ear as he looped a plastic cord round his hand and yanked his hand back, then tied it across his other wrist, pulling so hard that a yelp of pain escaped him. 'I told you to shut the fuck up, didn't I?' His hair was grabbed roughly from behind. Five, six, seven times his face was smashed into the metal floor with such force that he thought he was going to black out. Then a rag was forced into his mouth and strips of adhesive tape slapped over it. Finally a sack was forced over his head. 'That's you done, Shand,' said the voice near his ear. 'We're going to have ourselves such fun.'

I'm dead, Shand thought, *it's him and he'll kill me like the others. And I don't even know why. Nothing makes sense. It's all nonsense. Life is nonsense.*

'He's been attacking people in their home,' Austin said. 'Fairfield says he's working up to a rape, she's sure of it.'

'Laura.' McLusky's voice was flat with dread. 'The bastard is a mate of Laura's.'

'Seriously?'

'Year above her. But I've seen her with him, they go on digs together.' He spooled through his mobile, found Laura's number and dialled. 'She's even kipped in his van.'

'Fairfield said he uses his van to get women to give him their stockings, pretends his fan belt is busted.'

McLusky wrinkled his nose in distaste. Laura answered. 'Liam! Wonders never cease.' A lot of background noise, voices, clinking of glass.

'Where are you, Laura? In a pub?'

'No, I'm at home. Having a bit of a do here

305

with friends from college. Apropos of nothing. Did you want something?'

'Is Ethan there? The Canadian guy?'

'Liam, what is this? Have you been drinking?'

'Is he there?'

'He is, but you seem to have entirely the wrong idea. He's just a mate.'

'Give me your address, Laura, I need to see you.'

'Well, now is probably not a good time, I wouldn't be able to give you my undivided.'

'Just give me your address, Laura.' He insisted.

'You're unbelievable, you know that?' But she spelled it out for him. McLusky wrote it down and abruptly terminated the call. Austin looked at him questioningly. 'It's all right, she's with lots of people but he's there. Shared house in Redland, a party. Let's go.'

McLusky drove through the rain without saying a word. Redland. So near, and yet how far apart had they drifted that only now he found out her address or the circumstances of her digs. A shared house, how very studenty. McLusky had never lived in a shared house. As a student he had lived in a basement bedsit, alone, often drinking alone, even then.

'We're going to rain on her party,' said Austin. 'You'll be popular.'

'Yes. I bet he's the life and soul. It's up there.' McLusky was driving along a street of large Victorian terraced houses, cars, scooters lining both kerbs. 'Not a bad area. See? His camper van is right there, we'll need to pick that up.'

McLusky pulled up next to it. It had been

shoehorned between two small studenty-looking hatchbacks. 'I'll block him in, get out on my side.'

'You'll be blocking the entire road,' Austin objected.

'So? Get traffic to collect the camper and get it to forensics.'

While Austin made the call McLusky stood in the street listening to the music drifting across from the house. He did not recognize the tune, if it had one. Light spilled out from the large ground-floor window, all other windows were brightly lit up. A tangle of bicycles beside the door.

'D'you realize—' he fumed – 'we won't be able to turn down anything at all now until the rest of Avon & Somerset stops puking? We have a triple killer to find and here we are going after kids with an underwear fetish.' He rang the bell but could not hear it ring over the noise, so hammered open-handed on the front door. It was yanked open by a teenager with a freckled, slightly sweaty face and a freshly pierced eyebrow that looked infected. He was holding a can of lager. McLusky showed him his ID. 'Is it about the noise? It's still early, give us a break. Who complained?'

'No one complained. Where's Laura?'

'Who's Laura?'

Once inside McLusky left Austin as a dark sentinel by the door. The place was not as crowded as the noise levels had suggested. About forty people were standing in the kitchen door, along the hall, on the stairs and sitting on every available surface in the mostly candle-lit sitting room, where he found the source of the thumping music. Only one girl was dancing by herself in front of one of the speakers, holding a bottle of beer, oblivious to her surroundings. He scanned the faces, could see neither Laura nor his quarry; he pushed on through the hall, earning himself curious looks. Laura and Ethan were standing in the kitchen where a long kitchen table held both drinks and food offerings. They were part of a group of six, all women apart from the Canadian who visibly blanched when he looked up and spotted McLusky bearing down on them. Laura saw him too. She wore an ensemble of clothes that blended in easily with the dress code of multi-coloured ethnic, charity-shop chic and trendy trainers mix that everyone else was wearing.

She smiled thinly, with tiny shakes of her head. 'You're a marvel. Grab yourself a beer, then.'

As McLusky approached the group Ethan tried to slip away towards the door but he flung one arm out to block the young man's path. 'Oh no you don't. Stay right where you are because it's you I want.' He flashed his ID at him. 'I'm Detective Inspector McLusky. What's your surname, pal?' he asked.

'Gray.'

'Ethan Gray, I'm arresting you on suspicion of sexual assault, breaking and entering, and burglary. You do not have to say anything . . .'

Gray took off with explosive speed, nearly pushing a girl to the ground as he shoved past the table to the door. There were cries of dismay

308

and annoyance coming from the hall, then a brief commotion ending in a heavy thump. McLusky guessed rightly that Gray had run into the hairy arms of DS Austin. He went to check and saw the DS pressing his face against the front door while cuffing him. 'Caution him,' McLusky called over the music, 'he ran before I'd finished arresting him.' When he turned back into the kitchen the whole room was staring at him as though he was the most repulsive thing they had ever laid eyes on. The kitchen emptied of people.

Laura crossed to the table and angrily yanked open a can of industrial lager. 'Ethan? Him? You're sure about this?'

'Pretty sure.' He helped himself to a can of beer. 'You don't think I concocted it because I'm jealous?'

Laura sighed. 'No, I suppose not.' She held his eyes. 'But are you, though?'

'Am I sure?'

'No, not that.' She smiled. 'Are you jealous?'

McLusky helped himself to a can of beer before answering. 'A bit. No longer though.'

Twelve hours later in his office, McLusky found it hard to concentrate on what he was reading. Images of Laura kept intruding. He had only been able to stay for a few precious minutes but found himself going over every moment of it in his mind. Until last night he had always seen Laura in the context of their old life together. Even after she had moved to Bristol he had kept imagining her in the flat they had shared in Southampton. Now she had come dangerously alive for him and he felt like a human compass with Laura

309

being north. Last night he had stood by his bedroom window and stared towards Redland, had thought he could feel her being out there.

He tore his thoughts away from last night, logged off the network and left his office. This morning not one of the buffet casualties had made it in to work, three had been hospitalized. The catering company was being investigated while the regular canteen staff had decided to call a halt to the strike and were returning to work today. McLusky barely took any notice. At the CID room he stood in the door until Austin had finished the phone call he was making, then told him he was going out. 'I'm having another go at Michael Leslie.'

'Take your bible.'

'I'm taking forensic pictures of David Lamb's body. He can stick those in his bible as a reminder.'

'I thought you were going to go easy on him.'

'Compared to what I want to do to him, that's kid glove stuff.'

At the Leslie's home in Norton Malreward Mrs Leslie came to the door and made apologetic hand gestures. 'I'm afraid you had a wasted journey, Inspector. Michael has decided to move on. He has left.'

McLusky squinted into the sunshine for a few seconds, swallowed his anger and said quietly: 'I spoke to you not an hour ago. You said he was here.'

'He has left since then. He decided to go back up north.'

There was no sign of Richard Leslie's Jaguar.

'Where is your husband? Giving him a lift to the station?'

'My husband is at work. Michael left the way he came, by bicycle.'

'All the way up to . . . Bradford, wasn't it? You said he was half starved when he got here, how's he going to survive? You gave him money?'

'Enough to cycle to the moon.'

'You paid him to leave.'

She nodded. 'Should have done it ages ago.'

'How long ago did he leave?'

Pauline Leslie sighed. 'Can you *promise* me you won't bring him back?'

'Promise.'

'About five minutes ago.' She pointed down the lane. 'He went that way.'

Mindful that every blind bend could be hiding a religious man with cracked ribs wobbling about on a bicycle, McLusky drove carefully up the sunny single-track lane with the windows rolled down. After only a few minutes he had caught up with him. Michael Leslie had just struggled to the top of a rise. His bicycle was an old-fashioned one, with a rear-view mirror, mudguards, panniers and a rack piled high with bag, sleeping bag and odds and ends. The panniers were bulging and Michael Leslie was sweating. He stopped at the top of the rise and looked stony-faced when he recognized McLusky who had driven past and then blocked the road. Leslie tried to wheel his bicycle past him but McLusky laid a hand on his handlebar. Like a stubborn child Leslie pushed against him for a while without meeting his eyes, then desisted. 'There

311

is nothing else to say, Inspector. Everything is still the way it was.'

Leslie flinched when the inspector whipped a large photograph from his jacket and held it up to him. 'Not for him it isn't. Nor for his wife and two children. Because you won't help us.'

'No, not because I won't help you. God saved me and my brother from him. Perhaps that was a godless man. It is not my job to catch criminals. That is your job.'

'I need you to help me.'

Michael Leslie met his eyes at last. 'Are you saying that without me you won't be able to catch him?'

McLusky barely hesitated. 'Yes, that's what I am saying. You are the only one who saw him and survived.'

'You're a bad liar, Inspector.'

'He'll kill again. Do you really want that on your conscience?'

'But it won't be on my conscience. It is not me who is doing the killing and it is not my job to prevent him from killing again. I have prayed for him.'

'I need your help,' McLusky insisted. He felt like shaking him, hitting him.

Leslie grabbed at McLusky's hand and prised it off the handle bar. McLusky let go and Leslie pushed past him. 'I swore an oath on the bible.'

'Do you really believe you will go to hell if you break it?'

'Yes!' Leslie was getting back on his bike.

'Then do it! Break your oath and go to hell for it and save innocent lives!'

Leslie made no answer and started pedalling downhill, gathering speed.

'Nice day for a bike ride, Michael!' McLusky called after him. He flung the pictures of Lamb's body through the window into his car and thumped the roof with his fist until it hurt.

Nineteen

McLusky let himself fall on to his desk chair and lit a cigarette. He thought he could possibly spew smoke without the aid of tobacco, since his anger smouldered unabated. He opened the door of his desk and reached for the bottle of Glenmorangie that had survived two years of Bristol CID. It was a litre bottle a suspect had left behind and it had been helping Austin and McLusky celebrate the small triumphs of their jobs. The fact that after two years it was still half full seemed an adequate symbol of how he felt about CID work. He uncorked the bottle, put his nose to the neck and inhaled deeply. Then he returned the cork to the bottle and the bottle to the bottom of his desk. McLusky thought of it as incentivizing. The dread of a failed investigation now hung permanently in the air. He stared at the prepared mobile reserved for the killer and hoped it would not ring now. He had a few things to tie up at Albany Road but after that he intended to spend his time in St Augustine's Parade, phone in one hand, handcuffs in the other. It was the desk phone that rang. It was Sergeant Hayes; he had the ACC on the phone.

Anderson launched into the one-sided conversation with the gusto of a man unaccustomed to being interrupted or contradicted. 'I must congratulate you on apprehending the sexual deviant,

314

Gray. Canadian, is he? Let's hope we can deport him. They're not the kind who are cured by prison, he'll only pick up where he left off when he gets out. Most come out more perverse than they went in. Well done indeed, McLusky. No need for false modesty,' he said when McLusky tried to protest that his involvement had been marginal. 'Dreadful business, that food bug, quite serious, I believe. Lucky you and your sergeant were immune to the bug. You have CSI Denkhaus' full confidence and I'm putting you in charge of this investigation until he or DCI Gaunt return to duty. Are there any new developments?'

'There's quite a lot of forensics outstanding, tyre marks etc.'

'Good, good. Good work, McLusky, carry on.'

When he stepped out into the corridor it felt as though the missing CID officers had taken all the oxygen with them. If he did not get out of this place he was going to suffocate. He stood in the door of the CID room, for a moment feeling hopeless. Austin sensed him standing there, finished typing the sentence he had started, then looked up. 'How did you get on with Michael Leslie?'

'Our god-fearing witness is pedalling up north with all the answers in his back pocket.'

'He's leaving? Did you speak to him?'

'He won't talk. He has a good line in glib religious answers.'

'Charge him with obstruction?'

'Waste of time. Denkhaus thought we could compel him but he'd end up playing the martyr. He's too unstable.'

315

'Still no forensics on Lamb.'

'How are the relatives taking it?'

'I don't know. Did you not have the feeling they were quite a loose knit family? Anyway, they haven't given any statements, the press are camped on their doorstep of course but they're relatively cushioned out there. Lots of pictures of the house in the paper and speculation and some unkind comments.' He patted a folded-up copy of the *Herald* on his desk. 'A Dauphin deli van was spotted driving in and the *Herald* practically accuses his family of celebrating.'

'Shocking.' McLusky remembered having similar unkind thoughts when he witnessed the upmarket food delivery at the Steadman house after Barbara Steadman's death. What did we expect them to do, live off burgers as a sign of grief? McLusky made a show of patting his jacket and held up his airwave radio. 'I'm going out, everything's switched on and working.' Austin was just about to ask whether McLusky might share with him where he was going when McLusky added: 'Oh yeah, and I just had a phone call from the ACC, apparently we are flavour of the month, well done on catching Gray.'

'Fairfield's going to love that.'

'I tried to tell him but you know Anderson. But Denkhaus will give credit where it's due. Oh, and I'm now in charge.'

Austin's face lit up. 'What, did he make you acting DCI?'

'Nah, Anderson's not *that* mad.'

McLusky drove to a large supermarket across the river and went shopping: a baguette, some sliced bread, a tub of margarine, bottles of water and fruit juice, sliced cheese, sliced ham. Also a selection of mini cheeses, muesli bars and bags of peanuts. 'Looks like a picnic,' suggested the cheerful checkout girl. On his way out he stocked up on cigarettes, then he poured his purchases on to the back seat of the Mercedes and drove back into the centre, to St Augustine's parade. In one of the largest bus stop bays he parked and turned off the engine, then called the CCTV centre. 'Yes, we can see you. We'll try and keep this line free for you. How long are you prepared to stay there?'

'We'll see.' As long as it bloody takes, thought McLusky, as he terminated the call and reached for the baguette.

Three hours later he felt less enthusiastic about his vigil. He had informed traffic division about it but bus drivers were unenthusiastic about finding a huge black Mercedes in the bay and several traffic wardens had tried to move him on. He was covered in breadcrumbs from the baguette and since he had no knife there were now margarine stains and bits of cheese crumb everywhere. He felt slightly sick because he had started eating from boredom. He needed to use the toilet. Listening to so much of his old music had made him feel queasy with regrets and nostalgia for the past and he was tired of his own company. McLusky had been on several surveillance operations in the past but then at least there had been something or someone to watch and usually an equally bored colleague. All he could see now was the endless senseless milling about of people.

317

He was close to the statue of Neptune and he was sick of looking at that too. When it had stood by the waterside he had quite liked it, now it annoyed him intensely. At regular intervals the open-top buses crawled by and each time he lowered the window to catch snatches of the commentary droning from the PA system, buried under traffic noise. After a while noise was practically all he noticed, noise and movement and the stink of car exhausts. His thoughts drifted away from St Augustine's, across the river, beyond the city boundaries to the birdsong and the budding trees. Could it be that he was falling out of love with city life?

His mobile chimed but it was Austin on the little pink plastic one. 'I think we may have another one.' When McLusky did not answer for a few heartbeats he said: 'Are you there, Liam?'

'I'm here. A body?'

'No. Abandoned Range Rover in Anchor Road. Keys in the ignition.'

'Anchor Road? Any witnesses? No, don't even say it, no one noticed a damn thing as usual. Whose car?'

'Registered to a Neil Shand, address in Anchor Road. In fact his car was found outside his address, a posh penthouse in a riverside development.'

'I've heard of him, he's a big landlord, he's got properties all over, a lot of it neglected, and some of them death traps. It was in the *Herald*. He'll have plenty of enemies.'

'Am I meeting you down there?'

'God, no, I know what a Range Rover looks

318

like. You go.' A city tour bus growled past with the commentary turned up loud.

'You're in St Augustine's, I can hear the spiel about the statue. Sounds just like the recording. That's quite creepy.'

'Creep away, Jane. Keep me posted. I'm in a bus stop outside a travel agent's.'

Less well known to the press than McLusky, DS Austin enjoyed a brief moment of anonymity when he arrived in Anchor Road, but it did not last long. The nationals were happy to run with a series of abductions and violent killings and the extra spice of most of Bristol CID being out of action made it the perfect story. Officers had been drafted in from elsewhere in the Avon & Somerset area but only emergency work was being done. The prognosis was that three or four days should see most of the affected officers return. Reporters fired questions at him as he passed the scrum of them. He wondered why they always did that since they never provoked an answer. In the meantime Austin felt almost lonely without McLusky barking at all and sundry. Austin felt capable, thought he was a good officer, but he did not think he was ready to be in charge. This however looked so familiar he thought he could do it in his sleep.

'If this is what I think it is,' he told SOCO when they arrived, 'then there'll be bugger all on Shand's car.' Even as the words left his mouth he could hear McLusky's voice in his head, felt as though the DI was speaking through him, using him as a medium. 'I don't think our man even breathed on it,' he added.

The riverside development contained enough flats to keep them busy with knocking on doors but he thought he could already hear McLusky's voice saying something like *and none of them will have seen a damn thing because they were all staring at their tellies*. But at least, he thought, there'll be CCTV. He called McLusky. 'This time we'll have CCTV. Might throw something up.'

'I'm not holding my breath but it's different. All the others were snatched where there was none at all. Perhaps he's in a hurry. Though it's not because he feels we're closing in on him, I'm sure, because he must know that we're not.'

Austin turned his back on the SOCOs swarming around the Range Rover and entered Shand's building. He rode the lift up to the top floor where he knew Ian Jackson, the caretaker, was waiting for him with the spare keys to Shand's penthouse.

'I must ask you to stay outside, Mr Jackson,' Austin told him as he received the keys.

The caretaker was a thin man in his forties, with an unfashionable haircut, dressed in jeans, trainers and a blue shirt with the third button missing. 'If all you wanted was the keys,' he complained, 'then why did you have me stand around here for half an hour?'

'I did want to ask you a few questions,' Austin said. 'When did you last see Mr Shand?'

'Couple of days ago? In the morning, I think.'

'Was he alone?'

'Yes.'

'Does, erm, *did* Mr Shand have many visitors?'

'Not at all. He was a bit antisocial, if you ask me. Could barely bring himself to acknowledge people. Rich and grumpy, that one. Hardly went out, had his food delivered, looking down on the rest of the town from his penthouse.'

'Did you see anyone suspicious hanging around lately?'

Jackson scratched at a spot on his neck. 'Can't say I did. We have CCTV in the lobby and the lifts, it would show.'

'I'll need to see the footage of, let's say the last three days, for starters.'

'I can arrange that.'

Austin pulled on gloves and let himself in. He took three steps into the hall, then stopped, took out his mobile and called the SOCO team leader. 'We'll need complete forensics up here, top floor of the building. He's been in here.' While speaking he had taken a few more tentative steps forward so he could see into the large, bright reception room. 'Holy moly!' He terminated the call and called McLusky.

Only reluctantly had McLusky abandoned his lookout post at St Augustine's to inspect Shand's penthouse. Now he stood in the centre of the living room, hands buried deep in his pockets, with a look of disgust on his face. The room stank of alcohol. Everything he saw irritated him. The place had been trashed but, he noted, in a quiet way. Leather sofas and armchairs disembowelled and paintings slashed; table tops had been scored and scratched, plants decapitated, glass decanters of whisky, gin and vodka emptied on to the carpets. It was the kind of destruction

321

you could wreak without alerting the neighbours. On one wall, two-foot-high black spray-painted letters promised ONE LESS WANKER.

'The interesting one's through here,' Austin said.

Reluctantly the DI followed him into the kitchen. Before it had been messed up it had been an ultra-luxurious affair with a central island, six-burner gas cooker and every conceivable gadget. Now it had been not so much destroyed as vandalized. Across four doors of the kitchen units had been scrawled FUCK YOU MACLUSKY. The legend was surrounded by splashes of ketchup, sprayed from a squeezy bottle.

He looked at it dispassionately. 'He can't spell my name. You'd have thought he'd get that right at least. Lend me your mobile, Jane.'

'What's wrong with yours?'

'I'm using a crap plastic one that doesn't send pictures.'

Austin surrendered his iPhone and McLusky took a picture of the writing on the wall, then sent it to Phil Warren at the *Herald* with the caption 'Moron can't even spell. Killer of low intelligence. Print it, McLusky', then handed the mobile back.

Not long afterwards Austin's mobile rang. He answered it, listened, then said: 'I'm Detective Sergeant Austin, DI McLusky used my phone, it's genuine.' He put his mobile away. 'Warren checking.'

'How unexpectedly professional of her. It smells terrible in here.' In his car he had eaten

322

too much cheese and ham out of boredom and now felt nauseated by the smells of spilled bottle sauces, alcohol and emptied pickle jars. 'He's definitely branching out, he's not done this before.'

'Didn't have much chance with the others. Shand lived alone. But if he came up here he'll be caught on CCTV. I'll get on to it straight away.' Austin left to find the caretaker.

McLusky puffed up his cheeks and exhaled slowly, then shook his head. 'Waste of bloody time. He's not a moron at all.'

The caretaker's office was a windowless hole at the back of the ground-floor service area. The footage Austin checked with Jackson was in monochrome and made tedious viewing. They were limiting themselves to the last twenty-four hours but even speeded up it threatened to send Austin into a coma. People came, people went, singly, in couples. 'Resident,' Jackson commented each time. He put names to them. 'Visitors, seen them before,' he commented when an elderly couple rang a doorbell and were buzzed in. They were moving into night time. At exactly 10.30 pm a man appeared, wearing a hooded top, using keys to gain entry. Both Austin and Jackson reached out and tapped the screen. 'He's not a resident,' Jackson declared. They watched the grey figure enter; as it did, a gloved hand reached up and pulled the hood down even further.

'He knows there are cameras,' said Austin.

'They are quite obvious,' said Jackson.

The figure walked out of shot, his face having remained obscured. 'Where's he gone?'

'Not the lift. Must have used the stairs.'

'Can we see the footage?'

'There are no cameras on the stairs.'

'Marvellous.' Now I've really started talking like McLusky, Austin thought irritably. 'Why on earth not?'

'You've seen the age of the people who live here, no one uses the stairs. That's probably why.'

The figure re-emerged only twenty minutes later still wearing gloves. 'Must have worked like a demon.'

'Is it that bad up there?'

'Pretty trashed, though nothing structural. Just quiet malice.' Austin loaded the footage on to a USB stick and left. He was reluctant to call McLusky until he had something useful. He hoped the CCTV for Anchor Road would at last show how the killer spirited his victims away.

Austin had missed lunch. On the way back to Albany Road he stopped off at a minimart to buy a plastic box of sandwich triangles to prove he was not turning into McLusky. He had expected the CCTV footage to be on his desk but found nothing had been delivered. The CID room was empty. Somewhere in an office a phone rang and rang. 'Mary Celeste speaking, how can I help?' he said to the room. He ripped open the sandwich box and teased out the first triangle. Cheese and tomato. It drooped wetly as he eased one pointed end into his mouth. For the first time ever he noticed how the thin end of the wedge unpleasantly tickled the back of his mouth. He demolished the strangely insubstantial sandwich in sixty seconds, then picked up the receiver of his desk phone and called the CCTV suite.

'It'll be completely useless to you, we've looked at it, you can't see a thing. Someone took a pot shot at the camera with an air rifle. The camera is OK but it smashed the glass. It happens a lot, though usually they shoot out the street lights first.'

'Bit difficult on Anchor Road, too many. I don't suppose your camera caught an image of who shot it out?'

'Done from outside the frame, we think. We couldn't spot it, anyway.'

'When was it done?'

'20.59.'

'I want all the footage, from an hour before it was shot out until eleven,' Austin said and hung up. He eased another sandwich triangle out of the carton. It drooped unpleasantly in his hand and gaped open, revealing a pale tongue of industrial ham furred with butter. He opened his mouth wide to receive it, then changed his mind and stuffed the sandwich back into the box. Perhaps McLusky had a point after all.

In his car at his bus stop vigil near the statue of Neptune with his attendant bog-eyed fish, McLusky was staring at the special edition of the *Bristol Herald* – essentially a reprint of the lunchtime edition with a new front page – and blew smoke at the headline. NOW IT'S PERSONAL. The photograph took up nearly half the page; FUCK YOU MACLUSKY. Underneath he had been quoted almost word for word: 'The killer is obviously of low intelligence. The moron can't even spell my name.' The rest of the article was the usual filler, conjecture and rant against the useless police force, though Phil Warren's description of McLusky as 'last man standing' and 'all that stands between the city and a deranged killer' almost made him laugh.

But not quite. There was more to the queasy feeling in his stomach than his nutritional incompetence; it was the nagging feeling that not only was the investigation slipping away from him, but that perhaps this article had been one step too far. He was almost certain Denkhaus would not have authorized the release of the picture or at least argued against it. 'You're in charge, McLusky,' said McLusky quietly. He checked his mobile for perhaps the fiftieth time that day; it had charge and showed four out of five bars for signal strength. 'Call me, you bastard. I've called you an illiterate moron, surely you won't take that lying down. You and I know you're a clever little sod.'

It was getting late. Rush hour traffic was easing. The threat of rain had receded and been replaced with white clouds tinged with rose as the sun set over the harbour. Even the fountains looked less like a sewage works tonight. It was a fine evening; somewhere a man was being beaten to death, or perhaps electrocuted, while the man charged with finding his killer sat burping in a car full of rubbish, on the off chance the murderer might want to chat to him. McLusky called Austin on his plastic mobile. 'Why haven't you called me, what's with the CCTV?'

'I'm looking at it. It's useless.'

'You still working then? CCTV is always rubbish but why this time?'

'He's got his hood pulled down, obviously aware of the cameras. That's from the building. I just got the footage from the street. At 20.59 precisely someone shot out the camera with an air rifle. The glass shattered and through the shards you can see one tiny corner of the street and nothing appears in it. Nothing. The camera was working but you can't see a thing. And I've looked at the footage from before twenty times now, I can't see where the shooter was, it's just not there or I'm too stupid to see it. Shand was snatched between 20.59 and 22.30 because that's when our man enters the building with his key.'

McLusky sat straighter behind the wheel. 'Interesting.'

'Is it?'

'Our killer takes his time over killing his victims. If he's got Shand in his van he's not going to leave him in there while he trashes his flat. Even gagged and tied up a man can make noise. All it takes is someone walking past the van and hearing it. No, he drove him to his killing ground, then came back to trash the flat. That means it can't be that far away. Nine o'clock he knocks out the camera. Even if Shand turned up a minute later he only has an hour and a half to snatch him, drive him to his place and come back to Anchor Road. Half an hour's drive away at the most.'

'Roads are pretty clear around that time, that's still one hell of a radius.'

327

'Yes, yes, yes. Tomorrow you can go over all the CCTV in the entire area, follow every bloody van you see. Go home, Jane.'

'Yes, sir, thank you, sir. You still parked up next to Neptune?'

McLusky started the engine. 'Just packing it in.'

Anger, frustration, queasy stomach, neck and back ache, stress and niggling worries; Dr McLusky prescribed the same medication for all his symptoms, a night at the Barge Inn opposite his flat. Not even bothering to go home first, he parked the car and went straight inside. Behind the bar, Paul, the pub's bald landlord, had come to recognize McLusky's moods and knew the inspector had not come for pint, a pie and a chat. He nodded at him while pulling a pint of Guinness, took his money while it settled and wordlessly handed him his pint. Then he started pouring the next one, which he knew McLusky would come for within the next five minutes.

McLusky woke reluctantly and swatted at the hand that was shaking his shoulder. He had fallen asleep with his seventh pint untouched on the table in front of him. He had slumped into the corner of the bench seat gently snoring for the last hour. The pub was empty. The landlord went to collect beer mats and glasses from the last tables. 'You don't have to go home but you can't stay here, Inspector.'

McLusky passed a hand over his face, sat up straight and picked up his untouched pint, then set it down again as though it were too heavy for him. He got to his feet, picked up the glass once more and carried it to the bar, then made for the door. Paul called after him: 'Thanks Liam, good night.'

McLusky managed a grunt and pushed through the door into the dimly lit street. Behind him he heard the landlord bolt the double doors and a moment later the pub lights went out, leaving McLusky in an unusually dark Northampton Street. He looked up and saw that the street light in front of his house was not working. He crossed the street, still feeling asleep and probably drunk. The pavement was cluttered with recycling boxes and black bags of rubbish. He was crabbing towards his front door beside the entrance to Rossi's between two nests of bin bags when a shadow on his right exploded with movement. He reacted too slowly to ward off the blow; the wine bottle caught him across the back of the head and he felt his legs go under him. He landed face down in his neighbour's rubbish. The dark figure was on him in an instant, driving a heavy knee into his kidney area and grabbing his hair from behind with a gloved hand, pushing his face into the rubbish. 'Don't fucking move,' hissed a voice. 'I have a gun.' Cold metal was pressed hard against his cheek, McLusky heard it rasp against his stubble. 'I should do you right here, you annoying shit.' The hand pressed more heavily on the back of his head. McLusky fought hard not to throw up. The back of his head was whirring with pain and he felt as though he was falling, spinning through the air into darkness. He had the smell of rotting garbage in his nostrils and a high-pitched electronic screech in his ears that came from somewhere deep in his brain. 'I don't care how you fucking spell your name, unless it's on your gravestone. But you're not on my list, you know, and I cannot even be bothered. I've just come to tell you to shut up and stop insulting me or I'll simply put a bullet through you. Don't know what's keeping me, really. But I won't even waste a bullet on scum like you.' The gun was removed and he spat on McLusky's neck. Then the man pushed himself upright and kicked him in the ribs.

McLusky heard his rapid footsteps retreating. Moments later a small scooter engine started up, its prattling sound dwindling into the night. He vomited, just managing to push himself up high enough so as not to drown in the streams of dark liquid issuing uncontrollably from his mouth. Breathing was difficult. The world was still spinning but he crawled forward, across the vomit-streaked rubbish bags to his front door. He was still on his knees when he unlocked the door and pushed it open. Not until he reached the bottom of the stairs did he pull himself up, his head tilted down to the left. Nothing mattered, not the pain, not the nausea, not the breathing nor his shaking; only one thing mattered: the precious drops of his assailant's spittle on the side of his face, slowly dribbling down his neck now. He fell through his front door and groped along the wall to the bathroom. He grabbed several cotton buds from a plastic tub on the shelf and wiped them carefully through the area where he had felt the saliva land. Not having an evidence bag in the house he managed to get to the kitchen and stuff the cotton buds into a freezer bag and seal it. With the killer's DNA sitting in the fridge between the Cheddar cheese and the low fat margarine McLusky stepped under the shower, still half dressed, and while blood and vomit sluiced off him waited for the world to stop spinning around him.

Three hours later McLusky was still bleeding from the wound at the back of his head; reaching up to dab more kitchen roll against it made the ribs on his right side sing out in pain. He changed over to his left hand, which was barely an improvement. Having only one small shaving mirror in the house he had no clear idea of what the wound looked like, all he had to go by was the ragged imprint of blood on the wad of tissue. *Head wound.* It was an ominous expression. Breathing was painful and if past experience of injured ribs was anything to go by would become more difficult as inflammation set in. It took half an hour to sip the mug of sweet tea. *Head wound.* A stream of muttered obscenities helped him get dressed – bending down to tie his laces proved the most difficult – and dismissing the possibility of alcohol residue in his blood stream he drove himself to the A & E department at the Royal Infirmary, at this time of night only a five-minute journey.

He was surprised at how seriously his injuries were being taken. It was not long before he was being wheeled about, pushed in and out of cubicles, seen by nurses, then a doctor, had both his head and chest X-rayed and countless questions fired at him by a second doctor. A light was shone

331

into his eyes, he was invited to follow fingers and quizzed about his pains. His head wound was declared superficial, cleaned and dressed. The X-rays showed hairline cracks on three ribs.

'Bed rest. Three or four days.'

The doctor, wide awake, impossibly clean and coolly professional, looked too young to McLusky or perhaps it was just that he felt old and decrepit this morning. 'That's unlikely to happen,' McLusky told him.

'Please be sensible about this. Certainly if the headache persists. How does it feel now?'

'Much better already,' McLusky lied.

The doctor shook his head, not believing it. 'There is no point in playing the hero, if you're concussed and don't take it seriously the consequences of that could be disastrous. Is there anyone at home to look after you?'

McLusky had already learnt not to shake his head since it sent waves of nausea and pain through him. 'I'll be fine.'

'And you really should report this to the police. Do you know the person who did this to you?'

'First time we met.' He got painfully, geriatrically to his feet. 'But I'll make an effort to get to know him better.'

He left the hospital carrying a paper bag of painkillers and anti-inflammatory medication, unappreciative of dawn's rosy fingers in the sky. While he drove home he still imagined himself going to work after some kind of breakfast but once in his flat and stretched out on his sofa with his duvet on top of him the fight went out of him. Sleep, however, seemed an impossibility.

He had taken anti-inflammatories, set an uninviting pint glass of water beside him on the coffee table and dozed, chasing fruitless thoughts, calling himself names yet feeling strangely flat and unemotional. Even the effort of hating the killer seemed too much. Perhaps this was what depression felt like, flat, grey, tiring and pointless, he thought, and fell asleep.

He woke from uncomfortable dreams to the chime of his pink plastic mobile. He checked the time. It was 10.30.

'Where are you, Liam?' he heard Austin say. 'Denkhaus is back and wants a word.'

McLusky made a wrong move and his ribs complained noisily. His head felt much clearer though his exploded scalp still burnt. 'I don't think I'll make it into work for a while yet.' He gave Austin a heavily edited version of what had happened to him. 'I need you to come here and pick up his DNA. First make my excuses to the super. You can tell him about the possible DNA to keep him sweet.'

'Nothing will sweeten him, he looks like he vomited out his soul. A few others are back too, they all look haggard. I'll be round in a minute.'

Half an hour later Austin made his way past a recycling gang who were emptying containers full of glass into their wagon in ear-splitting cascades. After having rung McLusky's bell he had what felt like several minutes to peruse the display of vegetables outside Rossi's. He had discussed buying more food from independent shops with Eve but there were none within miles of his house and somehow it never happened.

McLusky had chosen this place wisely, and with a pub just across the street. At last the door release buzzed for an ungenerous split second and he was in.

By the time he reached the flat McLusky was once more sitting in a corner of his sofa where he had been sipping tea and nibbling toast. The place smelled charred. 'I burnt the first round,' he explained.

'Is that a hole in your head?' Austin asked. The dressing at the back of the inspector's head looked ominously large.

'All glued together again and I don't think I'm concussed. I'm tired but fine. He kicked me in the ribs, that's my main problem.'

'And he spat at you?'

'It was a gift. It's in the fridge in a sterile freezer bag. Let's hope he's known to us.'

'What about the bottle he hit you with?'

'He was wearing gloves, I could see it in the corner of my eye. Probably motorcycle gloves. After he ran off I heard a scooter drive off.'

'So he has a scooter as well as a van.'

McLusky pulled a face. 'Arrest every scooter rider in the city and check their DNA and bingo.'

'I have the feeling you're not serious.'

'Can't be done.'

'I'll get the sample off to the lab stat, the super has told them to drop all else.'

Austin retrieved the small zip-up freezer bag from McLusky's fridge and drove back to Albany Road where he handed it to a courier. While he had been out DS Sorbie had made an appearance, looking even more surly than usual.

'Is it true McLusky has been injured?' Sorbie asked. *Nothing trivial, I hope*, he wanted to add but stopped himself in time.

DI Fairfield too had returned to work. Austin went to see her with a preliminary forensic report on Ethan Gray's camper van. He did not mention that it had been sent to McLusky as the arresting officer. Fairfield scanned the first paragraph. 'Eeeyuck!'

'Quite, ma'am. He had two cameras installed which he used to record women who he had conned into giving him their tights. Quite a few of them were mad enough to get into the van to take them off in private. Or what they thought was more private. He also lent the van to fellow female students on digs if it was raining heavily while he himself slept in a tent. Everyone thought he was extremely chivalrous.'

'The disgusting little letch.'

'Must have been at it for years, he had a huge collection of women's underwear in two suitcases under his bed.'

'It was you who collared him, I'm told.'

'He ran straight into my loving arms.'

'Well done. Now, if you don't mind . . .'

Austin didn't mind at all. The possibility that they might identify the killer had injected a huge dose of adrenalin into the entire team. For the first time he felt they were getting closer to him. Not half an hour later the phone rang on his desk: Neil Shand's body had been found.

Twenty

'They must have thought he was just sleeping,' said PC Hanham who had been guarding the site. He stole a sideways glance at McLusky who looked pale and had a crumpled dressing on the back of his head where some of his hair had been shaved off. He thought that if it were him he'd have taken a week off but it was well known that McLusky was the obsessive type.

'Sleeping?' McLusky scoffed. 'I haven't seen a deader corpse for a long time.'

'Well, he was sitting up.' Hanham argued.

'It's called rigor bloody mortis, you'd have thought the public would know the difference!' But McLusky thought he knew exactly why it had taken so long for anyone to notice that the man sitting in the corner of the bus stop was in fact a corpse. Shand looked filthy, wrapped in some kind of sacking and death had given his face the peevish expression of an elderly drunk. The body looked like a tramp asleep and no one wanted to be bothered with a tramp, not while you were waiting for a bus and could not walk away. Coulthart had only just arrived and got ready to examine the body but had to wait until the screens had been set up, which had necessitated traffic police closing one lane of the busy Rownham Hill.

'That's the second bod that looked like a

336

homeless man,' said the pathologist as he came to a halt next to McLusky. 'And you're not looking too healthy again, if you don't mind me saying so. If you were a patient of mine I would definitely prescribe rest, plenty of fresh fruit and vegetables and other things besides.' Since there were junior ranks within earshot Coulthart refrained from mentioning that he would also recommend abstaining from alcohol and nicotine.

'Would you really? Most of your patients are dead, surely.'

After a rectal reading and cursory examination, Coulthart calculated that Shand had been killed in the early hours. 'Can't say what killed him yet. But as long as it is the same killer I expect you are not all that interested.'

'Not unless it's dramatically different. The killer owns a gun. He has not used it yet so I remain to be convinced that it's real. Real guns are still hard to come by unless you have criminal connections and our man is no criminal.'

'You make nice distinctions.'

'Something a scientist like you should appreciate.'

'Oh, I do, I do. I'll inform your office of the time of the PM.'

SOCOs were now swarming all over the place, there was a fingertip search in progress all along this side of the road and Denkhaus had just turned up and added his Range Rover to the long line of police vehicles.

Denkhaus entered the tent that now enclosed the entire bus stop. He looked fully recovered from his food poisoning and sounded it. But he looked exasperated and after a short exchange with Coulthart nodded his head towards the exit. 'A word, DI McLusky.'

Outside they strolled away from the tent and the uniforms towards the DSI's car. 'I'm glad to see you've fully recovered, sir,' offered McLusky.

'Yes, yes, yes. How's your head?'

'Fine, sir.'

'You were extremely lucky. He's obviously highly unstable and could have killed you.'

Walking and talking required too much breathing for McLusky so he stopped walking. 'Could have. Didn't.'

'Are you OK?'

'It's just my ribs. Shallow breathing is best.'

'This attack on you was exactly what I feared might happen. I wish you had found somewhere else to stay for the duration of the investigation. I blame myself, I should have insisted on it.'

'It was my decision. I'm alive. And we may have a good DNA sample. If we do then it was worth it.'

'It's generous of you to say so. There will be compensation, of course. And the moment our man's in custody I want you to take some leave.'

'Thank you, sir.' McLusky was impatient to get back to the deposition site.

'We'll have to find you some accommodation before tonight.'

'Leave it to me,' McLusky said. 'I have something in mind.'

'As long as you're sure. I'll leave it with you then. The ACC was very pleased you apprehended the sexual deviant who stole his wife's underwear. Good job.'

'We only picked him up, it was Kat Fairfield's work.'

'Yes, yes, yes. But it's your name he'll remember, and for the right reasons for once. I can see you're impatient to get back to work. Carry on.'

McLusky lit a cigarette and walked back to the tent, smoking carefully, mindful of his cracked ribs. He could not afford to cough.

Four hours later he found himself in the observation area of the autopsy suite at Flax Broughton, wearing not one but two nicotine patches. A coughing fit in his car on the way back from the deposition site had convinced him that it was time to stop smoking while his ribs healed. And who knew? Perhaps he would give up for good.

Neil Shand's corpse, now naked on the examination table, had retained its peevish facial expression. 'I think our killer is having a bit of fun here,' Coulthart said when McLusky mentioned it. 'I think he initially tied his jaw shut so it might set like that and he'd look more convincingly like a rough sleeper.'

'Exquisite sense of humour. But again he has gone to great lengths and risked a lot, too, by displaying Shand like that. He wanted him to look like a rough sleeper. We are looking into all Shand's affairs, especially anyone he may have evicted.'

'There must be hundreds,' Coulthart said.

'Yes, slightly fewer though that are van drivers and scooter riders.'

339

'Does he ride a scooter?'

'I believe he does, when he is not using his van. Rode off in one after he clouted me over the head, I think.'

'You look better than this morning, I must say. Let us proceed, then.'

Shand had been overweight by about five stone and his white midriff reminded McLusky of a bloated, dead dolphin he had once seen washed up on a beach in Devon. How Coulthart lived with the smell of people's insides every day he could not understand. As the pathologist made the initial incision he thought he could smell it even through the glass.

'Cause of death?' he asked.

Coulthart smiled; he had waited for the inspector to show a flicker of interest. 'What's it to you?' He flashed him a look over his glasses and turned to his young yet practically bald assistant. 'Daniel, would you put the X-rays up for the inspector?' A large monitor flicked on and a couple of chest X-rays, one frontal, the other side on, glowed blue and grey. 'Can you make that out? Every one of his ribs is broken.'

McLusky breathed in more deeply and his side ached and burned. 'It looks a mess.'

'Yes. Complete smashed-in ribcage, both lungs punctured in several places. I think we can safely say that he was trampled to death. From the looks of it he did not just kick him, he jumped around on him. The victim died of a heart attack soon after that.'

McLusky had come closer and closer to the glass, now he rested his forehead on it; behind

the reality of Coulthart's systematic disembowel-
ling of the corpse he saw images of a demonic
fairy-tale creature jumping about on Neil Shand's
chest. He felt the burning of his own chest inten-
sify and felt a similar sensation on his left, where
the mobile reserved for the demonic killer waited
silently in his jacket.

McLusky had tried Laura's number several
times during the day but not found the composure
to leave a message. He tried again at the end of
the day in his office, staring at an unopened packet
of Extra Lights on his desk. A split second before
he decided to give up, Laura answered.

'I was so busy all day,' she explained, 'and
hadn't even noticed the phone wasn't in my bag.
Anyway, it's only the second time you've called
me since I gave you my number. Want to arrest
another of my friends, is that it?'

'Laura, Ethan Gray was a . . .'

'I know, I know, just teasing. I'm glad you got
rid of the creep. I was more shocked by what a
bad judge of character I am. So, are you just
calling to gloat a bit?'

'I have a favour to ask.'

'Well, it seems I owe you one.'

'I need somewhere to stay.' He heard Laura
draw breath and quickly added: 'Just for a few
days. The killer we are hunting, he knows where
I live. Attacked me last night outside my place.'

'Jesus! Are you OK? Attacked how?'

McLusky gave a quick, sanitized account of
the ordeal. 'I'm improving rapidly. My head's
fine, it's my ribs that bother me most.'

'Of course you can stay here, Liam. Just pack

some things and come up. Sounds like you need looking after.'

Having thrown a few essentials like underwear, toothbrush and mobile chargers into a small holdall, he drove to Laura's house by a nonsensical, circuitous route, eyeing all scooter riders with suspicion and keeping a careful watch on his rear-view mirrors. When he found a large enough parking space and shoehorned his car into it he felt sure he had not been followed. As he arrived at the front door a girl opened it and nosed a bicycle past him, allowing him to enter the house unchallenged. She just raised one eyebrow, presumably as a kind of greeting.

'You don't even know me yet you just let me into the house,' he complained.

She gave him a sarcastic look. 'We've met, I'm Val and you're Laura's friend Liam. You arrested that weirdo Ethan. So you're welcome.' She swung into the saddle and pedalled away.

'Another satisfied customer,' McLusky muttered and went inside.

McLusky spent the evening talking. He talked to Laura at the kitchen table, he chatted to her housemates who came and went, he talked while they ate their enormous Chinese take-away and talked through the better part of two bottles of wine. It seemed to him that he had not enjoyed a normal conversation for months and if it had not been for the stiffness of his neck and shoulder and the burning of his rib cage he would have said he felt almost fine, nearly normal.

'Everything OK, Liam?' Laura asked.

He realized he had looked at her during a long

pause in the conversation. 'Yes. Very OK. I've just noticed something. I've just noticed I was enjoying myself. For the first time in bloody ages.'

'Well, good.'

'And we managed not to drag up any crap from our past, which makes a change.'

'I noticed that too. Are we about to spoil it all?' McLusky drained his glass. 'Try not to.'

'Good.' She stood up with a smile and her eyebrows at maximum elevation. 'Unfortunately Ethan's room has already been let again, so I'll make you up a bed in the sitting room. The sofa is huge and quite comfortable, apparently.'

Pauline Leslie hated her garden. It was large. It was full of features. It had everything she ever wanted, which was precisely the problem. She had always known it but her infuriating brother-in-law Michael had found it necessary to point it out: too much money and no taste. The house was the same, she had often suspected it. She would find things she liked the look of in magazines, then track them down and buy them for the house. They always looked out of place. Nothing fitted. She had no coherent vision. Sometimes she wished she could buy someone else's house with the garden finished and the house furnished and full of history, their history, not her own, God forbid. Pauline sipped at her vodka and coke as she toured her garden. This gazebo? No one ever went near it since from inside it all you could see was the house. She had loved the house when they bought it, now it

343

looked drab to her, too modern. It wasn't modern, of course, it was merely quite new. It would never mellow, never grow old gracefully. And this island bed? She had seen it in a magazine and told the gardener she wanted one like it. She had drawn the shape of it on a piece of paper for him. Today, the shape of the island bed made her sick; it was a stupid shape, it looked infantile and she had no one to blame but herself. Pampas grass, what had she been thinking? Rick always called it Pampers grass and of course he was right, it looked like shit in her garden. The naked girl with the jug that used to spout water had been Rick's idea; she knew it was tasteless tat but she hated it far less than her own attempts at being sophisticated. She sipped at her drink. This really needed another shot of vodka in it. Now that Michael had gone and stopped telling her that she was wasting her life with too much money and not enough God she thought she probably hated the bible-bashing twit less than she hated herself.

An engine noise approached the house, yes, definitely coming up the drive. Not Richard, she was not expecting him back until late afternoon. Not an expensive engine sound either. Sounded more like a delivery. She fervently hoped it was not the police again, she had seen enough of police officers to last her for the rest of her life. She could hear no doorbell; perhaps they would just go away and leave her in peace. But it didn't seem likely. Someone was calling.

'Mrs Leslie?'

'I'm in the garden.' She took another sip from

344

her far-too-weak drink and walked towards the house.

He was already there, just standing on her stone-flagged path with his silver gun and his sack and a carpenter's belt as though he had come to fix something. She did not recognize him at first but then it came to her: it was the delivery man from Dauphin's, the deli people. There was fear raging in her insides and a million thoughts whirred through her brain but her voice sounded calm. 'What do you want? You promised. You made a pact with Michael. You promised my brother-in-law not to harm my husband.'

The man advanced on her, the gun levelled at her head. 'Don't worry about your husband, Mrs Leslie, he is quite safe. It is you I have come for.'

McLusky could barely focus on the broken glass on the stone-flagged path and appeared not to hear what Dearlove was telling him, so the DC said it again. 'If it really is the last victim, like the graffiti in the house says, then perhaps we'll get a bit of breathing space.'

The sun had risen at last. McLusky looked up at the thin-haired DC. 'On the contrary, we might be completely buggered.'

Undaunted by the inspector's mood Dearlove said: 'We've got footprints now.'

'Yes and we have his DNA, too, probably enough to get a conviction. Have to find him before you can convict him, Deedee, and if he kills Pauline Leslie and then moves to Bangor to retire we might never find him.'

'Have they not analyzed his DNA sample yet?'

McLusky looked across at Austin who was standing on the veranda talking into a mobile and waving his free hand around. 'Austin is just giving them hell about it.' McLusky watched Austin stop gesticulating, the phone still pressed against his ear. 'Any second now, Deedee.'

Dearlove, too, looked across at the DS who was now listening motionlessly. Austin's shoulders slumped; he put away his mobile, scratched the tip of his nose and looked up at McLusky. He made his way past the SOCOs who were about to pack up and shook his head when McLusky raised questioning eyebrows. 'Not on file. IC1 male, but we sort of knew that. They're still working on it, might be able to tell us his eye colour eventually.'

'Marvellous. Naturally we are all happily convinced that it is our killer who abducted Mrs Leslie?'

Austin frowned at him. 'Aren't you?'

'I'm just saying that Mr Leslie has no alibi and has had plenty of time to bury her under a rose bush and conveniently blame it on the man who abducted his brother.'

Dearlove looked devastated. 'Are you serious, sir?'

'No. But I am suggesting that you'll never make inspector unless you stop taking things for granted. Or make DS, for that matter. And why has that broken glass not been bagged up yet? His bloody fingerprints could be on it for all you know.'

McLusky left them standing either side of the

smashed drinks glass on the path and went inside the house to take a last look at the legend spray-painted on to the carpet in the Leslies' sitting room: END OF THE LIST.

'Where is Mr Leslie?' he asked a PC standing guard in the hall.

'Sitting in his Jaguar on the drive.'

'Not about to drive off, is he?'

'Don't think so, sir. Just keeping out of the way. Been sitting there for ages.'

McLusky walked up to the car but if Richard Leslie noticed him he gave no sign of it. He tried the passenger door and, finding it unlocked, swung himself into the seat beside the grieving husband. Leslie gave him the briefest of sideways looks then returned to staring through the windscreen at the house. McLusky felt in dire need of a cigarette to occupy his hands. Instead he folded them in his lap and let his head sink back against the headrest. He knew he was tired enough to sleep, his whole body told him so but his mind was sharp and busy. 'We are naturally doing all we can to find your wife.'

Richard Leslie cleared his throat before answering. 'You didn't find the others until it was too late. What makes you think you can find Pauline?'

'I won't lie to you . . .'

'That's big of you,' Leslie interrupted. 'Don't even talk to me. Get out there and find her. Find *her*, not her body. Whatever you do, don't bring me her dead body.' There was a long pause. 'He had promised, Mike said he had promised. I suppose it's his little joke.'

347

'He wants to hurt you without breaking his promise.'

'But who? We've been through them all, every employee we've ever had, everyone who ever got fired, and there weren't that many, you looked at all of them.' Another long pause. 'Just go and do something. I can't bear you sitting here.'

McLusky got out and walked to his car while calling Austin on his plastic mobile. 'Find me at the bus stop.'

This time McLusky did not even detour to buy provisions. He did a half circuit of St Augustine's parade, waited for a bus to leave the bus stop and parked up. Once he had called the CCTV hub to let them know he was back in place near the statue of Neptune he turned the pink mobile off and took out the other phone. It was charged and showed three bars. McLusky stared at it. The end of the list. Perhaps Pauline Leslie really had been his last victim and the killer had no need to call him again. Perhaps he had run out of stolen mobiles. Or left the city. It could all be over already.

But McLusky shook off his doubts. It couldn't be over. This kind of killing had no end. The list was never at an end because there would be another list. Those who killed out of some kind of grievance or for some other murderous greed always carried on. It was addictive and just like drugs the effect wore off quickly. Nothing was achieved by the killings, the grievance remained, the need to feed the rage that burned inside them with another death returned. They were either caught or committed suicide or their mental state

348

deteriorated even further and took them far down other dark roads where no one followed.

Should have bought some food and drink. He checked his watch. For nearly three hours he had sat here now, staring at the mobile, staring out at the traffic. He shifted in his seat, winced at the flare-up of pain in his side but he noted that it was less fierce, less biting. Carefully he reached across to the glove box and let it fall open; somewhere in there had to be his emergency stash of cigarettes. Impatiently he pawed the content of the glove box into the passenger footwell: tapes, sweet wrappers, maps and crumpled bits of paper until he found the packet of Extra Lights with two emergency cigarettes. He put one gratefully to his lips and slid the packet into his jacket pocket. On top of the dashboard his phone rang and vibrated. He scrabbled frantically for it, spat his unlit cigarette at the steering wheel.

'McLusky.'

Three Harley Davidson bikes roared past so that he could barely make out the words. 'I am not sure why the fuck I'm still talking to you.'

McLusky's eyes swept across the scene outside. It was mid-morning, there were many people, too many people. 'Because you want to explain why you killed Pauline Leslie?'

'I could, but I won't. She's still alive, you see? I'm just off to pay her a final visit.' McLusky heard the growl of the motorcycles through the phone as they drove past the speaker. He could see them on the other side of the parade near the Hippodrome. And there stood a man by a scooter.

McLusky started the engine. 'Surely you will

want to tell me afterwards, if your list is now empty.' There was a tap on the passenger window and Austin's grinning face appeared. He was urgently waving a piece of paper at him. McLusky, tempted to drive off without him, cursed.

'Don't swear at me,' said the voice.

Austin, noticing which phone the inspector was using swung himself quietly into the passenger seat and even before he managed to close the door McLusky drove off. With no hand free to point and no eyes free to watch the distant figure McLusky barged though the traffic like a drunk in a dodgem car but soon ran into a wall of traffic waiting at a red light. Without a blue beacon, which would have alerted his quarry, he had to wait but now managed to point across the central island at the distant figure, already climbing on to his scooter.

'I wasn't swearing at you.'

'Better not be. Perhaps I should have killed you when I had the chance. If I ever start a new list, McLusky, I'll put you at the top, shithead.' The line went dead.

The lights changed and for a moment they lost sight of the scooter. McLusky simply dropped the mobile on to the floor. Austin snapped back in his seat and steadied himself as McLusky accelerated into a gap between two cars that had all but disappeared by the time they got there. McLusky worked his horn. The sudden braking threw Austin forward. 'We have a DNA match after all,' he managed to get out.

'How come?' McLusky's voice sounded as calm as though he were concentrating on a pinball

350

game and only mildly interested in what was being said while he bullied his way through the traffic.

'A girl was assaulted round here while you were on leave. We took about a hundred DNA samples from men who work in the area. His DNA was scheduled to be destroyed today but some bright spark double-checked first. Is that him over there? White helmet, grey scooter?'

'Damn, he's getting away through the lanes.'

Austin called in on his airwave radio. 'Alpha 12, can I come in, please?' He rattled off the description and their heading. 'Armed murder suspect. Divert TFU from *Dauphin* premises in St Augustine's to the pursuit.' To McLusky he said: 'His name's Terry Manson, he works as a delivery driver for the deli people. Tactical Firearms were on their way there.'

'Then I bet I know what he looks like.'

'Me too, could be the very guy who delivered at the Steadman house when we were there to question the husband. Where's he gone?'

'Can't see him. Which way did the bastard go, left or right?'

'He's just disappeared.'

'I'll go left.' McLusky overtook two cars, forcing an oncoming van to mount the pavement. 'He said he was on his way to see Pauline Leslie.'

'Do you have a beacon?'

'I don't want to alert him. He told me the woman is still alive. If he knows we're behind him he may not go there. Even if we manage to pull him he could simply refuse to talk and let her die wherever he has her stashed.'

351

'I ran Manson through the computer, he has no previous but his father has. Done for shoplifting in a supermarket. And guess who owns the supermarket?'

'Richard Leslie. Looks like it has to do with his dad, then. Still alive?'

'Died of pneumonia. At his home.'

'Did you check?'

'Neil Shand was the landlord.'

'There he is!' McLusky tapped the windscreen. Manson was riding along at normal speed, five cars ahead. He puffed up his cheeks and let out a long breath of relief. 'Thought we'd lost him.'

Austin gave their position and heading to control. In Hotwells, Manson crossed the river into Ashton Gate and proceeded north. They had been driving for nearly twenty minutes. Traffic was much lighter on this side of the river. 'If your guess about the radius is correct he must have his base within ten or fifteen minutes from here.'

McLusky was skilled at pursuit yet the size and blackness of his car did not lend itself to stealth. 'Just as well he's a typical scooter rider, no glass in his rear-view mirror and I've not seen him check behind once.'

'Things on his mind,' Austin suggested.

'I have things on my mind but I know exactly what's behind me,' growled McLusky. 'He's killing those he holds responsible for his father's death, I suspect. Pneumonia? I expect electricity comes into it, that's why he killed the Steadman woman they way he did, she had plenty of fluid in her lungs.'

352

'And a radiator round her ankles. Makes sense. And Lamb with his cuts in services and we're-all-in-this-together speech was just asking to be on Manson's list.'

'Yes. But when he promised not to hurt Richard Leslie he needed another way to get back at him.' They had passed the suburb of Leigh Woods, now going at a steady 40 mph when Manson slowed down. 'Shit, he's turning off here.' In front of them Manson curved off the road and into a narrow lane. Looking lazily over his shoulder he saw the black Mercedes approaching. He immediately accelerated hard up the lane while McLusky had to wait for three cars to pass before he could follow. 'He's clocked us, Liam.' Austin was giving their position over the radio and McLusky reached under his seat and set the blue beacon on his roof. He left the window open and air and noise rushed into the car as the five-litre engine responded to his flooring the accelerator. Almost immediately they came to a fork in the narrow one-lane track. McLusky brought the car to a stop and turned off the engine, then stuck his head out of the window. He could hear the prattling of the scooter being driven at high speed down the left fork. With engine restarted the Mercedes surged down the lane, which the car almost filled from side to side. Austin cringed deep into his seat, casting a glance at the speedometer; if anything came the other way at the same speed the collision would happen at a hundred mph. A house flew past, a Porsche parked in front. Fields to either side now, hedgerows, trees, a high fence

353

on the right, a 'For Sale' sign, more trees. Ahead the lane rose.

'That leads to the back of Abbots Leigh, I think,' Austin said.

McLusky slowed then stopped altogether, turned off the engine and listened once more. 'Nothing, he's turned off somewhere. The "For Sale" sign, what was that?' He did not look for a turning space but reversed at speed down the lane. It widened when they came to the high wooden fence and gate with the printed sale sign on top.

'What is that?' McLusky asked.

'I think it's an old timber yard or saw mill,' said Austin.

Both stepped out of the car and stood in the silence, the ticking of the cooling engine and a distant woodpecker the only sounds. Neither of them closed their doors. McLusky approached the tall wooden gate. Nothing could be seen, both fence and gate being eight foot tall. The gate consisted of two leaves meeting in the centre where they were joined through fist-sized holes with a thick dull metal chain. McLusky put his eye to one of the holes.

Austin had been right; on the other side lay a small timber yard, with long, low sheds covered in corrugated iron to the right and structures for timber storage on the left. A grimy van stood on the right, only just within his field of vision. 'He is here,' he said, looking up for a way in.

'He's got a gun, Liam,' Austin warned. McLusky ignored him, reaching up to test one of the planks in the fence. 'He's killed four times and nearly

354

killed you,' Austin continued. 'We should wait for the TFU.'

McLusky grunted and turned back to the car. 'You're right, of course.'

Back in the car Austin gave their position to the radio, then said. 'ETA fifteen minutes.'

'Yeah, right,' said McLusky. He started the engine, reversed a few yards, then threw the car into forward gear, floored the accelerator and drove straight at the fence. He was still accelerating as the Mercedes smashed through the wooden boards and only braked when they were far inside the yard.

There was complete silence as they stood in the soft evening light on either side of the car. The place was shaded by several tall trees, their branches overhanging the low, dilapidated sheds. McLusky shared all of Austin's misgivings but he could not bring himself to sit this out and let the Tactical Firearms Unit shoot the place up. Manson's scooter was there, his helmet on the ground beside it. While the first three sheds were all open-fronted the last one had a wooden door flanked by two grimy sash windows. There was no point in tip-toeing around. 'Manson!' The shout fell dead without echo in the yard and the deep breath needed for it had sent searing pain through his side. 'I've come for you!' he called and made straight for the door.

It opened on a dim, cavernous shed. Near the front stood a counter and a desk, covered in yellowing papers and dust. Another set of grimy windows and an open doorway gave on to the rest of it; beyond it in the dim light McLusky saw workbenches, machinery, ankle-high drifts of sawdust, off-cuts of every type of wood, stacks of timbers. Half-way down against the wall on the right stood a large old-fashioned fridge covered in scratches; a chain and padlock secured the door; next to it hung an open fuse box where Manson had accessed electricity; red and blue cables snaked away from it into the even darker back of the shed where he could just make out a crudely made wooden chair. It was rust red with the dried blood of Manson's victims.

'Watch my back, Jane.' McLusky stepped through the doorway. His headache had returned and his ribcage ached from driving and shouting. His stomach churned acidly and his skin pricked with sweat. He took a few steps inside the gloom and stopped. The place smelled confused; strongest was wood and resin but there was also a fungal smell and a hint of urine. Somewhere in this chaos was Pauline Leslie, dead or alive, and Manson was in here too, he could sense it. He spoke quietly. 'Might as well come out, Manson. I'm here, now, it's over.'

There was a long pause before the figure of Terry Manson slid into view from behind a large slant of oak planks. His silver semi-automatic was glinting as he held it steady, levelled at McLusky's chest. 'It's never over until I say it's over,' he said mildly. 'It's nearly done, though.'

'You sound disappointed.'

'Just tired, I guess. I came to Bristol to avenge myself on the bastards who let my father die without food or heat in a flat with nothing but a blow heater he could not afford to run. But if

356

you know my name you'll know that. And now at the end of it I just feel very tired of it. I don't even think killing them will give me any rest. I need rest. And I'm tired of you, too.'

'I'm doing my job. You understand that. I have come to arrest you.'

Manson waggled the gun as though to draw his attention to it. 'I'm the one with the gun, shithead.' Even the insult was delivered in a tired, conversational voice as though all the anger had drained from him.

McLusky took a couple of steps towards him. 'I don't think that's a real gun, otherwise you'd have used it. On me, or on them.' He stopped ten feet away from Manson when he saw him tense his hand around the weapon.

'The gun is real. But guns are vulgar and quick and sterile. They don't do much for your anger.'

'You're not angry at all,' said McLusky. 'You are just full of guilt for not having been there for your father when it happened.'

Manson exploded at him. 'You spiteful lying wanker!' He took two steps forward and his gun hand wavered as if undecided what part of McLusky's anatomy to discharge the weapon into. 'I was working on a cruise ship thousands of miles away. I am not responsible, *they* were. Now get back, and you there!' he shouted towards Austin who was waiting in the doorway. 'You too, get out!'

'Prove to me the gun is real and we'll do as you say,' McLusky said calmly.

At that moment the bulky shadows of two firearms officers in their bullet-proofs appeared at

357

the windows behind Austin. 'Backup is here, Liam,' said Austin urgently.

Manson seemed to deflate a little, his shoulders sagging, his eyes wandering away from McLusky's face towards his left. 'The gun is real.' He almost whispered it. He took aim and fired at the fridge just as firearms officers burst through the door, shouting commands. 'Shithead.' Manson stuck the gun into his mouth and pulled the trigger. McLusky jumped to avoid the spray of blood and brains as the back of Manson's head exploded into fragments and his body slumped to the ground.

It suddenly became very quiet in the room or perhaps McLusky had gone temporarily deaf to the world. Deep inside his brain a high-pitched electronic buzz started up, became louder, then disappeared. He walked over to the fridge. There was a bullet hole in the top-left corner of the door. He rattled the chain. The old-fashioned door handle prevented it from slipping down but it could be pushed up. Austin came to his aid and between them they managed to push it over the top. The door gaped open. Parcelled inside, tightly bound and gagged with gaffer tape, was Pauline Leslie, barely conscious. The bullet had missed her.

McLusky strode from the shed out into the yard. The van of the firearms unit had driven through the enormous gap where his Mercedes had flattened the fence. The front of his car was dented, creased and scratched and one of his headlights was shattered but McLusky thought he had driven worse-looking cars. He let himself sink into the driver's seat and for a moment rested his arms and forehead against the steering wheel. Then he straightened up and pulled the packet of Extra Lights from his pocket, withdrew the single cigarette left in it and lit it with his silver lighter. He drew the smoke deep into his lungs and exhaled without coughing. He started the engine and turned the car around just as the Range Rover of DSI Denkhaus nosed cautiously through the gap in the fence.

Denkhaus stopped beside him, let his window slide open and looked down at McLusky. 'Where are you going, McLusky?'

He took another drag from the cigarette. 'Not sure yet, sir. Manson is dead. Suicide. Pauline Leslie is alive. And I'm on immediate leave, remember?' Slowly he pulled away and drove over the broken fence panels into the green lane where he briefly stopped, his head leaning out of the window. McLusky sniffed. He thought he could smell freshly roasted coffee, his very favourite hallucination.

η